JOURNEY TO THE WATER

Journey to the Water

MADELINE CRANE

Copyright © 2024 by Madeline Crane
All rights reserved. No part of this book may be reproduced in any manner whatsoever without written permission except in the case of brief quotations embodied in critical articles and reviews.
First Printing, 2024

CONTENTS

Dedication - x

~I~

Prologue: The Citadel

1

~II~

The Temple of the Dragon

7

~III~

The Dragon's Peak

19

~IV~

Interlude One: Citadel Gate

27

~V~

The Isle of the Priestesses

35

~VI~

The Slope of Hanowa

51

~VI~

~VII~

The Abyss
63

~VIII~

The Emerald Sea
69

~IX~

Kannaoka, the Empty Isle
81

~X~

Betwixt Iron and Stone
95

~XI~

In the Hall of the Dead King
113

~XII~

The Tempest
131

~XIII~

Interlude Two: The Land of Ghosts
141

~XIV~

The House of the Weaver-Woman
155

~XV~

Nagara in Sunlight
173

~ VII

~XVI~

A Sky Without End

185

~XVII~

Svilsara of the Desert

197

~XVIII~

The Sacrificial Stone

213

~XIX~

Svilsara, As It Always Was

229

~XX~

Isra's Well

239

~XXI~

The City of the Dead

251

~XXII~

The Sorcerer's Tower

265

~XXIII~

Interlude Three: The Broken Road

273

~XXIV~

Among the Heretics

281

VIII ~

~XXV~

The Temple in the West

301

~XXVI~

The Ring-Fort

313

~XXVII~

The Standing Stones

325

~XXVIII~

Interlude Four: A Place Between

337

~XXIX~

Frontier of the Fallen Empire

343

~XXX~

The Burning Plain

357

~XXXI~

The Empty Tower

375

~XXXII~

The Last, Lonely Harbor

389

~XXXIII~

Interlude Five: The White City

401

~ IX

~XXXIV~

The Long Walk
409

~XXXV~

The New Phyreios
425

"Yþde swa þisne eardgeard   ælda scyppend
oþþæt burgwara   breahtma lease
eald enta geweorc   idlu stodon."

*(Thus the creator of men laid waste to this dwelling-place;
Bereft of the noise of the people,
The old works of the giants stand empty.)*

The Wanderer, Old English poem

***

*For Ian, who lent me the use of his first D&D character for this book.
For all those who wander, and especially for Kyle.*

~ I ~

PROLOGUE: THE CITADEL

Here stood the white city, its columns of pale marble bathed fiery red in perpetual twilight and its flagstone streets bare of dust, silent as a grave. He had been here for an age, he thought, because he could not remember where he had come from, and the sun did not move from the scarlet horizon, nor did the small, twisted trees confined to marble stands grow taller or shed their leaves. He needed neither to eat nor sleep, so he wandered alone in the endless, unchanging evening, waiting for the last of his memories to leave him at last.

He had already forgotten how he had come to be here, where he might have been before, and why his heart ached as he turned each corner to find it empty, the windows of the houses shuttered and the doors shut. If he could forget the ache, too, he might have been content here.

The streets lay on an orderly grid, north to south and east to the setting sun that never set. At the center, the temple stood watch over the city, its windows of many-colored glass glittering. He had tried the door a hundred or a thousand times, but it was far too heavy for him to move. Standing under the arch, one brown hand against the white stone, he thought he could sense watchful eyes gazing down at him. There had been another temple like this one, with its doors open to the desert air, and within had stood towering effigies of inhuman beauty whose stone eyes looked upon the people below without seeing. A shiver of fear and awe traveled down his back, and he took his hand from the door and placed it flat against his chest, a gesture that might have once held meaning, but no longer did.

He turned away from the temple. A gentle wind stirred the confined gardens of the central square, setting the trees to whispering. Under his bare feet, the steps were cold, untouched by the distant sun. *They should be warm,* he thought. *The wind should smell of dust and iron, and I shouldn't be alone.*

This was another memory, however brief and unclear, that he was certain to lose. No sand troubled the streets here, and no colored banners flew aloft, and the city was empty of everyone except for him.

He crossed the square and walked west into the faded light between the flat, rectangular faces of shuttered shop fronts and unoccupied houses. Between them, rows of tiny flowers, blue as a forgotten summer sky, curled their petals half-closed in readiness for a night that never came.

These flowers were the first to disappear as he went farther from the temple, followed by the doors and windows, and then the blank faces of the buildings themselves. The flagstones underfoot grew smooth and indistinct. Another step, and all was white fog, cold and intangible.

He held out one hand, curling his fingers around nothing. This had happened last time, and the time before—he had kept walking, then, chasing the indistinct memory of clouds of mist rolling over vast, green fields flooded with clear water. Surely, he had thought, that place was on the other side of the wall of fog.

He had walked and walked, and found himself some time later back in the citadel, standing before the temple's indifferent doors. Still, he pressed forward again, clinging to the small, forlorn hope that this time might be different, that there would be people on the other side, and a sky that changed with the hours and gave sun and rain to the earth below; that there was an end to this sterile, dead place and its cold marble walls.

If only he could remember where he had come from, or by which way he had entered the citadel. Fear rose like bile in his throat, and he swallowed it down, closing his eyes and reaching out his hands as he pushed forward through the expanse of white.

The edge of a marble flagstone caught his foot, and he stumbled and fell. Pain lanced through the palms of his hands. He raised his head, and the temple towered above, its columns like faceless sentries beneath their red-stained arches. He was back in the center square, just as he had expected.

He pushed himself to his knees and buried his face in both hands. Despair would not lead him to freedom, nor would it devour the last shreds of memory that spurred him to seek a way out, but it was unrelenting. If he allowed it, it would carry him by tiny crack and finger-hold, of which there were very few but just enough, to the top of the temple and off its domed roof to the steps beneath, but he would refuse it as long as he was able. Though he could not remember, he had the firm conviction that someone, somewhere, would mourn for him.

Lifting his head, he took a breath, the first in some time. A fall from the top of the temple might not end his thin, lonely imitation of life, then. The relief was fleeting, replaced as soon as it had come by a cold, creeping horror. Not even death would remove him from this place.

A flutter of movement caught his eye, and he looked up to the lowest archway over the temple stairs. An owl, its feathers shimmering in the low sunlight, alighted on the marble peak, shaking out its wings. Its face was round and white as a full moon.

It was the first living thing that he had seen since he came to the citadel an hour or an eternity ago. He stood, one foot at a time so as not to startle it, and crossed the square to stand beneath the arch. The owl bent its head to preen beneath its wing.

"Hello there," he said, and his voice was that of a stranger, and hoarse from lack of use. He had not spoken to anyone for as long as his troubled memory could recall.

The owl turned its moon face to him, tilting its head to one side and then the other. He stood still, not daring even to breathe, lest he frighten it away.

He had always been good with animals, hadn't he? He remembered an ox's soft muzzle under his hand, the weight of its huge head pushing against him. Despite its size, he recalled no fear.

The owl opened its hooked beak and spoke.

"Hello," it said. "Is that your face that you're wearing?"

Startled, he retreated by a step. It was an unusual thing, surely, for an owl to speak with the voice of a man. Bringing a hand to his face, he said, "I think so. Whose would it be?"

The owl ruffled its feathers in the avian imitation of a shrug. "I seem to recall seeing it before, that's all. It's rather impolite to steal another's face, you know, though you don't look like you're strong enough for that. Who are you?"

"I—" He opened his mouth to speak, but no name came forth, neither his nor that of some other man. He could not have told the difference had one come to mind. "I don't remember," he confessed, and the speaking of it summoned back the fear and despair he had tried so hard to banish. Again he placed his hand against his chest, and again it brought him no comfort.

"A pity," said the owl, "but perhaps it's for the best. Rest well, little one." It spread its obsidian wings, blotting out the dim red sun and reaching the full span of the arch, and moved to take flight.

"Wait!" he cried. "Who are you? By which way did you come? I must get out. I'll go mad."

The owl folded its wings again, blinking its jeweled eyes in annoyance. "So many questions. You'd be wiser to stay here, little one, where you're safe."

It must have come from somewhere outside the citadel. Despite the poor state of his memory, he was certain he had never seen the owl before. "I cannot stay," he said again. "Only show me the way out, and I'll not trouble you again."

"You don't even know your own name," the owl scoffed. "How do you expect to go anywhere if you don't know who you are?"

"I don't understand," he said.

"What is your name, little one?"

He closed his eyes, blotting out the shadow of the owl against the red sun. Images, as indistinct as a dream upon waking, flitted through his unsteady mind: a mountain the color of rust towering over a city not unlike this one, crowned in a wreath of clouds, and the same mountain lying low and hollow as smoke rose from the ruins.

"I can't remember," he said.

The owl leaned down, stretching its feathered neck, and fixed him with an unblinking, onyx stare. "Your name."

A name—surely he'd had one, once, and he could hear it now, called out across the field at sunset, summoning him home, or rising above the shouts of a crowd amidst a cloud of disturbed dust, obscuring all their faces, or whispered in the dark, soft and fervent as a prayer.

"Khalim," he said, and this time he recognized the voice in which he spoke. "My name is Khalim."

"Ah," said the owl. "Someone remembers you."

~ II ~

THE TEMPLE OF THE DRAGON

I have another tale to tell you, if you have the time to hear it. It begins after the passage of the worm, after the coming of the god-king, and after the loss of my heart.

I left the fallen stones of Phyreios before dawn, in the company of the warriors of the East. Under the clear autumn sky, a miasma of smoke and dust hovered over the rubble. A gaping black maw now lay open at the base of the mountain, where the great worm had gone back from whence it came, into the bowels of the earth. There it would sleep, and trouble us no more, until the last days of the world.

The few survivors made their camp where once a festering slum had marred the city's shining image. They had nothing but what they were able to carry from the ruins, and their cries of mourning pierced the predawn silence, but they lived, and they would rebuild. A god walked among them, and he would lead them to a golden age of peace and prosperity—a god who wore the face of my beloved.

How lonely it was to grieve among the grieving, and to refuse the beacon of hope that was offered. Their loss was greater than mine, for Khalim had not died. His hands sifted through the rubble like any other man's, and his feet traced the boundaries of the camp, but he was not there. For those who had not known Khalim, the distinction was one I could not explain, not without weeping or howling at the sky in rage.

And so I left before I could chance to see that face again, and meet the golden gaze of the god Torr in the place where my love's soft brown eyes had been. I gathered my few belongings: my ruined armor, three javelins, a tunic that had seen better days, and the canvas tent I had shared with Khalim on the mountain for so brief a time. I had with me the horse that was my friend Aysulu's parting gift, a black gelding as gentle as a pony bred for war could be. I named him Bran, after a raven-haired hero from the legends of my people. On the plain outside the ruin, my path and Aysulu's had at last diverged, as she rode out to meet the mustered men of the steppe, summoned far too late to prevent what had transpired.

I was to travel east, with the warriors of the Dragon Temple: stone-faced Jin and brash Heishiro; Yanlin of the quiet strength and Hualing of the sharp eye. We carried with us the prize of the Cerean Tournament, the Sword of Heaven, wrapped in cloth and hidden among Jin's belongings.

The other prize, the winner's purse, shared between myself, Aysulu, Khalim, and Garvesh the scholar, had either fallen beneath the earth when the mountain crumbled, or remained at the fortified camp in the high reaches. I would not take the time to fetch my share. Let another find it, and feed these people who remain in the ruin. While the mines that had once been the city's lifeblood lay buried, it might purchase what they needed to rebuild.

And so, as the sun climbed over the vast, iron-tinged desert and illuminated the wreck of Phyreios, we set off, walking in companionable silence. My fellow travelers had horses of their own, and rode intermittently throughout the day, but I could not bring myself to climb upon Bran's back.

"What's the matter?" Heishiro asked the first evening, as we made our camp in the shadow of the desert's wind-etched rocks. "You scaled the side of the worm with nothing but a sword and your wits. A horse with a saddle should give you no trouble."

That I did not enjoy the swaying of a horse's back, so unlike that of a ship on the northern sea, and that I feared his stamping hooves, I could not say to Heishiro. He would, without malice, call me a coward, and I could not abide it. I told him I was not afraid, and I would ride in the morning.

I slept alone in the small canvas tent that Khalim and I had shared for so short a time. On the inside of its rough walls was a record of our travels, mine across the frozen North and his across the flatlands, culminating in the city beneath the Iron Mountain. He could read and write no better than I, but his hands had been steadier, and the images he drew in charcoal from the cooking fire—of fields and forests and the creatures that walked among them—were finer than mine. The figure of the Iron Mountain, standing tall and proud as it once had appeared in the dreams that had summoned Khalim to the city, lingered in my own dreams, bringing with it the smell of smoke and blood.

All is not lost, I vowed silently in the dark. *I will travel to the temple, and the master who dwells there will grant me her wisdom, and I will find Khalim and return him to my side.*

In the morning, I pulled myself into Bran's saddle, and he accepted my weight with placid stoicism. He followed the other horses with no guidance from me, and so we passed most of the second day, until my thighs chafed and my back ached. Hualing told me I had done a fine job, and Heishiro mocked my bowlegged stance, but it was Jin's wordless nod of approval that I would recall the best.

Thus we passed the autumn, crossing the desert and entering the steppe, where we walked for weeks in a golden sea of grass, as beautiful as it was desolate, the sky pale and empty and the eight winds following our every step. It was a harsh land, a holy land. I had learned to treat it with the reverence it demanded when I had traveled with Aysulu, before Phyreios. When the sparse, dry snow fell, another set of mountains loomed in the distance, cradling the rising sun each morning in its peaks.

We arrived at the town at the base of the mountains in midwinter. This was a trading post, a wintering place for the nomadic folk, and the source of most of the temple's provisions. Above us, drifts of snow buried the roads, and we would have to wait until the spring thaw to make the climb.

To me, this delay was unacceptable. For months, I had made steady progress toward the temple and its master, day by day and step by step. It was a long road we had walked, under the desert stones and across the sea of grass, but I had held my goal in my mind, and the days had passed. Now it would be weeks or months before I could so much as visit the next waystation.

"Khalim is safe," Jin told me. "You heard as much, from his own mouth and that of the god. Nothing will befall him for a season."

I could not bring myself to confess that I did not trust the word of the god of Phyreios, who had stolen Khalim from me. Jin, I thought, would not hear it—he had seen the Ascended cast down and the Sword of Heaven remanded to his care, until such time as it was needed once more. His thoughts were of the balance of the world and the long ages to come. He had no time for the grief of one unfortunate lover.

Heishiro took me to the tavern under the hill, where the itinerant hunters and trappers who spent the summers in the mountains gathered to drink and ward off the cold. They were a tall, fine-boned people, their angular faces lined by sun and wind beneath their fur hats. Heishiro had a softer look about him, as he was younger than most of them and only a year or two older than I, his black hair glossy and his stubbled face untroubled by years of harsh weather. His eyes, though, had the same distant look about them as the eyes of the wanderers did. Those eyes said that this was only a brief respite, and each man would soon return to the road, searching for a home that would never appear.

I drank too much that night, and many of the nights that followed. In my restlessness, I found I could not sleep otherwise, and my youth spared me the worst of the pain the following mornings. I spent my days wandering outside the village, hunting swift hares in the snow. Once, I ventured too far with a storm gathering on the peaks above. The wind howled around me, and snow lashed at my face. The village disappeared from view, as did the mountain, and I could see nothing farther than the reach of my arms.

After an hour, when my hands and feet were numb and I had lost all sense of direction, a small golden light bobbed into view. I followed it, and I found it attached to Heishiro, cursing in several distinct tongues and clutching the lantern's pole in both hands.

"What in all the hells were you thinking?" he demanded over the sound of the wind. He grasped me by the shoulder of my borrowed coat and hauled me toward the cluster of dim lights that was the distant village, emerging one by one from the storm.

When we reached the tavern, and our frozen limbs had thawed, he regarded me with a grim expression. "I won't tell Jin," he said. "As far as he knows, you were here through the storm. But you must swear to me that you won't venture out into the weather again."

I spent more time in the village after that, learning to care for Bran like an archer of the steppe might, though I would never shoot a bow from his saddle. I draped warm blankets over his back in the evenings, took him walking over the frozen paths, and checked his hooves for stones when we returned. No songs would be sung of the bond between us, but we got along well enough.

As the snow at last began to thaw, Jin summoned me from the stable and took me with him to visit the village smith. Though the forge was a small one, tucked between the headman's house and the trading post, a hundred long, curved swords hung from its walls in neat columns, their steel blades blazing in the firelight.

The smith ignored me in favor of Jin, speaking to him in the language I was only just beginning to learn. Countless years bent his back and turned his skin to rough bark, but his eyes were sharp and clever. He examined the Sword of Heaven, his hammer ringing a strong, clear note upon the blade. Jin's own sword had grown loose in its hilt during the ordeal with the worm, and the smith set to work correcting it.

"You'll need a weapon," Jin told me. "Not today, and not while you stay with us at the temple, but you'll need it before long. I'd have you choose one now."

I had lost my axe during the tournament, when the fiery heart of a salamander had turned its head to a lump of molten metal and its handle to a cinder. For a brief time, the Sword of Heaven was mine to wield, but I had given it up as soon as the god Torr had asked me to pass it on to Jin. I had no desire to take it up again.

I turned to the swords on the wall. I thought this might have been a test, and I would be judged worthy by which weapon I chose.

Jin's face, square-jawed and black-browed, betrayed nothing.

Not a single axe hung from the smith's wall, so after some deliberation, I chose a steel knife with a lacquered handle. It would serve me as a weapon only in the most dangerous of straits, but as a tool, its value was beyond counting.

Jin only nodded, and paid the smith in silver coins stamped with the image of a palace I had never seen. He returned the Sword of Heaven to its sheath and wrapped it again in a length of cloth, hiding it from view.

Careful of Jin's watchful eye, I spent more time in the stable and less in the tavern in the weeks to come. The winter was passing, and in the time I had left, I would prove myself worthy of the temple's master.

Spring arrived in a torrent of rain, and when the floods had come and gone, we began the climb to the temple at last. The mountain turned from white to green as we ascended the narrow path, and rain fell each night and through most of each day, gentle but cold as the snow had been. Wind and water and the hooves of mountain goats had created most of this road, but in the places where the path was steepest, human hands had carved rough steps into the gray stone. We climbed above the clouds, past the rice fields cut into the mountainside in tiers like a giant's staircase, through gnarled trees and stands of grass many times taller than a man.

The mist parted at noon on the fifth day of climbing, and the temple appeared before us. Its tiled roofs jutted out from the mountain stone, and its columns, painted crimson, each had the carved face of a dragon. Around the base stood a cluster of small buildings—guest houses, Jin explained, for the pilgrims. One of them would be mine, for the duration of my stay here, with a chest for my few belongings and a simple paddock outside for my horse. I suppose I was a pilgrim, of a sort. I surely did not intend to remain here and live among these refined people.

They dressed simply, in tunics that crossed over the breast and loose trousers of rough hemp fiber, with simple cloth boots upon their feet to ward off the early spring chill. Men and women, from the old to the very young, dwelled and worked alongside one another, sweeping the paths to and from the temple, growing herbs and hardy vegetables, mending clothes, and preparing their meals. They created scrolls of beautiful script that I could not read, and painted meticulous reproductions of the beautiful, forbidding landscape about them. In mossy plazas open to the rain, they debated philosophy and read aloud the texts that the pilgrims had brought with them.

Some, like Jin and his companion, were warriors, trained in the arts of weapons and the open hand, and in the arcane arts that Yanlin practiced. Heat burned across the characters painted on their arms and flared from their fists, turning the rain to clouds of steam.

Jin placed the Sword of Heaven in a vault on the second level of the temple. There it would remain, until such a time as it was needed.

I asked him when I would be able to speak to the temple's master.

"Not yet," he said. "You will when you are ready."

Though my temper flared, I held my tongue. I was a stranger here, among the clouds in this foreign land. I would do as I was instructed.

Heishiro, I found out soon after, had never met the master either. "This year," he declared. "You will bring me good fortune, Eske."

He would become the greatest of warriors, he said, and he believed this temple's secrets would grant him what he sought, if he could only prove himself worthy.

When he was refused again after a number of weeks, he took up his sword and his armor and left the temple, to seek to sharpen his weapon and his mind elsewhere. I was sad to see him go, but Yanlin told me not to worry, and that Heishiro would return again before long. He always did.

In the meantime, I was instructed to work and learn alongside the temple's children. They marveled at my stature, and in the evening when the chores were complete, they would beg me to lift them and toss them in the air. I swept the paths and carried sacks of grain to and from the storehouses, and I learned to speak a little of their language. Strong drink was forbidden, and I had no time to feel its absence.

Summer came, bringing with it a heavy, damp heat, and still I was not permitted to climb the highest staircase. The aged men and women who instructed the children had me sit beneath a twisted tree and clear my mind of all thoughts—of Phyreios, of myself, and of Khalim. But instead of a mind clear as rainwater upon the fields, I dwelt on my failures, on the home I had left so long ago, and the monumental task I had undertaken. In the lands of my birth, only the shaman could cross between this world and the next. I had been my father's heir, destined to become chieftain, and I'd never had a reason to learn these magics. I would not return to my homeland, and the summer stars above the mountain peaks here were all strange to me, lacking even the northerly guides that would lead me back. I had placed all my hopes that the wisdom of the temple's master would provide me a way forward.

I could not learn to fight as the disciples of the temple did. They knew not the exuberant joy of the contest nor the fury of battle, preferring a calm mind and a disciplined body. The days passed, and I tried each morning to rid myself of all thoughts and failed at the task.

I asked Jin, again, when I would see the master, or if making myself worthy of an audience was something I could not achieve. My training continued, and my skills had improved, but I was no monk. I could not live as they did forever.

"What would you ask of me," I said, "in order for your master to see me?"

"That is not for me to decide," he told me.

Heishiro returned as autumn painted the mountains in fiery color. I worked to bring in the harvest, and carry it up and down the treacherous steps of the mountain path. In the village below, a festival took place, with music and a feast and a display of multicolored fire, and a chain of dancers wearing the shape of a many-legged serpentine dragon. As I watched the colored lights play across the enraptured faces of the children, I forgot my struggles, taken up in the beauty and joy that this harsh land had to offer.

The next day, I asked Jin a third time if I would be permitted to see the master.

With a brush and ink as shining black as his hair, he was inscribing a missive to some local ruler or another; he set down the brush and left the scriptorium to walk with me. "The last stairs in the temple are steep," he said, "and you will not be able to climb them so burdened."

I did not understand what he meant.

"Sorrow is a heavy weight to carry," he explained. "Guilt is heavier still. It is right that you should feel these things, but if you cannot lay them down, you will never be able to reach the peak, much less cross over to the other world."

"But I am here because of what happened in Phyreios," I argued. "I do this because of Khalim. Must I forget these reasons before I am allowed to make the journey?"

As we walked together, he led me away from the group of pilgrims, so we would not be overheard. "I have never passed through the barrier," he said. "You could search for an age and not find one who has. I have, however, met a creature from the spirit world, and on this very mountainside I faced him in single combat. Wicked spirits and desperate ghosts will use any weakness against you. They will wear the face of one you love, speak to you with their voice, and if your vision is clouded by the burdens you carry, you will be unable to tell the difference between the real person and the impostor."

He gazed out over the bare fields, watching the dry yellow leaves drift to the earth, seeing something from long ago. "Time will pass, memory will fade," he said at last. "What remains of those we love, after that?"

"I don't know," I confessed.

"I hope that you will, someday," said Jin. "It is also of equal import that you see yourself in the same way: as you are, and not as you wish yourself to be."

I shook my head. "It is customary for my people to boast, but if I have learned nothing else here, I know that I still have much to learn."

"Good. But that is not of what I speak. You see yourself as the center of the cataclysm at Phyreios, as though it was by your will that it took place—as though you alone must bear the burden of the lives lost. You are but one grain of rice upon the balance—one mortal man, living for but a brief flicker when compared to all the ages of the world. And yet, there will never, as long as this world and the next both last, be another Eske son of Ivor. You must know who you are, in order not to be deceived."

It was a riddle, and I had no love for riddles. Out of respect for the generous hospitality he and his people had shown me, I did not argue with Jin. I returned to my training.

"He's always speaking nonsense," Heishiro told me. "I love him like I would a brother, but I cannot abide him for long stretches."

I kept my wits sharp and my limbs strong by sparring with Heishiro while he remained at the temple. Nightmares haunted my cold, narrow bed in the pilgrim's house, and I still could not meditate as the monks did, but perhaps something had changed within me after this long year, for there came a day in the dead of winter that I was called up to the top of the temple to speak with its master.

I dressed in the manner of the temple, and shaved the sides of my head to expose the tattoos there. Yanlin gave me a warm coat, a paper lantern, a walking stick, and nothing else, for one could not carry anything up those final steps. I passed through the high, gilded doors, where a pair of dragons in gold lacquer faced each other on the red-stained wood, and I climbed.

The stairs emerged onto the mountain face. Here, trees could not take root, and the lichens that grew upon the stone in the lower reaches had gone dry and dormant for the winter. Snow blew across the uneven path, stinging my exposed skin. I covered my face with one arm and gripped my walking stick, and forged ahead unseeing.

My steps were true despite the wind, and at last I came to the top of the steps. The ruins of an ancient temple lay here, fallen so long ago that it had turned into a flat, circular plain, its once mighty columns only low piles of rubble, half-buried in snow. It had once been vast, towering over the countryside as it crowned the peak, but time and wind had laid it low.

I crossed this space, leaving footprints that disappeared even as I made them, and found myself face to face with the dragon.

~ III ~

THE DRAGON'S PEAK

With greedy hands, the storm tugged at my lantern. The dragon's sapphire scales caught its faint, wavering light and reflected it back like stars upon the sea. She raised her head, and the length between the quivering whiskers about her mouth and her crown of branching antlers was equal to that of a longboat from bow to stern. Her eyes, vast and dark and cunning, shone with the blue-white glow of reflected moonlight. Behind her, the vast coils of her body disappeared into the gloom of the storm.

As she reared up, the face of the lind-worm flashed into my memory. It had lifted its serpentine neck in the same way as it prepared to swamp my boat on that cold northern sea, and standing here upon the mountainside in the winter wind, I could feel the weight of the harpoon on my shoulder, hear the chanting of the oarsmen, and see brave Fearghus on the rudder. It had been the last time I had ever seen him. I recoiled backward with a start, and the lantern flew from my hand and went out.

I fell into a drift of snow, and it covered me with a thin, freezing blanket. Collecting my wits, I pushed myself to my knees. Snow clung to my hair and collected in my eyelashes, turning the world soft and white. Now, the only light in the storm came from the dragon's eyes, and they regarded me with a distant curiosity.

Understanding, not so different from dread, washed over me. This magnificent, terrifying creature was indeed the master of the temple, to whom I had labored for almost a year just for the chance to speak. I placed my hands in the snow, ignoring the ache of the cold, and pressed my brow to the ground.

The great head lowered, its writhing whiskers carving trails through the snow and exposing the carved stone floor of the ruined temple beneath. A steaming breath stirred my hair and the fur of my coat. I shivered, from the cold seeping through my clothing and from a deep, primal fear. In ages past, when the world was young, my forgotten forefathers lived in fear of dragons and their kin. Their language, customs, and wisdom had long since faded from memory, but the fear remained, coursing through my blood and turning my bowels to icy water.

"So," the dragon said, and her voice was inside my body, loud as thunder, louder than the beat of my heart or the thoughts in my mind. "You are the wanderer from the North."

I took a breath that tore at my throat, and hoarsely, I shouted above the noise of the wind. "Yes. I am a long way from home."

"Who are you?"

The question struck me like a hammer upon an anvil, more insistent than fear and more inexorable than desire. I had no choice but to answer with the truth.

I staggered to my feet, arms out in supplication as the wind clawed at my face. "I am Eske of the Clan of the Bear. I am a wanderer, yes, and world-treader, and champion of the Cerean Tournament." I gazed into the dragon's lidless eyes, and I said, "And I love Khalim. You may not know his name, but he was a healer, a traveler, a servant of the gods—a mortal man, for everything that might be worth."

The dragon's head settled back atop her coils, and she studied me, the weight of all the ages she had seen carried in that unblinking gaze. She had heard me, even though the winds howled and my voice could not carry.

"A great injustice has been done," I said. "And because I love Khalim, I mean to set it right."

The voice in my mind was softer, but no less painful to bear. "And who are you to decide what justice is? The people of Phyreios, sacrificed in the arena—will you seek *justice* for them, as well? Those crushed in their homes, under the body of the worm, what of them?"

Jin had informed his master of the events in Phyreios, certainly, but from the ache behind my eyes, the dragon was drawing the memories directly from me. "The ones responsible for the destruction of the city are gone," I said. I bowed my head, unable to bear the dragon's gaze any longer. "And I am only one man. Khalim was betrayed by the god he trusted and served faithfully all his life. If my love for him is worth nothing else, then let it be worth righting this wrong. I was told you had the wisdom that would aid me in my quest. I humbly ask for your help." Again I knelt in the snow and prostrated myself before the dragon, my face and hands numb from the cold.

The dragon uncoiled her tail, and the mountain shook. "Betrayed?" she intoned.

"Yes," I said, and my breath melted a tiny patch upon the stone. "Though he did not die, he was stolen away, and the god now walks the ruined streets of Phyreios in the body where Khalim once lived. I was promised he would be safe. I have no way of knowing if I was told the truth."

"If you wish to see your beloved again, you have no need of my help," the dragon said, close as a whisper and louder than the sea. "You have only to serve the same god for the rest of your natural life, and upon the hour of your death, you will join him in the place that god has made."

I raised my head. "I cannot do that. I cannot worship the one who stole Khalim from me."

"Then you wish to defy the will of that god, to defy the order of the world?"

A sharp ache shot through my jaw as my teeth ground against each other. Jin had warned me that I might not be ready to meet the master of the temple, but he had said nothing of preparing for the pain—it gripped my very bones and spurred me to run even as it made my limbs too heavy to move. "I do," I said. "He is not a wicked god, the god of Phyreios. He is nothing like those who enslaved the city for an age and brought about its destruction. I believe he will fulfill everything he has promised his people. In this instance, though, he did wrong."

Snow melted through the heavy fabric of my winter trousers and turned to ice against the stone floor. My hands shook, held out in an incomplete gesture, but the cold had faded from my awareness. There was only the dragon, beautiful and terrible.

Her whiskers curled in what might have been a smile. She raised her head to gaze through the snow and out across the distant, night-shrouded peaks, towering above me as tall as the sky, and I could neither move nor speak. "It is right for mortals to defy their gods from time to time," she said. "They grow stagnant, otherwise, and waste their lives in meaningless toil."

From the base of her coils, two mighty five-fingered claws emerged and folded together, an almost human gesture. Her great muzzle swung back to fix me again in her gaze. "I was worshiped as a god once, an age ago—did you know that? This arrangement, I think, is a far better one. I watch you mortals live out your brief, burning lives, and every so often one of you climbs up to ask me a question." Her nostrils flared, and she breathed a warmth over me that smelled of fire and molten rock disgorged from the earth. "Ask me your question, Eske of the North."

Forcing life into my frozen limbs, I got to my feet. "I intend to cross over into the other world, beyond the gate of bone and the river of memory. I will find the realm of the god Torr, and I will find my beloved and take him back with me. Failing that, I will remain there with him, for as long as he will have me. Will you help me?" I asked. "Know that I will perform any service, bear any hardship, and do anything you ask of me."

The mountain shook, and drifts of snow tumbled from the broken pillars that held them up and flowed like water from the temple floor. The dragon was laughing—not to mock me, but in genuine delight at the antics of the tiny mortals who lived beneath her. "You speak as if it were a simple matter of finding a ship and sailing out at high tide," she said. "To answer your question, yes, I will help you; I who fear neither death nor the gods, and will endure as long as the world endures. But I cannot open the way for you."

"Then tell me what I must do," I begged. The storm was departing from this peak, and with the lifting of the snow came a clearer view of the vastness of the dragon's coils, limned as they were in the faint luminescence of her eyes. Again fear gripped my chest; the old hunter's instinct that a much greater predator stalked the same land, visible only as a looming shadow.

"You will travel south to the sea," the dragon said, and with her voice clamoring in my mind I could muster no disagreement. "In the waters of Ashinya there stands an island, formed of a volcano that rose from the sea. The priestesses there maintain a temple to a goddess of the places between."

Another god. Doubt crept back into my awareness. I had left behind the gods of my people, who roamed the frozen plain among beasts as great as they; I had witnessed the death of the Seven Ascended beneath the arena of Phyreios; and I had turned my back on Torr, the First Hero. Would the goddess worshiped on the side of the volcano prove any different?

"And she'll help me, this goddess?" I asked.

The dragon's head lowered, and I saw myself, small and distorted, reflected in one of her eyes. "She may. She may not. I am a creature of the sky and the storm, and cannot predict the ways of the goddess of the deep. But she keeps the passages between worlds, as well as the blackest depths of the ocean, and you will not venture far without seeking her out. Pay your obeisance to the wise women of the island, and they will show you what you must do."

I bowed, back straight and hands at my sides in the way I had seen the monks do. "I will do as you have instructed."

As the wind returned, bringing with it the snow, it seemed that the dragon faded into the darkness, and I knew that I had been dismissed. I had been permitted one question, and it had been asked and answered.

***

I was eager to begin my journey—the southern sea was many weeks' travel from the temple, and I had lingered long in this beautiful, forbidding place. Winter still held sway over the mountains, however, and ice and snow covered the passages down the mountain. I spent the rest of the winter learning the stars of this strange new land, so that I could find my way south. The archer Hualing spent many a patient hour teaching me to read a map. My people had no writing, and I asked her why she could not simply tell me the route to take, so that I would need not rely on fragile paper and indistinct symbols to find it. She insisted, and I learned to recognize rivers and mountains drawn upon scrolls, but the names inscribed beside them remained a mystery to me.

My route was as simple as it was long: I had only to follow the pilgrim's road south until I found the River Mani, which I would know by the distinctive yellow moss that grew upon its banks. I could then follow it to the coast.

Spring came at last, and as the rains washed away the last of the snow, I prepared to leave. I was given two sets of the temple's simple clothing, a broad straw hat, and a cloak to keep the weather away. Along with my knife of folded steel, I had also a walking staff as long as I was tall, that could double as a weapon if the need arose. Heishiro helped me to repair Bran's saddle and balance the provisions we would need atop it; he was a wanderer as much as I, and had more experience with horses.

The map also went in my saddlebags, in case I had need of it. At the very bottom was inked a cluster of islands, with the largest one at the center, a mountain rising from the waves with a thin line of smoke rising from its peak. It was no more than two hands' breadths from the diagram of the temple, stretched across its own peaks.

When the sun broke through the high, gray bank of clouds, and the mud of the roads had solidified enough for a horse to walk unimpeded, I met Heishiro and Jin at the temple's gate.

"I hope that we will meet again, someday," Jin said, "and I wish you well on your quest."

With a clap on my shoulder, Heishiro added, "I'll miss having you around. Everyone here is boring. No offense, Jin."

Jin's face showed nothing, but I heard an exasperated sigh. "You are always welcome here, Heishiro. As you will be, Eske, should your path ever lead you back."

I thanked them both, bowing deeply.

"Your path will not be easy," said Jin. "It will not be unguarded, and steel alone cannot defend against spirit. I hope that we have made you ready for it."

I took up Bran's bridle, and he scratched at the soft ground, ready to be on our way at last. "If I may ask," I said, "when you fought the demon on the mountainside, whose face did it put on to trick you?"

Jin's eyes widened, only briefly, and he bent his head as though the memory was a heavy burden. "My father's." Collecting himself, he continued, "And so I understand the journey that you are about to take, and I do not envy you. I can only wish you good fortune."

I bowed again, and with this last blessing I set out down the mountain path.

"If you see your man again, tell him we said hello," Heishiro called after me.

Though he could not hear me, I promised I would.

~ IV ~

INTERLUDE ONE: CITADEL GATE

"I've remembered my name," Khalim said. "Will you help me?"

The moon-faced owl settled back atop the arch and preened the crook of one wing with its beak. Behind it, the red sun hung suspended in the sky, unmoving as ever. "Help you do what, little one?" it asked.

Khalim climbed three of the temple stairs, placing himself closer to the height of the arch standing athwart the steps, and stood with the grand, sealed door at his back. "Why do you call me that? I'm larger than you."

"Is that what you see?"

He nodded. He could hold the owl's body in his arms, if it would allow him, though the span of its wings was easily greater than his height.

The owl lowered its wing and studied him with one blank, black eye, smooth as polished glass. "Interesting. And what do you look like?"

The question was a strange one, considering that the owl stared him in the face, but Khalim did not argue. If he did, the owl might depart, never to be seen again, and take with it any hope he had of escaping this place. He held up his hands, spreading his fingers.

For a brief flash, he saw what he expected to see: brown skin, calluses, the frayed hem of a sleeve. Then his flesh turned pale and rigid—the same white marble that formed the steps beneath his feet and the towering temple at his back. Two black veins twined up each of his wrists. The threads of his clothing became ridges of stone, carved by the hand of a master in exquisite detail.

He drew in a sharp breath and curled his hands against his chest. They were frigid and bloodless, and his joints stiffened, resisting his will. The sudden cold weight in his belly was either fear or stone.

"What's happening to me?" he whispered.

"You're finding your place, little one," the owl said. "It's nothing to be frightened of."

Khalim shook his head. His body grew heavy, and even that slight motion made him sway on his feet. If he fell, would he shatter? "But this isn't my place," he said. "I don't want to be here. You said someone remembered me—I need to go back. I need to find him." He had recalled a man's voice, he was certain, but he could not conjure it again. His mind, too, was turning to stone.

The owl settled back upon its talons. "Why not? I suppose it's small yet, this city, but that will change with time. You cannot return from whence you came, and beyond the borders of this place lie the spirit wilds. You're likely to have your face stolen, or worse."

Khalim looked up. A lifeless chill crept across his shoulders. "So there are borders."

A crest of feathers around the owl's neck lifted and fluttered, and it lowered its head. "Ah, I've said too much. Rest well, little one. I expect I will not see you again."

It stretched out its dark wings against the crimson sky, and with two powerful strokes, it lifted from the arch and flew, quiet as a whisper, into the unchanging evening.

Willing his stiffening limbs to move, Khalim stumbled down the stairs to the street and gave chase. The white marble flagstones turned paler as he went, losing their gray veins, until they became a smooth, colorless surface. The owl receded as well, growing smaller until white fog enveloped it and it vanished from sight.

It was gone. Before Khalim stretched the vast sea of white, exactly as it had the last time he had ventured away from the city's center. He was alone once more, and now, he thought, he would never leave this place. He would become as one of the temple's pillars, unmoving as the distant sun, and thus spend the rest of eternity.

Weight building on his chest forced him to his knees. He covered his face with his hands, pale against the paler fog. *I'm not meant to be here,* he insisted silently, for no one remained in this place to hear. *I'm supposed to be where there are fields and mountains and rain and people, and there was a time when I wasn't alone.*

I wasn't alone, a voice in his memory repeated. *I never am.*

The voice was his own. Again he placed his hand against his chest, an impulse that had lost any meaning. Now there was only a hollow feeling and a cold, hard surface that once was flesh.

The void could not go on forever. The owl had come from somewhere, and it had returned there with only a beat of its wings.

What had it said to him? *How are you supposed to go anywhere if you don't know who you are?*

He cupped his hands, curling his cold, marble fingers as if he could hold on to his memories as they slipped by. If he remembered, he might find freedom. Otherwise he would turn to stone.

"My name is Khalim," he told the blank expanse. "I was born in Nagara, to Taherah the weaver-woman, and—" He stuttered, fell quiet, and tried again. "And in the summer of my fifth year, the year the star fell in the northern sky, I dreamed that the bridge on the river washed out and the ox drivers all drowned."

Memory washed over him in a flood: the bank of distant cloud, heavy on the air, the thick, green smell of the river and the roar as it rose, the lowing of the oxen and the shouting of men. Words poured from his mouth like water. All else, his labored breathing and the shaking of his shoulders, faded from his awareness. "I begged my mother to take me to the bridge. I cried and cried. When we got there, she called out to the men, and they stopped before the crossing. The flood came while they were waiting. I was relieved, but my mother was sad."

He could picture her face, wreathed in dark hair, her long nose and her soft smiles that never quite reached her eyes. He could not remember ever seeing her face free from sorrow. "She told me there was a god inside of me, and one day he was going to take me away, and he did. He took me to the great city below the mountain, and I did as he wanted, but I couldn't stop the mountain from falling or the city from burning."

The mountain had fallen on him, at the end, in the chamber that reeked of blood old and new, and the seven men and women with faces that shone wailed in useless lamentation at what they themselves had wrought. Part of Khalim had lain beneath the suffocating dark, while another had been pulled away to stand before another shining face, this one too bright to distinguish any of its features. He had begged, then, on what might have been his hands and knees, for another chance to save whomever could be saved, and for a little more time on the earth with the man who had loved him.

That god of the shining face, whom Khalim had carried with him as he left his home and traveled on foot across the desert to Phyreios, whose power had flowed through Khalim's hands as he mended wounds and chased away disease, and whose visions had tormented him ever since he was a child, had taken him from the rubble and placed him here. This was that god's place, his temple and his arches and his streets that led nowhere. It was a part of him, and Khalim was becoming a part of it, turning to black-veined white marble and losing all that made him *Khalim*.

"I did everything you ever asked," Khalim told the pale expanse, "and you took me away. I was young and in love and trying to help people, and you took everything from me."

He must have died there, under the rubble, but what did it matter? He had grasped a life from the brink of death before and pulled it back. Surely if the god he had borne had been willing, Khalim would still walk among the living, and yet here he was, a congealing lump of stone in an empty city.

Marble scraped against marble as he clasped his arms around himself, sobbing in grief and helpless rage. His body shook with the furious desire to lash out, to strike back at the god who had imprisoned him, but he had never struck anyone in his life and could not do so even in death. Here, in any case, there was only stone. Anger warmed him, chasing away the cold, and down his arms to his fingertips his skin softened into the semblance of flesh. With each rasping breath, his chest expanded a little more, and the heat in his belly grew. It would consume him, he thought, with nowhere else to go.

The fire burst from within his chest. Flames licked their way up his arms and down to the featureless pavement, staining the white stone black with soot. This was the realm of the gods, or a part of it, and believing something was enough to make it so.

Fear came first, and then the pain, crashing against him in waves. Searing brightness swallowed his vision. His hands scraped at his skin and clothing, trying to smother the flames, but still they spread, their hunger vast and insatiable. He was—had been—a healer, and he knew what a burn like this would do: skin melting like candle wax, blood boiling and fat sizzling as the flesh blackened and fell away. Someone in the distance was screaming, a hoarse, desperate cry of agony and terror. He was alone here, so it must have been his own voice.

I'm going to die. What that meant in this place beyond death, he could not guess, but whatever was left of him would not survive this.

That thought sharpened his resolve. He would not remain in the citadel, not as a statue nor as an ever-burning beacon or a pile of ash. Someone remembered him and loved him and hoped to see him again.

Eske. The name emerged from the haze of pain, and Khalim held onto it like a talisman. He took a breath, and then another, closing his eyes and forcing himself to pay no heed to the fire and remember himself as he had been, his skin warm and brown and unharmed.

The heat subsided, cooling like a bath left too long. The pain lessened to a dull throb and faded to another distant memory. When he opened his eyes again, a great gate stood before him, so tall that clouds, stained a soft red in the twilight, cloaked the upper edge of its peaked arch. Between the columns, a pair of heavy wooden doors fitted with iron sealed the passageway against whatever lay beyond. Other than Khalim, the doors were the only thing in the city not formed of white stone. On either side of the gate towered a marble statue, three times as tall as he was, an old man in a regal robe on the left and a young warrior carrying a shield and a curved sword on the right.

He knew their faces. Here was Lord Ihsad of House Darela, his weathered hands open in a welcoming gesture, and his beard carved with such fine detail that it turned the stone to soft wool. Beside him stood his son, Jahan, straight-backed and broad-shouldered, the hard angles of his face framing a kind softness around his eyes, exactly as he had been in life. Jahan had been a friend, Khalim remembered, and he had died just before Khalim had in the chamber beneath the arena of Phyreios.

His memory came in fragments, and the rest was fog, but Khalim thought that Lord Ihsad had still lived. How long had he been here? How many of the people he knew had left the land of the living while he remained in this place? Ihsad and Jahan must have come here long ago, for the city to have claimed them already.

"Jahan?" Khalim placed a hand—a hand of flesh, now, soft and yielding against stone—on the statue's sandaled foot. "Can you hear me? I'll get you out, I swear."

The statue's head lowered, inch by inch, the veins in the marble stretching and folding almost like skin. "You," it said in Jahan's voice.

"What happened to you?" Khalim asked.

"I met my death in the service of Torr, the First Hero whom my family honored even as the Ascended struck him from memory," said Jahan. "He granted me a place of honor—here, guarding the gate."

So the god had a name. In all their years together, he had never told Khalim.

"And what of you?" Jahan asked. "You were his most faithful servant. You brought him to Phyreios in our hour of need. Surely your place here is one of great esteem."

Khalim took a step backward, craning his neck to study Jahan's carved face. It was a warrior's face—stern, yes, but content in his duty and the violent fate it would bring, secure in the belief that he would prevent greater harm by the strength of his arm and his skill with the blade.

"You chose this," Khalim said.

"It was given to me, and I accepted it gladly," said Jahan.

Jahan and his father would not turn from stone to flesh again. They had become part of the citadel, and they welcomed it, as a gift the god had given them in exchange for their lifetimes of service. A similar gift had been given to Khalim, but he could not accept it, not now, after he had remembered how he had come to receive it.

"Will you open the gate for me?" he asked Jahan.

The statue's carved brows drew together in a slow, ponderous frown. "Why would you want to leave? You belong here, just as we do—all the more so, for your great sacrifice."

"A sacrifice is made willingly," Khalim said. "I'm sorry, Jahan. I cannot keep the faith of the First Hero any longer. Will you open the gate for me?"

The great doors shuddered, shaking the stone beneath his feet. With a terrible grinding of wood against stone and the creaking of its enormous iron hinges, it opened enough for Khalim to slip through.

"I am sorry, as well, my friend," Jahan said. "I hope to see you again one day."

Khalim touched the base of the statue once more. "Thank you," he said, and he passed through the gate and into the wilds.

~ V ~

THE ISLE OF THE PRIESTESSES

The road south was gentler than the one I had taken more than a year before, coming from the west, but it had its own perils. In the absence of the winter snow, the land turned to emerald green, and rain fell through the days and into each night. We made our way to the hill country, Bran and I, with only my broad hat and waxed canvas tent to keep us dry; we slipped in the ever-present mud and wound our way through narrow, rocky passes and over trees felled beneath the winter's weight. Though he was a steppe pony, accustomed to flat terrain and dry air, Bran performed admirably. I, on the other hand, misread the map, and it took us longer than the planned two weeks to reach the River Mani.

I had not spent a winter in the northern mountains for nothing, and I managed to keep myself and my horse fed and watered and relatively warm. The river, once it appeared, brought a renewed sense of purpose, and it gave me fish, after I had fashioned a net from the spare tunic the temple had given me.

It was the spring of my twenty-second year. I became accustomed once more to solitude, after so long in the company of others. To stave off madness, I spoke often to Bran, in the tongue I had learned from Aysulu and had spoken in Phyreios. He could not understand me any more than he would have in any other language, but it was a comfort to me.

The days grew warmer as we continued along the riverbank, and we passed bridges of rope and timber and villages built on stilts beneath the trees. The people stared at us but did not approach, and I left them to their toils of planting their crops and repairing their homes after the floods that had preceded me.

Summer came upon us before I was aware of it. The heat pressed down on us, and the air thickened; even at night, the oppression of it did not lift until nearly dawn, and the sun brought it back soon after. By noon on the fortieth day since we had left the temple, Bran's steps were slow and his breathing labored. He was ill, and I had neither the knowledge nor the means to care for him, and several weeks still lay between us and the sea.

I had yet to see another soul on the muddy banks of the Mani, but it would not have made a difference if I had—a steppe horse was an exceedingly rare sight this far south. Any other traveler would have known no more than I how to treat him.

I took him down the riverbank and into the snow-fed water, letting it cool his legs and belly. He rallied after a few minutes, and we continued on our way, but after another hour he slowed again, panting.

Aysulu would have known what to do. But she was half a world away, and I had not seen her in more than a year. I considered leaving Bran behind, or selling him to the farmers in their tall houses in the hopes that he would find his way into the hands of someone who could better care for him, but as soon as the thought came to me, I pushed it aside. He deserved better than that, as did Aysulu's friendship, and I feared that Bran was all that kept me from the madness of solitude as I traveled alone in this strange land.

Nonetheless, our progress slowed. Every hour, I had to stop and take Bran into the water to cool him down. My clothing did not dry in the periods between, and as much as I sweated under my hat, it did nothing to relieve the heat. Bran did not sweat at all.

The desire to travel faster pricked at me like insects crawling on my skin—in addition to the many real insects that clung to my arms and buzzed around my face. If I could only get to the port, I thought, my quest would be all but complete. It had already been one long year and two seasons since I had lost Khalim. Any further delay might carry him away from my reach. The god had promised he would be safe, but I put little trust in that promise.

I would not give up on Bran. As the sun sank over the hills the next evening, I tethered him to a tree close to the water and took my knife and my javelins into the woods to hunt. I would need food for the road ahead, however long it might be.

I followed a pair of tiny, swift-footed deer through the trees, keeping the river at my back. I had almost placed them within throwing range when they changed course and darted away, disappearing into the underbrush.

The ground shook with the footsteps of something large and impossibly heavy, its ponderous tread coming nearer. I returned the javelin to its quiver and climbed into the nearest tree, hiding among its broad green leaves.

Again, the forest trembled, the branch that bore my weight swaying like a ship in a storm. I held on to the smooth, wet bark and stilled my breathing.

The trees parted, and the creature emerged, its legs like temple columns and its ears like sails. The great dome of its head reached my hiding place among the branches. Its skin was thick and wrinkled and as gray as a thunderhead. I had seen something like it only once before: the rhinoceros that had trampled a man nearly to death in the Cerean Tournament. This creature stood even taller than that beast had, and in the place where a horn would have been there was a long, prehensile arm. It spied me with one eye and blew a discordant, trumpeting note through that trunk.

To my surprise, a second, much smaller creature followed the first, its trunk wrapped around its mother's ropy tail.

Curiosity came over me, and my task of hunting was forgotten. When the giants had passed, I dropped down from the tree, and I followed the path they had trampled through the undergrowth, staying a respectful distance behind, ducking beneath the trees. I had no desire to find out what such a beast might do to defend her young, should she come to believe I was a threat.

The trail ended at a rock face, where several more colossal creatures gathered. The one I followed broke off a loose stone with her trunk, dislodging a shower of white dust that she licked with a bright pink tongue and offered to her child. I tasted salt in the air.

More creatures came, and they ate off the rock and bathed themselves and each other in mud, finally moving off as darkness fell. I emerged from my hiding place, and with a stone they had discarded, broke jagged chunks of salt from the cliff and gathered it into the bottom of my tunic. I dropped much of it as I returned to Bran in the darkness, but we had enough to last the both of us a few weeks, if I were careful to ration it.

I saw no more of the creatures the next morning, but Bran breathed easier and his pace quickened, and even I found the heat more bearable. We continued on, and forest gave way to vast, tilled fields, and the shapes of walled towns formed out of the morning fog.

Seventy-five days since I left the gates of the Dragon Temple, I arrived at the port. I smelled the sea before I saw it, and when I arrived at the banner-draped walls of the city, the sound of waves crashing against the rocks below reached my ears. Tears sprang to my eyes unbidden, for more than the salt sting in the air—I had not seen any ocean since I had left the far northern shore in a hollowed tree, paddling the icy waters with my hands. The tide had carried me to the edge of the steppe, where Aysulu had found me, and together we had walked away from the coast and into the rocky embrace of the vast continent.

I collected myself and gave Bran's inquisitive nose a pat, and together we approached the gate. Guards dressed in blue robes and plumed helmets stood beneath the banners, and they examined my javelins and looked in my saddlebags before allowing me through. I could not follow their conversation, nor the din of commerce in the bustling town. Only one of the guards understood the language I had learned at the temple, and he told me the way to the harbor.

White gulls cried to one another over the market, and the sun shone upon the scales of fresh-caught fish, the ink-black hair of the fishermen, and the emerald waters I had walked so far to find. Beyond that far horizon lay the volcanic island on which I would find the women who served the goddess of the deep. If I raised the brim of my hat and strained my eyes, I could just make out a shadow at the very edge of the green expanse.

A ship lay anchored between the harbor and that shadow. Its pair of masts held three great red sails, secured to their spars by a number of dangling ropes; thirty oars emerged from its sides, held out of the water. From the prow, the figure of a woman leaned over the lapping waves, her wild hair and her arms stretched back over the oars, her wooden face regarding the bright sky with an expression of delight. A sailor climbed on her side beneath her right arm, scraping barnacles from the carved folds of her garment.

She was the largest ship I had ever seen, thrice as long and easily seven times as wide as my dragon-headed longship, with a vast, rounded hull that sat low in the water. My company of brave warriors, crowded as we had been then, would not have been sufficient in number to crew this vessel. More figures, shadowed underneath the towering masts, moved about on the upper deck.

"Magnificent, isn't she?" someone said, and to my surprise, I understood him. It was not quite my mother tongue that he spoke, and the accent was utterly unfamiliar, but the meaning was clear. I turned around.

Before me stood a man in an open vest and wide trousers tucked into polished leather boots. Sun and wind had darkened his skin and lightened his hair to the color of dry grass, marking him as much a stranger here as I was. A short, curved sword hung from his hip, and on his head sat a broad hat festooned with multicolored plumage. The tallest feather, blue as the summer sky, reached only to the center of my chest, for despite the thick soles of his boots, this man stood only four feet tall.

"Her name is the *Lady of Osona*," he continued, "and she has sailed the length and breadth of the world three times over. She is worthy of your admiration."

I could not disagree. "How do you speak the language of the North?" I asked.

I lost what he said next in the differences between his tongue and mine, but from it I gathered that his name was Hamilcar and he was the *Lady*'s captain. He had come from far to the west, and would return there again by way of the islands in the sea called Ashinya. "I'm in need of another rower," he said, "but the fishermen here are quite reluctant to leave the paradise that is their home."

Fate smiled upon me this day, or perhaps the goddess of the deep who lay beneath the emerald waters had granted me a boon. "Will you be traveling the isle where the priestesses dwell beneath the peak of a towering volcano?" I asked. "If that is so, I would be happy to row in exchange for passage for myself and my horse."

Hamilcar's welcoming smile turned somber. "You're going to Hanowa, then?

"If that is indeed the name of the volcanic isle, then yes," I said. "I must speak to the priestesses."

He held up a hand. "Say no more, my friend. Hanowa shall be our first port, and there is a berth for you and a place for your horse, if you are willing to work. If after you enter their temple, your journey takes you onward with us, you will be welcome again. For now, though, we should depart, and quickly."

He glanced over his shoulder, the feathers on his hat bobbing. Several of the guards in blue had entered the market, and by the set of their shoulders and their hands hovering near their weapons, they had grown watchful since I had passed through the gate.

I followed Hamilcar down to the rowboat that would take us out to his ship. Bran, steadfast as he was, refused to step off the dock until I covered his eyes with a strip of cloth and guided him into the boat. He spread his legs against the slats, locking his knees. We pushed off into the water as the first of the guards came down to the water's edge.

"Are they looking for you?" I asked Hamilcar as he handed me the oar.

He gave me a devilish grin. "Not yet, but one can never be too careful."

I understood him poorly, but I could comprehend this: I had just entered the service of a pirate.

We reached the ship, and Hamilcar's crew lifted us onto the deck. I had only enough time to find a place for Bran below before the anchor lifted and I was called to the rowing bench. His baleful dark eyes followed me as I left him alone to wonder what might become of him in this cramped, dark space.

I rowed through the afternoon and into the evening, when I was permitted to rest and feed my horse. I slept in a corner of the upper deck beneath a clear night sky.

In the morning, the black volcano towered above the ship, wearing a ring of clouds around the hollow in its peak. Around its base grew a jungle of strange trees, their bare trunks swaying and their high leaves whispering in the wind from the sea. Smaller islands, also formed of dark volcanic stone, circled the volcano.

The captain had me row him and a wooden chest he did not open to the beach. I insisted on bringing Bran, as well, and allowing him to set foot on solid ground. I could not follow everything Hamilcar said to me as I pulled the oars, but he did use the word *curse* and warned me to treat the women of the island with respect.

I brought us to a weathered dock jutting out from sand the color of ash, and we disembarked, tying the boat to a post. As soon as Bran's hooves touched the dock, he tugged his lead out of my hand and ran for the edge of the trees, where he turned and waited for me with his ears flattened. A short distance away, a young girl of seven or eight, a golden flower in her long, black braid, stood knee-deep in the surf, checking woven traps for fish. She stopped still with her hands in the water, her eyes following Bran with terror and curiosity in equal measure.

I called out to her, out of habit, in the language of the steppe. To my great surprise, she answered me in the same tongue.

"Who are you?" she asked.

I held out my hands. "My name is Eske. I'm looking for the seers of the islands. A dragon told me that they could help me."

She looked past me to the captain, and at his iron-bound chest of unknown treasures, and her small round face twisted into an angry frown. "You need to leave," she said, pointing an accusing finger at him. "The grandmothers don't want you here."

He put a hand to his chest, affronted. When he answered her, he spoke the same language he had used on the ship, the one that was similar to my mother tongue. "When have I ever given your grandmothers offense?"

There was some magic at work here. Though the captain and I spoke different tongues, the girl conversed with both of us.

"How can you do that?" I asked her.

She turned her wide, dark eyes to me. "Do what?"

"Never mind," I said. "I've come a very long way. I need to speak to the grandmothers. Can you show me to them?"

"I don't know." She pulled a small silver fish from her trap and added it to a length of string, from which several other fish already hung. "The grandmothers don't talk to just anyone. I'm supposed to keep bad people away. Like him."

The captain adopted a pleading pose, palms together in front of him, and he pulled from his vest pocket a pastry of fried dough wrapped around bright red berries—it seemed he had come prepared with bribes for the island's gatekeeper. He waded into the surf and held it out to her.

She stood half a hand's breadth taller than he. "I suppose I can ask," she said, taking the offered gift, "but you have to stay here." She put the pastry in a pocket of her loose dress, gathered one more fish, and knotted her string.

"You'll find the priestesses through there," Hamilcar said, wading back to me as I placed the heavy chest onto the dock. He indicated a gap between the trees with a sweep of one sunburned hand. "Kala will show you the way."

"What will you do while I'm away?" I asked.

He sat down on the lid of the chest. "I'll find a place to hide this, and then bring the crew ashore. You may find us when your task is complete." He reached inside his vest and produced a small sack of coins. "Give this to the priestesses, with my regards."

I thanked him and caught up to Bran, winding his lead around my hand to keep him close. I turned to find the girl, Kala, with her string of fish clenched in both hands and red berries smeared on her face.

"This is Bran," I told her. "He is a gentle creature, but you must not frighten him by walking close behind him where he cannot see you."

She reached out toward Bran's velvet nose, but fear stopped her before she could touch it. Placing herself on my other side, she put one small, sticky hand in mine, and led me into the jungle.

Bright golden fruit peered out between leaves of the deepest green, and birds with cerulean feathers called out from the tops of the tall trees. A scarlet lizard, a tiny cousin of the fire-breathing salamander I had once faced in the arena of Phyreios, skittered across the narrow footpath.

Our path sloped toward the mountain. Though the earth lay quiet and still beneath our feet, the volcano was no less mighty than the ones that sprang forth in fire and steam from the sea in my homeland. I approached it with cautious steps, keeping my eyes on the glimpses of its jagged, cloud-wreathed peak that appeared through the trees.

The island was not so large, and we soon came to the village at the base of the mountain: five small huts built upon stilts in a sandy clearing, with roofs of grass and leaves. Behind them, where the mountain's foot rose stark and sheer from the ground, a doorway had been chiseled into the smooth, black rock. The sunlight that streamed through the trees did not reach beyond its dark lintels.

Three old women in long, woven skirts, their hair snow-white and braided with beads of wood and shell, gathered around a cooking fire. I smelled roasting fish and something sweet and tantalizing, and I recalled that I had been so eager to reach the island that I had not yet eaten.

"Grandmother, the pirate is here again," Kala said, announcing our arrival.

The first woman looked up from the fishing net she was repairing, setting her needle beside her. "Well, did you tell him to leave?"

"I did," said Kala, "but he's still here."

"That's because you took his pastries, dear," said the woman beside the cooking pot.

Kala wiped scarlet jam from her face with one hand, succeeding only in smearing it further.

The first woman addressed me without looking up. "Tell your captain," she said, "that if he wishes to hide his ill-gotten gains on our island, he has to pay the fee."

I held out the sack of coins. "I believe this was intended to cover the cost."

The woman stood and approached me. Her skin was a weathered brown, her eyes sharp and discerning. Once-black ink, turned a coppery green, covered her exposed arms in a pattern of waves and winding currents. The image of a shark, huge-bellied and ancient, stared at me from her left shoulder.

I bowed, my hands at my sides and my back straight, as I had been taught to do at the temple. It seemed the correct thing to do; I had been a child when last I visited a wise woman. I wanted this one to find me worthy.

She took the pouch from me and placed it in a hidden pocket in her skirt. "Run along and tell the pirate he is welcome here for the fortnight," she told Kala.

The girl darted away, disappearing into the forest.

The priestess stepped back, her eyes measuring me from head to foot, taking in my salt-stained temple clothing, my own tattoos on my bared arms, and my stranger's face. "You are unknown to us," she said. "Who are you, child?"

"My name is Eske. I have traveled a very long way to see you. The dragon of the temple, in the winter mountains far to the north, sent me here—she said you could help me to save someone I love."

"Ah, and how is the Lady Dragon these days?" the woman asked.

"She is well," I answered. "She enjoys her position as a wise teacher above the temple."

The woman inclined her head, her face creasing into a smile. "That is good to hear. It has been some time since we have seen her. You are just in time for breakfast, young man, and then we can speak about your errand."

I sat down on a flat stone beside the fire, and I ate a strange but satisfying dish of fish and fruit, tart and savory and sweet as honey all at once, and drank tea as red as fine wine. The first priestess sat down beside me, while her companions returned to their tasks, weaving baskets and stringing fish on a line to dry, observing me through quick, shrewd glances.

"You are welcome in Ashinya, Eske," the woman beside me said when the meal was finished, "and to Hanowa, our home. My name is Luana, and I have served here at the base of the mountain for ten years."

"Thank you," I replied, "for the welcome and the meal. It has been a long road."

Luana nodded. "It has been some time since we've had a visitor. If the Lady Dragon sent you to us, we will do what we can to help you."

"If there is anything I can offer in exchange, it is yours," I said.

"That is kind of you. There are a few tasks for which we could use a strapping young man, but we will discuss that later. First: where do you come from? Who were the people who raised you?"

These questions, to me, had little to do with my quest, but I stilled the impulse to argue. "I come from a land far to the north—farther even than the temple of the dragon. I once thought that I had reached the southernmost part of the world, only to find that there was yet more world to see. My father is Ivor, chieftain of the Clan of the Bear. My mother..." I fell quiet. There was an old wound, there, one I had not uncovered since long before I had set out to hunt the lind-worm that fateful day. "My mother is Amaruq of the Seal People. My father won her respect and her hand through a great feat of bravery, and lost both before I came of age. She returned to her family many years ago."

The second priestess set aside her basket and folded her weathered hands into her lap. "And where is your home, dear?"

I squared my shoulders into an imitation of confidence, but I could not raise my head to look any of the women in the eye. "I can tell you about the land where I was born," I said.

"That is not what I asked."

I had thought as much. A salt-scented wind came in from the beach, stirring the trees and rustling the thatched roofs. Though this wind was temperate, my thoughts went to my father's longhouse, perched upon the sheer gray cliff, with its stout walls and roaring central fire. Smoke would pour from the chimney and mix with the smell of the ocean and the bite of the coming frost. I would look out over the sea with Fearghus beside me, claiming a moment of quiet as our feasting kin sang through the night.

Home was also the iron-rich mountain outside of Phyreios, in the fortress hidden from the eyes of the city. Khalim and I had shared a tent beside the stable. I still possessed the canvas, though I no longer used it. The charcoal figures we had drawn on the inside were all I had left of him, and they faded with each passing day and each change of the weather. It lay at the bottom of my pack, buried under my provisions.

Even if I returned to my father's hall, even if I journeyed back to Phyreios, I would not find home again. I could wander for a lifetime, a hundred lifetimes, and still it would remain beyond my reach.

Luana accepted my prolonged silence with a calm smile. She handed me a second cup of the red tea.

I accepted it and held the clay vessel in both hands, tracing my thumbs over the pattern of ocher squares etched into its sides. "I think I have no home," I said at last. "Not in this world."

"Then that is why you have come," the third priestess said. "You wish to look through the Dreaming Eye, and find it in the next."

I set the teacup aside, carving a small circle into the sand where it could rest without tipping. "I know nothing of the Dreaming Eye. I mean to cross over, and to retrieve the soul of one I love, whose body was taken from him. It is my hope that you can show me the way."

Luana's gentle smile fell from her face. The eyes of the two others fell on me with an almost tangible weight.

"Oh, dear boy," Luana murmured. "What's dead should stay dead. I know the Lady Dragon and her disciples must have told you that already, but I will say it again, in the hopes that this time you will hear it."

"He did not die," I argued. "His body still lives—his god dwells in it now, after sending him to the world beyond."

Luana shook her head, sunlight shimmering over her snowy hair. "I don't see how it makes any difference." Her smile returned, soft and maternal, but her words cut like a knife.

"Khalim loved his god. He trusted him, he spent his entire life serving him, and for his faithfulness he was banished from the world while that god uses his hands to rebuild a city without him. This was not a death, not even an unjust one, though an injustice it was. I intend to set it right." I got up from my seat and knelt in the sand at Luana's feet, bowing my head. "I have been more than a year on this quest. I will spend a lifetime, if I need to, but I need your help."

Her weathered hand on my cheek was cool. "You are very young, Eske," she said. "A lifetime is both longer than you can imagine and shorter than you will believe, when you are as old as I. There are other young men who could love you, and in the meantime, there are fields to be planted, fish to be caught, sea-ways to be plotted, and children to be cared for. There may be ways for you to cross over and carry your body with you, but those ways are hidden from us for a reason."

"Who is to say that, had he lived," the third priestess said, "you and your Khalim would not have grown apart? I myself buried one husband and bade farewell to the second, when I came to Hanowa. It is the way of things."

Did she speak the truth? Would Khalim refuse me, when at last I found him, or even after, in the future that I hoped for but dared not imagine? "That may be so," I admitted. "But I will not make that choice for him. If he tells me that he wishes to go on without me, then so be it." Each word was as heavy as iron, falling from my mouth, and I shivered despite the warmth of the sun. I would not be like the First Hero, denying Khalim the freedom of his own will. In the arrogance of youth, I believed my love was greater than that of a god.

I am not certain I was wrong.

"But I must find him, first," I said.

Luana stood, and she took my hand and guided me to my feet. "Very well," she said. "Understand this: we cannot help you to cross over. That knowledge is not ours to keep. But we will prepare the ritual, and you will look into the Dreaming Eye of the goddess Nashurru, and you will see what you will see."

I took her hand in both of mine and bowed, pressing it to my forehead. "I will forever be in your debt."

"Preparations will take some time," said the second priestess. "You must be patient, and perform the deeds that we ask of you."

I released Luana's hand and straightened my back. "I am ready."

~ VI ~

THE SLOPE OF HANOWA

My first tasks were menial ones: mending a roof and hauling water in tightly woven baskets from a spring in the forest to the urns in the largest of the houses. At every moment, my eyes wandered to the stone edifice behind the village and its yawning black door, and each time, the eyes of the grandmothers lifted from their own tasks and followed me. As much as the temple doorway sang to me, beckoning me nearer, I would not stray any closer without permission. I had learned my lesson well in the dragon's temple. My labors were a test, I was certain, and not simply the tasks that three old women might ask of a young man who happened upon their village. I would prove that I had both the strength and the temperament to be allowed to partake of their ritual. I could only hope that this time, I would not have to wait a full turn of the seasons.

Evening fell, and I ate another meal of fish and hung a hammock of knotted rope between two slender trees. When the priestesses had gone to bed, I followed the smell of the sea down to the northern beach and let the rising tide wash over my feet. The beach was soft sand that compressed under my weight instead of crumbling rock, and the wind blew gently, without a hint of the arctic chill that touched the North even in high summer, but I had found the sea again, and it felt something like home.

Khalim had never seen the ocean. If I could give this to him, even once, I would count my quest well fulfilled.

I slept easily that night, the rocking of my hammock lulling me like the motion of a ship. I dreamed of floating mountains of ice, the passing of whales in the deep, and the sense of unbridled freedom that a longship once provided me.

When I woke, I gathered my knife and my javelins and carried them back to the circle of huts. If the priestesses had no other tasks for me, I planned to provide all of us with meat from the forest.

"Are you going into battle?" the second priestess asked as soon as she saw me. Her name, she had told me the day before as I had repaired the thatching of her house, was Kani, and she was the eldest of the grandmothers. "Not without a meal, I hope?"

"I wouldn't dream of it," I said. I sat down and accepted the dish she offered me.

Luana, the first priestess, placed a piece of smooth driftwood onto the cooking fire. "You'll be going up the mountain today, Eske," she said. "The herb we need for the ritual only grows in the high places. We would send Kala, but the boars have grown restless of late, and the climb is too dangerous for her."

No harm would come to the girl as long as I remained to prevent it. Besides, I intended to hunt one of those boars, and thus repay the grandmothers' hospitality. I stood, reaching back to test the points of my javelins.

"Sit down, young man," the third priestess, Malea, ordered. "Finish your meal. You will need your strength for the climb."

She described the plant for me as a vine that clung to the volcanic rock, with white flowers and striated yellow and green leaves.

I finished eating and thanked the priestesses, and I went to fetch Bran from where he wandered the village outskirts, eating leaves and drinking from the spring. The sea wind kept the heavy air away, and he had much improved, his eyes bright and his breathing steady.

The path up the volcano wound narrow and overgrown through the forest, walked only by animals and one small girl, but it was clear enough. One of my javelins knocked against a low-hanging branch, and a pair of sapphire birds took to the air, flying around my head and screeching their displeasure. They departed and found another, hidden branch on which to sit and sing their raucous song.

My legs had grown accustomed to slopes after my year on the dragon's mountain, and I maintained a steady pace as I climbed toward the top of the volcano. I kept my footsteps quiet, listening for the heavy tread and snorting breath of boars. Even so, half an hour from the grandmothers' village, my footsteps picked up an echo. I stopped, and in the quiet I heard a stifled laugh and the rustling of branches.

"Who's there?" I said aloud, though I knew the answer. "Is it a boar, come to skewer me with its tusks?"

I turned as another laugh troubled a low plant, its trembling leaves as broad as a cooking pot. I took out a javelin and held the point in my hand to lift the leaf with the other end. There I found Kala, crouched in the undergrowth.

"What are you doing here?" I asked. "I'm going up the mountain to find the plant for the ritual. It's too dangerous for you."

Kala accepted my hand and got to her feet. "I thought you might get lost."

"Didn't the grandmothers tell you about the boars?"

She crossed her arms in the image of small, stubborn defiance. "But I always get the flowers," she said, "and you don't even know the way."

I did not fear becoming lost; the island was too small, and if I were to lose my way, I could find my way to the beach and walk by the sea until I came to the weathered dock again. The longer Kala maintained her obstinate pout, however, the more I doubted that she would obey me after disobeying the priestesses she served.

Better to keep her with me, then, where I could fend off any wandering boars.

"You may be right," I said. "I could use a guide. Have you ever ridden a horse before?"

Her eyes went wide, and she shook her head. I took Bran's lead and brought him closer. He nosed at her hair and the folds of her dress, looking for hidden food. Careful and reverent, Kala stroked the soft plane down the front of his face.

When their introductions had finished, I lifted Kala into the saddle, tightening the straps and placing her feet in the stirrups. "Hold on," I instructed, guiding her hands to the pommel. "If a boar appears, Bran will carry you to safety."

We continued up the narrow path, Kala holding the saddle as instructed as she rocked back and forth with the horse's gait. I kept his lead close and my eyes open for a sign of danger.

"Did you get to see the dragon?" Kala asked. "Is she beautiful?"

I conjured the image of the dragon in my memory, and felt again the bone-deep terror that had seized me on the mountain peak as she had examined me, laying bare my frailties with her great, shining eyes. "She is, in a way," I said. "Her scales shimmer like the ocean in the sun, and her antlers scrape against the clouds. She is wise, as well, and I am honored to have received her guidance on my quest. It's a quest for true love, you know."

"It is?" said Kala.

I thought of my own sister, though she had been much older than Kala when last I saw her. By this time, she must have been a woman grown. When we were children, I would tell her stories, and she would listen in rapt attention—my first audience, and perhaps my best, excluding my present company. She liked the stories of monsters foremost, followed by any with young heroines, to whom I always gave her name: Ylla.

"My love is trapped in the other world," I told Kala. "I mean to rescue him. He is kind and sweet, even to a warrior and a brute such as me. He saved my life, when I fought a monster in the arena of Phyreios—far north of here, beyond the sea. You'd like him. He is beautiful, and his hair is soft as a feather, and he is among the bravest of all the men who have ever lived."

In telling her of Khalim, I did not tell her of his frailties, or of the encroaching madness of the god-touched; how in the middle of the night he shook and sobbed in my arms in terror of his visions. Nor did I tell her how afraid I had been then. *Let Kala think of him as the hero of this story,* I thought, *and let me remember him the same way.*

Kala soon complained of sore legs, and she climbed down from the horse without waiting for me to assist her. I had no warning but the quiet rustle of leaves before the boar appeared.

Its mad dash through the forest had stained its long, gray coat a mottled green. Four tusks emerged from its snarling mouth, stark white even in the shade; the larger tusk on its left side had broken some time ago into a sharper point. It lunged for Kala, tossing its enormous snout, its tusks raking the air.

Bran kicked and ran up the path. Kala screamed. She still clung to one stirrup, and she stumbled through the brush. The boar screeched in displeasure and circled about for another charge.

I took a javelin in both hands and charged after it. As it turned toward me, I drove the spear point into its shoulder, biting through hide and flesh. The boar twisted away and wrenched the shaft from my hands. I needed a greater weapon, a winged spear that a better rider than I could wield from horseback, but I carried no such thing.

I roared a wordless challenge. The boar lowered its head, aiming its tusks at my midsection. I reached for another javelin.

The island shook. At my back, the volcano groaned, stirring from a long slumber, and the surrounding din of birdsong and buzzing insects fell silent. The boar shook its great head and dove into the trees, tearing furrows into the soft earth.

The mountain quieted, but above the trees, a column of steam wound its way into the sky. The volcano had woken, and it would not soon return to sleep.

I found Kala and Bran a short distance away, Kala's hands bloodless around the stirrup. She had taken a tumble, and dirt clung to her skinned knees, but she was otherwise unhurt. Bran stood with his legs apart and his head lowered, only raising it as I came near.

"You did the right thing, holding onto Bran," I told Kala. "I'll take you back to the grandmothers."

She wiped at her streaming eyes and running nose with the back of her hand and sniffled. "I wasn't scared."

"I know," I said, and I lifted her back into the saddle.

When we returned to the village, the priestesses stood on the beach, their faces turned toward the cloud-wreathed mountain. I helped Kala down to the sand, and she ran and clung to Malea's skirt.

"We have nothing to fear," Luana said. "Not yet. But we will make our preparations in anticipation of the appointed time. You must return to the mountainside in all haste, Eske."

Malea put her arms around the girl. "Something stirs beneath the sea. It will reach our shores before long."

I returned to the forest. By the time I retread the path as far as I had come before, the day had turned to evening. Beneath my feet, the volcano lay at rest, between sleeping and waking. In the distant lands of my birth, mountains like this one rose in jagged peaks form the ocean, spitting fire and ash into the clear winter sky, too dangerous to approach and too steep to summit, should one have had the courage to take up the challenge. We warned our children and young warriors not to make the attempt, even if the mountain in question had not erupted in a lifetime, for it could wake again at any moment.

The trees grew sparse, and the volcano's crown of clouds settled over me, coating my skin in cold mist. I found a path through the black rock, carved by rain and hard stone chisels. Here grew the flowering vines the priestesses had sent me to find, clinging to the marks of tools and the thick red lichen that grew in the shade. I gathered it in handfuls, winding the stems into a tight bundle that I tucked into my quiver, in the space left by the javelin the boar had taken from me.

I climbed farther in the quiet of the mountain's rest, taut as a held breath, and at last I pulled myself up to the mouth of the volcano. A vast, hollow space stretched out before me, round as a bowl and painted in green foliage. A lake lay at the bottom, as brilliant blue as the morning sky and so clear that I could see down to the black stone below, riven with fissures. Bubbles escaped from these deep, dark cracks, hinting at the unrest beneath. No living person had touched that lake since the volcano had last awoken an age ago—the slope was too steep, and the lichen provided no handholds. The faint smell of brimstone hung in the air.

In the last light of the evening, I climbed down to the trees and found a dry branch to serve as a torch. I reached the village just as the faint edge of the sliver moon dropped below the horizon. A small boat, its white sail decorated with lines of ocher paint, sat tethered to the dock, laden with baskets of provisions. In the distance, the *Lady of Osona* lay anchored, its sails silhouetted against the strange southern constellations. All who dwelled here, however transient, had prepared for a quick departure.

Luana took the herbs from me and placed them in a wide, shallow basket, and she listened to my account of the climb without speaking.

"Will it be enough?" I asked, filling the silence. "Will there be time before the mountain erupts?"

"The herbs will need to dry," she said. "Tomorrow night is the new moon. You will undertake the ritual then. You should eat, and rest, and gather your strength."

I concealed a sigh of relief. I had her approval, or as much of it as she would give me.

As I was instructed, I partook of what was left of the evening meal and went to my hammock by the shore. In the quiet, I thought to offer a prayer to Nashurru, goddess of the deep and the places between, but no words came to me. I had lost the will to pray when I last looked into the golden eyes of the god who had taken Khalim from me. I would make my petition to the goddess in the Dreaming Eye, and not before.

When morning came, Kala gathered the flowers from where they hung between the grandmothers' houses and took them away into the black stone temple. Though the sun shone bright and the sky was clear, even at the crown of the volcano, a shadow fell over the tiny village. The priestesses did not speak to me, and while countless questions filled my mind, I could give voice to none of them. The grandmothers fed me, and smiled, and allowed me to remain in silence. They watched me as I stoked the cooking fire and took the dishes down to the water to wash.

My long day of waiting concluded at last with our evening meal. A cold wind stirred the embers of the fire and whistled down the black corridor beneath the mountain.

"When I look into the Dreaming Eye," I asked, "what will I see?" It was the first that I had spoken that day, and my voice was harsh and unfamiliar.

Luana shook her head. "There is no way of knowing. Most will see Nashurru, for she keeps the passage between waking and dreaming. Some see the past; others, the future. You wish to look beyond the door into the other world, but whether you will succeed, I cannot say. Are you ready?"

I rose from my place beside the fire. Luana led the way, and Kani and Malea took up torches and followed.

Kala watched me, a mix of envy and fear on her face. She would not be present for the ritual.

"Wish me good fortune," I said.

She put on a determined frown. "Don't be scared."

"I promise." I drew a full breath, filling my lungs as the monks at the temple had taught me, and I passed between the basalt columns and into the belly of the volcano.

The passage opened into a circular chamber, with a platform around a still pool that covered most of the room. Glowing crystals set into the ceiling gave off a pale blue light that reflected in the water like a field of stars. Ahead of me, Luana went down a wide, shallow staircase and waded in. Her long, woven skirt trailed behind her. The water came up to her chest as she crossed to a pedestal at the center, but the surface of the pool remained smooth as glass.

Kani and Malea lit two braziers flanking the steps, and four more around the chamber's perimeter. Within the iron bowls, the vines I had gathered from the mountain burned, and the air filled with sweet, cloying smoke. I took another breath. I was no stranger to magical hallucinogens; the smell was not quite the same, but I could close my eyes and imagine I was confined in the hall during my rite of manhood, waiting for my senses to be confused and my mind open to the world of the gods before I took up a spear and walked into the forest, a solitary hunt both dangerous and divine. Young as I still was, the memory of that night had become so distant that it seemed to have happened to some other warrior.

Luana beckoned me to follow. I removed my boots and stripped to the waist. My feet disturbed the surface, sending ripples out to splash against the sides of the pool. Without the sun to warm it, the water was cold, and the hairs on my arms stood on end.

From the pedestal, Luana removed a small bowl of black stone. Holding it in both hands, she dipped it into the pool and filled it to the brim. Neither the stone nor the water within reflected any light from the incandescent crystals above. I reached the center of the pool and peered into the vessel; it was no longer a bowl, but a lightless chasm without an end.

The crystals took on new colors as the burning herbs coursed through my body, and Luana's face shimmered like the illusion of water in the desert. "Nashurru, goddess of the sea and the abyss and of the places between, cannot grant you passage into the other world. To our knowledge, no god can, but she may allow you to see into it. Though your body will remain here in the temple as an anchor, you must be on your guard. As a living being, you will attract the attention of wandering spirits, not all of whom are benevolent. The things you see may not represent the truth. Spirits often lie; some deliberately, and others because they are so far removed from life that they cannot speak a truth that you will understand. There may also be others—gods who grow strong out of fear, rather than worship."

"I have met such gods. How can I resist them?" I asked. My voice sounded as though it came from someone else, standing some distance away.

"Remember who you are, and remember what you are trying to achieve. You do this for love—focus on that." She took each of my hands and placed them on the edges of the pedestal, so that I bent over the bowl and gazed into its improbable depths. "Show respect at all times," she said. "Accept no gifts, make no agreements. Offer nothing you would not gladly part with. May your eyes be clear."

I fell into the Dreaming Eye, leaving my body standing at the pedestal and plunging into the deep ocean held within the bowl. Water closed in around me, cold and dark, though I still drew breath. I fell and came to a stop, floating above a rippling surface like a second sea lying beneath the one in which I swam. Before me lay an archway constructed of piled bones, its columns disappearing into the depths below. I kicked my legs and pushed myself closer. Skulls with three eye sockets stared back at me from the macabre heap, and spines with pointed spikes held up the arch. Clawed finger bones reached out to me as I drifted closer. Still other bones had the appearance of a human skeleton, though one far larger than I. These were the bones of gods, and of the mythical beasts they hunted across the plains of eternal summer in the stories of my people.

Here stood the gate of bone that Khalim had told me of the last time I had seen him. I studied its eldritch shape and swore that I would breach it, today or one day in the future.

The water beneath me surged, and I tumbled away from the gate. A pair of flukes, together as far across as the length of the pirate's ship, flashed into my vision before receding into darkness. Another wave pushed into me as that enormous tail turned.

Something massive moved in the depths, and it knew I was here.

~ VII ~

THE ABYSS

I kicked my legs and held out my arms to steady myself. My body moved as if I swam through mud instead of the water I saw all around me; as if I swam in a dream. Light filtered down from above and fell upon the gate of bone and upon the fin of a mighty whale that swam in the depths below.

A human hand, the same gray-blue as the whale's fins and as long from wrist to fingertips as I was tall, emerged from the darkness. Its arm, encrusted in barnacles and dappled in white and gray, followed. The figure unfurled its great length, and I found myself face to face with a giantess, her upper body bare and mottled with coral, and her waist tapering down to a pair of great flukes. Her hair was long sea-grass, and colorful fish darted between the fronds. Her face, angular and sharp-toothed, held a whale's huge, dark eyes. She studied me with one, and I saw myself reflected in it, tiny and distorted. Unhurried, she turned her head to fix me with the other.

Other things moved in the depths around her: things with needle teeth and glowing eyes, with lights that undulated through their translucent flesh, with hands and fins like clear glass disturbing the water as they came nearer.

I could not move. In the distance, my body breathed, though my consciousness remained submerged in this otherworldly sea. A terrible, deep note sounded through the depths, shaking the bones of the gate and stilling my heart for two terrifying beats. A question rang in that note, and in the wide-set eyes of the giantess. At last, I understood: I swam before Nashurru, goddess of the deep and the places between, and she wished to know why I had come to her.

"I must pass through that door," I said. The black ocean dampened my words, making them all but silent.

Nonetheless, Nashurru had heard me. She turned her face to regard me again with her left eye. A piercing, silver note shivered through the water, her long, ridged throat vibrating with it. It pierced my drug-addled thoughts and left in its wake the single question: *why?*

I abandoned my attempts to speak. Instead, in my mind's eye I conjured the memory of Khalim, as best as I could after more than a year—long-fingered hands and soft dark eyes and a wide, earnest smile. The image of his face was fading, and at that realization, grief welled up through my body, cold as the abyss. I grasped at all I could remember: the even rhythm of his breath as he slept, the sharp angles of his shoulder blades, the scar on his side where an assassin's knife had found him in a Phyreian alley.

Two great hands came together before me, churning the water. Nashurru's palms alone were as wide as the deck of a ship. Eerie blue light coalesced into a globe between them. She sang once more, and I felt as though my bones, here and in the chamber under the volcano, had turned to liquid and dissipated into the water around me. Within the light, the shadow of a city formed and brightened into a sharp, clear image.

A street of white marble stretched out into the distance. Houses of wood and stone stood in neat rows, and people in robes of bright colors passed in and out of the vision, carrying wooden boards and iron tools. The road ended at the foundations of a marble palace, covered with a temporary shelter of canvas stretched over wooden poles. A grand table stood under the shelter, its four sturdy legs carved with figures of hunting dogs and eagles—a table fit for a king. Atop it was scattered a collection of maps and figures, showing grids of intersecting streets and a drawing of a high dome with its supporting network of beams.

Familiar faces clustered around the table. There stood Reva, the head of the Phyreian miners' guild, her back straight and her hair like glossy obsidian; beside her was Roshani, princess of House Darela, in a riding costume of fine blue silk. Artyom of House Kaburh bent over a map, tracing an inked street with a blunt forefinger. His beard had grown longer since last we had met.

The vision turned to the head of the table, and for one wrenching moment I thought that I saw what I had come here to see. Tall and serene, with long brown limbs clothed in plain linen, iron circlet upon his curls, stood the god, Torr, in the body of my beloved.

Once, I could have told the difference between Khalim and the god he had carried in a glance, but I lingered in hope for the space of another breath. He lifted his head as though he could see me, fixing me with his hard, golden eyes.

I turned away. "Please," I begged the goddess. "Don't show me Phyreios. Nothing remains for me there."

She tilted her head to one side, and her deep green hair fluttered. Pressing her palms together, she collapsed the vision.

Torr had once judged me and found me worthy of wielding the sword he had imbued with his will, and I had believed myself inured to the measuring gaze of a god. Under the whale eyes of Nashurru, I felt myself fall short. I curled into the semblance of a bow, tucking in my head and holding out my open hands. Tiny silver fish swam out from the fronds of her hair and bit at my fingers with toothless mouths, and below me, the strange, terrible things in the deep rose to surround me with their flickering lights.

"Mistress of the sea, of the abyss and the places between," I said, "goddess of the priestesses of Hanowa, I humbly request your help. The one I seek is no longer upon the earth. He resides in the realm of the god Torr, or so I was promised. Will you let me see him?"

The waters trembled as the goddess sang another low tone. With a crack, a mighty tusk broke free of the gate and tumbled, end over end, into darkness. Light bloomed from her hands again, washing over me and illuminating the gate of bone with a pale, ghostly hue.

I raised my head. Again, the vision showed me a street of marble the color of fresh snow, but this was not Phyreios. The buildings were new, shining in the red sunset. Its streets showed no dust, no footprints, none of the debris of human habitation. Its small, manicured trees, planted at precise intervals, shed no leaves on the pavement. For all its beauty, the city was all but dead, and Khalim was not there.

The vision moved with me as I turned my head. I followed the main thoroughfare to a domed temple that shone in the low, red sun, and then in the opposite direction to a vast wooden gate, flanked by a pair of magnificent statues. My body, left behind under the mountain, drew a sharp breath when I recognized their faces. On the left stood Ihsad, lord of House Darela, and on the right stood his only son, Jahan, slain beneath the arena in the last, vile ritual of the Seven Ascended.

The gate shuddered open. Crimson light poured from it onto the flagstones, split into two beams by the long, thin shadow of a small figure standing at the feet of the statues. He stood with his head bent against a sudden gust of wind, holding his threadbare coat around him and shielding his eyes with his other hand. His feet were bare, and his jaw clenched with a familiar, determined tension.

Khalim. How could I have ever mistaken another—man or god—for him?

He slipped through the gap in the door. It closed behind him with a sound like a thunderclap, and he was gone, out of Torr's city and out of my sight.

The vision went dark. For the first time since I submerged myself in the Dreaming Eye and its alien ocean, the weight of its water enclosed me in a crushing grip. My breath came in gasps, struggling against the pressure that struck both my ears like a pair of daggers. Icy water, and the grip of a long tentacle from the deep, pulled me down into the dark.

My dream-body was as heavy as a stone. I reached up, driving my hands through water turned suddenly cold. Still I fell, dragged down the length of the goddess's flukes, as she gazed down on me with indifferent eyes.

I would not die here. I had seen one glimpse of my beloved, and it had bolstered my resolve. With a roar that none but I could hear, I kicked away the grasping tentacle. Inch by inch, I clawed my way toward the distant surface and the inhuman face watching me struggle, and I laid one hand upon her barnacled side.

She lowered her hand, wrapping her fingers around me as one would trap an insect. Her whale-song wove earth-shaking notes with aimless, sweet fluting, a tapestry of sound that swept over me in a wave. She drew me up to the level of her eyes, and my back and legs burned where her fingertips touched me.

I clenched my teeth against the pain. "Khalim has left the place of the god Torr," I said. "Can you show me where he wanders?"

Nashurru, as ever, said nothing. One last, low tone shook my body and the gate of bone, and all turned to black.

I awoke alone in my hammock on the beach. Though my ears rang, I heard the sound of waves, and the first rays of sunlight warmed my skin. I had returned to the waking world.

I stood and walked to the edge of the water, the place between the land and the deep, and I knelt in the surf and gave thanks to the goddess of the abyss for the vision she had granted me, however brief. Against the bright horizon, a great whale spouted and dove, raising its flukes to the sun.

But I also wept, there in the wet sand in the early hour, for the loss of that vision. A second time I had lost Khalim, and in my deepest thoughts I cursed Torr and Nashurru in equal measure, as shameful as it was. When the grandmothers woke, they found me there among the shallows, and they brought me back to dry land.

It was not until after I had hung my clothes to dry that I took notice of the fingerprints the goddess had left on my skin: the whorl of a thumb against my left thigh and the half-arches of a fingertip over my ribs on the right side, seared in white like the scar of an old burn.

~ VIII ~

THE EMERALD SEA

"What will you do now?" Luana asked me. Though the sun streamed bright and golden through the trees, a dark cloud had passed over me. Through the Dreaming Eye I had caught the briefest glimpse of my beloved, and now he was gone, departed from the place set aside for him by the First Hero and wandering across an unknown country. How foolish I had been to think that he would remain there and await rescue. My Khalim was many things, but patient was not one of them. He must have hated that pale, dead city. It had nothing that he loved in its meager confines; no growing things other than the scant, stunted trees, no open sky, no human beings. Once, he had told me that he had never been alone. Torr's realm must have been terrifying in its stark loneliness.

"My quest remains the same," I said. "All that has changed is that I now know I will not find Khalim in Torr's kingdom. I still intend to find him."

Luana's face was somber. "We can offer you no more help. Nashurru has shown you as much as she is willing, and we have not the means to allow you to cross over before the time of your death. If the mountain continues to tremble, we will need to depart from this island with all haste. I am sorry."

"I understand."

"Is that so?" Kani, eldest of the priestesses, demanded. "You have been told that there is no way for you to enter the land of the dead, and yet you persist. You have undertaken the ritual, communed with the goddess, and yet you are not satisfied. I fear you will remain so until you have turned to the forbidden arts, twisting your body and mind into something neither living nor dead."

She pointed one weathered, accusing finger at my chest. I backed away, holding out my hands in supplication and protestation of my innocence. "I swear to you, I will do no such thing. I have neither the talent nor the inclination for magic. I do not wish to defy death for myself or for Khalim. My only desire is to return to him the life that was stolen."

"You insist there is a difference between the two," Luana said, much more gently than her companion, "and I see how your grief has made it seem so. In time, you will understand that all deaths are the same. All are equally dreaded, equally unjust, and equally given."

My welcome here, granted to me by the word of the dragon, was wearing thin. I would not be permitted a second look into the Dreaming Eye. "I will not ask anything of you that you would not willingly give me," I said. "Allow me one last question, and I will depart from your isle."

"Ask it," said Luana. "We will not drive you from our shores so cruelly."

I knelt again in the sand, as much a capitulation to the weight of my task as it was a show of respect. I had the words to boast of my deeds, to tell of my long journey, but I had none to convince the grandmothers of my intentions. "Khalim wanders the world beyond," I said. "It might be some time before I am able to find him. How will I know where he has gone?"

Luana reached out and placed her small, brown hand on mine. "Only he could tell you that. It is not like this world, where islands are rooted in place and the wind and the sea obey the sun and moon. There, the world changes according to the will of the gods and of the mortal souls that dwell within it."

"There must be some way I can find him again," I said. If only I had been able to speak to him, to tell him that I had not forgotten him and I would come for him soon. If only I could have asked him what he meant to do.

"You said he was free of his prison," said Luana. "He wanders of his own will. Do you know where that will would carry him?"

I opened my mouth to speak, but I had no answer for her. Khalim had told me where he had come from, and how he had come to Phyreios, but now that he was separated from everything he had loved, I could not say what he would choose to do next.

Our acquaintance had been so brief. Already I had spent many times longer in pursuit of him than I had spent in his company. Despair washed over me, followed by a second wave of anger, like a rising tide. The gods had permitted the Seven Ascended to crush the people of Phyreios beneath their shining feet for generations, and they permitted the mountain of Hanowa to stir, threatening to cover the island in fire, but they did not allow me to love Khalim for more than the turn of a moon.

"I don't know," I confessed at last, and I bent to the soft sand, my hands sinking into its warmth. My body was heavy with exhaustion, as though it had endured great feats while my mind had left it to enter the Dreaming Eye. Grief carved a hollow in my chest.

"Think on it," Luana said. "But you must prepare to depart, as we will. We do not know how long the mountain will sleep."

Luana had warned me of duplicitous spirits and wicked gods, of which I had only managed a glimpse in the depths, and Jin had admonished me not to be deceived. Khalim had received no such warnings. If only he had possessed the good sense to stay where Torr had promised he would be safe. Now he wandered, unprotected, beyond where even the Dreaming Eye could see.

But when had he ever done as he was told? He had obeyed only the command of his god, and now he defied even that.

My anger lasted only the length of a heartbeat before it turned again to pain. If given the chance, I would follow him and speak not a word against him. I could not blame him for rejecting the gifts of the god who had stolen him from me. After I had seen the prison-paradise Torr had offered with my own eyes, I could fault him even less. I swore I would never confine him as Torr had done.

I picked myself up and went to Bran's saddlebags where they lay beneath my hammock. The horse himself had wandered down to the beach, where he chased Kala in the glittering morning surf under the watchful eye of the priestess Malea.

From my pack, I retrieved the small canvas tent that Khalim and I had shared on the mountainside. With utmost care, I unrolled the canvas onto a stretch of gray sand, and my heart sank to behold what had become of it. Weeks in the rain and damp on the road from the temple had turned the charcoal figures to translucent ghosts, their lines blurred and their shapes softened. Still, I could follow Khalim's road from a thatch-roofed house, across a rice field presided over by humpbacked cattle, to a wide, muddy river, and finally past the wind-etched rocks of the red desert. At the top of the tent, where the canvas creased, stood Phyreios, with the mountain behind it, vigilant over the city's spires.

I would not return to Phyreios, but I could find where Khalim's journey began, in the village he had called home: Nagara, on the banks of the river. There, I might find his family, those who had known him longer than I had, and I might gain some insight as to where he might go now that he was free of the pale citadel.

The grandmothers had nothing to fear, I thought. I could find my way to Khalim without any more of their aid, and without the use of the dark sorcery of which they spoke. If I could not trust the gods, then I would put my faith in Khalim's stubbornness, Aysulu's generosity, and Bran's steadfastness, and the need of a large ship for another rower.

I bade a sad farewell to Kala, and thanked the grandmothers again for their hospitality. Luana put a cool hand to my face and wished me good fortune, but Kani's sharp eyes held only suspicion. Above, the volcano hissed like a great serpent, disturbed again from its rest.

I took Bran around the island to the eastern beach, where the crew of the *Lady of Osona* lay in the sun, passing bottles of liquor among themselves and crafting fans of palm leaves. Their rowboats lay heavy in the water, burdened for a swift departure, and the ship herself waited a short distance out with her oars high.

The captain got up from his place beneath a shady tree and greeted me with a broad wave and a winsome smile. He beckoned me closer.

"I need to sail west," I told him, gesturing toward the declining afternoon sun, "to the green country south of the desert. I can row."

He looked up at me with a frown. Our languages were distant cousins, not brothers, and I feared he hadn't understood a word.

At last, he said, "West, then!" and a number of other things I could only guess, but he spread his arms wide, and the sailors cheered.

A tall man with a sun-darkened face and a scar across one high cheekbone handed me a bottle of sweet brown liquor. Once I had swallowed half of it and the island swam pleasantly about me, another sailor with hair in tight black curls against his head, tied away from his handsome face with a scarf the color of golden spice, took me by the arm and led me to a table where others were engaged in a contest of arm wrestling.

He pushed me into a wobbly chair, set into the sand at a precarious angle. Opposite me sat an elderly man, his face like worn leather and his arms like the knotted branches of an oak. What teeth he had remaining were capped in gold and silver. He set his elbow on the barrel between us and held up his hand.

I glanced at the eager faces of the surrounding sailors. Years at sea had made this man strong, but I was a third his age and a warrior born. Another man, a redheaded fellow as broad as I, gave me an encouraging smile.

I placed my hand in the old man's and began to push against him.

Pain shot through my leg. I cried out, and my grip faltered. The old man slammed my hand against the barrel, and he jumped to his feet and laughed in delight.

I did not need to understand the words of his triumphant boast to fathom what had occurred. He had kicked me, his bony foot connecting with my shin. I laughed as well, as did the other sailors, and I knew that this, too, had been a test. I had lost the contest of strength, but gained their esteem.

We returned to the ship before evening. The volcano was quiet again, but the sailors watched its cloud-ringed peak until the night covered it completely.

"It's coming from the west," I heard them say. "All the islands are shaking. Something stirs in the deep."

"We'll be clear of it soon," Hamilcar promised them.

That first night I spent on board the ship, I dreamed.

I floated in the abyss before the gate of bone, with blackness pressing around me and the shape of the goddess Nashurru moving in the depths below. My body ached with the chill of the water, my limbs stiff and shivering. I kicked my legs and reached my arms toward the gate, but no matter how I moved, I came no closer, and the cold pierced my bones and filled my belly with ice. My chest contracted, trying to breathe and sucking against nothing. The bright white of the bones grew soft as my vision faded. At last, I could withstand no more, and I inhaled frigid water.

I would die here, I thought, and my bones would join the gate as Nashurru looked on, indifferent. I would never see Khalim again.

A strong hand reached down from the surface and gripped mine, and I was hauled out of the darkness. I coughed and spat seawater onto the deck of a ship—not the pirate's ship, with its twin masts and its crimson sails, but a longship. It was *my* longship, the one I had wrecked on the far northern sea so long ago. Its oars sat still, its benches empty, and its figurehead, the carved imitation of the sea serpent I had sailed out to hunt, gazed out over a flat, gray horizon.

In the bow sat Fearghus.

He was exactly as I remembered him: copper hair cut short and caressed by the wind, freckles across his nose, a cloak of deep blue around his strong shoulders. To me, he seemed young. It was I who had grown older.

"The eye is open," he said.

The sky stretched out, dark as iron, over the still water. Not even a bird moved in that gray expanse, so far were we from the land.

"I don't understand," I told him.

Fearghus only shook his head. "Wake up, Eske," he said, "before you no longer remember how."

And wake I did, in my rope hammock hung belowdecks, beside where Bran slept between two bales of hay and in the company of a pair of goats. He lifted his head and sniffed at my offered hand. Satisfied that I was not in danger, he returned to his uneasy sleep. The motion of the ship unnerved him, and neither the view of the surrounding water nor his confinement below gave him any comfort.

He no longer struggled to breathe, but it may have been foolish for me to bring him aboard. I might have left him with Kala on the priestesses' island, to spare him the discomfort and bewilderment of a long voyage. I could not explain to him that dry land would come soon enough and he had no reason to be afraid, not in any tongue he could understand.

For better or for worse, I would not give Bran up. If I lost him, I would once again be alone. The sailors slept around me, their hammocks clustered like the fruit that hung from the islands' tall trees, swaying with the motion of the sea. Even surrounded by others, their sleeping bodies nearly touching my shoulders, an unseen wall separated me from them, and only Bran and I stood within it.

I climbed the ladder to the upper deck. Even at night, the air was warm and close, and the clear sky glittered with its strange southern stars. Dawn waited just below the horizon.

The eye is open.

I did not know what these words meant, but they weighed on me as heavily as the barrels I had taken to the hold the previous evening. The gods sent dreams to their servants, yes, but I was neither a shaman nor a prophet—and now, I served no gods. Such dreams had plagued Khalim, and each night that he had woken shaking and sobbing, I had wished that I could have taken that burden from him, but it could not have been mine to bear.

Why had I dreamed of Fearghus? He had perished at sea, and I had only myself and my own hubris to blame. I took some small comfort in the knowledge that he would hunt and fight with his ancestors and the gods of our people, and be given an honored place for his death in the struggle against the lind-worm. I spent the months alone, after, wishing that I'd had the good fortune to join him.

The night sky granted me no answers. I returned to my hammock, and the sea lulled me back to sleep, this time without dreaming.

A portion of the distance between myself and the ship's crew was that of language, and it was the first I overcame. I spent the next morning's shift on the oars seated beside the broad, red-haired fellow who had arbitrated the wrestling contest.

"You once rowed a longship, didn't you?" he said, and though his accent was unfamiliar, I understood him clearly.

His name was Halvor, and he was once a raider of the North—though not as far north as I had once made my home. At the edge of the tundra, on the harsh western coast, where storms brought rain and snow in equal measure throughout the year, stood the halls of his people. The longship he had once crewed, and the chieftain who had commanded it, had both been lost in a battle upon the waves, and he chanced to find the *Lady of Osona* and her captain some weeks later.

Under Halvor's tutelage, I learned the distinctive language of the ship. The crew numbered forty strong, twelve of them women, and few shared a mother tongue. Thus they spoke a language that combined all of them, along with what was spoken on the isles and in the kingdoms of the South, and thus they communed with each other and those with whom they traded and fought as they crossed the breadth of the world year by year. They ate well, and shared both their ill-gotten gains and their legitimate earnings in equal portions.

When my mastery of the ship's own idiom proved sufficient, I met with the captain. He went by the name of Hamilcar the Great, and I heard no one dispute the title, though it was known that the name was an assumed one. He had won the *Lady of Osona* in a game of chance on one of these clustered islands, and had been plying his trade as a pirate ever since. Despite his small stature, his presence commanded the ship: he was fond of expansive gestures, often involving sweeps of his feathered hat, and his wardrobe consisted of fine silks in garish colors. He slept in a small cabin beneath the topmost deck, and what space was not devoted to his cot and a small table was packed with maps of the seas and charts of the stars, a treasure no less valuable or more easily won than stolen gold.

"It is good to meet you properly at last, Eske," he said. "Halvor says you are a strong rower. Tell me, how long will you remain with us? Where do you intend to go?"

I told him all I could. "I seek a vast green country, south of the citadel of Phyreios. I'm looking for a particular village—Nagara, it is called, though I doubt any here would know of it. It would take a man six months to walk from there to the citadel, crossing the desert."

Hamilcar pulled a rolled map from a shelf behind him and spread it out on the tabletop. Lines of red ink marked islands and coastlines, and rows of cramped black lettering filled the spaces between them.

With an open hand, he gestured to the upper portion of the map, a blank space marred only by the wandering ink line of a river. "From your description, that village lies somewhere here. I'm afraid I've never set foot in this land, though I have heard tell of Phyreios." He traced a finger down to the end of the peninsula, where a port was marked in red. "If you wish to stay with us, we will reach Hali by the end of the year. You can make your way over land from there."

"If you'll have me that long, then I will stay," I said.

He grinned, showing his teeth. "The grandmothers of Hanowa saw fit to help you. I could do no less."

I bowed my head. "You know of their ritual, then."

He held out his arm across the map, showing me the inside of one bare wrist. There, the familiar pale imprint of the goddess's fingertip shone in the light of the hanging lantern. "I, too, have looked into the Dreaming Eye," he said.

"What did you see?" I asked.

He raised an admonishing finger. "I cannot tell you, and I will not ask it of you, either. The visions of the Dreaming Eye are only for those who see them." He rolled the map with dexterous speed and returned it to its place on the wall. "So, Eske, you will sail with us to the port of Hali, and until then, a share of our supplies and our treasure is yours. If the gods smile on us, the winds will be in our favor, and the danger of the quakes will pass. It has been quiet of late. We will hope that it remains so."

I thanked him, and I returned to my bench to row. I was no stranger to the oar, and I had to work enough to justify what both Bran and I ate from the stores. I was grateful for it, for I slept well and did not dream.

In my long travels across the steppe and the hill country, from the desert to the snow-capped mountains, I had forgotten the enchanting song of the sea. At all hours of the day and night it was loud in my ears, drowning out the song of grief; the absence of Khalim and the reopened wound of the absence of Fearghus. Once, my longship had freed me from my father's wrath and the burdens I was to carry as the son of the chieftain. The *Lady of Osona* was no longship, but on her deck and even at her oars, my spirit was light.

I would come to the port of Hali, and then to Nagara, before long. Until then, my sorrow remained quiet.

Two short months passed as we rowed from island to island. Our next port was to be the isle of Kannaoka, the largest in the vast archipelago and home to a lady by the name of Sarika, whom Hamilcar was eager to see. Sarika, he said, was tall as a tree, and her hair shone like fine silk in the sun. He had among his possessions a comb of jade, wrapped in a cloth to keep it safe from salt and sand, and he intended to give it to her.

He also intended to gain some treasure on the island. A rival captain, Agaton of Lore, had hidden a vast store of coin and jewels somewhere in Kannaoka's uninhabited jungle, between the villages on the shore and the city atop the hill. Among these riches, the sailors said, was an enchanted weapon. One tale said it was a spear, another a sword with a single, fine edge, and still another a curved bow—word traveled fast between islands, and each teller added their own embellishments.

Kannaoka, wearing its fabled city as a shining crown, appeared upon the horizon late in the evening. That night, a great wave lifted the ship, waking the sleepers and rousing me from where I dozed on my watch. The storm we anticipated would follow did not appear, and the next morning was clear and bright as the sapphires Halvor swore would be found in the buried treasure of Agaton.

It had not been a storm that had sent that wave, but the trembling of the earth.

When we drew near to Kannaoka's shores, we found the harbor empty, and the village there silent. Our ship was alone.

~ IX ~

KANNAOKA, THE EMPTY ISLE

"Where is everyone?" Hamilcar asked the crew, the island itself, or the gods, giving voice to the unspoken question that those of us gathered on the dock held in common.

No one answered.

A high tide had carried our rowboats to the harbor. The six thatched-roof houses and solitary central structure stood well clear of the water, raised up on wooden beams against the possibility of a flood. A wind from the sea moved across the sand, scattering dust against sealed doors and covered windows.

I led Bran by his halter onto the beach, keeping my hand below his chin so he could not turn his head and see the terrifying expanse of ocean surrounding him on three sides. He relaxed as soon as his hooves left the creaking planks of the dock, and so did my grip, but I remained wary. My free hand went to the knife tucked into the sash that held my tunic closed.

"I don't like this," Halvor muttered.

A thick forest, its emerald leaves casting shadows dark as night, separated the beach and its villages from the slope of the island. The city on the hill shone bright and serene. From this distance, it also appeared empty, but even the sharpest eyes among the crew could not be certain.

I gave Bran's lead a gentle tug, and we walked inside the ring of long-legged houses. The sand lay white and smooth, disturbed only where we trod. Any footprints in the sand, any record of where the inhabitants had walked, were lost to wind and time.

"Do you think there was a fight?" asked another sailor. His name was Devdan, and he was taller than I, with a face chiseled from shining brown stone. A scar on one cheekbone twitched toward his eye as he surveyed the village.

"No blood," Halvor replied, "no weapons. Nothing's damaged."

I stood at the center of the village, Bran tugging at his halter as he spied fresh young leaves at the forest's edge. The southernmost house, closest to the beach, leaned toward the water. The beams on which it stood had cracked, showing a jagged opening like a mouth full of splintery teeth, large enough for me to put my fingers inside.

Hamilcar came up beside me, the feathers in his hat bobbing with a frenetic rhythm. "This is Sarika's house," he said.

I let Bran have his way and climbed up the ladder to the door. The wooden latch came free, and the door swung open with the creak of swollen timbers. Within, the house was dark, its central fireplace cold and clear of ash. A bed of rope stretched over a frame stood against the far wall, and two small hammocks hung nearby; all three had been stripped of their bedding. An imprint in the dust on the floor marked where something large and rectangular had been removed from the foot of the bed. I looked for foodstuffs, to determine how long the occupants had been gone by their decay, but not even the cookware remained.

I climbed back down. Halvor and Devdan reported similar findings: the villagers had packed up their belongings and left—by sea, judging by the empty harbor—and nothing and no one remained behind.

All of the houses stood on cracked legs.

Beside the forest, Bran snorted and shook his head. The metal fastenings of his harness rang like tiny bells. Without another sound, he planted his feet wide and ducked his head.

I had only the space of a breath to understand what this gesture meant before the earthquake struck. It kicked up a cloud of fine dust from the beach and rustled the trees like a summer storm. The houses groaned as if in pain. Waves swept over the dock. I thought myself upon the mountain outside Phyreios once more, with the great worm chewing its way from beneath the earth and Khalim's god coming to take him from me.

The vision passed. I ran across the heaving ground to Bran, stumbling in the shifting sand.

Just as quickly as it had come, the earthquake was gone. Waves tossed the ship once more, then let her fall. The village still stood, though the houses leaned a little farther, and the cracks in their legs opened wider. Another quake, perhaps two, would fell them.

Hamilcar brushed dust from his hat and surveyed the scene, his lips moving as he counted his crew. When we were all accounted for, he said, "Well! That was strange. I thought we had sailed past the quakes."

"There's never been one this far west," Devdan said, his voice low and grim. "Not as long as I've lived."

Silence returned to the beach. But for the circling of the disturbed birds above the forest, the rest of the island was also still, even the distant city.

This village was not meant to withstand a quake—a flood, yes, or a storm, but it relied upon the earth to give it strength. Its people had fled before it fell on their heads.

"Take everything back to the ship," Hamilcar ordered, "and raise the anchor. We'll find Agaton's hiding place and be on our way."

He chose Halvor, Devdan, two women by the names of Mirala and Kelebek, and myself to go with him into the forest and search for buried treasure. We carried shovels and picks, as well as blades to cut through the underbrush. The others rowed our cargo across the shallows to return it to the hold. There would be no exchange of goods and good company with the people of Kannaoka, not here. The hope went unspoken that we would find them on another island.

A footpath led through the trees behind the village, sloping upward as we walked away from the beach. The birds and the scurrying creatures had hidden themselves away after the quake, and the only sound was the whisper of the wind through the trees. I kept a tight hold on Bran, and he followed at my heels, his head lowered and his ears flicking.

"If I know Agaton, which I do," Hamilcar said, forcing cheerfulness, "he will have hidden his riches somewhere auspicious. He has never once missed an opportunity for pomp and ceremony."

The path forked, and he chose the left-hand side that curved away from the route to the city, because the flowers growing along it were huge and scarlet. By all evidence, he had no idea where Agaton of Lore had hidden his treasure. So we walked, and the sun climbed above the forest, and the birds began to sing again. If not for my racing pulse, I could have forgotten about the earthquake.

Kelebek held up a hand bedecked in silver rings, her bright silk sleeve catching the wind. "There's someone ahead," she whispered.

I followed her gesture with my gaze. A hunched figure stood beside the path, its face obscured behind a low-hanging branch. Its clothing was dark and stained with green.

We approached with silent steps. The green in the figure's clothing resolved into a pattern of creeping moss. A few more paces, and we could see it for what it was: a carving of stone, worn by the weather, with a pair of wings extended to shelter an indistinct face and clawed hands clasped as if in prayer. From the bottom of its flat, blank face extended a tangle of carved hair or tendrils that reached down to the scaly, moss-covered feet gripping the edge of its low pedestal.

On the ground beneath it lay three baskets. The two largest held an abundance of fruit, rotting and swarming with flies. The last, much smaller, held beads of silver and stone, strung into bracelets. An offering had been left for this forgotten, neglected god, only to be forgotten again.

"This was left a week ago, at least," said Devdan.

Hamilcar nodded. "That tells us how long the villagers have been gone."

"I don't think so," Kelebek argued. "This is a hunting path, not a road. People don't come this way often."

"Who else could have left it?" Devdan asked.

"Agaton's pirates?" offered Hamilcar. "Though I've never known him to be the faithful sort. Come, friends, the day grows old. I'd rather not spend a night in the woods."

We left the offerings and the idol where they lay. Even Kelebek, with her penchant for jewelry and her profession as a robber of the seas, did not touch the beads. I knew not whether this faceless god would have minded if she did, but I had no wish to find out. I had learned that even forgotten, nameless gods still held power, and they guarded that which they saw as theirs with jealousy.

Following our captain's intuition, or perhaps his imagination, we ventured deeper into the forest, in single file with Hamilcar at the head of our column. The trees thinned, and coarse gray stones emerged from between them, crusted with brown lichen. The crest of the hill, with the stone wall of the city encircling it, shone through the canopy to the north. Something moved on the battlements, but I could not be sure if it was the top of a watchman's helmeted head or a bird flown in to roost.

There were footprints here, sunken into the mud of the forest floor, following the same narrow path. Whoever had left them had been carrying something heavy.

The trail ended at the sheer stone face of a cliff, far too steep to climb. Sunlight warmed the stone, and a few small lizards watched us from their perches with glassy black eyes, too comfortable to bother running and hiding.

"Now," Hamilcar said, "which way would Agaton have taken his spoils? To the north, closer to the city?"

"What about that structure, there?" Mirala asked.

A stone's throw to the south, against the wall of stone, stood a temple much like the one on Hanowa. This one was rough gray stone, rather than lightless black, but the pillars flanking its open door stood just as proudly, and the arch above had a familiar curve.

Hamilcar's face brightened. "Ah, yes, of course. He would hide it in the ruins."

Crumbled stone and rotting vegetation held the temple doors in place, and the smell of stagnant water wafted from beneath the arch. I tied Bran by a long lead to a nearby tree. Kelebek found a dry branch and lit a torch, and we descended rough-hewn steps into the wet, decaying darkness.

A layer of mud on the stairs showed the passage of humans and animals. At the bottom, the corridor opened into a vast, domed room. Scorch marks on the walls indicated where the previous crew of pirates had hung their lights, and two empty barrels that stank of liquor further proved that they had once passed through here. Faintly, the smell of seawater cut through the underground temple's humid miasma, and waves crashed against rock somewhere beneath our feet.

Agaton had chosen this place for its impressiveness, and not for its abundance of hiding places. At the back of the vast chamber, two of the remaining flagstones had been disturbed, forming a peak like a tent.

Between Halvor, Devdan, Mirala, and I, we lifted each stone and set it aside. I took up a shovel and set about digging into the soft, disturbed earth.

Soon, Halvor and I stood deep in the hole, the edge of the floor level with our eyes. The first treasure to emerge was a small chest, wrapped in oilcloth to keep away the damp. I handed it up, and Devdan cut through the seal of wax and opened it. Golden coins, from the size of a fingernail to the size of his palm, each stamped with the face of a different ruler, glittered in the torchlight.

I dug out another chest, this one packed with rough jewels the deep green of the shaded forest, and another, containing only a knife with a gilt handle and a blade spotted with rust.

As the others tallied up our newfound riches, I found one last object hidden in the muck: a soft, oblong package of waxed canvas. With my steel knife, I cut through the heavy stitching, and the cloth fell away. Beneath lay a spear, its head carved of horn and as sharp as the day it was crafted, the barbs curved like the claws of a great beast. The shaft, formed from some dark, rigid wood, reached from my feet to the top of my head. A wrapping of leather strips marked the balance point at its center.

I climbed out of the pit and lifted the weapon in my hands. Despite its size, it was almost weightless. I could send it flying with a gesture. An electric shiver passed through my body, and I felt the weapon's will.

It was an ancient cunning, as old as the movement of the earth and the passage of the tides. I recognized the fiery temper of a dragon, balanced against the patience borne of watching kingdoms rise and fall and rise again. The horn and claws had not been taken by conquest, but given willingly, to one whom the dragon had held in high esteem. With this knowledge came a sense of foreboding, and of anticipation: something was coming, and the dragon's wisdom asked if I would be willing to act when it arrived.

With my steady hand, I told it that I would.

The riches of the pirate Agaton lay at my feet, and my companions pored over it, dreams of finery and rich foods and expeditions to distant shores passing between them in whispers and echoing from the cavernous walls. My thoughts were only of the dragon spear, and how if I'd had such a weapon in my possession on the far northern sea, I might have slain the lind-worm and kept my boat and the lives of Fearghus and the others.

Even the gods could not change the past. I had it now, and it sang to me, a song of dragon flight and the hands of heroes. I was the last of many to carry this weapon, and many more will wield it after me. When the dragon who had given it shape had hatched from its stone egg, the world had been young, covered in water and fire. With reverence, I replaced the oil cloth covering the spear and fashioned a sling out of rope to carry it on my back.

"I don't need a share of the treasure," I told Hamilcar. "I want only this weapon."

He looked up from the figures he was scratching in the mud with a twig and gave an expansive shrug. "If that's your choice, then, you can have it. Gods know we won't find a buyer for months."

"My friend," said Halvor, gesturing at me with a large coin, "you need to learn the value of money."

This was not the first time I had abandoned a share of a chest full of coins. I had no use for them; as long as I worked, Bran and I would eat, and I could hunt and forage for enough to trade when I at last reached my port.

Hamilcar had us fill in the cavity and replace the flagstones, but not before he inked a message to Agaton, folded into the waxed cloth that had protected the treasure, and placed it beneath the floor for the other pirate to find. I could not read the words, but I could guess what it said: a boast proclaiming Hamilcar the better pirate.

He sent me to ride back to the dock and fetch more sailors to help carry the treasure out. The earth had lain still since we had left the beach, but the danger remained, especially under a mountain's worth of stone. We had to depart with haste.

I climbed the slippery stairs and emerged, squinting against the high sun, into the forest of Kannaoka.

Five men in armor stood around the temple door, their boots crushing the moss and the sun glinting off their mail shirts. The one farthest to my left held Bran's halter, and his arms strained as the horse pulled away from him. The other four held spears tipped with sharp iron, crossed to impede my passage. They wore helmets wrapped in pale green cloth, and each had a sash of the same color that held a curved knife. They were the first people other than the crew that I had seen on the island.

"I don't mean any harm," I said. "Give me back my horse."

The man at the center took up his weapon and leveled it at me. "By the order of King Sondassan, you are to be taken to the city," he said. "Come quietly and you—and your horse—will not be harmed."

"Are there more with you in the ruin?" another man asked.

The sailors moved about behind me, but the temple's darkness concealed them. "No," I said, loud enough for them to hear. "I am alone."

Once again, the birds had fallen silent. The forest loomed over me, painting the cliff in dark shadow and speaking to itself in a fearful whisper of leaves.

The soldiers were as broad as I, though shorter by half a head. I wore only my clothing from the temple, mended and patched after months on the road and on the sea, and I carried only the dragon's spear and my knife. My odds were poor, but I thought I might prevail should I attempt to fight—and if my companions in the ruin came to my aid, we could overpower these men. I moved a hand to the weapon on my back.

The man holding Bran shifted his grip on his own spear and held the head to Bran's neck. Bran pulled away, hooves tearing at the moss, but his bridle held him in place. His rolling eyes found me and stared.

I would not risk Bran. I held up my hands to the men and, inch by inch, slipped the strap over my head and lowered the concealed weapon to the ground. The soldier at the center picked it up, and three of his companions circled around me, closing off any routes by which I might have escaped. Another man took my knife from my sash and placed it in his own.

They marched me through the forest, the man with my spear ahead, the man holding Bran behind, and the others in a rotating formation at my sides. The forest opened into a well-worn footpath that climbed from the harbor to the city. I kept my face forward, resisting the urge to look for Hamilcar or back at the ship. Surely the soldiers had seen it by now, its tall crimson sails open against the southern sky, but I would not draw their attention to it. I hoped for an eventual rescue, if I could not free myself, but I would not have the crew captured on my account.

The city rose above me in stark, flat gray, and the height and breadth of its walls turned all thoughts of escape to despair. Watchmen paced the battlements, with only their hardened leather helmets visible from my vantage point far below. A wooden portcullis with sharpened points groaned open, and the din of commerce and daily life drifted through the gate. Kannaoka was not as empty as it had appeared.

In all my travels, I had not learned to love the sight of walls and edifices of stone. Phyreios's high wall had not saved it from destruction, nor did it contain the worm when it emerged from under the mountain. A wall could turn away arrows, but it would not protect anyone from the dangers that lay within.

I was to find that there were many dangers inside the walls of this city.

The soldiers took me down a paved street and into a central square full of people. They wore silk and fanned themselves with palm fronds, and they looked at me with suspicion, a measure of contempt, and, strangely, relief, as if they had been waiting for me to appear. They whispered to one another, heads bent. At the other side of the plaza stood a squat, rectangular palace, carved from a single, enormous block of stone. A pattern of leafy vines climbed its doors, etched in gold, and five columns stood on either side of its great door. Behind the palace towered the husk of an unfinished building, a lattice of scaffolding propped against its walls of quarried stone blocks. Through the empty hollow where a window would be, the carved figure of a man in a jagged crown stared at me with accusing eyes.

A deep, metallic ringing filled the square and its surrounding thoroughfares, and the gathered townsfolk ceased their hushed chatter. Before I could locate the source of the sound, I was taken away, past the steps to the palace and down a shady alleyway. An iron gate set into a chiseled doorway opened at the approach of the soldiers and closed behind me, separating me from Bran and the man who held him.

"Where are you taking my horse?" I asked, but the soldiers did not answer.

My escort, now only four, led me down a long corridor hazy with smoke. Torches reached out from iron fastenings on the walls, and the hall was barely wide enough for three to walk abreast. The ceiling hung a mere hand's breadth from the top of my head. I bowed my shoulders, dropping my chin to my chest.

The corridor rang with the sound of metal tools on stone. Somewhere beyond the walls, which were not as thick as they appeared, diggers worked in an extensive network. Echoes reverberated near and far, shaking dust from the ceiling. The stone beneath my feet trembled with their efforts. It was as though the whole structure quivered with an inhuman pulse, but it was no earthquake, not yet.

We arrived in a wide room lined with cells, each behind a heavy iron grate. All were empty. The first soldier opened the door on the right, and the other three shoved me inside without ceremony. The door closed with a sound that made dust and flakes of rust rain onto the floor.

The soldiers left, taking with them my spear and my knife and the single torch that lit the dungeon. A slit in the wall above my head let in a thin stream of daylight. I tried the door, but it was locked, the bars fitted tightly into the stone. My cell contained only a bucket and a slab carved out of the wall, not quite large enough to lie upon. I was alone. Either the other prisoners had been put to work at the interminable digging I heard even now, or I had been the only one to invoke the city's ire.

The light from the window traced a slow path across my cell, disappearing when it reached the bars. I sang a rowing song, loud and raucous, to drown out the sound of digging and in the hopes of disturbing an unseen guard enough to summon him to me. I remained alone. Night fell, turning the dungeon black.

I lay on the slab, my knees bent and my feet against the adjoining wall, and tried to rest. My throat was raw from singing, and hunger had begun to sap my strength, but sleep did not come. The window showed only darkness. I was farther from the open sky than I had thought.

A light appeared in the corridor at what must have been midnight, though it seemed to me that years had passed. Three men entered the dungeon: two soldiers, mailed and armed as the ones who had brought me here, and the third dressed in a robe the color of fresh blood. His skin was dark and rough as the bark of an oak tree. A circlet of shards of black volcanic glass, wound in copper wire, sat atop his white hair. Around his neck hung a jeweled collar, green gems reflecting the light of the torch he carried.

The soldiers stayed in the doorway, and the old man advanced. I shielded my eyes against the invasion of light as he examined me.

"Who are you?" I demanded. "Why am I being held here? I am Eske of the Clan of the Bear, hunter of the great lind-worm and champion of the Cerean Tournament. I have walked the length and breadth of the world and gazed upon the Dreaming Eye. I will not remain here against my will."

The man's face cracked into a broad grin, showing a row of white teeth worn short and flat. "A champion, you say? Yes, I think you'll do nicely. King Sondassan will be pleased."

~ X ~

BETWIXT IRON AND STONE

He smiled at me, a paternal, placating expression through which the devious hunger in his eyes shone. His obsidian crown shimmered like water.

"After months of delays, the gods smile upon our city at last," he said. "Where do you come from, champion? What thread of fate brought you here?"

I stepped back from the bars and crossed my arms over my chest. "If there is a task you wish me to perform in exchange for my freedom, then let me hear of it. I have no time to waste lingering here."

"In due time, my friend." In the flickering light of his torch, the shadows on his face deepened. He appeared as an ancient thing, carved of wood and long buried.

Even at this hour, the ring of metal tools against stone came through the walls surrounding me. The digging continued. I entertained a brief fantasy that some unknown benefactor was about to break through my cell from the other side. Though I had briefly claimed the attention of one of the gods of these southern isles, a sudden rescue seemed too much to ask.

"I've given you my name," I said. "Tell me who you are and why you have taken me prisoner. I've done nothing against you."

"No, my friend, you haven't. But you will do much for me and for King Sondassan, ruler of this, the greatest of the isles, now and forever." His hand went to the largest jewel on his collar, nearly the size of his palm, in a gesture of obeisance to the absent king. "I am, by his grace, high priest of Kannaoka."

"Your lord is a generous one," I said with a nod to his jewels, "and clearly you serve him with valor. I don't see why you would need me."

"That is where you are wrong, my friend." His smile widened, creasing his face further.

I liked neither this man nor his smiles, nor his insistence on calling me *friend*. I gripped the bars with both hands, testing their strength. They were as rigid and unmoving as the stone walls. "What do you want?" I asked again. "I am undertaking a quest of great import. Tell me what it is that will gain me my freedom, and I will do it and be on my way."

The high priest nodded, folding his hands around his torch. "Tell me of your deeds, champion. I wish to know how useful you will be to my king."

If a retelling of my adventure would allow me to return to the ship, then I would give it. I hung my arms through the iron grate and looked into the high priest's small, dark eyes. They glinted like volcanic stone in the firelight.

"I am a warrior of the far northern reaches, where the sun does not rise in the winter, nor does it set in high summer. On a longship I fought the worm that hunts among mountains of floating ice, and I traveled across the vast steppe to the holy city, Phyreios. I was named champion of the great tournament, and I was there when Phyreios fell along with its gods."

The high priest bent his head. "So Phyreios has indeed fallen," he murmured. "We had been told the mine had collapsed. It was believed to only be a rumor, an excuse the merchant ships gave to justify the high price of iron."

"It was much worse than that," I said.

The terrible smile returned, and he asked, "What then? Kannaoka is a long way from Phyreios, and the iron shortage is a year or more old. Surely you have done other deeds since then."

All around the dungeon, the diggers carved at the island's very foundations. A faint tremor passed through the stone under my feet. The sound of the picks went silent and began again, louder and more insistent.

"I spent a year at the Temple of the Dragon," I said, "and then I came south. I sought the help of the priestesses of Hanowa, and now I travel west. Is that sufficient?"

"And what is the quest that brings you here?" he asked, his tone light and inviting.

I would not be taken in. I would not speak Khalim's name aloud to this smiling, scheming man who kept me here and had yet to reveal why. I feared what he might do with the knowledge.

When I did not reply, his smile faded, but his eyes glinted with some curious pride and satisfaction. "Well, whatever it is, I'm sorry to say that your travels will end here. All is not in vain, however: you will play a crucial role in what is to come. You will help King Sondassan ascend to godhood, and Kannaoka will reign eternally over the waters because of you, Eske the champion."

I straightened, pulling my hands inside the bars. "And how am I meant to do this?"

"Sondassan is the greatest and wisest of all kings," the high priest said. "He is advanced in years, and in his wisdom, he will not leave Kannaoka without his guidance. Your blood, champion that you are, will not be sufficient, but it will grant him a stretch of precious time—long enough to finally unearth the god who sleeps beneath the island and take its strength and its divinity. He will live forever, and it will be in no small part due to your help."

He bowed, and he smiled, and revulsion turned my empty stomach.

"You cannot do this," I said.

"Of course not." The wavering red light of the torch turned his face into a skull covered in bark, his eyes sunken and his mouth a black hollow. "King Sondassan will do it, with my help and with yours."

I gave the bars a futile push. "You don't understand. What you do here—this is why Phyreios fell. Seven gods together were not powerful enough to put down what they had called up."

"That may be so," sad the high priest, "but you are a champion, not a scholar—if indeed the tale you tell is true. I will trust my own readings of the heavens and the wisdom of my king before I listen to a barbarian from the North."

He raised a hand, signaling to his guards. Their postures straightened, and they raised their spears from the ground, their eyes forward and staring at nothing.

I struck the iron grate with my palms. "Listen to me!"

The high priest turned and stalked back to the armed men, his scarlet vestment trailing on the rough, dusty floor. Darkness fell once more upon my tiny cell. He arrived at the doorway, and his guards turned toward the stairs with a single, synchronized pivot.

"I saw it with my own eyes," I called after him. "Not even the blood of an entire city could grant them control of the great worm when it burst forth from the mountain. The Ascended all died along with their people."

He paused, but he did not turn to look at me. "I will hear no more of your insolence. You will be fed and given water when I see fit to order it, and your blood will be spilled three days hence, at the rise of the full moon."

He mounted the stairs, and all the light went with him.

"The earthquakes are an omen," I shouted into the blackness.

The only answer was the incessant ringing of picks beyond the walls of my prison. I felt my way back to the shelf that served as my bed, and the stone hummed beneath my hands; a warning of the cataclysm to come. King Sondassan's ill-fated workers were digging their way to certain death.

I had lost my new weapon almost as soon as I had gained it, and I had lost Bran, as well. I prayed to no one that the soldiers would see the use of a good horse, rather than offering him up to be sacrificed or butchered for meat. Captain Hamilcar and his crew had been safe, the last I saw them, and if their gods were kind, they would sail far away by the time Kannaoka fell.

The night stretched on, the rhythm of the diggers marking out the passing minutes. I slept a fitful hour and dreamed of the great worm, its putrid, pale flesh and the piercing sound of its roar. In Phyreios, I'd had Khalim and his god and a handful of the best warriors who had ever walked the world, and I yet lived to tell the tale, as much as it fell upon unhearing ears. Now, I was alone.

I would find Khalim again, even in death, I promised the dark and the broken earth. As long as I was still in possession of my life, however, I would use it to complete my quest and find him. If I had any choice in the matter, I would not allow my tale to end underneath Kannaoka.

The digging stopped at last, and I slept again. It resumed with the reappearance of the sun through my narrow window. The light showed the other cells to remain empty, and I suspected I knew what had become of any others who might have shared the dungeon with me.

The sound of booted footsteps came down the stairs. A soldier, a short sword at his belt and a shirt of mail over his narrow shoulders, carried a shallow dish into this empty chamber. He was younger than I, thin and wiry, with the scars of adolescent pockmarks still on his clean-shaven chin.

He stopped an arm's length from my cell and held up the dish. It was half full of a thin, pale gruel, watery where it wasn't fibrous. I had not eaten in a day, but this would do little to satisfy my hunger.

"Stay away from the bars," the young soldier commanded. His voice shook, belying his confident posture and grim expression.

I sat up from my unwelcoming bed and held out my hands to show they were empty. He was armed, and I was not. I could best him hand to hand, I thought, but the iron grate prevented that.

He came forward and slid the dish between the bars and onto the floor of my cell. Before I could rise, he stood and stepped back, staying well out of my reach.

"Thank you," I said. There was no reason to provoke him. With my hands visible, I went to collect my meager rations.

"Is it true?" he asked.

I returned to my place on the slab. "Yes, all of it," I said before he could elaborate.

The soldier rested a hand on the pommel of his sword and shifted his weight between his feet. He had nothing to fear from me; even if I could have drawn him near and overpowered him, he did not possess the keys to my cell. I had nothing to gain from him.

"I meant about what happened in the city of Phyreios," he said. "What you told High Priest Ucasta."

My false confidence dropped. I stared into his eyes without pretense. "All that is true. I swear on the gods of my people." The oath was bitter in my mouth. If ever I had felt the presence of the gods of the North, that time had long passed. "I swear on the love I hold for those lost in the cataclysm. Your king and your high priest will doom Kannaoka."

"The villagers all left," said the soldier. "They fled in their boats when the island began to shake. We here in the city are forced to remain, and more of us disappear with each turn of the moon."

"They were wise to leave."

A frown troubled his young face, and his hand gripped his sword, as though he could fend off the coming cataclysm with it.

I left the dish of gruel on my makeshift bed and crossed my cell. The soldier took an instinctive step away.

"Why is he doing this?" I asked. "Your king. There is no power in the world or beyond it that is worth the deaths of so many."

His shoulders went up in a shrug and then dropped, heavy and resigned. "Haven't you ever wished you could cheat death?"

The question lingered in the still, underground air like a memory, or like the smell of blood. I heard again the words of Luana, priestess of Hanowa: *what's dead should stay dead.*

I wanted to shout that I was nothing like King Sondassan, that my desire to bring Khalim back was selfless and righteous and far from an old man's desire to live forever, but I held my tongue. I did not have the time to argue, and neither did Kannaoka, and what little the king and the high priest knew of me had already condemned me to death.

What I said was, "I would never sacrifice the lives of others. I risk only my own."

The young man shook his head. "We are a small kingdom, and King Sondassan doesn't yet have a suitable heir. Without leadership, we risk conquest by any number of the other islands." He recited something he had been taught, but the words no longer held weight. He did not believe them now.

"There will not be a Kannaoka left to conquer if things continue as they are," I insisted.

"What can I do?" he asked, a question more directed to the gods than to me. "I am tasked with feeding the prisoners and making sure the door from the palace is secured. No one will listen to me."

Fear was written across his face. He had already seen the villagers flee and the city folk bleed for their king, and he would witness more horrors before the end.

"Someone will," I said. I could not be sure if I tried to convince myself or him. "You must try."

His brow creased into a troubled frown, but he nodded, and he turned away to the stairs. The door that I knew stood at the top was little more than a stone's throw away, but it might as well have been on the other side of the world.

"What's your name?" I called after him. If I was about to place my fate in his hands, I should at least know that.

He stopped, letting out a breath and running a hand through his thick, dark hair. "Ajan," he said. "And yours?"

"Eske. Good luck, Ajan. If there are true gods here, may they watch over you." It was a blessing that had once been given to me at the gate of burning Phyreios, and it was all I had to give.

Ajan left, and I remained in my cell. I ate the slimy gruel and waited. A thin beam of daylight traced its slow path across the floor, interrupted by the passage of soldiers and the shadows of their feet. Until the very end, I had learned in Phyreios, there would be enough men in armor to subdue the dwindling population. After that, these men would end up just as dead as anyone else.

All the while, the sound of picks striking stone grew louder. The diggers were coming nearer.

That evening, when the light had gone from my window and the prison was dark and gray, I received another visitor: a woman, nearly as tall as I, dressed in a shirt of mail links that shimmered darkly where the small lamp she carried shone on them. A length of deep green silk tied up her hair and wound around her head, and another was tied around her shoulders. At her hip hung a mace with a polished wooden shaft and a head of iron spikes. Her eyes were dark, her features sharp and her shoulders broad. She held her head high and favored me with an imperious crook of one brow.

"So," she said without so much as a greeting, "this is going to get worse."

I stood up from my cold slab and put my hands against the bars. "You can't even imagine."

"There's a lot I can imagine. How do I stop it?"

After a day of languishing in my cell, I found her directness refreshing. "Set me free," I said, "and I will do whatever I can to help you. I am a warrior of no small renown."

Her look was impassive. Unlike Ajan, she stood close to the cell door, unafraid of my reach. "You can help me? Against the priests, the household guard, the city's soldiers, and the king himself?"

"Leaving me here won't improve your odds," I argued.

I guessed she was my elder by some ten years, but the dim firelight and the careworn lines on her face aged her more. Her posture faltered.

"My name is Mara Suryan," she said. "Since you are a stranger here, you do not know the weight of that name. For generations, my family has served the daughters of the house of Kannaoka, ever since the days of the virgin priestesses of the gods of stone and fire. I have under my command a company of twenty women, and we are charged with protecting King Sondassan's heirs: his twin granddaughters. They are twelve years old."

"An immortal king needs no heirs," I said.

Mara nodded. "Once, he doted on the children, and would die before allowing even a hair on their heads to be harmed. Now?" One callused hand rubbed at her brow. "I'm not certain he could recognize them. Even if he did, what love remains in him would only make their blood more potent as a sacrifice, if Ucasta is to be believed."

If ever the Seven Ascended had loved their people, that love had long been forgotten. As they walked the streets of Phyreios among its citizens, all they had seen were the means of perpetuating their power and divinity, and to that end, one's blood had been just as good as another's.

"Thus far, I have kept the princesses safe from the priests," Mara continued, "and from the designs of the nobles and the captains of the military, who sense that the death of the king must be near and wish to take the throne by means of a forced marriage. I cannot do this forever. And if what you say is true, I do not have much time."

"Then the king is not so hale and hearty as the high priest implied," I said.

Mara's eyes fell to the dusty ground at her feet. "He is not. Each sacrifice grants him another day—a week—a month. Someone like you might give him enough life to sustain himself for a season, or so Ucasta claims; a season in which the delvers will crack the foundations of the island and call forth the old god who slumbers there."

My cell shook with tiny tremors that rattled my teeth and rained dust onto my shoulders. Deeper down, the island groaned with a voice of stone on stone.

"I came here on a ship," I said. "Do you know if it is safe? Has it left these waters?"

A hint of a smile cracked the stony angles of Mara's face. "Is that your ship lingering just out of reach?" she asked. "I assume they are well, provided their stores are good. They have evaded the king's attempts to capture them. With the villagers gone, we don't have enough boats."

So Hamilcar and his crew had not left me here. Relief washed over me—I was not, as I had assumed, alone—followed by a cold wave of fear. The forty souls aboard the *Lady of Osona* could mean forty more chances for King Sondassan to destroy his people.

But Hamilcar knew what he was about, and if it was his decision as captain and the will of the rest of the crew to wait for me, then I would not disagree.

"If you can find a way to contact that ship," I said, "there are forty capable fighters on board. Add to that all your guards, yourself, and me, and we may have a chance."

Her face remained expressionless as she considered it. She was a warrior, from her head to her booted feet, and the guardian of two young children; if she were afraid, she would not betray it.

"I'll do what I can," she said at last.

"That is all I can ask of you," I replied.

She glanced over her shoulder, back the way she had come. More footsteps had come to the unseen door at the top of the stairs.

"I've stayed here long enough already," said Mara, "and I won't be able to return. You will have to trust me."

"My life is in your care," I said, and I went back to my cold, unyielding bed and sat with my head in my hands. The light departed with Mara, and darkness filled the prison once more.

A soldier I did not recognize brought me more of the gruel. It filled my belly even if it did not nourish me. Neither Mara nor Ajan visited my cell that night, nor anytime the day after, and when the earth shook I feared one or both of them had been sacrificed already. The ringing of picks filled my ears, and the corner of the slab beneath me bit into my back. I closed my eyes and thought I was crushed beneath a mountain of stone, as I had been when the ritual chamber of the Ascended had collapsed.

I awoke in the evening, as the sun set and the full moon that signaled my doom rose beyond the confines in my cell. The digging had stopped, and the march of soldiers replaced it, above my head and through the tunnels behind the dungeon walls. They moved with a singular purpose toward a place in the rock somewhere below.

Ajan appeared at the stairs, accompanied by another soldier, who carried a torch. In Ajan's hands were a length of chain and a pair of manacles. His companion stayed in the center of the room, and Ajan took a ring of heavy iron keys from him and opened my door.

"Hold out your hands," he said.

If I struck him in the face, I could take his weapon, and I might subdue the other soldier before he could cry for help. I hesitated, curling my hands into fists.

"The pirates are here," Ajan whispered. "And High Priest Ucasta has ordered the princesses to be sacrificed. Mara and her women will be in the ritual chamber."

I offered up my wrists. He closed the manacles around them, leaving them unlocked. I drew my hands to my chest to keep them in place.

"Wait until we reach the chamber," he said, and then, much louder: "This way."

He tugged on the length of chain connecting my hands and led me out of my cell.

I kept my head bowed, being led as I was to the slaughter, and I followed Ajan into the bowels of Kannaoka. Two other guards fell in behind me, mailed and armed as he was, to prevent my escape. They need not have bothered—the way back led only to my cell. The only way to go was forward. Beneath my feet, the earth tensed and trembled; not a quake, but the warning of one. Whatever slept beneath the island stirred, close to waking.

The tunnel constricted, the ceiling almost scraping the top of my head, and then it opened into a massive underground chamber. Its walls bore the scars of picks and shovels, and hewn logs supported the ceiling. Rubble and dust lay in heaps on the floor. Four iron braziers spilled dim light and thick smoke into the room.

Carved into the center of the room was a shallow indentation, blackened with old blood. Around it, etched into the stone and painted with more blood, lay the sigils of this foul ritual.

Mara stood to my right, her face set in grim resolve, flanked by two more women in chainmail with their hair covered in silk. Behind them, a pair of young girls clasped each other's hand, their delicate faces identical and painted red from the edge of their rich, dark hair to the ends of their small noses. Two lines of white paint curved down their necks from their ears, meeting at their collarbones. Their garments were sapphire silk, with a golden sun embroidered on one shoulder and a moon on the other, the rest a field of stars. Heavy jewelry in gold and silver weighed down their wrists and ankles. Their hair, decorated with strings of pearls, fell almost to the backs of their knees.

They were dressed for a ceremony. I assumed I was to be sacrificed first, and they would follow after the appropriate words and gestures.

Dust fell from the ceiling like a soft rain. This cavern would collapse before long, one way or another. Ajan's knuckles were white where he grasped my lead, and he trembled. "Gods," he muttered, but I knew not to whom he prayed.

Two more lightless tunnels led out of the room, one on the right-hand wall and the other opposite the way I had entered. High Priest Ucasta, in his jeweled collar and his crown of glass, took his place on the other side of the dry, bloody pool, his scarlet vestment dark and his face skeletal in the smoky light. On his either side stood his lesser priests, dressed in the same red, their collars polished wood instead of jewels. I counted eight of them, and ten more guards, standing in ranks behind.

A desiccated corpse knelt beside the pool. It held a lacquered walking stick, its hands reaching out to grip it with the fragile stiffness of death. Its arms were mottled skin stretched out over bone, emerging from a voluminous robe as white as untouched Northern snow. A golden crown encircled its hairless, bent head.

The corpse took a deep, shuddering breath and looked up. He was no corpse, not yet—this was King Sondassan, and he clung to life by the barest thread, staving off the coming of death with blood and dark magic. His sunken eyes fixed me with a gaze of pure, unholy hunger. If ever they had possessed the power to recognize his family, his trusted advisors, or the members of his court, that power was long gone. He saw only the life-force that would let him live another hour, another day.

"I fear even my blood cannot help you, Your Grace," I said aloud.

The king only continued to stare, but Ucasta's sinister smile split his weathered face as he bowed, half-mocking, in my direction. "Your blood, champion, will finally summon the ancient god of this magnificent isle, so that a new god may take its place. If it reassures you, we will lay a stone in the new temple in your honor."

Sondassan raised a bony hand from his walking stick, pointing at me with a finger like a knotted twig. Though white clouds covered his eyes, he could see me.

"You're already dead, Your Grace," I said. "Don't condemn your people to die with you."

His mouth opened, showing gray gums and a tongue like a grave-worm. A gasp, thick and rattling, came forth from his throat. Alas, it was not his last breath. He still lived, and he still believed he would become a god.

Ucasta lifted his arms, beaming with wicked pride. "Bring forth the sacrifices!"

"Very well," I said, and the cavern echoed and amplified my words. "You shall see why they call me champion."

I threw off my chains, and they fell in a cascade to my feet. Shifting my stance, I turned to the guard at my left. My fist found his windpipe where it emerged above the collar of his mail, and it cracked under the force of my blow. He gasped and sputtered, blood turning his spittle pink. I took his sword from its sheath as he fell.

Ajan drew his own sword, his eyes wide with fear. He turned on his fellows with no allies but Mara and me, and in that moment, I admired him.

"Take the princesses to safety!" Mara ordered. Ajan and the two other women obeyed, ushering the girls to the tunnel behind me in a rush of silk and a clatter of jewelry. Whatever was to happen, they should not see it, and the farther they could get away from the bloodthirsty thing that was once their grandfather, the better.

One of them asked a question in a language I did not recognize, high-pitched and afraid.

My other guard drew his own sword and swung at me, a high, wild arc that missed my head and brushed against my shoulder. I felt nothing. Battle-rage was already upon me, singing its keening song in my ears. I pushed past the soldier's sword arm and drove my blade into his abdomen, splitting mail rings and flesh alike.

"Seize them!" Ucasta cried, and the guards behind him filed out to obey. The earth under our feet gave one slight lurch, like a dream of falling that wakes the dreamer in an instant. Though the men exchanged frightened glances, they pressed forward, unsheathing their swords in a hiss that filled the echoing chamber.

Mara took three long strides and met them on the stretch of uneven ground before the dry pool. She took the first blade on her mailed arm and answered with a crushing blow of her mace, sending the first soldier sprawling. He did not get up again.

I ran up to her undefended side, turning the sword over in my hand. With all the force of my rage, I struck the leftmost soldier across the face, crushing his nose beneath my iron pommel.

He cried out and stumbled backward. Blood ran from his nose and tears poured from his eyes, and he brought a hand up to wipe them away.

Another guard stepped into his place. He was nearly as young as Ajan, his face a twisted mask of fear and anger. He struck with a reckless, overhand swing, and our blades met with a deafening clash of metal.

All at once, the echoes in the chamber ceased. It was as though I had been struck suddenly deaf, and I feared the high priest had cast some foul magic upon me. The cavern convulsed. My hearing returned with a roar of crumbling stone and rushing water. Though the earth calmed, the sound continued, and it resolved into words—words I could not understand in an inhuman voice that shook a cascade of gravel from the ceiling and rattled my very bones, but words nonetheless.

High Priest Ucasta was chanting. The ritual had begun.

Sondassan's whitened eyes closed, and he raised his head, his robes stirred by the labored motion of his dying breaths, one after another. The braziers darkened, and an indigo glow illuminated the carved sigils around the pool. Ucasta's obsidian crown glittered in the eerie light. Around him, the lesser priests murmured in an undulating harmony.

A high-pitched tone assaulted my ears, and I found it difficult to breathe, my chest constricted and heavy. The air felt as thick as water.

Noticing my distraction, the soldiers surrounding me seized my arms and dragged me to the ground. I had one guard on either side, and a third tried to hold my legs, but I kicked him away. The clattering of chains made its way through the unholy din, and I struggled, my muscles straining and fallen rock digging into my chest. I inhaled smoke and dust, and I coughed, my eyes tearing. Another soldier knocked my sword from my hand.

The island groaned as if in agony, a sound that crawled across my skin and into my very bones. I thought I heard water flowing, the ocean flooding the tunnels below, but it might have been only the chant, growing louder and deeper as the room grew darker.

A shout of surprise went up on the other side of the cavern, behind the pool and the priests. The guard holding the chains dropped them near my head, metal ringing against stone not unlike the digging that had hounded me for three days. He drew his sword, stepped over my arm and the man holding it, and ran toward the tunnel and the people emerging from it.

"What's all this?" cried Captain Hamilcar of the *Lady of Osona*.

True to her word, Mara had contacted the ship, and now the crew had arrived to attempt a daring rescue. Hamilcar, being the man that he was, had chosen the most dramatic moment to arrive rather than removing me from the prison before the ritual, but I could not protest.

Iron clashed against steel at the far end of the cavern. Mara's boots left my field of vision as she pushed her way past the soldiers.

I pulled my legs beneath me and twisted my chest, throwing off one of my captors. I grasped the other's sword, still sheathed at his hip, and drew it out. His eyes shone white.

I swung. The blade bit into the soldier's neck, cutting through flesh and colliding with bone.

He collapsed onto my arm. I tugged it out and scrambled to my feet. Across the bloodstained pool, Mara knocked Ucasta's head back with a vicious underhand swipe of her mace.

The chant quieted, though it persisted—the lesser priests, their eyes closed in prayer, maintained their part in the harmony. Ucasta's crown slipped off his head and shattered into a rain of glittering black shards. He dropped to his knees and fell over the lip of the pool.

Blood ran from his nose and mouth, and it dripped in thick rivulets onto the stone. It flowed into the dry pool, mingling with the black flakes of older blood.

The bluish glow that permeated the room grew brighter. King Sondassan took one strong, deep breath, and he looked at me with clear eyes.

~ XI ~

IN THE HALL OF THE DEAD KING

Hamilcar and his crew descended upon the priests, knocking them down and silencing their chanting. The earth heaved, and steel clashed. Halvor and Kelebek raced to the edge of the bloodstained pool, armed with curved swords and small round shields. After them came Issa and Adama, brothers from the southlands, Issa with his dark pate shaved and Adama's hair twisted into braids beaded with silver that caught the eerie glow of the room. Their swords came in matched pairs, one in each hand. Halvor also carried my new spear slung on his back. Languishing in the dungeon, I had thought it lost forever, and that I would never see the brave folk of the *Lady of Osona* again.

It was Hamilcar who reached Sondassan first. He raised his fine-pointed sword, taking up a fighter's stance before the risen corpse. Even as withered as he was, the king stood head and shoulders above Hamilcar, straight and strong as a young warrior, and his walking stick was as long as a sword.

Sondassan raised a hand, and light flashed through the chamber. It seared my eyes with a blue-white fire. Unseeing, I pushed against one of the soldiers in my path and knocked him down. Another grasped my arm with both of his, his weapon forgotten. With a strength born of battle-fury, I lifted him up, found his belt with my other hand, and threw him into one of his companions. The others struck at me with blades and fists, but their blows had grown faint and far away. The air trembled with magic, and the cavern shuddered as if from a bad dream.

The light faded. I blinked to clear the spots from my eyes. Hamilcar knelt before the king, one hand gripping his sword and the other clutched at his abdomen. His breath came in gasps like a drowning man's, and his face, yellowed and twisted in pain, had the look of a man many years older.

Two bright points shone in Sondassan's eyes. Though his arms shook under the weight of his robes, he strode forward with a strength and steadiness greater than even Ucasta's blood had allowed him. Behind him, the pool drained, blood flowing away to somewhere deep below.

The bedrock lurched underneath me, throwing me to the ground. My hands caught my weight, and a shock traveled up to my shoulders, but the pain would come later. On my either side, the soldiers I had not yet bested fell upon the quaking earth. The island gave a groan of pressure and agony, almost human but for its depth and volume.

My hand found the hilt of a sword. I took it in both hands and staggered to my feet. Three of Ucasta's soldiers—King Sondassan's, now, as he was alert in a semblance of life while Ucasta lay dying—advanced, their legs buckling and their swords blunting against the cavern floor as they used their blades to keep themselves upright. I crashed into the first soldier, my sword against his arm. His own weapon fell from his hands and disappeared into the shadows.

I struck again. The rings of his mail burst in a shower of metal fragments. Blood bloomed like a flower on the white tunic underneath. He gasped once and dropped to his knees.

Kelebek clashed with another guard, her golden bangles glittering in the chamber's unearthly light. With a crack, her shield knocked aside her opponent's curved blade. Issa and Adama, back to back, defended against two more of the king's guard. I had lost track of Halvor.

Hamilcar still lived, though Sondassan's magic continued to claw at him. All the blood and color had drained from his face, leaving him pale as ice, his unfocused eyes blinking and straining against the cavernous darkness. He put his boots beneath him and stood, his arms wheeling for balance. Kelebek stepped in to cover his undefended side with her shield.

Another soldier came up to my left, an unmarred, new blade in his hand. He might have been younger even than Ajan; all the guards in the chamber were young, bare-faced, unproven. With a snarl, he charged forward, slashing at my ribs.

I backed away, avoiding the first blow. The second I met with the sword I had taken from his fellow. He had his own battle-fury, a volatile mix of panic and rage, and it gave him a burst of inhuman strength. My sword wrenched from my hand and clattered away into the unnatural, violet gloaming.

I was stronger than the young watchman, and my fury was greater than his. His next strike came down at my head, and I caught it in my bare hand, blood running black over unfeeling flesh. I threw the sword aside. With my uninjured hand, I lifted him by the collar of his hauberk, the chain shifting and stretching with the pull of his weight, and threw him. He landed somewhere out of sight.

Mara's mace felled another guard, and in the fray I found myself between her and Halvor. The latter unslung my spear from his back and handed it to me without a word. It hummed like the taut string of a bow, singing a song of battle.

When I threw it, it leapt from my hand like a hunting hawk given the order to pursue a rabbit. It found its roost in the chest of Sondassan's flanking guard, bursting his mail and knocking him to the ground.

Sondassan turned to me, his eyes furious and glowing with blue-violet light. His mouth twisted into a snarl, or perhaps a triumphant smile—his bloodless lips and decaying teeth showed no emotion I could recognize. He raised his hand again, and the light in his eyes erupted into cold fire. A voice like the grinding of stone shook his throat. The stone beneath our feet answered him with a crash and the rush of surging water.

I clenched my jaw and squared my shoulders against his magic, but it was Mara who received it when the light flashed. Her mace hit the ground with a metallic ring, and she fell, both hands holding her chest as she gasped for breath. A gray pallor covered her face, and veins stood out from her neck, her pulse struggling through them. She put one hand on the floor to steady herself, but her arm collapsed beneath her, and she hit the stone and lay there, unmoving but for the uneven rise and fall of her chest.

The dead king laughed, a sound like wind through dry branches. He raised his hand again, one crooked finger pointed at me.

Instinct raised my hand to reach for another spear to throw. I only possessed one, and my quiver of javelins remained where I had left it on the ship, but my outstretched fingers met the jagged edge of a dragon's horn and curled, impossibly, around the leather-wrapped shaft. Its weight, cold and rigid, fell into my palm. Sparks of white light kissed my fingertips and cast long, wavering shadows on the cavern floor.

I threw the spear a second time.

It struck the decaying King Sondassan just below his heart. Silence filled the room, smothering the clash of steel and the breaking of stone. A pool of darkness formed where the spear's point entered his chest and spread like black fire to drain all the light from the chamber. I held my breath.

A thunderclap shattered the oppressive quiet. Lightning followed, searing and blinding. I covered my face, but still it robbed me of my sight. In darkness, I waited for the killing blow to come, for one of the few soldiers who remained to drive his blade into my back, or for Sondassan himself to cast his evil magic upon me and finish what he had set out to do.

The earth gave one last, painful groan, and the stone beneath our feet cracked. My vision returned in patches and spots. I rubbed at my eyes, smearing dust and blood across my face, and gazed into the terrible rent in the island, black against black. The fissure ran through the sacrificial pool, splitting it in two. From within came the roar of the encroaching ocean.

Within that narrow chasm, the forgotten god of the island woke from its long slumber. Its flesh stretched and strained against the stone that confined it, and a single, luminous eye opened, yellow as firelight and wide as the span of my arms, embedded in its surrounding mass of writhing tendrils. Its slitted pupil contracted in sudden awareness, gazing at the people standing above it.

There was another clap of thunder, and the halves of the shallow pool fell together, closing that great eye and cocooning the god once again in stone. The island lay still at last.

The braziers that had lit the chamber sputtered to life, casting small pools of dim, soft light on the now-solid floor. Where King Sondassan had stood, a fine cloud of dust hovered in the air and fell into the pool, mingling with the last of Ucasta's blood. The echo of his final, rasping breath passed through the cavern and faded into silence.

Mara picked herself up from the floor, and with a shaking hand she recovered her mace. Sweat and stone dust streaked her face and clung to her clothing. "Seize Ucasta's priests," she ordered. "The king is dead."

One by one, the soldiers moved to obey: first Mara's women and Ajan, and then the few others who remained, turning from where they faced each other toward the cowering priests.

I held out my hand. Once more, my fingers curled around the shaft of my spear. It was heavy now, content to lie still. It had done what it had been created to do: it had slain the tyrant and freed the people of Kannaoka.

I took it in both hands and touched it to my brow in thanks. Now I had a weapon equal to the Sword of Heaven or my friend Jin's enchanted blade. It was more precious to me than life. With it, I thought, I would soon find my way to Khalim and best any obstacle in my way.

"It's good to see you alive, Eske," Hamilcar said. Some of his ruddy color had returned to his face, but he still swayed on his feet, and he labored to breathe. "I was worried we'd lost you."

"I would have borne you no ill will for saving the crew and leaving me behind," I said, "but I am grateful beyond words for your rescue."

Hamilcar waved a hand, dismissing me, before gathering it into a fist to still its tremors. "Nonsense. I wouldn't have hired you on if I'd thought you weren't worth keeping."

Kelebek approached the body of High Priest Ucasta and nudged his fine red robe with her foot. "I don't like this place," she said. "When can we leave?"

"We can leave when the distinguished lady in command allocates some of the palace treasury to us as payment for our help," Hamilcar announced, favoring Mara with a winsome smile and a tip of his hat.

She paid him no heed. "Up to the palace," she said. "Place these men in the same cells as those they sacrificed. Keep them under guard."

My rage had left me, and exhaustion took its place. My arms ached where the soldiers had seized them to wrench me to the ground, and my left hand throbbed and bled. With heavy steps, I left the hollow chamber, now solid and quiet, and left the god beneath to its deathlike slumber.

As morning came, bathing the sea and the island of Kannaoka in pale golden light, I found myself in the throne room. A vaulted ceiling of cold gray stone stretched out far above my head, and pillars carved with the figures of warriors and ships supported it on two sides. Each column showed a thin, webbing crack, and the flagstones on the floor lay at odd angles. The throne, standing on a dais opposite the palace doors, was as tall as a tree; a chair fit for a giant. It would have dwarfed King Sondassan's withered form, but he had not sat here in some time. Kannaoka was now without a ruler—but, perhaps, it had been without for a long time before my weapon had finally slain King Sondassan.

At the base of the dais sat Kannaoka's twin princesses. Their gowns were gray with dust, and tears had streaked their ceremonial paint, though they had long since ceased their weeping. They stared wordlessly at the bedraggled crowd gathering before them, their hands clasped to each other and their eyes wide with fear.

Two of Mara's soldiers opened the heavy doors, and fresh air stirred the dust for the first time in months. The city lay under a watchful quiet, waiting for the next calamity. I sat at the base of the dais, beside Hamilcar and his crew and a good distance from the princesses, wrapping my bleeding hand in a scrap of dirty cloth torn from my tunic.

The soldiers came first: men in shirts of chain and brightly feathered helmets, swords at their sides and spears in their hands. Their leader was a tall man with a short, silver beard and shrewd dark eyes that took stock of the room from beneath the ridge of a hammered iron helm. Its plume, the sapphire blue of the island birds, fluttered as he strode across the uneven floor.

From the center aisle between the two rows of columns to the western end of the hall, the scions of Kannaoka's noble families gathered. Their angular faces were clean-shaven, and silver thread decorated their oiled black hair. They wore the finest silks I had yet seen in all my travels, all in a spectrum of rich jewel colors.

They murmured amongst themselves, and only a little of their conversation reached my ears: *is it true? Is King Sondassan dead? And High Priest Ucasta, as well? How could this have happened?*

Mara placed herself between the princesses and the gathering of men, and her companions formed a grim-faced line, shielding the girls from view. The pair of them were very small and very young in their filthy gowns, and they spoke only to each other, in whispers with their heads bowed close together.

I understood little about this city upon the hill, still standing after the final quake and much diminished after months of blood sacrifice, but I knew enough to tell that there was to be a question of succession. While Sondassan had named the twins his heirs while he was still their loving grandfather, they were not yet old enough to assume the throne. In the meantime, every one of the nobles and quite a few of the soldiers had some ambition of ruling.

I had not slept well for three days, and had eaten nothing but a bit of thin gruel. My battle-rage had dissipated and left me exhausted. At that moment, my hammock on the ship seemed the height of luxury.

"All our hard work, and the great risk to our persons—especially yours, Eske—deserve a reward." Hamilcar said. Sondassan's strange magic had aged him ten years, though this brief rest and swig from a flask he produced from inside his vest had restored a few of them. "In order to receive that reward, we need access to the royal treasury, and the treasury won't be available until there is a functioning government overseeing this unfortunate island. We wait."

Kelebek had already fallen asleep, back to back with Adama, sitting on the ground beside the dais. Halvor and Issa crouched beside them, glowering at the crowd as it grew louder and angrier.

I got to my feet, grimacing at the pain in my arms and legs. Beside the throne stood a gong, a great bronze disk hanging from a frame of iron. A mallet hung from one corner of the frame. With my spear in hand in case of an unexpected threat, I climbed onto the dais and struck the gong.

It filled the room with such a deep, reverberating sound that I braced for another earthquake. As it faded, however, there was only quiet. The crowd of men turned to me as one, their glances sharp and accusing.

Mara held up one hand to call their attention. The other remained resting on her mace, which bore a dark stain of dried blood—the blood of the high priest. "It is good of you all to assemble here," she said. Her voice carried through the hall, and her face was as still as a mask. "What you have heard is true. King Sondassan is dead, as is High Priest Ucasta. According to our laws, the princesses Mindarya and Marisaya will take up their grandfather's crown when they come of age. Until then, in the absence of the king, we will need to rebuild."

"And how is it that both these illustrious men perished, and in the same evening?" came a voice from the crowd. It belonged to a handsome man of about thirty, his neck adorned with a silver collar and his eyes cold and suspicious.

Mara fixed him with a gaze that suggested she had long ago measured him and found him wanting. "King Sondassan died, Lord Reisim, the way we always knew he would: his time ran out. As for the high priest, he set his designs on Sondassan's heirs, intending to sacrifice them to fuel his foul magics. I slew him to preserve the lives of the princesses and the integrity of Salmacha's throne."

"The same throne that you now stand behind, Mara Suryan," Lord Reisim said with a curl of his lip.

"I am standing between you and these girls," said Mara, "and this is where I will stay."

The leader of the soldiers stepped forward, placing his plumed helmet under his arm. "Our laws require a regent, Mara. You know this."

Now that they stood together, the resemblance between Mara and this man was unmistakable. They shared the same sharp nose and dark eyes beneath a heavy, troubled brow.

"I know, Uncle," Mara said, confirming my suspicions. "But whom among these men can I trust? My duty is to the princesses, and to them alone."

I surveyed the gathered crowd. They had begun to murmur again, and they shifted like a school of fish approached by a shark, forming circles around those that might have been their leaders. One of them shouted above the din: "I am the king's second cousin by blood! After the princesses, I am next in line. I should be regent."

Lord Reisim scoffed. "And have two young women be all that stands between you and the throne, Lord Hadast? I'd expect them both to be lost at sea within the week."

Hadast bristled at that. He was older than Reisim, his long hair more gray than black and his face sun-darkened and lined. Around him gathered other men of a similar age, and they whispered among themselves, casting sharp, sidelong glances at Reisim and at Mara.

"The princesses are only a few years from their majority," Lord Reisim said, speaking to the crowd. "It's better that they be married—one or both—to ensure there is a strong hand to guide them."

"Absolutely not," Mara declared. Her expression was withering, and her words carried an old anger. This was not the first time the nobles had proposed an early marriage for Sondassan's heirs.

Mara's uncle raised a fist, and the soldiers behind him stood as one and turned to him. "Mara protects the daughters of the house of Pallis," he said. "Not once in twelve years has she shirked her duty. I am commander of the king's forces, and I will support the regent she chooses."

He turned to her and added, under his breath, "But you must choose quickly. I would not see this court divided, not after everything else that has happened."

"Will you rule, then, Ilossa?" Lord Hadast cried. "Will you and your niece place a house of common soldiers on Sondassan's throne?"

"Enough." Mara's hand tightened around her mace. "There was a time when the daughters of the house could rule, in the days of the old gods when House Pallis served as kings and priests alike."

A confusion of baffled voices filled the hall. "That hasn't been done in a thousand years!" Lord Reisim shouted above the noise.

"That may be so," said Mara. "But my house remembers it, even if yours does not. We still guard the king's daughters, so that none may touch them until they are ready to marry, though they no longer take up the duties of maiden priestesses." A pointed look at Reisim punctuated this last statement.

"Bring forth the highest ranking priest who yet lives," Ilossa ordered. "Ucasta is dead, but those under his command learned the old laws just as he did. Not so many years have passed since they turned their attention to new gods. They will remember if they know what's good for them."

Two of his armored men bowed stiffly from the waist and left the throne room. The gathered noblemen whispered to one another, and the room grew warmer, and I longed for a place to lie down and rest.

When the soldiers returned, they brought with them a tall, spindly man of middle age, his head shaved but for a fine gray thatch around his ears. He wore the brown robe of Ucasta's underlings, and a spreading purple bruise at his left temple told of his experience in the ritual chamber below. The soldiers dropped him at Mara's feet, and he remained on his knees, his hands raised in supplication.

"This is Chanjask, Ucasta's second," one of the soldiers said. "He claims he will do whatever is asked of him."

Chanjask touched his brow to the floor. "Ucasta led us all astray," he said in a plaintive whine. "Please, tell me how I can be of service."

"The ways of the old gods must be restored so that the princesses can lead us safely out of this time of calamity," said Mara. "Recite for us the law of the gods of stone."

With his hands still outstretched, Chanjask obeyed. "The scion of the house of Pallis will rule, and his sisters and daughters will serve the gods beneath the stone and the gods under the sea. Should the king perish without an heir, then the priestesses will guide Kannaoka, so long as they remain unmarried and bear no children."

"And if they do bear children?" one of the nobles asked. I could not see if it was Lord Reisim.

"Then the eldest son will be named as heir," Chanjask intoned.

Ilossa slammed the butt of his spear against the floor, a sound almost as loud as the gong. "It is decided, then. Mindarya and Marisaya will rule us as priestesses. We will commence an election for a ruling council in the days to come, to see that they are guided by wisdom and that the crimes that have been committed here are well repaid."

An uncomfortable murmur passed through the crowd. How many of them had given up their servants, their neighbors, or their children when Ucasta's priests had come looking for blood? How few had resisted?

The soldiers shuffled Chanjask aside, placing him beside the pirates and me as the princesses stood to accept their new position. Mara knelt before them, offering up her mace, and Ilossa's men bowed their heads and raised their spears.

The priest straightened his brown robe and his polished wooden collar. "I remember you," he said, just loudly enough for me to hear. "You were the prisoner, the one with the lightning weapon. Are you pleased with your handiwork?"

"I did what had to be done," I answered.

Chanjask put on a look of exaggerated sorrow. "Ah, yes. Ucasta believed he was doing what was best for the kingdom, as misguided as he might have been. You saw how we have narrowly avoided war between the nobles today."

"It seems this was long overdue," I said. "Sondassan looked as though he should have died years ago."

The priest nodded, his eyes darting back and forth. He took a step closer, hunching his shoulders and turning away from the group. "Yes, he had been ill for some time, though he kept it concealed. But even if he had been hale and hearty at his ninety years of age, I believe he would have sought Ucasta's help anyway. King Sondassan wanted to win the age-old battle against death. He wanted to live forever."

He spoke as though he had not been present for every step that had led us here: serving the high priest, spilling blood into the pool, and chanting along with his fellows. He was a slippery one, this priest, and I feared he was well on his way to escaping punishment for his deeds.

"And you and your high priest intended to grant his wish?" I asked.

Chanjask shook his head in a mockery of regret. "Alas, such a thing is impossible. Death comes for every man, whether he be a king or a pirate. Despite all his searching, High Priest Ucasta could not find a way to restore a soul to its own body once it had been severed." He leaned in, gesturing for me to do the same, drawing me into his talk of conspiracy. "His success was in preventing the separation from occurring in the first place. King Sondassan remained alive, his body preserved, and thus he could still guide our great kingdom."

"But you needed blood to maintain him," I said. That Sondassan had done little guidance in his last days, lying like a corpse in the chamber below, I did not mention.

"It was an unfortunate necessity," said Chanjask. "Once the old god under the island had been called up, its sacrifice would have sustained him for a hundred years."

When that hundred years came to an end, I knew, he would need more blood. I had seen the same thing in Phyreios. The Ascended had ruled for a thousand years, or so the people living under their tyranny had said. The gods they had slain were beyond counting, and many more were the number of human beings who, willingly or not, had given their blood.

Something else Chanjask had said lodged in my mind like a fish hook. "You said it is impossible for a soul to return to its body?"

His eyes caught the climbing sun with a sharp, intelligent gleam. "Ucasta had not yet achieved it, though he claimed he was nearing it by the day. He acquired a tome some years ago, a record of the work of a Western mystic. It was quite helpful when Sondassan came to him with his requests."

"A book," I said. "I have no use for books."

He put a hand to his chin and looked me up and down. "Hm. I suspected as much. Worry not, stranger. I will help you."

I frowned. "I never said I needed help."

"My mistake," he said. "I suppose it will be of no interest to you, then, that with the book, Ucasta could preserve the body and soul of the king, and with it, I could retrieve a soul for you and place it in the correct vessel. Failing the original body, would you prefer a gem? A lamp? Another body? It would be a simple matter to sacrifice one of the prisoners—"

The thought of Khalim being imprisoned in an object, or placed in a stolen body after its occupant had been murdered, turned my stomach. I cut him off. "No."

It was almost a shout. Silence struck the room, and all eyes turned to me.

I cleared my throat and squared my shoulders, looking away until the gathered noblemen lost interest and returned to their scheming. Chanjask, for his part, had backed away several paces, and his furtive glances told me that he was trying to escape. His face cracked into a smile of feigned innocence as I closed the short distance between us.

"I will not permit you to commit such evil," I said into his ear.

He lifted his arms in a long-limbed shrug. "It's quite a large tome. I'm sure that whatever you want with the soul in question, you'd find some wisdom in its pages." With another step backward, he added, "Ucasta kept it in a locked chest in the new temple. I can fetch it for you."

He had no intention of returning with the book. I placed an arm around his bony shoulders, my hand clenching around his upper arm and holding him in place. "We'll go together," I said.

His smile faltered, and fear rose behind his eyes. "As you like," he said, feigning ease. "It's only a short walk."

I nodded to Hamilcar and the soldiers, and I marched Chanjask out the great doors of the palace and onto the grounds. Once, this place might have been beautiful, this walled garden maintained for the exclusive use of the royal family. Paths of marble wound between overgrown shrubs and alabaster planters filled with dry earth. A single scarlet rose, missing most of its petals, stared out like a bloody eye from a climbing vine covered in thorns, clinging to a tall, white pillar. I feared the palace gardeners had met their fate in the tunnels below. As in the palace, the flagstones had cracked, forming tiny mountains and valleys among the scattered brown leaves on the path.

The unfinished temple, all flat, quarried stone placed at sharp angles, lay open to the sun. Chanjask and I climbed the carved stairs to the second level, where Ucasta's book lay inside a locked chest beneath a length of fine white silk and a collar of rubies. A tent canvas stretched overhead took the place of a roof, keeping the chest out of the weather.

It wasn't much to look at, Ucasta's book, its plain leather cover dyed a uniform, faded black, and the binding stitched with sinews. Chanjask scowled briefly when I took it from his hands and opened it.

The image of a man's body, flayed and spread out on a bed of cramped, shaky text, greeted me from within its pages. Death and I were no strangers, but the illustration disturbed me—the terror in the man's eyes, the hollow cavities in his body where his heart and stomach would have been, the inscrutable writing surrounding him, and the soft, warm texture of the page, as though I touched the skin of a living person.

On the facing page was inked the meticulous image of an archway made of piled bone: the hollow-eyed skulls of giants, stacked atop one another and supported by vast, curving spines and the long, layered bones of the limbs of great beasts. Every detail appeared exactly as I remembered it from the vision of the goddess Nashurru.

I slammed the book shut between my hands, prompting another scowl from Chanjask. "Shall I start reading it to you?" he asked.

I should have cast the book aside, or set it aflame, but doubt stayed my hand. I had climbed the dragon's mountain and gazed into the Dreaming Eye, and yet I had come no closer to finding my way beyond that pale gate. This book was an evil thing, I knew, and both the dragon and the goddess of the deep would undoubtedly command me to rid myself of it.

But they had not brought Khalim back to me, and Chanjask claimed that this book would.

I would set it aside, I decided, and use it only as a last resort. I could not leave it in Chanjask's slippery hands, not now while Kannaoka and its princesses leaned over the precipice of chaos.

"I will be taking this," I said.

"You can't even read it!" he argued. "Are you really going to steal an artifact from me, after everything else you've done here?"

"Where I come from, this would be considered rightful spoils, along with any other treasure you have here," I said. "But if you disagree, I would happily challenge you for it." I reached for my spear.

Chanjask held up his hands in surrender. "So be it," he said. "I wish you luck in learning its magic. There are few who can help you, and even fewer who might be willing."

~ XII ~

THE TEMPEST

I tucked the terrible book inside my filthy tunic, where it clung, cold and sticky, to my skin. With my arm around Chanjask's shoulders, I marched him back to the palace. Much of the crowd had dispersed by the time we entered the throne room. Two clusters of young men in brilliant silk robes, patterned in saffron and ocean blue, remained, speaking to each other with wide gestures and pointed frowns. Their talk was of the cracks in the streets and the half-built temple, and what might become of it; Kannaoka's god had returned to sleep beneath the stone, and only men would oversee its rebuilding. Chaos would mark the days to come, despite Mara's best efforts and the crowning of the twin princesses.

Selfishly, I thought of Phyreios, and what might have happened if it had been left to its own devices when it had shattered. Worthy men and women had survived the calamity, all equals to the same task that had been set before Mara and her allies. If the god Torr had left the city, and left Khalim to live his life as it should have been, what might have become of them?

The gods had never granted me the gift of foresight. What insight I had been given had come to me in the vision I'd seen in the deep, of a peaceful Phyreios rebuilding from its very foundations.

I found Hamilcar and his shore party in negotiations with Mara, with the princesses looking on. I remanded Chanjask into the custody of two of the armed women, and he cast a withering glance over his shoulder as they led him away. I would not learn of his eventual fate.

Standing on the dais, Hamilcar was almost tall enough to meet Mara's eyes, and he favored her with his most charming smile, one hand resting on his sword.

If she noticed his flirtations, she did not acknowledge them. The long day without any sleep had made itself apparent, and her eyes were sunken and her mouth drawn. In one hand, she held a flat stick, and in the other an iron stylus with which she pressed a row of figures into the soft wood. She turned the stick to show it to the princesses, and first one and then the other nodded in approval.

That done, she handed the stick to Hamilcar and sent him on his way. He hopped down from the dais and led the party, with me trailing behind, to the eastern wing of the palace. A soldier standing before a heavy iron door accepted the carved figures and, after some time spent in the chamber behind the door, gave him a heavy leather sack as large as two hands. When he opened it, a hoard of gold and jewels caught the light from the high windows. Colors brighter than the robes of the noblemen scattered across the walls and the tiled floor, slipping into the cracks left by the final quake.

Pleased with this trade, Hamilcar drew the sack closed and tossed it to Kelebek. She was both surprised and pleased when its weight fell into her hands.

We left the palace, then, and I found Bran tethered at the entrance to the palace's dead garden, dusty and thirsty but alive. He caught sight of me and tugged at his lead, and I untied him and held his head in my arms. It was with great regret that I informed him we would again have to board a ship, and he would be confined to the hold once more.

And so, as the sun sank over the quiet western sea, I returned to the *Lady of Osona* a free man, having escaped death at the hands of the high priest and having played no small role in preventing the sinking of Kannaoka. From the deck, I turned one last time to the island, where a procession of lights wound from the city down to the abandoned temple where the pirate Agaton had hidden his treasure. I had my spear, and the book of dark sorcery, and—upon Hamilcar's insistence—a small pouch containing my share of the treasure.

"Keep this safe," he said. "If you don't, you'll wish you had."

I promised him that I would. That night, I slept at last, and in the morning I took my place at the oars as we followed the rumors of the villagers of Kannaoka. I stored the book at the bottom of my pack, and there it lay. Revulsion kept me from looking at it, but something else stayed my hand each time I thought to rid myself and the world of it. I was cursed, not by sorcery but by faint hope, to take it with me.

We spotted the signal fire the next evening, its column of smoke like the stroke of a painter's brush across the sky. The villagers of Kannaoka, having fled before the priests could take their children or the earthquakes could bring their homes down upon their heads, had taken their canoes across the sea to a cluster of shady isles three days' journey away. There, they had set up camp and waited for their fellows to join them and for the quakes to either subside or drive them farther on. This was a known refuge, this chain of sandy beaches and freshwater springs beneath a canopy of tall trees. I could think of many worse places to wait out the impending doom of one's home.

A group of five village leaders greeted us as we brought the rowboat into the shallows. Among them was Sarika, the tall lady of whom Hamilcar had spoken. From his description, I had expected a giant, but she was a slender, strong woman not quite as tall as I. She welcomed us, clasping Hamilcar in her arms and lifting him from his feet, and invited us to stay and feast upon fish and fruit liquor with her people before they returned home and we went on our way north to the continent.

I went to my bed that night with my belly full and my head pleasantly light, and I dreamed of a gray sea under a flat, blank sky.

When I awoke, the morning sun streamed through the palm trees above my hammock. Hamilcar's crew and the villagers sang, calling back and forth across the sandbars, as they gathered their belongings and readied their boats. We would sail north, Hamilcar said, and before long we would find ourselves on the shores of a vast, green country, the land that my Khalim had called home. It must have been a gentle land, I thought, one of soft rains and bountiful harvests. My homeland was harsh, and my people scratched out a living among the mountain stones and struggled with one another for everything we had, and it had made me a warrior. I feared I would be too much a stranger in a country that produced healers.

But I was grateful for the chance to rest, after the days in which I had languished in the dungeon beneath Kannaoka with only a stone slab for a bed and only the earthquakes for company. I had been reunited with Bran, and he spent a pleasant day among the villagers, eating fruit and leaves from the trees. He had been raised on dry steppe grasses; such a bounty as these islands provided must have been more than he had ever dreamed of as a foal. When I tried to lead him back to the ship, he planted his feet wide and tossed his head, snorting his displeasure. I had to lure him up the plank with a basket of vivid pink fruit, the name of which I was told but cannot recall, and plenty of soft-spoken promises that his time in the hold would not be so long. He stared at me accusingly, his dark eyes wide and baleful, as I tethered him to his place below the deck. He would not acknowledge my presence otherwise for a full day, despite my frequent apologies.

We bade farewell to the villagers, and they burdened their deep canoes with the provisions they needed to repair their homes and pushed out into the surf. Sarika, a jade comb in her shining hair, bent down to kiss Hamilcar farewell. The promises he whispered in her ear made the color rise in her face.

I spent the first day on the oars, pulling the *Lady of Osona* out of the shallows until a favorable wind caught our sails in the early evening. The work distracted me from my worries—about the book, about the people I might encounter when I reached land, and whether they might reject me, and about Khalim, wherever he might be wandering. He had passed beyond death, beyond sickness and injury, but not beyond all danger, and I could not reach him. Now that my own life was safe enough, fear gnawed at my belly and turned my hands cold even in this tropical summer. I slept uneasily, awoken by the slightest creak of the ship's timbers or change in the water, and I dreamed often of drowning.

My pack hung from an iron hook beside my hammock, and the weight of Ucasta's tome thumped against the hull as the ship swayed, reminding me of its presence. I thought to ask Hamilcar to interpret it for me, as he was fluent in the writing of many tongues, so that I would know if anything between its strange skin pages was worth my attention. In order to do so, however, I would have to touch it and look upon it again, so it remained where it was, a secret guilt of which I never spoke. These were the forbidden arts that the priestess Kani had accused me of wanting to seek out, and I despised the thought that she might have been correct.

I have no need of this book, I told myself. *I am going to Nagara, and there I will find some connection to Khalim, and thus I will find him in the other world.*

The book remained where it lay, unread and untouched, but not unremembered, in the weeks that passed.

When the next full moon set beneath the sea in the west, morning failed to come.

The sun rose, but it was so obscured by black clouds that I might as well have awakened in the middle of the night. A wave lifted the ship and dropped it from such a height that I was thrown from my hammock and dashed upon the floor. I gained awareness in time to cover my head with my arms. My elbows struck the planks, sending sharp pain into my wrists and shoulders.

Adama and Kelebek had been sleeping in hammocks beside mine, and I helped them to their feet. Kelebek's hands bled from where she had broken her fall. Together, we pulled ourselves hand over hand toward the stairs and onto the deck.

Rain lashed at the planks, and in an instant it soaked me to the skin. Salt spray stung my eyes, and my bare feet slipped on the sea-drenched deck. Another wave crashed over the bow, knocking Halvor into the rail. Captain Hamilcar, his hat wet and its plume clinging to the brim, shouted orders as he gripped the helm, but the wailing wind snatched up his words before they could reach my ears. The timbers creaked and complained, and the sails above strained as the wind tore at them with greedy hands. Thunder rolled in from the east, ending in a deafening crash.

I was no stranger to storms. My grip was strong and my feet were sure. The sails had to come down before we lost them for good—or, worse, they took the masts down with them. With one last look to assure me that Adama and Kelebek clung to the rail, I set off across the deck.

Even the worst of the earthquakes under Kannaoka could not compare to the pitching and rolling of the ship. I fell to my knees and crawled on all fours, my fingers gripping at the timbers.

I reached the mast as the first crack of lightning split the sky, turning the world to white. Momentarily blinded, I groped forward and found a length of rope hanging before me, and I unspooled it and tied it around my waist, its wet fibers biting at my skin. I knotted it twice, feeling the rope strain, and slung the rest over my shoulder.

The mast towered above me like a vast, bare tree. I had climbed to the sails of my longship on many an occasion, as the spring winds ravaged the northern seas, but the *Lady* was a much larger ship, and the climb far more daunting. I tore my gaze from its dizzying height and looked instead at the rigging before me.

Once, I had scaled the side of the great worm as it laid waste to Phyreios. With only a sword and the texture of its filthy hide to aid me, I had reached the crest of its head. If I had completed that feat, I thought, then a rope ladder would make this task an easy one, even in a tropical storm.

I was wrong. My memories of the weather at sea had faded, becoming distant and small in the years I had spent far from shore. As soon as my feet left the deck, my stomach flew into my throat, and my heart fell to my belly. I pressed my body into the rigging.

The sound of tearing canvas, louder even than the thunder, shook me from my fearful stupor. I had to make this climb—I could do no less after the crew had risked their lives to rescue me from Kannaoka's dungeon, and if the mast came down, dragged into the sea by the sail, I would suffer no less than any other soul on this ship. Bending my head against the driving rain, I willed my hand to open, my arm to reach.

I forgot the discomfort of my wet clothes and the roar of the oncoming thunder. My hands ached, the strain of holding my weight to the rope curling them into painful claws. The cut I had received in the hollow chamber opened, blood mixing with rainwater and running down my wrist, but the pain did not matter, so I forgot it as well. There was no ship, no storm, no sea below. Only the climb existed.

Lightning flashed twice in quick succession, and a thunderclap followed close behind. The worst of the storm was yet advancing upon us. Wind tore at my hair and my clothing, and the rigging shook beneath me. I lifted one hand and found my grip before moving one foot, over and over, not daring to look farther than the next few inches of rope.

At last, my hand met wood: the main sail's yard, to which the canvas still clung. It groaned and squealed like an injured animal as the sail pulled it back and forth. Far below, a towering wave crashed over the deck.

I stepped through the ropes, hooking both feet into the rigging. The wind seized me by the shoulders, pulling me away from the mast, and I dared lift only one hand to remove the coil of rope from my shoulder and loop it over the yard. One hand and one knot at a time, as the mast waved at the sky like a spear in the hand of a triumphant warrior, I fashioned myself a harness and climbed onto the swaying beam.

I could not stand even if I had wished to. I crawled, hand over hand and knee in front of knee, to the first knot where the sail was still affixed. I thought to untie it, but that would remove both my hands from their grips, and I was neither brave nor foolhardy enough to risk it. Wrapping both legs around the beam, I fumbled for my steel knife. Rope fibers stretched and split under the blade, and the sail tore away with a roar of wind. It flew like a flag, still attached at two more points.

With both legs and one arm wrapped around the yard, I returned the knife to my belt. I would be useless if I were to lose it.

Hamilcar steered the ship into the oncoming wave, and it crashed over the bow, drenching the crew below. Rain ran into my eyes. I inched forward, shouting a wordless challenge and a desperate prayer for our safety into the wind even as it stole my breath from my lips.

I heard the sail shaking before I saw it, and felt the straining rope with one hand. I secured myself to the yard, drew my knife, and drove it into the center of the taut fibers.

The rope snapped. My knife twisted out of my hand and fell into the lashing rain, never to be seen again. Pain shot across my right forearm as a loose end of rope struck me with all the force of the wind. My hand jerked back, and I slipped over the beam.

My harness tightened across my chest. The backs of my knees, scraped raw from twisting over the rough wood, stuck painfully to the yard, my trousers torn through. I had not quite fallen, not yet.

Thunder assaulted my ears. The world had become a drum, beaten by the hand of a god. Lightning, blue-white and brighter than fire, followed after.

The main sail tore its last knot and flew away across the waves.

~ XIII ~

INTERLUDE TWO: THE LAND OF GHOSTS

Khalim was lost.

Thirty-one steps from the gate of Torr's citadel, he had turned to see the way he had come. The white marble walls had already disappeared, smothered in blue fog behind the dark shapes of trees. He had not looked back a second time.

Unfamiliar stars glittered from a black sky. The forest encircled him with darkness and the smell of green things growing, each tree tall and wide as the mountains of iron, the loam under his feet soft and deep. This place, he thought, had been old even when the earth had been young.

He had walked for some time now, in a night as endless as the white city's scarlet evening. He felt neither hunger nor thirst, a small mercy granted to him so far from the place of his erstwhile god. A cold, damp wind tugged at his clothes. He had acquired, in the center of his tunic, a ragged, burnt hole, through which the chill cut at his skin. It was the memory of the conjured lance of Malang, the war god of Phyreios, who had recognized the god inside Khalim and sought to slay him for good. The lance had burned, searing a mark across Khalim's chest that he had spent the last of his strength healing, and the force of it had taken him off his feet. In comparison, he far preferred the cold.

Voices filled the wood, chattering in languages he did not understand, mingling with the calls of birds and the distant, threatening growls of unseen beasts. The undergrowth shifted like water, and shadowy shapes darted in and out of sight.

There were people, too—shades in the shapes of men and women, barely brighter than the night around them. Khalim had called out to them, again and again, but none had answered, nor had they ceased their wandering to acknowledge him. Now, one crossed Khalim's path and stopped, staring into his face with blank, black eyes, searching for something.

"Who are you?" Khalim asked.

The man only shook his head, drawing his loose robe around him and shivering. "No, no," he said. "You aren't my son."

He turned away, muttering a low, rhythmic prayer, and the forest swallowed his shadowy form. In the space of another breath, he was gone.

"Good luck," Khalim called after him.

How long had that man been wandering here? The eternal night stretched on, and Khalim's memory of the citadel grew fainter with each step he took, and it was so, so cold. His home had always been warm, even in the rainy seasons, so warm that Phyreios had felt wintry whenever he'd walked into the shade. The door to his mother's house had only a curtain hung across the door to keep out the insects.

I'm never going to see her again, am I? Even when she passed on into death—or had she already?—he had no way of finding her. She might become like the shadow of the man, searching endlessly for her son, hoping that by random chance and the whims of the absent gods, their paths might cross just once.

But Khalim had known they would not meet again when he had told her goodbye, beside the bridge that crossed the river and joined with the road north. She had not wept, then, but he knew she would, after he was gone and would not see her. It had not been a vision that had told him he would never return, but a terrible, icy weight that had dropped into his belly as he walked over the bridge—his first taste of cold.

As much as he had wanted to turn and run back home, he hadn't looked back, not once in the six months that he walked over the rice fields and through the desert, chasing the far-off Iron Mountain. The god he carried had commanded him, and he had obeyed. This was what it had earned him: an eternity of wandering in the wilds of the world beyond. The shades of others pushed against him as he went, each touch a breath of winter wind, and not one spoke to him. A few of the faces limned in pale starlight were almost familiar, but he could not recall their names.

The citadel had been safe, and it had been small, and hadn't that been what Khalim had desired all along? He had only dreamed of leaving Nagara in the worst of his visions, as the First Hero urged him onward with images of the fall of Phyreios. He had wanted a house of his own, a place to do his work, and to take care of his mother. He had wanted, with all the ardor of a lonely youth, a husband or a wife, though the touch of his god had frightened most everyone away—everyone save Eske.

Khalim found a place between the roots of a great tree, beneath a branch with leaves as wide as the span of his arms. Here, the wind did not bite so harshly, and when he tucked his legs underneath him and wrapped his arms around his shoulders, the shelter was almost warm. He would rest, he decided, and choose a path forward from here. He had been walking for days, now, perhaps weeks. Years might have passed without his awareness, a possibility that made him want to weep, but he rested his head on his arms and took several forced, unnatural breaths. He would not return to the citadel, even if he could. He would sooner wander until the end of the world than return to that empty prison.

He shivered. Once, he had believed that his god would protect him from any harm. He was alone now, and the moon-faced owl's warning rang in his ears: *you're likely to get your face stolen. Or worse.*

The brilliant stars wheeled in erratic spirals above the trees. The ground shook as something colossal walked by out of sight, a great dark shape that shadowed the sky and passed on as quickly as it had come. It carried a lantern as large as a house, burning with a flickering violet fire. In its light, the passing shades were illuminated in purple and blue, their troubled faces shining.

Khalim had not become a shade. To his own eyes, his hands and feet were the hue and texture of flesh, and though the darkness muted their colors, the threads of his clothing had not turned to shadow. Given enough time, would he too become a silhouette, or did each shade see itself as it was in life, and Khalim as a ghost?

He wanted to leave this place. He wanted to find that man again, and help him find his son, but the man was gone. He wanted to find the place where all these people had come from and offer them some comfort, but even if he had not lost the ability to heal when Torr had left him, what help could he give a ghost?

He was lost, and he had been lost for a long, long time.

Time passed. The stars turned overhead. He got up and made his way a little farther across the latticed roots, climbing their damp sides and stumbling into the deep, loamy valleys between them. Somewhere, someone was weeping, but each time Khalim thought he had found the source of the sound, it drifted farther away.

Still the shades wandered by, following paths only they could see. Khalim's path was a winding one, each turn chosen at random as he passed each towering tree. If he had circled back around toward the citadel at last, it did not appear from the gloom. He pressed on.

A crumbling wall of overgrown masonry, dark gray under the perpetual damp, emerged from the tangle of roots. It was hewn of dark rock that glistened with rot and mica, and half-buried as the roots of the trees pulled it into the soil.

Even thus consumed by the forest, it stood twice Khalim's height. The carved faces of men, stern-faced and bearded and covered in moss, gazed on him with hollow eyes. A shade leapt from the overhanging ledge and landed beside him without a sound. He wore the shadow of a broken mask, blank and faceless over the left side of his face. His clothing was wisps of shadow, wrapped around him like a shroud, and the exposed side of his face twisted into an expression of fear and rage.

"You," he hissed.

Khalim stepped back, his heels catching against a serpentine root. "Who are you?"

The man held out his hands, grasping at the air. He smelled of smoke and burnt flesh. "You," he said again. "False prophet of a false god. I will cast you down in the name of the Ascended."

"The Ascended are dead," said Khalim, and then, again: "Who are you?"

He did not know this twisted half-face. The mask made the memory of his heartbeat quicken in fear, and a ghostly pain shot across his ribs. The man reached for his belt, but his hand closed around nothing. He had not carried whatever weapon he sought into the land of the dead.

"It's all right," Khalim continued, his voice soft. "I'm not going to hurt you. Do you have a name? Do you remember it?"

The man laughed, a dry, rasping rattle. "You *killed* me, sorcerer. You called down fire from the sky and burned me where I stood. I remember."

Khalim remembered, as well—the assassins in the alleys of Phyreios, and in the long grass upon the mountainside. One had struck him with a poisoned blade. Another had cut Eske down and raised his dripping knife for the killing blow.

There, Khalim's memory faltered. He could recall only a flash of blinding light, and the grim certainty that he had done something for which he would never be forgiven. He'd not had the time, afterward, to regret it, or to ask why the power that had only ever healed had so cruelly taken a life. He had lived only one more day.

He knew now that Torr was a war-god, a ruler-god; a god of high walls and straight roads and terrible, final judgments, so unlike the gods of forest and field that Khalim had lived beside in his youth. He would kill and heal with the same hand—Khalim's hand.

"I'm so sorry," Khalim said. "I didn't know what would happen. I didn't want you to hurt Eske, but I didn't mean for you to die. I'm sorry." It sounded hollow. He had wanted the Serpent gone, and had given no thought to the consequences. Another apology, one placing the blame on the god, died unspoken on his tongue.

The Serpent laughed again, mirthless and dry. "I hope your death was as painful as mine."

Khalim said nothing.

"I failed in my duty to kill you," the Serpent said. "My gods have barred me from their paradise. I see now that they were testing me. I'll bring you to them, and I'll receive my reward at last."

He reached out, one hand gloved in shadow grasping for Khalim's clothing. The uncovered half of his face stretched and distorted, baring his teeth, which shone white in the darkness of his face.

Because he would not be confined to the prison of the dead Ascended any more than he would remain in Torr's city, and because he was a coward as well as a murderer, Khalim turned and ran into the forest.

How strange it was to run without breathing. He climbed over roots and beneath overhanging branches, pushing his way past ghosts that stumbled once as he touched them and continued, unheeding, on their endless wanderings. The wind tore at his hair and through the hole in his tunic, cold as death.

Only when he was lost again, far out of sight of the crumbling wall—the only landmark in this expanse of endless trees—did he turn to look behind. The Serpent had not followed. He had become just another shade, as Khalim surely was to him. Would he wander forever, searching for Khalim like the man looking for his son?

Khalim crouched among the roots, placing his head in his hands. He could not blame the Torr for the Serpent's fate, not while his chest ached with the memory of the terror and rage that had possessed him when he had seen the poisoned knife raised above Eske's head. He had failed to save a life before, for want of time, but he had never taken one until that terrible day. He'd never held a weapon.

Did you know that this would happen? he asked his absent god. *Is this what you intended, when you gave me the visions of Phyreios in flames?*

His only answer was the rustling of the wind through the trees. And then: "Help me!"

A small, high voice cut through the gloom. It whimpered, weak and quivery with terror, the voice of a small child or a trapped animal.

Khalim got to his feet. The sound came from somewhere behind him, farther ahead along the way he had fled the Serpent. Across the ground, a web of knotted roots waited to ensnare him.

If I caught my ankle, would it break? Would it hurt?

He found the thickest root and climbed atop it, following it to the base of its tree. The trunk stood wider than the citadel gate, too large to see around. "Where are you?" he called out.

The high-pitched whimpering continued. Khalim chose left, placing his hands on the furrowed bark to keep his balance as he picked his way over the roots. Fans of thin leaves grasped at his hair, and the branches were heavy with strange, elongated fruit, crooked like the fingers of an old man.

On the other side, nestled in a hollow of roots, lay a heavy iron trap. Its serrated jaws closed around the leg of a shade, small and slight. The cries came from beneath a plate of white bone, like a mask, over the shade's face. Behind the mask lay two glassy, dark eyes that mirrored the starry abyss above. Small, human hands scratched feebly at the trap. It turned its bone mask and small, bright eyes to Khalim, and emitted a piercing cry like steam escaping from a pot.

It was a child, or the ghost of one. Khalim held up his hands, showing they were empty. "I'm a healer," he said. "Or, I was, I suppose." He no longer had his magic. His hands fell to his sides, cold and ineffectual.

Khalim might not have been the healer he once was, but he could set a bone and bandage a wound. He knelt beside the trap.

The iron teeth had pierced the shadowy skin, and ink-black blood trickled between them. *So it is possible to be injured here, in the world beyond the world.* A pair of long fins held the trap steady against the forest floor, and the rounded edges of its heavy hinge gave it the look of a large-eyed, toothy fish breaching from the water.

The child cowered, falling into terrified silence.

"Hold still," Khalim said. "I'll get you out."

He placed his fingers between the iron teeth. The jaw resisted, rusted metal creaking in protest, and gave way with a screech. His hands slipped, and it snapped shut again, a hair's breadth from the ends of his fingers.

The ghost was free. Khalim hadn't thought he had held the trap long enough, but the child sat beside the clenched metal jaw, examining its wound through its pale mask.

"May I see it?" asked Khalim.

The child—a little boy, maybe seven years old, with tousled hair made of shadow—remained still. Khalim crawled closer and took the injured leg in his hands.

"You're lucky," he said. "It's not broken. It will heal up in time. All I have is my shirt, but it's clean enough. There wasn't any dirt in the citadel."

No answer came. Perhaps this spirit could not speak—plenty of the shades only moaned, and others made no sound at all, but Khalim was certain he had heard the boy cry for help.

How many more of these traps lay between the roots, waiting for someone to pass through in the dark? Who could have placed this one here?

I am a healer, he thought as he tore strips from his clothing and tied them around the bloody mess. *I don't know anything else, but I know that.*

That done, he stood up and held out his hands. "Can you walk, little one?"

Small, ice-cold hands hooked around each of his thumbs, and the boy placed his weight on his legs and fell forward into Khalim's arms. He was light, like a bird, and trembled with a fast, nervous pulse.

"In that case," Khalim said, "I'll carry you for a while. We can look after each other."

The child weighed almost nothing. His arms draped over Khalim's shoulders, and his legs clenched around Khalim's waist and through the crooks of his elbows. The mask was cold and damp against his shoulders.

"I suppose I should keep walking, then," Khalim said, mostly to himself. "I won't get out of this place otherwise. You don't mind, do you?"

In a soft, sibilant voice, the boy said, "Where are you going?"

His mouth was hidden behind the mask, and his small, glittering eyes met Khalim's.

"So you do talk," said Khalim.

A narrow pass between the trees opened up before him, and he climbed down. "I don't really know," he confessed. "I was in the citadel for…I'm not sure. For a long time. Then I came here."

The stars were spinning faster, as though the eternal night sped though an hour with each passing second. Lights danced across the forest floor. Far in the distance, obscured by the trees, the purple glow of the enormous lantern bobbed as its hulking bearer continued its mysterious rounds.

"I suppose I'm looking for someone," Khalim continued. "He's probably not here in this world. I hope not. But I want to find a way to tell him I'm all right. And I'd like to tell my mother I'm safe, or as safe as I can be. She always worried about me."

The boy nodded, his mask scraping against Khalim's ear. "I can help you."

"Do you know this place?" asked Khalim.

The boy stretched his neck forward to look Khalim in the face. Beneath the edge of the mask, he smiled, showing a row of pointed teeth. "I will show you the way."

A soft, cold rain fell over the trees, though the stars remained unshadowed, and threads of silver light traced their way over tangled roots and muddy earth. Khalim shivered. The form of the boy had grown warm, draped over his shoulders like a cloak.

"Where are we going?" he asked. His voice was flat and muffled, swallowed up by the forest.

"Out of the wilds," came the whispered reply, a soft hiss in Khalim's ear. "There's a path up ahead."

The stars gave little illumination, and the rain filled the air with a fine mist, obscuring where the path might have been. "What's on the other side?" Khalim asked.

"Other places." The bone mask found a spot in the crook of Khalim's shoulder, left bare by his ragged clothing, and came to rest there, sending a chill through Khalim's chest and down his back. When the boy spoke again, his sharp teeth brushed against Khalim's skin. "Places with people. Gods' places. You'll see."

"I just came from a god's place."

Khalim climbed onto the ridge of another huge, dark root, its surface rough and splintery under his feet. Before him lay a space between two trees, a window of night sky overhead, and something that might have once been a road. Broken stones emerged from the mud, clasped tightly to the earth in a net of roots and fallen branches. A small, scurrying creature, only a shadow in the surrounding gloom, caught sight of him and dashed away to hide beneath a hollow log. The small, glittering eyes of its young stared out from the darkness, fearful and silent.

"Oh, but you left," the boy said. "You left to wander the wilds."

Khalim jumped from the root to the wet ground beneath. Water collected in a glassy puddle at the base of the tree, reflecting the stars like a mirror, though rain still fell on his face. "Yes, I did. I couldn't stay there. I was turning to stone."

Water slicked the remains of the ancient highway and made it shimmer in the starlight. It wound through the trees, twisting back and forth around them. The forest, then, was older than the ruin. In the distance stood a tree so large that twenty men could not reach halfway around its trunk. It must have been older than the world, Khalim thought, older than even the gods. In comparison, he was but an insect, so small that neither his presence nor his absence would be noticed.

"Jahan was happy to become a statue," he said aloud, "to keep watch by the gate. But I'm not like him. He's—he was—a warrior. He sacrificed himself to save others. I don't think I'm as brave as he was."

Now that he stood upon the road, it stretched on in either direction, gray stone breaking through the undergrowth in jagged ridges and wind-worn curves.

"Where to now?" he asked.

The boy lifted one arm and pointed to the left. Khalim adjusted his small burden and kept walking.

In life, he had never questioned why the god of the citadel had chosen him. It had always been a fact, like the sun rising in the morning or the rains coming twice a year. It was the will of the gods, and even if one had wanted to risk their displeasure by questioning it further, there had been rice to plant and harvest, and newborn calves to wash, and clothes to mend, and injured ox-drivers to look after. Now, he had nothing but time and the long road that wended through the wilds.

Why me? he thought, but as in life, there was no answer.

The wheeling sky disappeared behind a thick canopy of branches, as ancient trees clawed at each other in wide arcs over the path. A curtain of vines, each as thick as his arm, brushed against the choking roots. One of them must have been a snake, but it stopped moving as soon as he turned to look at it.

"So where did you come from, little one?" he asked. He had someone to talk to, now, after he had spent so long alone in the citadel. He had been on the brink of madness, then, before the moon-faced owl had found him.

Maybe he already was mad, and that was why he couldn't keep track of time. Past, present, and future had collapsed into a single, endless moment, and he watched it play out as the stars spun across the sky, far beyond his reach.

That had always been the worst thing about his visions: to witness the city crumble and burn and to cry out into the suffocating silence, smothered under an invisible weight. Worse still, when all that he had seen had come to pass, he'd been exactly as helpless as he had been while asleep.

The boy rested his head on Khalim's shoulder. The hard ridge of the mask dug into his flesh. "Not far from here," the boy said. "You'll see it soon."

The rain stopped, or the branches overhead grew so thick and wove themselves together so tightly that nothing, not even starlight, could pass through. The broken paving stones had become nothing more than thin, gray crescents above a soft, smothering blackness. The huge columns of the surrounding trees faded into a wall of shadow.

Silence covered Khalim like a thick cloth. "I can't see," he whispered.

On his back, the boy had grown feverishly hot, and sweat trickled down Khalim's spine, turning to ice as it met the air. A dull ache settled into his hands and feet.

Is this what winter feels like? Eske had told him of the dark season of the North, where rain fell as tiny flakes of ice and the sun didn't rise for many weeks. Khalim almost hadn't believed him. It had sounded like a myth, the sort of place where the unjust and wicked dead would be punished for their misdeeds in life.

Perhaps Khalim had met his own punishment. He'd left the citadel, against the advice of the moon-faced owl and of Jahan, all turned to stone. He had not been blameless in life. *I tried, but I couldn't save Phyreios. I didn't act in time. I let Reva hide me away, as though my life were more important than all the lives in the city. I thought more of Eske than I did of my duty. I killed the Serpent in a gout of fire.*

The boy's sibilant whisper cut through his guilty thoughts. "Keep going," he said. "Not far now."

Khalim forced his feet to take a step, and then another. His limbs were heavy and clumsy, and the broken road no longer pressed into his feet. He pressed his elbows into his sides, holding the child closer for fear that he might drop him. "How much farther?"

"Not far," the boy said again. "You'll see it very soon."

"See what?" Khalim asked.

A point of light, burning red like a single ember in the gloom, flickered into view. A second soon joined it, and a pair of scarlet eyes stared into Khalim's own. With ponderous lethargy, a hulking form rose from the forest floor, lifting the eyes into the treetops.

It was enormous, and it was close, looming over him as tall as the walls of Phyreios. Its mouth opened into a terrible rictus grin. The light of its eyes shone on two rows of needle-sharp teeth, white and glistening, and the smooth planes of a mask of bone, the huge mirror of the one worn by the child on Khalim's back.

~ XIV ~

THE HOUSE OF THE WEAVER-WOMAN

The *Lady of Osona* surged forth, carried on the crest of a great wave, and fell into the storm's eye. I hung from the yard, my head spinning and my limbs contorted into painful shapes. I pulled myself up, forcing my arms to stretch and my legs to unfurl, and I crawled back to the rigging. Though the ship lay still, as if in a deep, dreamless sleep, my vision blurred and tilted with the memory of the storm. I cut myself free of the harness and descended to the deck.

My rope-burned feet touched the soaked timbers, and I fell to my knees, shutting my eyes and gulping air for one long moment until rain once again brushed against my shoulders and the back of my neck.

With the sails raised or missing, and our cargo tied down or lost, we had only to endure. I went below deck.

Bran stood with his legs splayed and his head hanging low, his eyes flashing white in the thin beam of deceptive sunlight that followed me into the hold. I approached him slowly, speaking soft words in the language of the steppe from whence he came. He had met storms before, the torrents of wind and dust that tore across the flat, empty plains, but never had the ground beneath his feet tossed him about with such violence. A bright, wet laceration on his shoulder showed where he had knocked against the rough beams of his enclosure.

He allowed me to come near, and after nosing at both my hands, let me touch his face. The light faded from the hatch, and the wind began its shrill lament once more. Halvor called me to the oars.

I left Bran in the dark, my heart wrested from my chest to remain in the enclosure with him, and took up my place beside Halvor. The wind howled across the deck.

"Pull for your lives!" Adama shouted, and we did, driving the *Lady* into the rising waves. Roiling seawater pooled at our feet. It grasped at my ankles and tugged at my ruined clothing. Behind me, Bran screamed in panic, and I could do nothing to comfort him. On we rowed, thrashed by water within and outside the hold. The pain in my arms faded, as did my worry for Bran and my concern for my own life. There was only the oar.

True, clear daylight, red-tinged with the sunset, shone at last in the storm's wake. A cheer went up from the sodden hold, answered in kind by another from the deck. We had survived, all of us, though we had lost a sail and a good portion of our cargo.

Bran, too, had survived. As pain and exhaustion caught up to me, I stayed awake with him, and I sang him a song of the open sky until he stood still and his breathing evened.

From here to the great port of Hali, at the southernmost tip of the continent, I rowed in double shifts to carry the wounded *Lady* safely to land. Without our main sail, the strength of our arms and the steadfastness of our hearts moved the ship. I slept from the afternoon until midnight, exhaustion turning my hammock as soft as the bed of a king, and if I dreamed of anything but storms and a ship's dark berth, I do not remember it. I forgot, as well, the evil book and the magics that might have been contained within. My thoughts were on my work, and only occasionally drifted toward land, and the task that waited for me there—finding Khalim's homeland, and something of him to guide me on my way.

At the start of the new year, when tempests gave way to heavy, quiet rain, we arrived at Hali. A long finger of land stretched out before us, pointing south into the sea, with a city of red bricks standing beyond it, in the palm of the continent's hand. I packed my few belongings, the book and my spear among them, and led Bran to the deck.

I hesitated there, before I stepped off the ship. The life of a sailor was a hard one, harder even than that of a wandering warrior, but it had its own triumphs. My heart ached at the thought that I would never see any of these brave people again, and that I would leave the ocean behind, perhaps forever. It called to me, a tempting song of wind and waves, promising adventure and a distraction from my cares. The sea is a cruel lover, demanding all one's thoughts and attention and endless labor, but she gives much in return.

As I led Bran onto the dock. I tried to hear instead the song of the bright green wood that surrounded the city like a collar of emerald silk. The wind came down from the mountains beyond, soft and cool, promising more rain. My destination lay somewhere on the other side, nearer to Phyreios, where a god ruled the city and wore the face of my beloved.

I went to find Khalim, and so I said farewell to the *Lady of Osona*, her crew, and the sea.

"We go west," Hamilcar told me. "If ever your road leads you there, you are welcome to join us again."

He made me show him my share of the treasure from Kannaoka, to prove that I still had it, and I swore to him that I would spend it wisely.

My first coin was given in exchange for a fruit that Bran stole from a vendor near the dock, emboldened by solid land beneath his hooves and tempted by the sweet smell. I kept a better hold on him after that.

The language of Hamilcar's crew served me well in this new country, though I had to point at the provisions I wanted and had no hope of haggling for a better price. By the time night fell, I had secured a week's worth of travel rations and a room at an inn. The innkeeper, a toothless old man dressed in a long tunic of grass-green cotton, greeted me with an expansive wave. He offered me a drink, malt liquor that smelled of wet earth, and pointed curiously to my tattooed arms.

"I come from far to the north," I explained, "where I was a warrior of great renown. Many of us are marked like this, to grant us the favor and protection of the gods."

The old man smiled. "You are indeed a strange man to behold. But you came from the south—from the islands."

I accepted the offered drink and took a long draught. "I have been wandering for a long time."

He nodded, and his weathered face turned pensive, though he did not share his thoughts with me. He had the wiry limbs and sunburnt face of a sailor; he might have thought of his own wanderings.

"For now, my journey turns north again," I said. "I am looking for a village called Nagara, between here and the citadel of Phyreios. A young man lived there—he was blessed by the gods, and had the power to heal any ailment. Do you know the way I might take?"

"The highway will take you into the mountains," he replied, tugging at his white wisp of a beard, "but beyond that, I do not know. I once had a traveler in my inn who told a story like yours. He said he met a boy in the river valley who possessed a strange talent for magic."

I placed my hands flat on the tabletop and leaned toward him. "What else did he say?"

"It has been ten years or more—it was before the year of the great storm, and it has been seven years since then. He was a pilgrim, and he had just come from the peak of Mount Abora. Before that, he had seen the headwaters of the great northern river."

Then it was that river, the lifeblood of this green country, that I had to find, tracing the path of this nameless pilgrim all the way to the village where he met the boy who could heal. Ten years past, Khalim would yet have been a child, but already aware of the power he held and the terrible destiny that came with it.

The next morning, the wind came from the sea, smelling of brine and distant storms. The *Lady of Osona* lay anchored a short distance from the harbor, and a new, scarlet sail hung from its main mast. Soon, she would depart again, to cross the waters without me.

My road turned north. I saddled Bran and rode out of Hali on the cobbled street that led into the mountains. A blue fog crowned the distant peaks, among them the sacred mountain of Abora, its long shadow falling across the highway.

The sun set a little later each evening, and as I followed the pilgrim's road, the rains moved north ahead of me. The farmers in the foothills were generous with their bounty, and the goatherders upon the cliffs taught me which of the hardy plants that grew among the rocks were good to eat for both men and horses. In each of them, I saw a little of Khalim: an easy white smile in a brown face; a crown of soft, dark curls; hands callused from work instead of fighting.

They had not heard of Nagara, the village in the river valley where once lived a boy with the power of the gods. The road through the mountains was a long one, and human settlements grew farther and farther apart as I left the coast behind and the air grew thin and cold. The people with whom I spoke had grown old in the same town in which they had been born, or they had married into the next one down the road and never returned.

I met a woman in a herding village on a vast, flat plateau, where the trees grew low and twisted in the thin soil, their outstretched branches battered by strong winds. She gave her name as Sarata, and though she had been married to a man of the plateau for five years, she had been born in the low country. A flood, she said, had washed away her home in a single night, and now so little remained of her village that it was as though no one had ever lived there at all. She missed the summer heat, which never quite reached the altitude of her new home, and she missed her dear younger brother, who had drowned that fateful day.

"I had thought this was a gentle land," I told her. "I see now that I was mistaken."

She gave a shake of her head, setting the polished wooden ornaments at the end of her braids rattling. "The rain waters the fields and floods the riverbanks, for the gods are both kind and cruel. You'll meet them on the road, if you look."

I asked of Khalim, and she told me of a neighbor afflicted by a disease of the blood. With each passing year, it sapped his strength, until at twenty he was as feeble as an old man. His father carried him on his back up the river to see a healer, passing through three villages on the way—farther than anyone Sarata knew had ever traveled, until her own journey two years later. The young man returned still weak, but walking on his own feet beside his father, and they told a story of a young healer who had driven out the affliction with only a touch.

"Where can I find the place where this healer lived?" I asked, but Sarata only shook her head again. She had never traveled there herself, only heard tell of it, and now she could not even guide me to the place where her village had been, to give me a place to start.

I thanked her for her story and for her hospitality, and I spent the evening with Bran in a shelter leaning against Sarata's house, along with five ill-tempered goats. I understood their dislike of me, as I had eaten one of their fellows in a savory stew prepared by Sarata's husband.

I set off the next morning on the winding road down the opposite face of the plateau. The steep decline eased as Bran and I passed into the foothills. As we finally crossed into the lowlands, the dry season swept across the forest, turning it from deep green to the yellow-brown of the kelp that grew in the warm waters of the south.

I heard the river before I saw it. Even at its lowest depth, it sang in a deep rumbling voice a song of ancient power, of the blessings it granted to those who lived on its banks and the wrath it visited upon them in turn. Here was the god that Sarata had told me I would meet, and it was as benevolent and cruel as Khalim's god. How fitting, then, that this land was where he and Khalim had met.

The first village upon the dry bank offered me a place to sleep in exchange for a deer, and the old men in whose house I stayed knew the village of Nagara by name. I had only to travel west for seven more days, they said, and I would find it just over the hill from a roadside shrine.

I asked them if the shrine honored the god of Phyreios, but neither had heard of such a god or such a place. The god of the shrine was a god of the rice fields, and had nothing to do with a faraway city in the desert.

On the sixth day, I found this god of the fields just as the men had said. I had imagined a towering statue, gazing out over the green, but the carved figure stood only two feet tall upon a smooth stone pedestal of the same height. Rain had reduced his face to nothing but the ridge of his brow and the hollows of his eyes. In his arms were sheaves of grain, and beneath his feet were gentle ridges that were once the carved shapes of defeated serpents. I bowed my head as I passed, but I did not offer a prayer. I had no words for this god in any of the tongues I knew, only a voiceless hope that I had at last arrived at my destination.

An unseasonable rain fell, and a fine mist rose up from the ground. I climbed the hill and emerged from the fog to witness a sky half obscured, the sun shining through the clouds upon a dozen small houses of clay and stone. Water sluiced down their thatched roofs into shallow channels carved into the earth, and their eaves hung low over their curtained doors like half-lidded eyes. The river lay at the bottom of the hill, making its slow way to the distant sea, its surface spotted with raindrops. Beyond the village, the shadowed shapes of the villagers moved between tilled rows that stretched out to the horizon. They carried baskets of grain, and they scattered it in handfuls.

I crossed the river by way of a rope bridge, its timber walkway swollen with water. Under the awning of the first house, a man of middle age, his thick, black beard carrying a single streak of white, filled more baskets with brown rice. He caught sight of me as I approached and left his work, shielding his eyes from the sun and rain with one hand.

"Hello, traveler," he called out. "It isn't often we see someone brave the mountains and the forest to come here, of all places. What brings you to Nagara?"

To hear the name of this place spoken by another lifted my spirits. "There was a young man who lived here," I said, "by the name of Khalim. He had the gift of healing. Do you know him?"

"I do. If you're looking to be healed, I'm afraid he is no longer here. He left for the north more than three years ago, and we yet await his return."

Over the months I had crossed this country, I had rehearsed my tale, making it grander than it had been but not so grand as to not be believed, smoothing over the mistakes I had made and casting Khalim as a hero his countrymen might admire, but all of it fell away. Though I had sailed many miles and walked many more to reach this place, a terrible dread came over me in place of my anticipated relief. I could only bow my head. "I'm looking for his family."

The man's friendly face dimmed. "Then it is as we feared," he said. "Khalim will not be coming home."

I had brought to this quiet village the news it had feared for three long years: that their favored son had been lost to the wide world. I intended to bring Khalim back, but how could I explain that to this man? To say that Khalim had not died, and yet was not among the living, and that I had dedicated myself to performing feats of bravery and magic that not even the wisest of sages had attempted, would only serve to convince him that I was mad. He might not trust a madman's report of the fall of Phyreios, and he and his fellow villagers would not wait forever before sending out an expedition to search for Khalim. These people were strangers, but I did not wish for them to share in my most vivid and terrible memory, of seeing another's eyes looking out from Khalim's face. Letting them believe he had died might have been a kindness, but it was a bitter one.

"My name is Roda," the man said. "I am the smith here, though today I distribute the seed grain."

"Eske of the North," I said. Roda had no use for any of my titles or the boasts of my deeds.

"Come with me, Eske."

He brought me to the last house on the muddy path through the village, where a woven tapestry of red vines on a blue field hung across the narrow door.

"This is the house of Taherah, the weaver-woman," Roda told me, and I could guess his next words before he spoke them. "She is Khalim's mother."

He left me there, alone, beneath the dripping overhang of the roof, staring at the curtained door. I would have no help in this endeavor.

I had climbed the side of the fell worm as it lay waste to Phyreios. I had climbed the mountain to commune with the ancient dragon of the temple, and I had sailed out to hunt the sea-serpent amongst the floating towers of ice, but this was the harshest test of my courage that I had yet encountered. I stood there, willing my arm to lift and my hand to knock upon the lintel, but I could not do it. The rain departed and returned again, whispering a soft rhythm against the thatched roof and beating against the surface of the river.

At length, I would have to announce my presence or be discovered here, lurking at the door. I tapped my knuckles against the frame.

A callused brown hand pulled aside the covering, and a face that was at once familiar and strange appeared in its place. She was perhaps forty years old, her long, black hair covered with a loose veil, and as tall and elegant as the carving of a goddess or a long-dead queen.

She looked me up and down, the fine lines of her face creased in confusion. I was dressed in a tunic given to me at the temple and boots and trousers acquired from Hamilcar's crew, a steppe horse in tow and a spear on my back. Roda had said that few travelers ever came to Nagara. I must have been quite the sight to behold. I opened my mouth to explain myself, but no words came to me.

Understanding flickered into Taherah's huge, dark eyes. Tears welled up beneath them as she took in my strange appearance, and she let the curtain fall over the door. I heard a single, strangled sob as she walked away toward the back of the house.

It was to her that I was obligated to speak. I would wait for her return. I let Bran wander and graze, and I sat in the narrow dry space beneath the roof and the outer wall of the house, resting my feet and considering what I might say of Taherah's son.

The storm moved on, taking the rain and the shadows with it. Low, slanting sunlight painted the forest in yellow and gold, and the river shone blue. On either side of the village, the rice fields lay rich and dark, and the heavy air smelled of fertile soil. A young woman leading a humpbacked white ox, a pair of baskets strapped to its sides, stopped to stare at me for a moment, her head tilted to one side. More oxen followed her, their shapes like small clouds floating close to the ground, the people walking unhurried between them. The song they sang drifted across the fields to my ears, and it told a story of benevolent gods granting food to the people who worshiped them, giving them all that they needed in exchange for a season's worth of work. If such were the gods of this land, then it was no wonder that Khalim had placed his trust entirely in the god who had chosen him. How could he do otherwise, when he had received such gifts? If I had spent my youth as he had, in a green country where soft rains fell, and where neighboring villages did not take up arms every year to seize what little the others possessed, I would have grown to become a very different man—perhaps, I thought, a better one. One who might know what to say to Khalim's mother, who had waited so long for news of her son.

But I remembered the river, and the flood that had taken the village of the kind Sarata, and I thought that Torr in his benevolence and cruelty might have been the equal of these gods.

The villagers returned from the fields before nightfall, when the sky cast a bloody glow onto the river and more clouds gathered on the eastern horizon. Darkness covered the forest, and the hill with its weathered shrine cast a long shadow. It was then that Taherah opened her door once again, her eyes dry and circled in red.

"You should come inside," she said, and she let the curtain drop and disappeared into the shadows of the house.

I obeyed, glancing behind once to look for Bran and finding him nibbling at the grass growing beside one of the neighboring houses, content. A small, round face appeared in the window above him, staring at the strange creature that had accompanied the stranger into the village. I lifted the curtain and went inside.

A central fire, little more than embers, smoldered in a hollow dug into the floor. A three-legged iron stand held a small copper pot above it, and something that smelled of sharp spice bubbled within. I had not eaten for most of the day, but my belly had turned to stone; I would not have been able to accept anything offered to me.

On one side of the door, Taherah's loom stood as tall as I, a half-finished cloth of gold and orange threads stretched between its beams. The flickering embers turned the pattern into moving flames, and I watched it, transfixed and desperately delaying the inevitable conversation I had come so far to have.

Opposite the loom was a narrow bed with a soft woolen blanket tucked in at the corners. Its neat folds suggested it had not been touched in some time. This had been Khalim's bed, and it awaited his return, keeping watch by the door.

"Tell me your name, stranger," Taherah said. She sat beside the fire, tucking her skirt around her legs, and gave the pot a stir with a scorched wooden spoon.

I knelt on the floor, out of the reach of the fire's warmth. The small house was suddenly too large, its shadows deep and black and cavernous. The empty bed and the empty space by the fire yawned, huge and hollow, at the edges of my awareness.

"I am Eske, son of Ivor, of the Clan of the Bear," I said. "I met your son in the great city of the desert."

"Then he did reach the city from his dreams." The spoon tapped against the edge of the pot, ringing a soft, mournful note. Taherah glanced up. "Did the disaster come to pass? Did he save them?"

The smell of the small cooking fire became the miasma of smoke and dust that had hung over Phyreios at the end. I closed my eyes. "He saved many," I said. "Not all. Not enough. But without him, many more would have been lost."

"He is dead, then." It was not a question. She had known for some time—a mother's insight or a version of Khalim's gift of foresight.

The moment I had been dreading had arrived. "No," I began. "He did not die."

Before I could explain further, Taherah said, "Then why is he not with you?"

"When the task was done, and the survivors looked out over the ruin of Phyreios, the god Khalim carried took it upon himself to lead them. He sent Khalim away, to the land of the dead, and he rules the city still." Each word was a weight, and speaking them aloud only stacked them upon my shoulders. I bowed my head.

A troubled expression creased her brow. The embers cast tiny flames into her eyes—the same soft brown eyes that Khalim had possessed, but the god wearing his face had not.

"I loved your son," I said. "I love him still. What happened to him was an injustice, and I mean to set it right."

Taherah looked at me, taking my measure. Even with the shadows hollowing her eyes and deepening the creases beneath them, she was younger than I had expected. She would have been younger than I when she had borne Khalim. "You cannot defy the gods," she said. "I have tried. It always comes to naught."

"That may be so. But I will do everything in my power to bring Khalim back. If I should die in the attempt, then so be it." I drew in a shaky breath, my eyes stinging from the tears I held back as much from the smoke. I'd had three years, give or take a season, to mourn and commit myself to my quest, and I wished to offer what meager comfort I could, not to receive it.

"He was my husband's last gift to me," Taherah said to the fire, and to the empty house and her memories. I had all but disappeared. "The plague took him, as it took so many others, and left me alone. Khalim came six months later. He almost never cried. I thought he was ill, that I would lose him just as I'd lost his father.

But he lived, and he grew strong, and I thought that all was well. I was young, I had suitors, but I had no place in my heart for anyone but my son."

I listened, keeping still and silent, even as my feet went numb beneath me and the last light of the sun vanished from the doorway. How often had Khalim knelt here, learning at his mother's feet? I imagined him there beside me, but the effort only sent a sharp pain through my chest and worsened the burning in my eyes. I had come here to find him, and I had only found absence. The place he had left behind was no substitute for the man himself.

"He was only five when the star fell," Taherah continued. "I saw it while he was asleep, red like fire and blood, aflame in the northern sky. A bad omen. But I had work to do, and a little mouth to feed, and so I forgot about it."

She raised her head, startled to find me there. She had forgotten about me. "I did not think of the star again until Khalim began to dream," she said.

The rest of the tale of the falling star I knew already. It had landed near Phyreios, in the form of a lump of enchanted iron, and the Ascended had forged it into the Sword of Heaven, the tool of their own destruction. They could no more resist the will of Khalim's god than a mortal man could.

One person had defied that will. Khalim had left the cold, empty city where Torr had placed him. How much greater was the power of a god in his own sanctum than it was here under the sky?

Taherah stared into the fire, seeing nothing. It was as though she had gone far away, and left her body behind to stir her copper pot and keep my sad company, the hollow shades of both of us and of Khalim sitting in silent vigil.

"I am sorry to have been the one to bring this news to you," I said into the crushing silence. "I would have liked for Khalim to have introduced me to you. I would have liked to show him the land that I came from."

The ghost of a smile passed across her face. "I'm glad he found you. I'm glad he wasn't alone."

Shame bent my head and curled my shoulders inward. If I had been more worthy, if I had acted sooner, Khalim would not have been alone in Torr's prison-paradise. I would not burden Taherah with these thoughts, but they chanted their terrible rhythm in my skull nonetheless. "I hope that I may still bring him back," I said, drowning the litany out, "and that when my long journey is done, you and I will both see him again."

I waited for her to tell me that my quest was mere vanity, as so many others had done before, but she said nothing.

"When I left Phyreios, I went to the far eastern mountains," I continued, "where warriors train under the guidance of a great, serpentine dragon. The dragon sent me to the islands of the south, where I underwent the ceremony of the Dreaming Eye, and looked into the other world, where Khalim was taken." Unthinking, I placed a hand against my ribs, where the mark of the goddess's fingers remained.

Taherah's eyes lifted from the fire, and she studied me with a look that reminded me of my own mother, who could tell without fail whether I was lying. "What did you see?" she asked.

I shivered, the memory of the plunge into the black water seizing my body with an icy hand. "I saw the citadel, the cold and empty place where Khalim was meant to stay. He has gone from there, and now he wanders." I took a breath, to steady my nerves and reassure myself that I still could breathe, that I had not fallen into another dream of drowning. "I came here to ask for your help. One day, I will find a way to cross over, whether by magic or might. I will find Khalim. But—"

My words faltered. Taherah waited, her mouth a thin line and her pot forgotten. The spice began to burn, stinging the back of my throat.

"Our time together was so short," I admitted at last. "I had not the foresight to ask him where he might go if he had all the realms of the gods to choose from. That's why I came here—to find someone who could tell me more of him than I was able to learn."

Taherah smiled, and this time it lingered and touched the dark pools of her eyes. "He would not choose a place," she said. "He would find where he was most needed, and he would stay there as long as he could help. That's why he went to Phyreios."

"Of course he would." The god Torr had chosen Khalim for a reason, and it was for the same reason that I loved him and his mother mourned his absence with a silent, crushing sorrow. Where Taherah and I had seen the young man, however, Torr had seen a tool, worth no more consideration than an axe or a hammer, to be discarded when another would be more fitting for the task at hand. What thought did a god have for the value of one mortal life, when there were thousands more in his care?

"As for the rest," Taherah continued, "you likely already know. He would want to be near other people. He liked the rain. For his god to place him in an empty city would be cruelty. I'm not surprised he left."

She placed her wooden spoon through the handle of the pot and removed it from the fire. Getting to her feet, she added, "I don't believe you will succeed, Eske son of Ivor. But if you see my son again, promise me that you'll tell him I love him. And I know he did the best he could."

"I will not swear it in the name of any god," I said, "but I do swear it."

"And tell him I'm sorry," she said to the dark room. "I would have spared him all of it, if I could."

As would I, I thought, but I could no longer speak. Sorrow and rage constricted around my throat, each a great hand with fingers strong as iron. I would not let Taherah see me weep. I'd had years to tend to my own grief, and hers was newborn and ravenous. I was thankful for the dark.

"Do you eat meat?" she asked, as though I were an ordinary guest, stopping by for an evening meal, though her voice was soft. "Khalim never did. Once he learned to heal, any flesh made him ill. He explained it to me once, how he could feel it wanting to be whole again, but I never quite understood it."

I found my voice again, swallowing the obstruction in my throat, and told her I would eat whatever she offered. We dined in silence, as night drew the shadows closer and gathered them around the fire, but neither of us ate much. If I looked away from the light, the smell of spices and dried meat placed me back at the small house in the shadow of Phyreios's forge, lacking only the smoke of the ironworks and the presence of my companions.

"You came all this way to find me," Taherah said when we were finished. "I'm not sure I can thank you."

I shook my head. "I should thank you—for your hospitality, and for telling me of Khalim."

"Where will you go now?" she asked.

"I don't know." I would have liked to give her an answer, to promise her that I had a path to follow and a plan to carry out. Instead, I had only the hollow space that Khalim had left behind in this house, and an empty place in my heart to match it.

I had, also, a book I could not read and its looming threat of blasphemous magic. I pushed the thought from my mind, but the image of the flayed man, his eyes wide and white with terror, lingered.

Taherah was quiet, and the fire showed only the soft outline of her face and her folded hands, the rest all covered with night. "You may stay here," she said, "as long as you require it."

"I am a stranger to you. I would not burden you any more than I must."

Though I could not see her face, I could feel her gaze find me in the dark. "You are no more a burden than Khalim was, and for all the pain the gods gave me for his sake, he brought me only joy. Any help I give you is only what I would give to him."

It was not the green land and the gentle rain that had made Khalim who he was, but this house and this woman. He had known only love, generosity, and as much safety as the hostile world could grant, and he had offered the same in turn—even to those who had wished him harm.

Despite the warmth of the embers, the distance between Taherah and me had grown cold. Both she and the house longed for Khalim, and I was a poor substitute. "I will stay a short while," I said. "And I will hear anything you wish to tell me of your son."

The hour had grown late. I went out to secure Bran beneath the overhanging roof of the house, to keep him out of the weather. I would need to seek out drier climes soon, or he would fall ill again.

Taherah gave me Khalim's bed by the door. A rice-straw mattress still held the indentation of his body down its center, waiting for his return. Years of washing had worn the blanket smooth and threadbare, fading its colors into soft uniformity. Too much time had passed for it to smell of anything but rain.

There, in the narrow bed beside the weaver-woman's door, in the hollow space that did not fit me, I dreamed again of the gray coastline under the strange green sky.

~ XV ~

NAGARA IN SUNLIGHT

No sooner had I drifted off than I found myself underwater again, submerged in an icy sea. Darkness crept from the depths toward my feet, and only a thin, green band of sunlight gave me any indication of where the surface might lie. In the way of dreams, I knew at once that this was no ordinary ocean, and I curled my body and dove, looking for the huge presence of the goddess of the deep and the gate of bone that she kept.

I saw only darkness. Nashurru did not rise from below to clasp me in her huge, cold hands, and neither did the priestesses of the temple under the mountain keep my body safe as it slept, to ensure I did not drown. The frigid water sapped the strength from my limbs, and I kicked weakly for the surface. My chest ached for want of breath.

The sun's thin light disappeared as my vision faded. Pain like hot knives shot through my ribs. At any moment, I would be forced to breathe, and I would inhale water and perish. Was this, then, how my quest would end? I held no illusions as to my own mortality, but I had always anticipated a glorious death, not drowning alone in strange water with nothing to mark my passing, not even a bloodstain or a broken spear.

How had I come to be here? The last I remembered, I was conversing with Khalim's mother, in a house beside a field of rich, black earth, as safe from harm as I had ever been. I was dreaming, and I'd had this dream before.

The pain drifted away as though it had never been, and the cold subsided. I stretched my arms toward the thin ray of light and kicked away from the encroaching darkness below.

I broke the surface with a gasp. The flat, blank sky glowed a sickly green, with neither a sun to provide light nor clouds to obscure it. The sea around me was iron-gray, its waves breaking upon my shoulders.

The next wave rolled underneath me, carrying me skyward and on toward one distant horizon. A rocky spar emerged from the water, surrounded by spindly evergreen trees, and at its feet lay a beach of slate shards worn smooth under eons of rising tides.

When I washed up on that beach and staggered to my feet, I was dressed in scraps of mail and waterlogged leather, as I had been when I landed on a different rocky beach, so long ago. I had dreamed of Fearghus, when last I dreamed of drowning. I hoped that I would find him again, here beneath this strange sky, as much as I dreaded the questions he might ask me if I did.

The eye is open, his dream-self had told me. His words carried weight, as they often had in life. Fearghus had always been a better leader of men than I, and certainly a better fit for the head of our tribe, but an accident of fate had made me the son of the chieftain and not him.

On both sides, the beach stretched out, gray and empty. If human feet had tread it before me, they had left nothing behind, not even the wreck of a boat or a forgotten scrap of fishing net. Before me rose a palisade of sharp rock, each pointed like the head of a spear.

I approached the rocks and found a gap between them. A short stretch of flat stone gave way to a sickly, stunted forest. Naked boughs clawed the green sky, and the trees rattled like dry bones as the wind swept through them.

At the edge of the trees stood a stag, broad and towering. Its antlers were the branches of a tree, gnarled and rough and hung with bright moss. A heavy brown coat, shaggy as a steppe pony in winter, covered it from the base of its antlers to its tail. It lifted its head and stared at me.

It had a human's eyes, mottled green-brown surrounded by white sclera, sharp and intelligent. With a shake of its enormous antlers, it turned and walked into the wood.

I followed it, shouldering my way through the dead trees. The bark yielded to my efforts like flesh, but it was cold as death—cold as a Northern winter. I drew my hand back in surprise. Crumbling brown leaves and dry needles littered the ground.

The stag walked with heavy footsteps as the trees parted before it, not even turning its oak-crowned visage to acknowledge me. Its shoulders stood higher than my head. A chill wind passed through the branches around us and the ones growing from its head, whistling like a hunter's call for his hounds. I thought to return to the beach, in the hopes that I would find the longship I had seen in my previous vision and Fearghus along with it, but the way I had come closed behind me. There was only the dead winter forest, the stag with its soft human eyes turned toward its unknown destination, and me.

"Do you wish for me to follow you?" I asked.

It did not answer. On the stag went, and I walked at its shoulder. Before us, the trees leaned away, trembling in the wind.

And then the forest was gone, and I stood at the creature's side in a field of tall, golden grass, and the air tasted of an oncoming storm.

The stag turned to me, and its antlers obscured the fading light from a darkening sky. "The eye is open," it said.

"So I have been told," I replied.

"It cannot be closed again," said the stag. "You must go forward."

"Where should I go?" I asked. "I've traveled half the world, spoken to gods and priests and adventurers, and yet I'm no closer to finding Khalim than I was when I left Phyreios."

"Where should you go?" the stag echoed. "What will you do?"

I gave a resigned sigh. The air was heavy as fog, though my sight remained clear. "Then you have no answers for me, either."

"Nothing will be given to you, Eske of the Bear Clan."

I awoke, then, to the sound of calling birds. A thin line of bright sunlight fell from the door across my eyes. Tendrils of mist curled around it. Even in the dry season, Nagara lay under a blanket of moisture.

Pale dawn crept over the house. I lay in Khalim's narrow bed, beneath his worn blanket, hoping against all the evidence of my eyes that I would feel his presence here with me. The straw mattress hollowed around his absent body. The house, too, was hollow, too large for its occupants and waiting in vain for his return. I found myself holding my breath.

I'd thought that I'd find him here, in the place of his birth—the place he had spent the first almost twenty years of his life. I had believed I would see him in the faces of those who had known him far longer than I had. And yet, even here, I was as far from him as I had ever been. I had found only the grief of his mother and an empty space.

Taherah slept in the adjoining room. I got up and paced before the door, unsure of how to comport myself as a guest. Around the cold, damp remains of the fire, I found a ceramic vessel of water, a basket of some kind of fine meal, and several strong-smelling herbs in jars, but I feared I would ruin my host's supplies by attempting to cook them. I would hunt, I decided, outside the village, and thus repay her generosity. I would also put some distance between myself and the yawning absence of Khalim in this house.

My hands found my spear in the dark space under the bed, and then my pack, heavy and angular. I still had High Priest Ucasta's book, though how long it would survive in this damp, I could only guess. The cover burned like a fever when I took it out, hotter than the surrounding air and swollen like an infected wound. In surprise and disgust, I dropped it. It landed on the earthen floor with a muffled sound.

I retrieved it from between my feet. The sensation of heat had left, fleeting as a dream, and the book was cold and solid. I thought of throwing it into the river, or burying it in the spring mud. It was nothing but an added weight on my shoulder and a shiver down my back whenever I chanced to think of it.

A curious impulse came over me, and the book opened in my hand. The spine creaked softly in damp protest. I looked away, fearing the terrified, staring eyes of the image I had seen before, but the flayed man did not appear. Instead, a stag crowned with the branches of an oak tree stood beside a river of black ink, its eyes white and serene.

Nothing will be given to you, Eske of the Bear Clan.

I touched the drawing with one finger, tracing the line of the stag's back. A returning touch, light as the soft breeze from the door and gentle as a lover, pushed back at me from the page.

I drew my hand back. The book fell once more to the ground.

"Who's there?" came a voice from the small house's only other room. I had woken Taherah.

"Only I," I called out.

She did not answer. In her half-dreaming state, had she expected to hear the voice of her son? Her grief, huge and suffocating, filled the house. There was no room for her and I and it in the confined space.

I picked up the book once more and wrapped it in an oilcloth, returning it to the bottom of my pack. Still it called to me, promising answers to the questions I had not yet formed in my mind. If I could find someone both skilled with letters and worthy of trust, what harm could come from gaining the book's knowledge? I could always burn it, afterward, if I saw fit. It had come from the West, or so the priest Chanjask had claimed. Somewhere beyond the setting sun, some nameless sage had seen the gate of bone, and had dreamed the same dream that now haunted me even in my waking hours.

I waited until Taherah had dressed and emerged from the back room to inform her that I would spend the day on the hunt in the forest, to repay her and her fellow villagers for their hospitality. I asked that she look to my horse from time to time, more to prevent injury to curious children than for his care, and promised that I would return before nightfall.

I mentioned nothing of the book or my nascent plan to leave Nagara and head west.

"Of course," she said, "but there's no need for you to do this. We have enough food, and you're the only traveler who has set foot in Nagara for a year or more."

I assured her that it was my wish to hunt, and asked only for a few provisions I could take with me. As the sun climbed higher, and the village folk left their homes for the fields, I departed for the tree-covered hills. The steady, quiet rhythm of Taherah's loom followed me out her door.

I crossed the rope bridge and wandered past the god overlooking the town. I placed a strip of dried fruit at his weathered feet. I would not ask him for his help, but neither would I deny him, being a guest in his lands. I imagined that Khalim might have done the same.

There was a second reason why I wished to depart, for the West or elsewhere. I had walked the paths Khalim had walked, spoke to those who knew him, and slept in his bed, and I could not bear it any longer. It had been some time since I had shared my grief with anyone. I found I wished to be alone with it once more.

In blessed solitude, I stalked a deer for most of the morning, finally catching it by noon. Though my spear flew from my hand as it had in the chamber under Kannaoka, it did not summon lightning as it had then.

I could not depart for the land where wicked sorcerers worked to command the souls of the dead without at least greeting the rest of Khalim's countrymen, as few as they were in number. They deserved to hear the news of Khalim's loss, and I would not place this burden on Taherah.

I dressed the deer, my offering of apology for all I had failed to do, and placed it over my shoulders to return to the village.

Word had spread from house to house while I was away, and by the time I returned in the late afternoon, a small crowd had formed beside the bridge, watching for Taherah's strange visitor to return. I was accustomed to being a stranger, having spent so long away from my people, but their stares stopped me on the opposite bank. Khalim had looked at me in much the same way, when first we met, with guileless, wide-eyed curiosity. *You're a long way from home*, he had said, and now I was even farther. My chest ached, and I longed to turn back to the forest. I pressed on instead.

The river-folk were a tall people, but I was half again as broad as the young farmers, with blue spirals tattooed on my paler skin. Dressed in clothing borrowed from the Dragon Temple and from Hamilcar's crew, I was a strange sight indeed—and I had arrived on horseback, with news of a faraway city none of them had ever seen. Their stares carried no judgment, but heat rose to my face nonetheless.

Roda broke away from the group and met me halfway across the bridge. He offered to help carry the burden of the deer, but I refused. I had brought it this far.

"We have enough food for a single traveler," he told me, echoing Taherah's words from early that morning. "You need not to have gone to all this trouble."

"I'm happy to do it," I said. A sudden fear struck me as I adjusted the weight of the carcass, and I asked, "Is it not permitted to hunt the deer?" I knew so little of their gods and the commandments they might have given. Khalim had eaten no flesh, but that had been a peculiarity of his own.

Roda smiled. "Not at all. But you are a guest. I would not have it said that Nagara treats its guests so poorly."

I assured him that I would say no such thing. "I only wanted to repay your hospitality," I said.

"Then we shall hold a feast in your honor," said Roda, "and in honor of Khalim."

He believed Khalim was dead. I had only told Taherah the long tale, and she was not among those gathered by the bridge. Would she tell them, when the wound of her loss had begun to heal? Would she cast me as a madman in her retelling, a fanatic who beat his fists uselessly against the barrier between life and death, surely to call down the wrath of every god who took notice of him?

Two gray-haired women took the deer from me without so much as asking, lifting it from my shoulders and carrying it away to be butchered. My part in this was done, and I was to get out of the way.

I returned to Bran, tethered outside Taherah's door, and cared for him in the way that Aysulu had taught me so long ago. I brushed his coat from his ears to his tail, and I checked his hooves for stones and his iron shoes for damage. We had traveled for so long in lands that had never seen a horse, and the metal was wearing down, and the leather of his harness deteriorated from use and humidity, cracking at the joints.

Bran had eaten a feast of his own from the tall grass that grew around Taherah's house. A small pile of dried berries lay beside the path, at the far reach of his tether, and a young girl in a sky-blue dress left another handful, watching Bran and me with huge, dark eyes. I beckoned her closer, my hand on Bran's neck, but she turned and ran into the house at the edge of the field.

The rhythm of the loom continued behind me at a frantic pace, as though weaving could drive out grief by force and speed. She would leave her work if I entered, and feed me if I asked it of her, but I knew I would not be truly welcome. She, too, preferred to nurse her sorrow alone.

The air filled with the smell of smoke and spices. I wandered to the center of the village, where Roda directed several youths in the placement of a long table. Its weight swung precariously between them as they looked for a level place on the soft earth.

I asked if I could help, but the table thudded to the ground, rocked once, and was still.

"No need," Roda told me. "There will be more things to carry later. You traveled for many days to reach us. You should rest."

I had traveled for several weeks—or, from another view, for nearly three years—but I did not correct him. Instead, I said, "If you have the time, I would like to hear all that you remember about Khalim."

Roda paused, and a frown creased his heavy brow. Years at the forge had thickened and knotted his arms. He crafted only the tools of plowing and planting, and he had never made a weapon more formidable than a hunting knife. "I'm not sure what I can tell you that couldn't be better told by Taherah," he said, "but I will say what I can. I offered to marry her, after her husband died, and raise the boy as my own, but she refused me as she did all the others. I bear her no ill will. The plague took much from all of us."

He paused and stroked his beard with one hand. "We had thought that it had taken Khalim's mind, in the months that Taherah carried him. He did not speak for almost five summers, and then, only to his mother. We learned later that he had not been harmed. He did not speak because he was listening."

My eyes burned, and I looked away. This was a punishment I inflicted on myself. Had I not learned in Taherah's house that speaking of Khalim would not summon him here?

Roda pulled back his sleeve and showed me his arm, where faint, white scarring dappled his skin from his elbow to his wrist. "I was burned down to the bone," he explained. "It was an accident. Red-hot iron. Thanks to Khalim, this is all that remains; this, and the memory. He was nine, I think, and by then he would speak to anyone, but he always was quiet."

I swallowed the tightness in my throat and managed to thank him. He left for the storehouse, the youths in tow, to fetch sacks of last year's rice for the feast. I moved to follow, but my pulse raced and my chest constricted, a sudden fear that something terrible was about to happen sweeping over me, my vision constricting to exclude all else but the path before me. I fought the impulse to warn the villagers and to flee into the forest.

I closed my eyes and covered them with my hand, and I breathed in the heavy, pungent air until my heart had slowed to its usual pace. I had nothing to fear. I stood among people who had never known war, whose harvests were plenty and whose gods were generous. The earth was solid beneath my feet, and the river flowed on, confined to its banks.

It was only as I opened my eyes again and found tilled earth and small houses with heavy, overhanging roofs instead of tents and a wooden palisade that I understood what had become of me. Much time had passed since I had last helped with the preparations for a feast: on the side of the Iron Mountain, after my companions and I had driven away the tribe of reavers the Ascended had sent into the hills after us. We had celebrated into the night, until an earthquake passed under the mountain and signaled the beginning of the end, and the god Torr spoke through Khalim for the first time. I feared that this moment of respite and celebration, like that one, signaled the arrival of another calamity.

Now that I had identified the memory, I could keep it from creeping into the present, but it remained in my mind like a shadow over the sun, dark and untouchable.

In an effort to turn my thoughts elsewhere, I entered the largest building in the village, from whence smoke and the smell of cooking meat poured into the wet air and across the fields. It was twice as large as Taherah's house, and it stood away from the river—the last house on the road west.

Heat washed over me as I entered the curtained door. Inside, the shadowed figures of four women and two men moved in a faint haze of smoke. A low, wide fire smoldered underneath a huge ceramic basin. The meat I had brought could only make up a small part of what bubbled tantalizingly within. Already there was enough food to feed a town twice the size of Nagara.

Hunger overtook my shame at the relative insignificance of my offering, and I asked what I could do to help. The eldest woman directed me to a steaming clay oven, handing me disks of flat dough. Soon, flour and ash streaked my sweat-drenched arms.

"For twenty years, I was the village midwife," she told me. "Khalim is—he was—a young man. He had no business in the birthing of children. I only asked for him once, when the mother and the baby were certain to die."

Khalim had told me this story, that same night on the mountain, of a baby born breathless and blue that he had restored to life. He had called it the greatest thing he had ever done.

That story gave rise to another, as a young woman beside the cooking pot told of an ox with a broken leg that Khalim had restored, and one of them added a tale of his small son, who had fallen out of a tree. The people of Nagara remembered Khalim as a healer, and nothing more. He had shared so little of his own thoughts, as Roda said, so how could they do otherwise?

I sat beside Taherah as the feast was served in the early evening, when the sun turned the river to liquid amber and a cool wind promised more rain. She ate little, and she kept her head bowed. We did not speak for a long time, we who had for so short a time had the honor of knowing Khalim.

"Will you be leaving, then?" she asked at last.

Already I could feel the weight of the book on my back. "Soon," I said. "Perhaps tomorrow. I have a long journey ahead of me."

She set her dish aside, her hands worrying at the hem of her headdress. Though she watched the river, I suspected she did not see it. She had again gone somewhere else.

"Do you remember what you promised me, yesterday evening?" she said.

"That I will tell him that you love him," I said, "that he did the best he could, and that you are sorry for not sparing him." I remembered it well. I would carry it with me as long as I lived.

"You would be welcome here, if ever you were to return," she told me.

I knew that already, just as I knew that I would not come back, not until the vast and terrible task before me was done.

~ XVI ~

A SKY WITHOUT END

Taherah left before the feast had ended to return to her empty house, and I followed some time later, after the night was half-gone. I slept again in Khalim's bed by the door, and despite the lingering heat of the day, it remained cold.

I shared the house with the only other person who remembered Khalim for who he was—not the healer, nor the prophet, but the man—save perhaps for our companions who had competed with us in the Cerean Tournament. Garvesh had remained in Phyreios, and Aysulu had returned to the steppe with her horses to find her scattered people. Now only Taherah and I remained, in this house filled with grief.

I left the house early in the morning and took Bran to Roda's smithy, where he again distributed grain to the planters. The caravans that crossed the desert between Phyreios and the river valley had brought no iron for the better part of two years, but he had an old woodcutting axe and the rusting blade of a plow that possessed iron enough to reshoe Bran. I had not the heart to tell him that the mine of Phyreios had fallen along with the city, and the iron would be a long time coming.

And thus I said farewell to Nagara, to Roda and Taherah and the good people who had been my beloved's kinsmen, and turned west. I left behind the place that Khalim had called home and that he had left, so long ago, and to which he had never returned.

With the morning sun at my back and my saddlebags heavy with grain, I believed I would not have to journey far to find a sage or sorcerer who could interpret my dreams and find a way to the gate of bone. Whether I would show such a learned person the book I carried or not, I had yet to decide—the book was, to me, only proof that I was not the first to dream of the stag with antlers of wood, nor to seek out the gate to the other world. Its contents mattered little.

Still, I carried it with me, its weight on my back heavy with shame and fear. If Taherah had known that I possessed such a thing, would she have cast me out of her house, for fear of what its evil magics might do to her son? Would Roda have driven me empty-handed across the bridge from whence I came?

And had I deceived them, by accepting their hospitality without telling them what I had brought into their midst?

Khalim had thought me a good man. I told myself that he still would, when at last I found him again.

The days grew longer as I crossed the valley. The river turned away to the sea, and the distant peak of Mount Abora faded into memory. The green hills erupted in color as spring bloomed into summer, bloody red and royal purple and the blushing hue of dawn, as though the sun rose above and below the horizon at the same time. The air hummed with the chorus of thousands of insects. Through the lowlands, I pursued the setting sun, while somewhere far to the north Phyreios slept quietly under the watchful eye of its god, its mines empty and silent. Farther still lay the lands of my birth, with winter retreating from their rocky shores like a cloak drawn back.

I found first the remains of a village, no more than a few rotting posts overgrown with weeds. Beneath them lay the ruins of something far older: ridges of pale stone rising from the sod, and a pair of weathered columns alone in what was once the village square, and before that was a temple to some forgotten god.

A week later, I found a living village, its goats and oxen left to roam the surrounding hills. A child directed me to the house of his grandmother, the oldest person yet living there. Her eyes were clouded, but she milked the cows with practiced ease, and her keen ears alerted her to my approach.

"I'm sorry to trouble you," I said. "I'm looking for a wise man or woman, who knows something of spirits and of dreams. I seek a gate made of the bones of giants, and a stag with two trees growing from its head."

She shook her head, the snow-white hairs that had escaped from her braids trembling in the summer winds. "I've never heard of such things," she replied. "If you are here to tell us a tale, then do so while you pull weeds from the fields. Do not interrupt my work."

Bran and I made our way to another village, and then another, and the people there were friendly enough, but they were as unlettered as I and had their own tales of the land of the dead, tales that would not help me in my endeavor. I strayed away from populated lands after that, and began the climb into the western mountains on an empty footpath between two sheer cliffs that stretched on for days. In that time, the sun never touched the ground beneath my feet. I was grateful for dry days and cold nights, as was Bran, and I slept without dreaming.

The better part of a year passed between Nagara and the far side of the great, flat-topped mountains, each like the stump of a felled tree as large as the world. Layers upon layers of red and gray rock towered above me, dusted with glittering white snow. The wind tasted of frost, and it carried fine dust that stung my skin and set Bran's tail to lashing.

Winter would arrive before long. For now, it remained in the North, fenced in by the farthest mountains where my people made their home.

The plateaus flattened at last into a blinding expanse of pale yellow desert, blank as an unwritten vellum page, with the sky above a deep, shimmering blue like an ocean inverted. These were not the iron-tinged sands of the desert surrounding Phyreios, where a similar sky burned through rarefied air; this was a low desert, close to the sea, where the approach of winter would grant only the barest of reprieves from the sun's unrelenting heat.

Like a lighthouse upon a sea of dust, the great caravanserai stood at the edge of the desert. A stone building, three stories tall, towered over the flatlands. From its great southern gate wound a single file of men riding camels, saddled between cloth-wrapped parcels and woven baskets. The village of Nagara could have fit easily between the high walls, with room left over for half their rice fields. Not since the port of Hali had I seen so much land given over to civilization.

I still possessed the power of language, though the long weeks of solitude with no one but Bran with whom to converse had turned my voice hoarse. I spent half the money I carried on supplies for myself and my horse and one night in a room on the second floor. I relinquished Bran to a stable hand, offering another gold coin for his shoes to be checked and his tack repaired, and followed the innkeeper up a set of carved stairs and underneath a series of graceful arches. But for the seams between sections of pillar, I would have believed the entire complex carved out of the surrounding rock.

I went below for an evening meal, and shared a table with a wiry man of middle age, his long black beard plaited in a single braid and his clothing the same sapphire hue as the cloudless sky. He was a cloth merchant, and a seller of the particular indigo dye that adorned his robes, and by his account he had been quite successful. He gave his name as Kosa, son of Aym, and I answered him in kind.

Taking a westward heading, he explained, I would walk for ten days across stone and gravel before finding an oasis built upon a deep well. After that would come the sand: fine-grained and as deep as the sea, with winds like a winter storm over the cold Northern ocean—this last was my interpretation, as this man had never seen any ocean, nor had he experienced any winter like one I might recognize. Winter in this desert meant rain, but it was not the blessed return of green life that the word promised elsewhere. It would come in torrents, Kosa said, and the plain would flood before one could hear the water coming, carrying with it entire camps and caravans.

"If you must go, keep to the high places," he told me. "Make your camp on stone."

I promised him I would. I had seen treacherous landscapes before, and once crossed the northern sea in a canoe made of a hollow log. Whatever dangers this new desert might bring me, I thought in the hubris of my youth, I would prove myself greater. I had come, by that time, almost to the end of my twenty-fourth year.

That night, I slept on a thick carpet beneath a heavy woolen blanket, as the faint sound of music drifted up from the courtyard. I dreamed of Phyreios and awoke before dawn, the image of hard golden eyes lingering even as I got up to gather my provisions.

Bran and I set out into the desert as the sun cast a pale light on the mountains behind us, both too heavily laden for me to ride. Our burdens would grow lighter as we consumed our food and water, but our first days on the dusty path would be slow ones.

We reached the oasis on the morning of the tenth day, just as Kosa the merchant had said, and just in time to witness a flash flood tear away the embankment that was to be our path into the ocean of sand. "Turn south," the merchant women around the well said, "but beware the demons of the desert. You cannot trust your eyes so far from the traveled roads."

In the tongue of the merchants, the desert was called Shunkare. Save for the few days of the year when the rains came, the air burned to breathe and carried dust into the lungs, slaying the unwise and unmasked while it painted the sky in streaks of violet with each rising and setting of the sun. Endless drifts of fine sand stretched out before me, carved by floods and drying in place like ridges of ice upon the sea.

From that sea, islands jutted out toward the blinding sky. Pillars of white rock, etched sharp as spears in the wind, glinted in the sunlight. Each possessed a wide base, buried under the sand, or so the merchants told me. I traveled from spire to spire, crossing the dust only by daylight and only when the sky was clear, my eyes fixed on the distant horizon to watch for floods. With vigilance and the mercy of the gods of that treacherous expanse, I would take a long route around the deepest basin and avoid sinking into the sand, buried alive and unmourned. I would then reach the coast by spring.

Other villages stood upon the rim of the basin. The first was a waystation, built around a single well, and the imperious, veiled woman in command accepted some of my gold in exchange for two skins of water that tasted of dust. The next clustered around a mine carved out of the wind-scarred rock, as deep and wide as the mine of Phyreios, though the laborers there dug for water and not for iron.

The season of floods came to an end, and the season of dust loomed as a haze on the horizon. I had cloth to cover my face and Bran's, and a shelter that would keep out the worst of the night winds. The desert was a stern teacher, I found, but it was not my enemy. I believed I had learned its lessons well.

Within another three days, I was lost.

The dust arrived, and the air and the sky turned a dull white. The sun faded to a distant beacon in the fog; it was all I had by which to navigate the pale void. Bran and I huddled in my tent as sand rained down on us. Sand was in my clothes, between my teeth, in the water, and in each dwindling ration of food. When the itching quelled enough for me to finally sleep, leaning against Bran's flank with the canvas pressing against the top of my head, a persistent cough woke me each hour until dawn. Bran fared a little better, but he drank water faster than I did, and our stores would soon run dry.

Setting my course by the dim lamp of the sun, I pressed forward, holding in my mind's eye the image of the next waystation. I had seen it the day before, a dark silhouette of rounded tents and thin, wind-battered trees, but now the dust had swallowed it. I pushed on, back bent against the wind and sand stinging my eyes and hands, the only parts left uncovered by necessity. Bran's shape grew indistinct, even as he walked no farther from me than the reach of my arm.

Evening fell, and neither the oasis nor the end of the storm lay within reach. My tent shook and buckled, and a trickle of sand entered at three different corners. Neither Bran nor I slept well that night, but we were accustomed to hardship. We kept watch together as the dust blew over our shelter.

A blessed clear sky greeted us the next morning. Sand had buried the tent, and I considered leaving it behind, but the thought of another storm without it drove me through the sweltering task of digging it out. By midday, my arms were burned, and I had drunk more than my share of water. A haze of pale dust settled over the earth, its colorless expanse stretching out from horizon to horizon. The waystation still did not appear.

I still had the sun, and I could not have wandered so far from my intended path in the storm, as slow as I had gone. As the midday heat subsided, the shimmering images of the rocky spires at the edge of the dust basin swam into view, and I turned toward their limited shelter.

The sky turned from dusty blue to a deep, bloody purple, and the wind sang with a distinctly human voice—high and keening, in a language I did not recognize.

I had been warned not to trust my eyes, and my ears were no more reliable. But as I pressed on, the voice grew louder, and its cries formed a few words I understood: *desert* and *full moon, sandstorm* and *destroyer*—the last a term that Kelebek of the *Lady of Osona* had used to describe the tempest we had endured in the southern ocean.

I crossed a stretch of coarse sand to the next formation of rock, a spire like a chimney three times my height. At the level of my eyes, an iron hook had been driven into the stone, and attached to it was a length of dust-laden rope.

I followed that rope to its other end. On a stretch of flat stone knelt a hunched human figure, dressed in a loose, tattered robe, with one bony wrist encircled in a knot. Thin hair clung to a skull-like head, facing away from me toward the basin. Between their emaciated figure and their shapeless clothing, threadbare and stained with dust, I could not tell their sex; their keening voice rang thin and shrill as the wind. Heat and malnutrition had aged them before their time.

The rope was loose enough to allow one skeletal hand to slip through, but the figure remained upon the rock, the wind tearing at their sparse hair. How long had they sat here in the heat? Now, night approached on swift wings, bringing with it a dry, winter cold. If the sun hadn't slain this poor soul yet, exposure and a lack of water surely would before morning came again. I had seen cruelty in my time, but this was beyond imagining. It would have been kinder to kill them outright. Even if they had wished to leave this place, there was nowhere else to go.

I approached with one hand on Bran's halter, uncovering my face and holding my free hand away from my weapons. "Stranger," I called out, in the hopes that a little of my sailor's cant would be understood, "I'll set you free. My shelter is small, but you may share it."

The wailing song stopped as I came nearer, and the figure turned to me with a look of bewilderment in their sunken eyes. With slow, careful movements, I set the claw barbs of my spear against the rope, and its fibers split at the touch. The gesture, I thought, would carry meaning even if my words could not.

Their eyes widened. "What are you doing?"

I looked about for a threat, for this person's captors to appear from behind the rocks and attack me, but there was nothing but sand and sky. "Who did this to you?" I asked.

A shake of the head was their only reply, and they turned back toward the dust basin, peering out into the encroaching dark. They began again to sing.

I was not the expected rescue, but while I was here, I would make myself useful. I set about laying down my burdens and removing Bran's, building a small fire, and dividing out two portions of barley cakes and dates, one of packed scrub grass and dry leaves, and three of water. The stranger's share I set out within the reach of their arm before retreating back to my side of the fire. Their eyes followed me as I moved about the camp with a strange, dull lethargy, pupils huge and dark even as my fire cast a bright red halo upon the tower of stone.

Bran and I ate, and I put up the tent, and neither rescuer nor captor appeared. The sky turned ink-black and the stars shone bright white; with luck, the next dust storm would stay away tonight. I weighted Bran's tether with a stone. Having been confined for so long, he was happy for a night outdoors.

My strange companion had tired of singing. "You can shelter with me, if you wish," I said, gesturing to the tent. "You'll die of cold out here."

Despite the dullness in their eyes, they looked at me with a fury sharp and cold as a spear-point. "You've ruined everything," was their reply.

"What?" I had offered food, water, and shelter to a stranger in the desert, as I understood was right to do. To have it refused was surprising enough—to be blamed for some transgression was beyond my comprehension.

The stranger turned away, too disgusted by my ignorance to bear looking at me. "Begone from here, unbeliever," they said.

My tent was already pitched, my fire built, and beyond the reach of its light lay only darkness. Even unwanted, I would remain here until morning. "Eat," I said. "Drink some water. Then you can tell me what's wrong."

They said nothing, and made no move to approach the offered food. I would not sleep with an angry stranger just outside my door, so I stayed by the fire, and set about mending a hole I had torn in my protective robe. The poor light made for clumsy stitches.

Dragging the rope behind them, the stranger crawled toward the fire and picked at the food with bony fingers. They tasted water from my small clay cup, the taut skin of their face twisting at the taste of it. "The great serpent was to be here at sunset," they said.

I waited, searching my garment for additional tears, but no further explanation came. "I didn't know there was a serpent in the desert," I offered.

"Of course you didn't," the stranger said. "You're an outsider. An unbeliever."

"Well, I believe you. I've seen great serpents before, and even a dragon, and I know they keep their own time. It might still come." Only wind stirred the plain of dust, but the night was yet young. "What happens when it gets here?"

I received a derisive snort in reply. "He will eat me, of course. And the great kingdom of Svilsara will prosper for another year."

~ XVII ~

SVILSARA OF THE DESERT

"He will eat you," I echoed, thoughtless as a reverberation in a temple dome. The words made no more sense coming from my mouth.

The stranger nodded, and picked at the offered barley and dates with bony fingers and crumbling nails. "I have been preparing for this day since the hour of my birth."

I drew my legs underneath me and sat back on my heels before the fire. "My name is Eske, and I come from far to the north," I said. "Tell me of yourself and your city."

In between bites, my strange interlocutor provided something of an explanation of the circumstances in which we found ourselves. Her name was Fenin, and for the previous seventeen years of her life, she had been kept apart from almost all others in a small house in the center of the city of Svilsara, permitted to leave only with three escorts. She had carnal knowledge of neither woman nor man, a detail she emphasized despite the discomfort I could not keep from my face. In that house at the center of the city's blooming garden, she had been provided with everything she could want: the finest of clothes and delicacies, a room full of books, and next year's sacrifice as a companion. Leisurely reading and ritual music consumed her days, and she walked each morning a full circuit around the city wall, a trip that by her description took less than an hour.

"Svilsara is the greatest city upon the earth," she said, though neither Phyreios nor the port of Hali could be circumnavigated in so short a time. I made no remark of it, nor of the fact that here she was, tied to this rock and dressed only in rags, without even straw sandals to protect her feet from the sun's heat or the night's chill. She ate in tiny, nibbling bites—she was missing several teeth, and her gums were the deep purple of a sailor's long lost at sea. Each movement of her jaw prompted a grimace of pain, stretching paper-thin skin over the delicate bones of her face. Her garment barely concealed a belly huge and distended from malnourishment.

Night drew in around us. Fenin's eyes came into focus, the ritual drugs wearing off. She kept her gaze fixed on the stretch of stone between herself in the fire. "This is your fault," she told me again. "Everything was in place until you came along." It was not whatever substance she had consumed this morning, but seventeen years inside a beautiful cage that had persuaded her to remain here.

"I'm sure it will come along in its own time," I said. "You should rest. I'll keep watch for the serpent."

She shook her head, her wisps of dark hair falling around her ears. "It is my responsibility to greet him when he arrives. If he arrives," she added with a pointed look at me, sounding like the petulant child she was despite her aged appearance.

"He's likely on his way," I said.

Her swift, sharp glance told me she did not believe me.

If she would not rest, then neither would I. She was so frail that I feared she might expire if I took my eyes from her. The wind would eat away her meager flesh and etch her bones to dust, and no traveler would find any evidence that she had ever lived. I decided that the serpent must have been a lie, and nothing but the weather consumed each year's sacrifice.

But why was Fenin half-dead to begin with, starved over the course of months or even years, when the sun would slay even the healthiest of unprepared travelers and deprived captives alike in hours? And why did she believe, against the evidence of her eyes and the obvious pain in her mouth, that she had been treated like a great khan's pampered bride for her entire life? She took the blanket I offered and wrapped it around her narrow shoulders, grimacing at the texture of the rough wool between her fingers.

I finished my mending and drew my robe around me, and I added more wood and dried camel dung to the fire. My fuel was precious, but Fenin would accept no shelter, and she would certainly die if I let the fire burn out.

I could leave her here, and save both time and provisions, and all evidence of my negligence would be gone in a day—but Khalim would not have left a starving girl to the elements, and I could not show my face to him one day with the knowledge that I had done so. The only thing left to do was to wait until morning. I would take Fenin back to Svilsara, the city of books and green gardens and virgin sacrifices, and demand an explanation from whomever placed her here.

"So, this city of yours," I said, drawing her attention back from the empty desert. "What do people do there? Is there a well? A mine? Good land for grazing?"

Her sunken eyes blinked twice as she favored me with a blank stare. "The serpent provides all we need," she said.

Not even the monks of the temple could boast so of the dragon on the peaks, and I could not believe that this serpent, if it was indeed more than a myth, was quite so benevolent as she had been. "You must have some learned men there," I said, "and women, as well, with all your books."

Fenin might not have been strong enough to lift the book I carried, but perhaps there was someone in her city who might have both the knowledge and the strength to help me. Renewed in my decision to wait out the night with her, I fed the fire and sat with my back against my pack.

"The elders of Svilsara are the wisest in the world," Fenin told me. "No others could have made contact with the great serpent and gained his blessings."

"Do you think so?" I could not help but ask.

She must have heard the doubt in my tone, because she gave me a brief glare before returning her eyes to the benighted desert, from which no serpent emerged.

"They must be wise," I said, trying a different tack, "and crafty, to entice such a being with only one sacrifice per year. I've never met a great serpent, though I have met a dragon, and I've fought a great worm that required the blood of hundreds and thousands to emerge from its mountain."

"You know nothing, unbeliever," Fenin spat.

Gently, like the rocking of a ship in shallow water, the stone beneath us shook.

I thought it the trembling of my own overtired mind, but Fenin pulled herself to her knees and sang once more, her keening cry offering herself up to be devoured, begging the serpent to come near.

I jumped to my feet and seized Bran's halter, and I banked the fire and smothered it with sand, afraid a spark might fly out and catch my tent. Bran awoke and nosed at my clothing, his ears flicking and his eyes wide in what remained of the light. One hoof scraped an anxious rhythm on the rock.

The last embers of my fire went out, and the black desert night fell over us like a shroud. Fenin continued to sing, and as long as she did, I knew she still lived. The quake slowed, thrumming away into the earth beyond the reach of my senses, and stopped.

A shape moved around the sacrificial stone, black against black, darting in from the unseen expanse of dust. The smell of burning sand, absent since sunset, followed behind it.

I reached for my spear. Thin tongues of lightning licked at my fingers, casting an eerie, pale light upon the scene. Fenin knelt upon the rock, her skeletal hands lifted in supplication. A shadow, tall as a man and growing taller, loomed over her.

"Who goes there?" I shouted into the darkness. "Step back from her and show yourself. I have a weapon."

The figure straightened, turned, and stalked toward me and the remains of the fire. I held Bran at arm's length and brought the spear to my shoulder. Its faint crackling light fell on the curve of a sharp smile and reflected in a pair of liquid black eyes. My hand tightened around the shaft as the figure bent over the smothered embers and reached out a shadowy hand.

Blazing yellow burned my eyes and turned the world, for an instant, into brightest day. I turned my face away, lowering my weapon to shield my face. Bran whinnied and stamped his feet. I held him fast.

The spots faded from my vision, and my eyes adjusted to the new light. My fire, now relit, flickered and sputtered under its layer of sand, staining the dusty stone a dull orange. Fenin, her eyes wide and glassy, knelt on the other side.

Standing beside her was a sharp-featured young man, dressed in a robe as black as the night. He grasped both Fenin's wrists in one hand, and in his other, he held a curved knife that caught the firelight and reflected back a blood-red gleam. He turned to me and smiled, stretching his lips a little too widely over teeth that shone as white as the distant sickle moon and as sharp as his knife.

"How fortunate I am this evening," he said in a voice like the wind hissing over the dunes. "I asked for one sacrifice, and Svilsara has given me two."

Fenin's eyes closed, and she knelt without struggling, her hands stretched toward the sky above her captor's curled fist. The blanket dropped from her shoulders and pooled around her in darkened folds.

"I'm not a sacrifice," I said, a needless clarification that I nonetheless was compelled to make. Whatever devilry Fenin's city had concocted and inflicted upon its citizens, I wanted no part of it. "I am a warrior of the North. Unhand the girl, and I'll let you depart from here in peace."

His smile only stretched wider. "I might have known."

In the wavering light of the half-buried fire, the man's eyes shone a polished, dark amber. The sharp-toothed grin split his face from ear to ear. I had thought him tall when he had appeared, but now he towered over me, his robe undulating like waves in a benighted sea. As I followed his impossible ascent with my eyes, my vision swam, and I tightened my hand around the shaft of my spear and planted my feet upon the stone.

The wind blew sand across my vision, and I turned my head, blinking it away. When I looked again, the man was gone, and in his place was the shining, scaly hide of an enormous black serpent. In great coils, its bulk spread across the rock, hiding Fenin and her captor at its center.

The great snake of the desert, for which Fenin had waited all evening, had arrived. It was quicker than lightning, more silent than a shark in water.

I had fought worse. I threw the spear.

A thunderclap echoed across the night sky. Lightning flashed white-violet against the obsidian scales, and I closed my eyes again, bright spots crackling against my eyelids.

As it had in the chamber under Kannaoka, the spear returned to my hand, its weight solid and reassuring. I placed myself between the serpent and Bran, certain that its yet-unseen head had reared back in preparation to strike.

Bran flattened his ears and scratched at the dust. He watched me, not the serpent, turning his head to regard me with one eye.

I brushed sand from my face. When my eyes opened, the serpent and the man were gone. There was only Fenin, kneeling on the rock, her sunken eyes huge with surprise and grief. The fire sputtered beside her.

"He was here," she wailed. "He was here, and now he's gone."

A cold wind stirred the sand. "What happened?" I asked.

Fenin wept, dry, rasping sobs wracking her shoulders. She gave me no answer.

The only footprints in the sand were mine and Bran's, and the wind swept them away. Of the serpent's huge coils, or the tracks of the man with the sharp smile, there remained no sign. The fire's light reached only an arm's span past the edge of the rock, where the sea of dust formed gentle waves exactly as it had before the serpent had arrived.

"I fear there's some evil magic afoot," I said.

Fenin ignored me.

"You should rest." I approached her and drew one edge of the fallen blanket to her shoulders. "I'll keep watch. In the morning, I'll return you to your city."

She wiped at her face with the backs of her hands. "How can I go back? The serpent has rejected me. Without my sacrifice, he won't protect Svilsara anymore. The city will fall to invaders."

"If your elders are as wise as you say, they'll know what to do," I said.

I built the fire up a second time, coaxing it to a size that would chase the cold wind away. Keeping it alight until morning would burn through almost all my remaining fuel. I placed a second blanket on Bran and the third and last around me before sitting across from Fenin. She stared into the fire, her hollow eyes shadowed, reflecting the flames in two burning points.

"Who was that man?" I asked. "Did you see where he went?"

Her eyes flicked upward. "What man?"

My compassion for this strange, starving girl had worn thin. "You blame me for the serpent not eating you," I said. Most others might have been grateful, but I had not found myself in the company of most others. "I can't help that. I'm trying to keep you alive long enough to find out what happened. The least you could do is cooperate a *little*."

She crossed her arms, drawing the blanket around her. "I don't know what you're talking about. The only man here was you."

Evil magic, I thought. The air tasted of lightning, dry and sharp, but that might have been my doing. "What did you see when the fire went out?"

"The serpent came and encircled me with his coils, That's what put the fire out. Then there was thunder and lightning, and he was gone. I didn't see another man."

"And you didn't hear him speak?" I asked. "He had you by both wrists."

Her expression grew troubled. "I don't know what you're talking about. No one else was here."

One of us was going mad. I wanted to blame Fenin, but my confidence faltered with each of her insistent words. I reached out a hand to the fire, reassuring myself that its warmth was no illusion. Bran stood where I had left him, and there lay my tent, one of its poles sagging under its weight. Somewhere in the distance, a night-bird called for its mate, and the wind continued its thin, sad song. All was as it should have been, but it offered me no comfort.

If I slept that night, it was in fits and starts, never resting long enough to dream. The sun woke me, and I struck my camp and buried the last embers of the fire. I put Fenin in Bran's saddle—she was surely too weak to walk, and I could not wait for her to finish picking at a single barley cake—and we set off among the stone columns, seeking the ill-omened city.

She did not speak that morning, and she avoided my eyes, though she accepted the offered food and the help onto Bran's back. I detested and distrusted her elders more and more with every step. If it was their serpent's will that Fenin live another year, then who were they to disagree? Gods demanded blood, that

I knew well, whether in battle or directly as a sacrifice. The great beasts of the world, gods in all but name, took their own price from the flesh of men. Neither gods nor beasts thought as men thought, or desired the things that human beings desired; why they spared one life and took another was not for us to comprehend.

I would leave her in the city, I told myself. I would not let her starve on the rock, or succumb to sun and heat, but my part in her confounding predicament would soon come to an end. If she was returned to the sacrificial stone afterward, it would be with her own consent.

We crossed the shifting sands in a haze of dust. The city appeared at midday, a shining crescent atop a far western hill. As we came nearer, it resolved into a wall of pale stone encircling five sky-blue towers, like the fingers of some azure giant emerging from the earth. Tiled roofs in white and red-brown lay beneath the spires, warming in the midday sun. The ever-present layer of sand that clung to Bran's coat and tangled in my hair had left the roofs and colorful plaster walls untouched. At the foot of the wall, the hill rose at a gentle slope. An invading army could march up its sides and assault the gate with nothing more than the sand to slow their assault.

The gate was solid iron, ponderous and foreboding. A pair of guards stood upon the battlements above it, their armor gleaming in the sun and their surcoats a spotless white. We approached, Fenin riding Bran as I held his lead, and a shout went up. With a turning of well-oiled gears and heavy chains, the gate crept upward.

I tugged on Bran's halter, and we made our way forward under the massive stone arch. Only a beast like the great serpent, if indeed it existed, or the worm that had lain waste to Phyreios could break through such a wall. The indefensible hill was of no consequence.

Within, the desert heat loosened its grip, and I could smell water, though a series of clean, blue houses obscured my view of the rest of the city. The road that branched left and right from the gate had been swept, and even the flagstones shone. I was suddenly aware of the days of sand and sweat that clung to my skin, and I scratched at my head and grimaced at the grit that worked its way under my nails.

The gate shuddered closed behind us, and a third white-clad guard approached. He carried a small, round shield polished mirror-bright and a short spear with a winged head. Even to my uncultured eye, the metalwork appeared of fine quality, the etching at the tops of his bracers and the spear's wings carved by the hand of an artist.

"Lady Fenin," the man said. A frown troubled his handsome face. He was about my age, taller than I in his cloth-wrapped helmet, his thick beard combed and his teeth white and even. "You've returned. What happened? Who is this stranger?"

"All in good time," Fenin said within an authority I'd not yet heard her use. "I must speak to the elders."

I looked over my shoulder. Despite the lingering heat, my blood turned cold.

In place of the emaciated girl dressed in rags that I had met upon the rock, a priestess in a robe of white silk and a collar of pearls sat straight-backed and proud in the saddle. Her hair, thick and dark as the desert night, fell in a single braid to her waist. Her sunken cheeks had turned round and rosy, and her full-lipped mouth moved without pain.

This healthy young woman was, indeed, Fenin: there were her sharp cheekbones, though much less prominent, and here were her suspicious dark eyes, brighter and less sunken. The imperious pout she gave the watchman was the same she had given me.

Some kind of sorcery permeated the air here, crafted to deceive the senses and confuse the mind. I adjusted my grip on Bran's lead, pulling him close. He tossed his mane, raining dust on the spotless flagstones.

Two guardsmen in polished armor escorted us into the city. Blue and white walls cast off the desert's heat, and well-watered flowers bloomed from every window. A clothesline cast across the thoroughfare held tunics of bright, patterned silk dyed blazing orange and verdant green. Our small procession passed by a woman and her three children, all dressed in silks, with gold baubles dangling from their ears and hanging around their necks.

We passed through a market square, where brightly dressed townsfolk exchanged gold coins for sacks of grain and baskets of fresh fruit. The smell of warm spice bloomed under a gentler sun than the one under which I had toiled in the desert. The merchants smiled, their teeth shining in their youthful faces, and with hands bedecked in gold they gave sweets to the children and greeted Fenin with hesitant waves. She held her head high and did not acknowledge them.

From the market, we walked under a carved archway and climbed a slight incline to the center of the city, where a second wall separated the holy places from the rest of Svilsara. A wooden gate, carved with an intricate, spiraling pattern of leafy vines, opened on quiet hinges. Our guards stayed behind as I led Fenin and Bran through, and another pair left their posts on the other side to take their places. Rows of meticulously shaped trees flanked the marble path through the garden, and more flowers bloomed in their shade, vivid pink and fiery orange. Small white doves sang to one another among the branches.

The path took us out of the trees and around a shimmering, circular pond almost as wide as one of Nagara's rice fields. Huge golden fish, each as long as the span of my arms, swam in lazy circles beneath white lotus flowers. In the desert, this was a king's ransom in water; it could supply a hundred travelers like me, or maintain a hardy crop for a season. It was a perverse thing to keep it here solely for its beauty, though I could not deny that it was beautiful. Sunlight slanted through clear water to the pebbled bottom, where strands of long grass swayed in the wake of the fish.

Behind the pond stood a temple of white marble, six towering pillars raising a high arch over its cavernous door. Its peaked roof shone in the sun, so bright that I could not bear to look at it, and neither dust nor fallen leaves troubled the four steps from the path to the doorway. An attendant in a white robe greeted us at the bottom of the stairs.

Fenin dismounted, folding one leg up and around Bran's neck and sliding to the ground. I held out a hand to steady her, but she shook her head and waved it away. Along with her silk raiment and collar of pearls, she had acquired supple leather sandals that laced up to the knee. Her gown flowed from her shoulders, as spotlessly white as the marble temple, showing her rounded arms and their soft skin.

The attendant bowed. His garment matched hers, though his possessed voluminous sleeves and crossed modestly over the breast. His head was shaved but for a single long braid growing from the top of his head, threaded with silver and falling to his shoulder. It swung into his face as he bowed, catching the light.

"Lady Fenin," he said. "You've returned. What has happened?"

Fenin straightened her dress and assumed the same imperious look she had given the guards at the gate. "This is a matter for the elders. I must see them at once."

I, too, looked forward to meeting these elders. I handed Bran's reins to the guardsman at my side. "See that no harm comes to my horse," I said, "or I'll ensure that the same harm befalls you."

He accepted the lead, his eyes wide, and nodded. Assured that I had frightened the man into obedience, I went to follow Fenin into the temple.

The attendant placed his slight form in my path, holding up a hand to my chest. "Outsiders are not permitted within," he said.

"You have been allowed into the inner grounds because you escorted Lady Fenin, but you must wait here."

I would not remain in this vast, decadent garden while the men within deliberated my fate. "I've brought the lady this far, haven't I? And I have news of the desert that your elders will want to hear."

He glanced from me to Fenin and back again. He wasn't much older than she, and the desert had not troubled his soft skin and unlined face.

"Let him pass," Fenin said. "The elders will deal with him."

The attendant narrowed his eyes, but he bowed and moved to one side of the doorway. As I entered the temple alongside Fenin, he followed behind us, sandaled feet whispering against the marble floor. Two more young men, identically dressed and with the same curious hairstyle, appeared from the shadows before my eyes had time to adjust from bright daylight to the temple's shade.

Two rows of pillars supported a vaulted ceiling. Here, the stone was a soft yellow, and it had the texture of sand. Sunlight streamed in from a pair of high windows, one on each side of the long chamber. Besides the pillars, and the five of us casting long shadows, the room was empty. Where rugs or benches might have provided worshipers with a place to rest, there was only bare floor, and a blank wall stood at the far end of the hall instead of an altar.

The first attendant approached the left-hand wall and lifted a hand, pressing it flat against the blank expanse of sandstone. A door appeared behind where the altar should have been and swung away on hidden hinges.

This hall of worship, towering and hollow, separated the worshipers from the elders within. I scowled, unable to keep my disgust from my face. The elders governed Svilsara, and it was they who selected the sacrifices to the great serpent, arranging for the continued prosperity of the city with the blood of others—yet they hid behind a secret door in a temple few could visit, while a fortune in water lay untouched in their honor. Even the Ascended had shown their inhuman faces to their people, walking among them and hearing their petitions even as they used their blood for a terrible ritual. My father, chieftain of the Bear Clan, for all his faults, would have considered it his solemn duty to overthrow a fellow chieftain who hid away in this manner.

I wanted to meet these elders. The narrow doorway forced us to walk in a single file: two of the attendants first, then Fenin, followed by myself and the attendant who had greeted us at the door. The cramped sandstone hallway led underground, sloping away from the door and its patch of sunlight. My eyes stung, and I tasted smoke on the air, though my vision remained clear. I rubbed a hand across my face, dislodging more sand from my skin.

Fenin walked with slow, processional steps, her hands pressed together in front of her and her expression piously serene. She had made this descent before. Fear and relief in equal measure troubled the corners of her mouth and formed a slight crease between her brows. She had come home after she had expected to die in the desert, and was surrounded once more by familiar things. If my reckoning of her circumstances was correct, she was the first sacrifice in an age to return to the city. The shadow of doubt had followed her home.

The corridor opened into a windowless room. Half a dozen torches mounted in iron brackets on the walls provided light, illuminating a high ceiling crossed with arches. Four tall-backed chairs, carved of white stone, sat facing the center of the room. A stone pillar stood behind each of them.

Each throne held an old man. They wore white robes with wide sleeves, layers upon layers of silk that covered their hands and feet and pooled on the floor. Their beards were also white, combed and plaited with golden beads. A rug patterned in red and violet lay under their chairs.

Svilsara stood beside no waterways, nor did it lie on the well-traveled caravan roads that crossed the desert. The people in the marketplace had stared like they had never before seen an outsider. Had the serpent truly provided all the wealth in this cavernous room, the water for the garden, and the silk that draped everyone from the priests to the children? Unseen smoke brought tears to my eyes, and I wiped them away. My dusty feet left no marks on the carpet.

I recalled the strange man in the desert, and Fenin's serpent, and how both had disappeared without leaving a trace. I could not trust my eyes.

At the dragon's temple, during my long penitence there, the warrior Jin had warned me of the wicked spirits of the world beyond, who could deceive one's sight and win over one's confidence with falsehoods. Here, in the world of the living, I had steeled myself against the schemes of men and the strength of beasts, certain that I would have more time to prepare for the machinations of spirits.

I had been mistaken—or I had underestimated the magics that a mortal man could craft. I studied each of the bearded elders in turn, searching their faces. They were as alike as brothers, with the same pale brown skin and soft white hair, with brows that met over aquiline noses. The desert had been as kind to them as it had been to Fenin's new face. Despite the color of their hair, not one appeared older than fifty. They met my gaze with serene, unreadable expressions, devoid even of the surprise and confusion that had come upon the guards when they had seen me.

I took a breath of smoke and dust and pushed away all thoughts of the desert and this strange room and its wealth, as I had been instructed at the temple. I had not the skill for it then, and I had not improved much since, but I let my mind settle on the solid stone beneath my feet and the comforting weight of my spear on my back.

In a steady, sonorous voice, Fenin recited a series of honorifics, greeting the elders and giving thanks to the serpent for Svilsara's prosperity. Her voice faded from my awareness, and I achieved something resembling focus.

And so, as Fenin knelt upon the rich, red carpet, her arms held up in the same supplicating pose she had assumed on the sacrificial stone, I saw the room as it truly was.

Thick smoke hung in the air, foul and greasy. Darkness fell over the cramped chamber, which was now only a little taller than my head, its walls black with soot. Fenin's glossy hair and snow-white raiment disappeared, and she became as she always was, with a dusty rag wrapped around her skeletal figure. The elders, too, were shriveled and starving, their beards faint wisps and their sunken faces like bark, their clothing threadbare and stained. Where the fine rug had lain was only a moth-eaten, brownish remnant. Even the young attendants, standing by the door, became thin, weathered shadows of their former selves.

This place was an illusion, all of it. If I were to have the good fortune to escape the temple and see the light of day once more, I suspected I would find the entire city in a similar state, its riches stripped away and its people frail and sickly.

~ XVIII ~

THE SACRIFICIAL STONE

Alas, my mind was not like water, as the Dragon Temple acolytes had encouraged. The illusion, so quickly drawn away, fell over my eyes again just as quickly. The filthy, smoke-filled room became clean and bright, and its occupants, save for me, were once more dressed in fine white silk, showing no sign of their long starvation.

The illusion hid, as well, any sign of the ritual used to cast it. The bare walls held no sigils, and the floor had been swept clean. I breathed in smoke and smelled no hint of either blood or incense.

"Please, wise elders," Fenin said, her head bent and her palms raised to the men on their thrones. "Help me to understand. I saw the serpent, but it vanished. I swear I did only as I was instructed." Her rich hair fell over one rounded shoulder, catching the torchlight like black glass.

The old man on her left stroked his beard with one hand. Rings bedecked his long fingers, dark jewels glittering. "The serpent has never refused a sacrifice before," he said.

"Never in all our history," agreed his neighbor.

"I've brought you this man," Fenin continued, sitting up and placing her hands in her lap. She gestured to me with a sharp motion of her head. "He is an outsider and an unbeliever. He was present before the serpent appeared."

The elders nodded, in the slow way that men do when they wish to appear wise. With a jeweled hand, the man on the far right indicated that Fenin should continue.

She hesitated, catching her bottom lip between her even white teeth, showing neither the decay I had witnessed in the desert nor the accompanying pain. "I fear he has displeased our benefactor. The serpent—" She turned her head to me, but turned away before our eyes met. "The serpent may not return until he is dealt with."

So this was how I was to be repaid for finding the girl, feeding her, and bringing her home. I lifted a hand to the strap that held my spear over my shoulder. The attendants moved from the doorway to flank me, but they kept their hands folded as if in prayer.

If they chose not to seize me, then I would not instigate a fight with them. I let my hand drop.

"You were correct to bring him to us, Lady Fenin," the third elder said.

The fourth narrowed his eyes at me. I could not guess what he saw, here within the illusion of health and prosperity. "Who are you, stranger?" he demanded.

In Kannaoka, I had introduced myself as a champion, and it had only encouraged the high priest to spill my blood. I would not make that mistake a second time. "I am Eske, a traveler from the North," I said. "I'm on my way to the coast. I found Fenin in the desert, and she appeared to be in some distress, so I escorted her here."

"Did *you* see the serpent?" the first elder asked.

"I can't be certain," I replied. "I believed that I had, but the desert has a way of confusing the senses."

The elders bent their heads, conferring amongst themselves in quiet murmurs. Fenin wrung her hands and twisted the fabric of her garment between her fingers. Something troubled her about this deliberation. Despite her eagerness to be consumed upon the rock, and her equal willingness to offer me up as a second sacrifice, the thought of one or both of these outcomes did not please her.

I could not cast blame on her, though I could not say what had become of the fanatic in the desert. Her doubt was nearly as shocking a change as the fullness of her flesh and the length of her hair.

At last, the fourth elder declared, "We will summon the serpent."

"Take Lady Fenin to the Sky House," said the second elder, "and this man to the house on the edge of the garden. We will send for them at a later time."

The attendants marched Fenin and me back through the narrow corridor and into the temple proper, their eyes fixed straight ahead and their hands folded. Even Fenin refused to look at me.

I was given over to the custody of the armed watchmen outside the temple, while the attendants whisked Fenin away to her secluded residence, a home to which she was never meant to return. Bran remained with the guard outside the temple, who held his tether with both hands and watched him with fearful eyes. Either he had taken my threats about Bran's well-being to heart, or he had never seen a horse before and did not know whether they were carnivorous. Bran ignored him, pawing at the grass with one hoof. When I came near, he stuck his nose under my arms and inside my robe, looking for food.

The garden's trees gleamed with ruby-red fruit, and the grass was as deep a green as the forest beside Nagara had been in the rain. The pond shimmered. Bran had neither eaten nor drank since I had left his side. Was all of this an illusion, as well? How cruel, I thought, to conjure the image of this garden in the middle of the sea of dust, and surround it with emaciated people who could only look and never enjoy it.

The watchman handed me Bran's lead and led me across the garden. The enormous fish turned in lazy circles as I walked by, and I wondered if they, too, were starving, or if they were only light and trickery.

Beside the inner wall, a house stood under two trees that bent under the weight of thousands of strands of purple flowers. I walked over fallen petals behind the watchman. Much like the rest of the city, the walls were painted a soft sky blue, and its low, rounded doorway and two circular windows faced the garden's green expanse. Ceramic pots stood like sentries atop the flat roof, holding leafy ferns and flowers in gleaming white and yellow.

This was far too fine a place for a filthy traveler such as myself. I could not begin to imagine what it might look like in truth.

Inside, I found a central fireplace of white stone, an iron cooking pot on a stand, and an assortment of ceramic dishes glazed in intricate, geometric patterns, all deep blue and gold. A large basin of water stood beside the door, and a woven curtain separated a small, low bed from the rest of the room.

"It's a beautiful house," I said, determined to at least present the appearance of a grateful guest. "And such fine craftsmanship. Who makes the pottery?"

My escort frowned, as if I had suddenly spoken a language he did not understand. "The serpent provides all we need," he said.

"It must be difficult for him to operate a potter's wheel without hands or feet," I said.

My attempt at a jest was met with the same bewilderment. "You must stay here," the watchman told me, "until the elders send for you. Do not wander the garden."

I promised him I would remain in the house, though I intended to break that promise if the elders required my blood. I would take Bran and flee the city, even if I had to open the gate with my own strength.

For now, I would wait. My guard left the house, and I bathed in the basin as best I could, washing days of sand from my skin and hair. I washed my clothing, as well, and watched in wonder as the water in the basin remained clear and unsullied. What degree of cleanliness I had actually achieved, I could not say, but the sand no longer itched. I hung up my robe to dry in the sun and went to investigate the rest of the house.

Several of the covered dishes contained food—spiced meat, rice, and fresh vegetables. After weeks of the same dry barley cakes and jerky, I devoured it all, and it was the best thing I had tasted in recent memory.

A few minutes later, I was hungry again. It was no wonder Fenin and her people were malnourished. They must have eaten something underneath the illusory smells and textures, or none of them would have ever reached adulthood, but it was far from sufficient. I fed myself and Bran from our dwindling stores, and counted how many days of rations we would have if we left for the coast at first light.

"What do you see, my friend?" I asked Bran, who had refused the green leaves and the garden's water. "What did you see when the serpent came?"

Of course, he gave me no answer.

Barring any attempt at sacrificing Bran and me to assuage the serpent's foul mood, I resolved to depart in the morning. The bed in the garden house might have been an illusion, but I had not slept the night before, and many days had passed since I had lain my head anywhere but the ground. I slept through the afternoon and into the evening, waking after nightfall.

Outside the house's small windows, hundreds of tiny lights bedecked the garden and marked out its paths, a mirror image of the starry sky above. More light poured out of the temple's windows, pooling on its steps. Fenin's voice, high and strong, led a chorus of chants.

My guard had left, though others stood along the path from the inner wall to the temple. If I kept to the shelter of the trees, I could avoid the men in the dark, and learn the name of the god this city worshiped—the god who demanded blood and gave only the image of safety and sustenance in exchange.

I dressed and slung my spear over my shoulder, and I promised Bran that I would soon return. He snorted and tossed his head. To offer him and myself some comfort, I placed his bridle over his head and his saddle about his girth, in preparation for a swift departure.

In the shadows beneath the trees, I crept past the pond, where the long, smooth sides of the fish drifted gently near the bottom, limned in soft, pale light. The song of the gathered priests drifted over the garden. I had heard its strange tones before, when Fenin had sung to call the serpent from the sea of dust.

I reached the temple and positioned myself beneath one window, out of sight of the open door. I raised my head to peer over the casement, and the light of a hundred torches seared my eyes. Fenin and the elders were nothing but undulating shadows within.

"Beautiful, isn't it?" came a voice from behind me.

I dropped to my knees, reaching for my weapon. The bright lights within had seared my eyes, and the benighted garden lay under an impenetrable shadow. "Who's there?" I whispered.

A human shape resolved out of the gloom, tall and slender and dressed all in black. An angular face at last came into view, and along with it, a sharp, too-wide smile reflected the light from the window. He was paler than the men and women inside, almost the color of sand, and from his hood emerged a handful of stray curls, dark and glossy. He might have been beautiful but for that smile.

He was more human than he had appeared on the sacrificial stone, his grin a little less like a snake's, but he was unmistakable. "You!" I said through my teeth. "Who are you? What do you want?" I freed my spear from its sling and held it in both hands, placing it between myself and the sharp-toothed stranger.

"They can't hear you," he said. Though the voice emanated from his direction, his mouth did not move, maintaining its viper's grin. "I thought I'd give us a moment to speak, while the good people of Svilsara finish their performance."

I got to my feet and left the patch of light beside the window. My eyes grew accustomed to the dark, but the stranger remained shadowed and formless, his black robe woven from strands of night. If I took my eyes away, he would vanish into the darkness.

Or, I thought, *he might turn into a snake.* The same sorcery that had turned Fenin hale and healthy could make a man appear as a serpent, or a serpent as a man. "What is it you intend, stranger?" I asked. "I'll warn you once: this city may be an illusion, but my spear is not, and neither is the arm that wields it."

"It's been some time since I've met one who could appreciate my handiwork," he said. He spread his arms, his voluminous sleeves trailing shadows, indicating the temple, the garden, and the whole city. "What say you? Have I not built a paradise on the earth?"

I took another step closer. "This is your doing?"

"All of it," he said, his eyes two tiny points of light in liquid blackness.

"Then unhand these people," I said. "They suffer and starve without knowing it. They cannot even seek better conditions because of your trickery."

He folded his arms into his sleeves, shadows undulating around him. "No, I don't believe I will. I've maintained this place for two hundred years. You entertain me, little warrior, and so I've let you live. I may change my mind if you try my patience."

Two hundred years. No mortal sorcerer could conjure a fantasy this broad and all-encompassing, maintaining it for generations. "You're a god. A greedy, blood-hungry god, unworthy of the worship you receive," I said. "It's of no matter to me. I've done battle with gods before."

The stranger clapped his hands in delight. "Ah, you flatter me, little warrior. Alas, the gods of the desert are set in their ways, and they refuse to name me as one of their number. But I do not mind. I have my city, and that is all I require."

"A true god would provide for his people," I said. Even the Ascended had done that. "You only trick them into thinking they have what they need."

"Oh, but they do," he replied, and this time his lips moved, as though he had just remembered that they should. He still had too many teeth. "They live out their lives in peace and happiness. Some die sooner, yes, but they are honored to do so, and their short lives are even more blessed. They need neither work nor fight, and yet the city is safe from invaders, and there is food on their tables and rich clothing on their backs. What more could a mortal soul want?"

In the temple, Fenin and the priests continued to sing. Someone beat a drum, low and steady like the pulsing of an enormous heart.

"These people are starving and dressed in rags," I argued. "They are sick, and no deception can keep away the cold night or restore their bodies."

He shrugged, a languid unfurling of his arms that caused the shadows around him to whirl and eddy. "You may be right. I doubt the good people of Svilsara would agree, though. Would you like to go and ask them?" His teeth glinted. "Offer them the choice—to continue as they are, or to starve in the desert with no one to protect them. I think you know as well as I do how they will answer."

Unbidden, my own teeth clenched, sending a sharp pain into my ears. "Dispel the illusion, first," I said, "and then they may make their choice as free people."

"Free, like you?" he asked.

I frowned. "I go where I choose. I speak to whom I choose. If a place no longer suits me, then I leave it. Your magic denies this to the people of Svilsara."

"But you, little warrior, are a slave to your belly, to the whims of the wind and the weather, and to whatever other fleshly urges that might strike you. The people here are protected from all these things."

"You've protected them from nothing." I assumed a fighting stance, raising my spear. "They still hunger, they still thirst; the sun still burns their skin. You've only drawn a veil over their eyes."

"Go on, then," the shadowy man said. "Present the choice to these people. See what they say."

"Cease your magic, and I'll do it," I said.

A flash of light erupted from the window behind me, and the chanting ceased. The drum pulsed twice more and fell silent. The ritual had ended. The light dimmed, and the temple was dark.

The stranger folded himself up in layers of black fabric, diminishing until nothing was left but a wisp of smoke that faded into the surrounding darkness. The garden's false greenery was a deep gray-blue in the starlight.

Fenin emerged from the temple first, carrying a lantern in both hands. Only a slight tremble in her arms suggested the truth, that she had not the strength to carry it. Behind her came the elders, two by two, their backs straight and their hands folded over their long, white beards. Their attendants took up the rear, each with a silver candlestick. Golden light bathed the garden, turning the trees to emerald and reflecting in the tranquil pond.

It fell upon me, as well, where I stood beside the paved path, well away from the house where I had promised to remain. As one, the procession turned to me. Fenin's eyes widened in surprise. "You're not supposed to be here," she said. "What are you doing?"

My mouth opened to tell her that I had met the god of Svilsara, whatever he was, in this garden of his own making, and he had admitted that all the luxuries of this desert paradise were but shadows. I bit my tongue. As loath as I was to admit it, he had been right: with the illusion still in place, Fenin would think me mad.

"I went for a walk in the garden," I said. Too late, I returned my spear to my shoulder, and the eyes of the elders and their attendants followed my hand. "I am a wanderer by nature. I never intended to go far."

Fenin's dubious look was fleeting. With her face as still as a mask, she intoned, "The serpent has spoken."

"The serpent has spoken," echoed the elders.

I waited in silence to hear of my fate.

"Eske of the North," Fenin continued, "you are an outsider and an unbeliever. Your presence has angered the great serpent and risked his wrath against Svilsara. Because we are faithful, the serpent will not rescind his blessings if we obey his command. At first light, you will be taken to the sacrificial stone, where you will be devoured. Your blood will undo the harm you have done to us."

His control of Svilsara was absolute. He had only to give the word, and the whole city turned against me. He knew I would not raise a hand against these starving people, even as they proclaimed I was to die.

Let it be so, I decided. Let me go back to the rock upon the sea of dust, away from the innocent victims of the serpent's lies, and let him come to me in that desolate place in either of his guises. He would not be the first god, or pretender to that title, that I had met in combat.

I bowed my head, putting on the image of contrition. "Your serpent is wise in all ways," I said, imitating Fenin's cadence. "I have seen now that your city is the finest in all the world, and its peace must be preserved. I am sorry for the trouble that I have caused you. I will go to the sacrificial stone."

The lie was bitter in my mouth. I swallowed the acrid taste and added, "Will you permit me to bring my horse and my possessions, as further offerings to the serpent? I would not have your city sullied by things of the outside world."

In the singular long day of our acquaintance, Fenin had never once trusted anything I'd had to say. But she had never met an outsider before, nor anyone without faith in her god. Such a person was impossible for her to imagine, even as he stood before her.

She gave a sharp nod, lifted her lantern another inch, and said, "Very well. All these things will be offered, and the serpent will be pleased. The city will be cleansed."

A the sun rose over the eastern edge of the sea of dust, Fenin's attendants tethered me to the stone where I had found her, with Bran tied beside me and the remainder of our supplies in a pile just out of reach. Morning set the dunes alight with a blinding glare. I closed my eyes and waited for the serpent.

***

The priestly attendants had affixed my hands to the iron ring more securely than they had done Fenin's. In a small, perverse way, I was grateful for the rope chafing my wrists. The people of Svilsara were like children—naive, trusting, and sheltered from the world outside their walls—but in the end, they had doubted my false repentance, and took measures to ensure I would not escape before I fulfilled my promise to be eaten. If they could doubt me, then perhaps they possessed the capacity to doubt the serpent and his illusions.

The desert sun bore down upon my head, its heat like a burning iron on my face and the exposed skin of my arms. My thin traveler's robe did little to protect me, and my flesh reddened and burned.

"Come on, you foul creature," I shouted into the expanse of dust. "I'm waiting."

The god of Svilsara, the demon of the sands, did not appear in the guise of man or serpent. His arrogance had compelled him to seek me out in the garden, and it would make me wait for his own good time.

Bran's lead was longer, and he moved into the shade of the stone, snorting his displeasure. He was thirsty, as was I, and the food and water we had remaining lay just out of our reach. Everything I owned in the world was piled in a small heap at the edge of the stone, with my spear balanced on top.

I tugged at my bonds. The rope was a fraying braid of rough fibers, their ends digging into my flesh, and the knots held fast. I pulled hard, dropping my weight to the ground, but despite the creaking of the iron ring and the bruising strain on my wrists, the rope withstood my efforts.

Bran regarded me with one black eye. His look said that I was a fool and I had doomed us both. I believed he may have been right. Sweat dried on my skin as quickly as it appeared. Without water, I would not last the day. Inch by inch, the sun climbed toward noon. Many, many hours lay between me and the relief of evening, the brief respite before the chill of the desert night.

I pressed my back against the stone, letting the tiny sliver of shade relieve the burn on my neck. My eyes fell upon the dragon-tooth head of my spear, glinting darkly in the sun. It had returned to my hand when I had thrown it. If I had the will, could I summon it now?

I reached out, the rope pulling taut over my head. I stretched my fingers and willed the weapon to move. It remained where it was, still as death, indifferent to my plight.

"You helped me free the people of Kannaoka," I said. "You are a dragon's flesh and bone, a dragon's gift to one who would throw off the yoke of an oppressor. Help me now, and I will do everything in my power to free Svilsara. This I swear."

It fell from my saddlebags and rolled a step toward my feet. Hope flared in my chest. A tremor under the earth put it out. I had not summoned my weapon, and the serpent was on his way, with all his needless fanfare.

A plume of dust bloomed upon the pale surface of the desert, rushing toward the sky like water pouring over a cliff. Beneath it, the serpent's body glinted as it undulated across the plain. It reminded me of the sea serpent of the North, with its scales and spines shining in the sun, and the thrill and terror of watching it approach. My hands curled around an imaginary harpoon.

Dust washed over me in a wave, clinging to my skin and stinging my eyes. When it cleared, the serpent had vanished, and the strange, tall man with his snakelike grin stood on the rock beside me.

"Hello again, little warrior," he said, his lips unmoving and his amber eyes hard as flint.

I acknowledged him with a nod. "You've certainly kept me waiting."

His sigh was almost human. "That's the trouble with you mortals," he said. "You want everything to happen so quickly. You have no patience. It's what makes you so easy to bend toward obedience."

"You're trying to convince me that the people of Svilsara deserve what you've done to them," I said. "It's not going to work."

His brows went up, and his smile widened, splitting his face in half. If he ever opened his mouth, I expected to see a serpent's forked tongue between his lips. "Oh? Here you are, tied to the sacrificial stone, waiting to be devoured." He swept an arm out to indicate our surroundings. "I did not place you here."

"You told them to do it," I said.

He nodded. "And they obeyed of their own volition."

My eyes fell from the man's uncanny visage to my spear, still lying upon the rock. I tried to make my mind like water, to think like the dragon who had made this weapon and the champion who had first received it, but my skin was afire and my mouth full of dust.

The spear turned on the stone, sweeping an arc barely an inch across. I could call it to me, I was certain, but I needed more time. I needed to keep this arrogant, petty god boasting of his deeds.

"You've denied them their own volition," I said. "One day, the veil will be lifted, and they'll realize you've fed them worthless food and their city is a ruin, and they'll turn on you."

He laughed, showing human teeth that all shone white in the desert sun: four sets of incisors and double the expected number of sharp canines. "I am immortal, little warrior. Each year, the blood of their chosen sacrifices sustains me, but I will endure even without it. Your blood, on the other hand…"

The spear twitched.

"You haven't been eating their rations," he continued. "You've grown strong on your travels. Your blood will last me a good many years. Does that please you, little warrior? Your sacrifice will allow me to keep my people happy and safe. Isn't that what you want?"

"So that's why you had them bring me here," I said. "You're not the first petty god who has desired my blood, and I'm sure you won't be the last. What makes you think you'll be the one to take it?"

His robe blurred at the edges, drifting away from his body like thick smoke rising from a fire. Sunlight shone through his face as his form faded into the air. "Because you have spent a night and a day in my city and among my people. I know your mind. You cannot stand against me."

"I think you're mistaken," I said, and my spear flew from the ground and into my hand. I let the shaft slip through my fingers and gripped it just below the wicked barbs of its head. With a turn of my wrist, I cut my bonds. The rope fell slack around me.

I brought the spear to my shoulder and turned to the man. He may have been a god—I was not entirely convinced—but he wasn't powerful enough to resist an enchanted weapon.

Where he had stood, only a swirl of pale sand remained. The sea of dust was blank and flat, the only sound the howl of the scorching wind. "Where are you?" I cried. "Show yourself!"

"Who are you looking for?"

That voice, at once familiar and strange, cut through the roar of my blood racing through my ears. I knew that voice, but I would never, ever have expected to hear it here, in the middle of the vast desert.

My arm fell from my shoulder. The point of the spear struck the ground, striking a tiny chip from the stone. The shaft remained in my hand, though I could no longer feel its weight, and the pain of the heat and my ever-present thirst became dull and distant.

I turned. There, standing beside Bran in the shade of the stone pillar was Khalim. He wore the clothes in which he had traveled to Phyreios, a thin coat over a plain woven shirt and trousers rolled up to the knee. His wild curls shone where they caught the light, and his soft dark eyes looked at me with amusement and concern.

"Eske," he said. "Are you all right?"

This was an illusion. I should have anticipated it, after what I had seen of the city. If the serpent-god could create a blooming garden in the desert, with shimmering ponds and great fish to populate them, then he could easily conjure the image of one man.

I gripped the spear, but I found I could not lift it. My limbs were weak. I stood as if on a towering precipice, and if I were to move, either the rock beneath my feet or my own body would crumble away into nothingness.

"You're not here," I choked out, the words like stones in my throat, rough and heavy.

Khalim—the image of Khalim—smiled, and my heart dropped into my belly. "Of course not," he said, "but I could be. You could have whatever you wanted."

~ XIX ~

SVILSARA, AS IT ALWAYS WAS

Jin had warned me of this at the temple—of devious spirits that haunted the world beyond death, luring the unwary into certain doom. He had described them as less than gods, but what was a god to a man who lived in the shadow of an ancient dragon who refused all those who would worship her? The thing that had placed itself as a god over Svilsara was far beneath his acknowledgment.

And what was a god to one such as I? The Ascended, hungry for blood and willing to destroy their thousand-year reign to obtain it? Their master, who could not prevent the destruction of the city, and yet thought it right to rule over it afterward? The gods of my people were hunters and wanderers, warriors and magic-workers, and the great beasts that roamed the vast, icy plains of the world beyond. Here in the desert, so far from the lands of my birth, they held no sway. There was only the demon serpent and his false faces.

He still wore Khalim's face, and his long-limbed form and his well-worn clothing. I could not raise my eyes to meet his. My arm was strong and my aim was true, but the spear had become an impossible weight. Even if I could have lifted it, I could not cast it at someone who looked like Khalim.

His bare feet crossed the burning rock. Without lifting my head, I watched his shadow approach Bran and untie the tether around his neck. Bran snorted, tossing his head.

"You've been traveling for a long time, haven't you?" the man who was not Khalim said. "When was the last time you saw me?"

I answered against my will, the words harsh against a tongue dry as dust. "Four years, come autumn."

"Four years," he echoed. "Your wandering could be over, you know. You could live with me in the city, in the house in the garden. No one would ever separate us again."

I swallowed an obstruction in my throat, my dry tongue sluggish. I needed water. My last full skin lay on the stone, a few steps away, but I could not move.

"Come with me," Khalim's voice said.

I managed the barest shake of my head, a weak, wavering refusal. The serpent's only power was that of illusion; no magecraft held me in place, and this was not Khalim. Khalim wandered the paths of gods and spirits while the body he had once inhabited remained in Phyreios. I repeated these truths in my mind, a litany of disbelief, but my body refused them. I longed to take his hand, to touch his face, to place myself deeper into the lie. My spear dangled from my hand, as useless as the arm that carried it.

His footsteps were soft on the scorching surface of the sacrificial stone. With my eyes lowered, the world had become three bands of color: the red of the stone, the pale yellow of the desert sand, and a thin line of the fathomless blue of the sky. I turned my face away before he could enter my field of vision.

"I know you don't trust the city," he said, gently and without pretense, exactly as Khalim might have. "But I think you'd come to like it. It could be home."

He paused, standing beside me, and reached out a hand. His fingers brushed against mine. "I could call it home," he added, "if you were there."

How easy it would have been to forget my quest, to forget the past years and imagine that the terrible day in Phyreios had never happened. Against my better judgment, I looked up. I would find some flaw in the man-serpent's imitation of Khalim's face, I thought, and that would break the spell.

He was precisely as I remembered him. Stubble shaded his jaw, and his dark hair caught the sunlight. That same smile had driven me to the far corners of the world. The god of Svilsara had never met Khalim, nor had he ever visited Phyreios or the village of Nagara. He had taken the image of Khalim from my memory. My skin crawled at the violation.

I understood, now, why the ancestors of Svilsara's elders had taken the serpent's bargain, exchanging their health and freedom, and those of their children and their children's children, for the shallow image of prosperity. They must have struggled before they had found this god, here beneath the merciless sun with no neighbors to help them when their wells went dry, all while the wind blew stinging dust into their eyes and against their blistered skin. I did not claim to be a leader of men, but I might have done the same, had I been offered a way to relieve the suffering of those who had trusted me to protect them—like Khalim had, in those last days.

Svilsara's god offered me the same choice. A relief of pain, in exchange for the world as it was, where the sun burned, and dust scratched my throat, and I had not seen Khalim in almost four years.

A stronger man than I would not have hesitated to reject the comforting lie. And it was a lie, all of it, from the image of Khalim to the house in the garden to the promise of a life spent in peace. My only value to the creature in Khalim's guise was whatever power could be extracted from my blood. If I followed the false Khalim back to Svilsara, how long would I live there before either the god or his followers slew me in my sleep? Would I be allowed even a day, a week, a month of the promised illusory bliss before they brought it to an end?

The illusion smiled again with Khalim's mouth, and the threat all but flew from my mind.

I looked away, the sun reflecting on the vastness of white dust making my eyes ache. "Do you promise me that?" I asked, more to the shimmering air than to the figure beside me. "A home in the city, and my love as I remember him?"

"All of it and more," he said.

"Lead the way, then," I heard myself say. "I will follow."

He moved across the stone, bare feet stirring the dust. An unseen hand gripped my chest, and I struggled to breathe, taking in painful gasps.

Bran's harness rattled as he tossed his head. I lifted my spear. My hands, numb and awkward as they were, gripped the weapon with a practiced, unthinking ease. It rested lightly against my fingers, like a bird ready to fly from my hand. Energy shivered up my arm.

I took two unsteady steps toward the pile of my belongings. Bran regarded me with one eye, his ears flattened.

In Khalim's guise, the god of Svilsara made his way to the pillar with its iron ring, where Fenin and I, and hundreds of sacrifices before us, had been tethered by hope and faith more than rope. He turned to me, smiling expectantly, rooting me to the spot where I stood.

"We need water for the journey," I said, gesturing to the bags at my feet.

He nodded, turning away to reach for Bran's halter.

I closed my eyes and inhaled dust, letting it burn my throat. Then, as Khalim's—the god's—tousled hair hid his face, I lifted the spear to my shoulder and threw it.

A sound like thunder shattered the desert stillness. The sky darkened, as though the sun had blinked like a great, burning eye. Bran reared back, his hooves striking at empty air. He backed away, his eyes rolling and his nostrils flared.

At his feet lay a crumpled body wearing Khalim's clothes.

My spear returned to my hand, and my fingers wrapped around it, preparing me for another throw without my conscious approval. Khalim's face turned to me, and I could not look away. Even in sorrow and betrayal, he was beautiful.

He had gone pale, struggling to breathe around the wound in his chest. Blood spilled over his grasping hands. "Eske?" he whispered.

"You were never here," I said aloud. "Your body is in Phyreios, and your spirit wanders the world beyond. I didn't hurt you. I didn't touch you. You were never here."

My knees hit the stone before I realized I was falling. A crushing weight pressed down on my shoulders. My own breath came in strangled sobs.

Khalim's face shifted and changed, and before me lay the strange, black-robed man with his serpentlike mouth. Even that image did not last. The face cracked and crumbled away into sand, black smoke spiraling up from his robes as they, too, dissipated into the air. A black scar remained at the foot of the pillar, a smear of soot barely a hand's breadth wide on the burning rock. In a few hours, a day at most, the wind would scour the surface clean.

The serpent-god of Svilsara was dead, as much as any god can die, and all his works would soon follow. In the city, Fenin and her attendants would see each other and themselves for the first time, and look with unclouded eyes upon what little of their home remained. They would grieve, but worse would be the confusion—having lived so long in the illusion, not one of them could have had any hope of explaining what had become of them.

It was a cruel thing I had done.

But as the wind took up the last of the dusty remains of the god, I had no thought of the people of Svilsara, lost and alone in this unforgiving landscape. I could only weep, for myself and for

Khalim, and the unshakable certainty that despite what I saw before me, I had done him terrible harm.

The midday sun burned overhead, and the heat bore down on me with searing claws. I needed water, shelter from the infernal heat, and a plan to make my dwindling supplies last until I reached another waystation, but my limbs were as heavy as stone.

I wept without tears as the sun began its descent and the black scar upon the stone turned to soft gray. Bran stepped into my view, his iron shoes loud against the rock, and put his nose to my ear.

I forced my hand to rise and stroke his sweat-lathered neck. He was as thirsty as I, and I could not abandon myself and perish under the sun without endangering this noble creature. I got to my feet, and on weakened legs I retrieved some water and food for both of us.

The weight on my body lifted, breath by breath. The smell of water brought back hunger and thirst in equal measure, and my strength returned. I stretched my tent over the rock, and Bran and I rested in the shade.

I had four days' worth of food for myself and my horse. I could stretch it to six, perhaps, but I could not negotiate with the three days' supply of water. Svilsara was remote; they engaged in no commerce, and their goods were all illusions. They had called this safety.

Fenin had lived to see seventeen years, and the elders she served many more, so they had some provisions, if not much. It might have been enough to see me on my way, but how could I take from them, when they had so little?

How could I do otherwise, when they had tied me to the rock and left me to die?

Their supplies would run out whether I partook of them or not. *The serpent provides all we need,* they had said. They did not have the skill to hunt or to till the earth, and I had just killed their serpent and doomed them all to die.

The mark on the stone had all but disappeared. The image of Khalim, lying upon the stone with his hands clutching the wound and his face contorted in pain, remained. I had carried his memory here, where it had been used as a weapon against me.

Then let it be used for some good, as well, I decided. *Let me try to save Svilsara.*

The sun made its way westward, and I gathered my belongings and took Bran across the sand to the city. I arrived as afternoon turned to evening, and dust painted the desert sky red.

Under that sky, where the wall of white stone had stood against the real and imagined threats of the world outside, only drifts of sand encircled the city. Beyond that, half-buried hovels sprawled across the dunes. Most had only three or four walls, open to the air and dust, but a few still possessed crumbling timbers that had once been a roof. The blue plaster that had lent Svilsara its particular charm was nowhere to be seen. The sun had long ago leached any color from the hunched buildings. Age and weather had pitted and scarred, the thin, brittle walls, and the streets were no more than footpaths carved into the sand.

The hands of neither gods nor men had cared for this city in an age. A chill wind, harbinger of the night to come, whispered its way through empty houses and down buried staircases. I dismounted and crossed the ridge that marked the outer wall, keeping Bran close at hand. He flattened his ears, his eyes darting from one deepening shadow to the next.

But for the wind, the city was quiet. I wandered toward the inner wall and the garden, past darkened windows and empty doorways. I risked a glance inside one house, beside what had appeared to be the grand staircase leading to the center of town. The fading light caught the dust hanging in the air and touched upon tattered curtains, a filthy tabletop of jagged splinters, and a moth-eaten basket of rotting, unrecognizable fruit spilling out onto the sand that covered the floor.

My stomach turned. I ducked my head and hurried Bran to the temple.

Here, where a lush green garden had demonstrated every blessing the serpent had offered, there was only more sand. The temple of the elders stood above it, barely taller than my head, its magnificent vaulted ceiling only open air. Black soot stains around the windows offered the only evidence that anyone had used the building in a hundred years or more. The house in which I had stayed—the house that the serpent had promised me—was nothing but a ring of wind-blasted stones, half-covered in sand.

At the center of the garden, around an empty, shallow hollow that must have been the fish pond, the people of Svilsara huddled together against the oncoming night. In the dark, I could not count them, but I guessed there were perhaps fifty, men and women and children, clutching at their thin, dust-stained robes with skeletal fingers. A pair of chipped clay lamps spit foul-smelling smoke into the air and cast baleful shadows on the hollow eyes and sunken cheeks of those sitting nearby. A tiny child suckled on the hem of his dirty sleeve, his head huge and heavy above narrow, knife-sharp shoulders. I could not tell his age.

I had done exactly the thing I had hated their god for doing: I had taken away their choice to live with or without the illusion. At the sight of them, I could no longer believe that the truth was better than the lie. They were a cursed people, now, at the edge of death.

"You!" a familiar voice rang out. Fenin rose from the far side of the gathering, one hand holding her rags over her distended belly while the other pointed an accusing finger at me. Around her, the elders' wizened hands shook as they pleaded silently with the sky.

I held up my free hand in return. "I mean you no harm," I said, but my words meant nothing. I had already done them harm.

"You are a demon from the wastes!" Fenin screamed across the dark expanse of the ruined garden. "Begone from here! The serpent will strike you down and devour your flesh!"

"Your serpent is dead," I said. I had not the strength to invent a convincing lie, not after what had transpired upon the sacrificial stone, and not with a hundred shadowed eyes staring at me, accusation and hatred in the reflected flames that burned within them.

"Impossible," said the wavering, raspy voice of one of the elders. "The Serpent is eternal. A god cannot die."

If only this old man pretending at wisdom knew how wrong he was. He and his fellows had not lived long enough to have been the ones who had first made this arrangement with the serpent, but under their auspices, Svilsara continued to offer blood in exchange for imagined wealth and protection. I could not blame them for the city's suffering, but neither could I forgive them—not that it mattered, in the end. Mine was not the forgiveness the elders should have been seeking.

"You can believe me or not," I said. "It makes no difference. Your serpent is not coming to save you, and you'll need food and water and shelter before nightfall. I'm leaving to seek out others who might help. If you wish, you may come with me. Otherwise you can remain here and wait."

A second elder waved a bony hand, as if to dismiss me like a puff of smoke. "We are protected here. You will only lead us to our deaths, demon."

"Sit down, Lady Fenin," a third said. "We must pray."

Fenin looked at them, and then at me, thin wisps of hair drifting around her ears. Her hands clenched in the threadbare fabric of her robe.

"You're going to find help?" she asked.

"I swear it," I said. "I will do it or die in the attempt."

And then the young woman, who had been willing to die for her people once, glanced over their starving faces and chose to risk death once more. She gathered up the hem of her clothing and squared her narrow shoulders. "Then I'm coming with you."

~ XX ~

ISRA'S WELL

Two others stood with Fenin: young men, one in the tattered remnants of an attendant's white robe, and the other carrying a pitted, splintery staff that had once been enchanted to look like a spear. Had I met either of them before the illusion broke? Their gaunt cheeks, thin hair, and missing teeth were nothing like the bright, bronze faces that had greeted me in suspicion yesterday. Except for Fenin, everyone here was a stranger.

The elders remained, kneeling on the dusty ground. They bowed their heads, turning their faces from me and from their defecting subjects. In rasping, wavering voices, through toothless mouths, they sang a hymn to their dead god. I could not bear to watch them any longer. I left the barren garden in search of enough provisions to survive in the desert. My fragile, courageous new charges followed me in a single file, sunken eyes bright, not daring to speak.

We visited the hollow shells of the garden houses, moving in a circle around the inner wall. I found most of a sack of grain, its corners torn out by rats' teeth, and a package of what appeared to be splintered wood that, upon closer inspection, revealed itself to be dried meat. A cistern of dusty, brackish water beside the temple filled my empty skins. I thought I might take the rest of it—more water skins lay nearby, neglected and covered in sand—to punish the people of Svilsara for leaving me to die, but I left it where it was. I was no god, to choose who might live and who might succumb to thirst in the desert. Even if the others chose to do nothing, and met whatever fate the sun and wind had in store for them, I would not take from them their only hope at survival.

We would travel by night, I explained to my young charges, and thus avoid the heat. In the ruin of another house, I found three moth-eaten blankets that could approximate warm clothing. If they belonged to someone, that person stayed in the garden, bowed down before the powerless elders.

We departed from the remains of the gate. Only the flickering lights at the top of the hill gave any evidence that anyone still lived in Svilsara.

"Should we go back?" Fenin asked. A voice like a little girl's had replaced the imperious tones of the priestess. "What will happen to them?"

"They will follow if they wish to," I told her. "If they are unwilling, we cannot force them."

"When we find help, I'll come back," she said.

She could do no such thing if she did not survive the journey. I allowed my sickly charges to ride Bran in shifts, sparing a little of their wavering strength. When the sun rose behind us, casting soft, rosy light onto the haze of dust that hid the city from view, I set up our shelter and distributed a little food and water. If they ate too little or too much, they would die under my care. Looking at their swollen bellies, I doubted I possessed the wisdom to ensure their survival.

"I don't know what happened," Fenin whispered to the young attendant as they crawled under their blankets. "I was beautiful once, and nothing hurt."

"You will be again," he said. "All will be well."

***

"Perhaps we will see the serpent out here," Fenin said the next evening. "Perhaps he will return to Svilsara when he sees our devotion."

The serpent would never come again. The only thing that would save Svilsara would be years of grueling work—work that her citizens had not the strength to perform. Fenin sat in Bran's saddle, and Astin the guardsman clung to one stirrup, his steps dragging furrows in the sand. Tolma, the priestly attendant, had fallen behind. I tugged on Bran's halter and waited.

"My legs hurt," Tolma said between panting breaths.

"You'll ride next," I said. "Just a little farther."

They complained of pain each evening when they woke and each night when they lay in their beds, when they ate and when they walked. They were like children, unable to understand why their teeth ached and their limbs shook.

I had done this to them. No—their wicked god had done this to them, and I was right to have slain him. Still, they suffered, and I'd had no small hand in it. Aside from allowing them to ride, I could not ease their burdens.

So we walked. I kept us heading west, toward the setting sun and the distant coast. Four days out of Svilsara, the waystation appeared: a tall building with a single spire, black against the violet evening sky. Night fell, and the structure faded into darkness, only appearing again at morning when the pale sun illuminated its sharp corners. Around it, the desert undulated, a vast and forbidding sea. A cluster of low buildings appeared around the spire the following evening.

"There," I told my charges. "That's where we'll find help."

Tolma's weathered face creased into a suspicious frown. "Outsiders," was all he said.

The others nodded in agreement, and they looked at me, expectation in their hollow eyes.

"I'll keep you safe," I promised.

Guilt burned in my belly. The image of Khalim, lying upon the sacrificial stone, came to my mind unbidden. I shook my head to clear it away.

We arrived in the early morning, when the first gray light turned the sand to silver and the tall plaster walls a pale blue. A solitary figure, dressed in a green robe that dusted the path behind her, left one of the outbuildings and headed toward the central structure, a basket of clean, white linens slung over one arm. She was of middle age, her hair covered in a shawl of the same vibrant green, a color I had not seen since the illusory garden. A vest laced in the front held her garments together.

She spotted us—Astin slumped in the saddle, Fenin and Tolma lagging a few paces behind, leaning on one another, and me leading Bran—and beckoned us closer with a wave. A slim brown arm emerged from her voluminous sleeve.

We entered through a fence woven like a basket, scarcely taller than my knees. A pair of goats bleated in surprise when they lay eyes on my horse and ran behind the nearest outbuilding. Before I could explain, three more women appeared, whisking my charges away to a low house lined with cots at the northern end of the compound. They offered me a bed, as well, and tea with honey and salt to cure prolonged thirst, but I refused. I was well enough.

"I come from Svilsara," I said. "Have you heard of it?"

The first woman shook her head, shaking the fringe on her green mantle. "You have the appearance of an outlander," she remarked.

"I come from the North," I explained, "but Svilsara is seven days' walk east of here, at the edge of the sea of dust. I fear that my three companions are all who yet live from the city, but I hope that the rest can yet be saved. Will you help me?"

She took me into the temple, for that was what the tall edifice was: a shrine to the goddess of wheat sheaves and mothers, whose vague, moonlike face smiled down upon me as I entered the carved doors. Her green-robed priestesses sat me down on a bench beside a tall, white pillar supporting the vaulted ceiling. This place was too much like the temple of Svilsara's elders, or rather the illusion of it. The snake god must have entered this place before he crafted his mirages, and perhaps this smiling goddess had been one of the desert gods who had scorned his company. An altar stood at her feet, covered in green silk, and an open book lay beneath a beam of sunlight from an east-facing window.

I sat as I was instructed, laying my spear and my pack beside me. "Svilsara is alone in the desert," I said, "surrounded on all sides by the sea of dust. For a time, they lived in prosperity, but as of late their supplies have failed, and the people are weak, sickly, and starving. I am but a traveler, but I agreed to take any who would come with me to seek aid elsewhere. We were fortunate to come upon this temple before our provisions ran out."

The lie was bitter on my tongue, but I had no choice. I had slain a god, and Fenin's people had spilled human blood for generations to secure their imagined safety and wealth. Neither truth would endear us to the holy women of this temple.

"The young woman you brought with you says otherwise," the priestess said, a slight, unreadable smile crossing her face. "She says your presence angered the gods, and Svilsara has fallen under a curse."

"That may also be true," I said. Here, with the morning sun streaming in through windows of colored glass, my encounter with Svilsara's god had become like a distantly remembered dream, impossible to recount even if I had wanted to.

"If there are others, we can send an expedition with supplies," said the priestess.

I bowed my head. "I would be in your debt."

She smiled, a mirror of the statue towering above, and stood, brushing out her skirts. "If you are well, then you will labor in our garden for a time, in exchange for your keep and that of your friends."

I could hardly call Fenin a friend, but a few days' work was an easy price to pay for the fulfillment of my oaths and repayment of my debts, as well as a roof over my head and a real bed beneath it. I slept that night and dreamed again of the oak-headed stag, walking silently through a forest that bent and shifted in his wake. In the morning, my body was heavy, and a many-branched shape lurked at the corners of my eyes, disappearing whenever I turned my head.

I went to work in the garden, as I had been bidden. This small community of green-robed women had been constructed around a deep well: the well, they said, of the goddess Isra herself. It was Isra's will that the water be given to any who asked for it. It also irrigated an expansive garden of small, hardy vegetables and a date palm on either side of the temple. Thin, yellow-green leaves trembled in the harsh desert wind, remaining no matter how long I stared at them. This place was no illusion.

I pulled water from the well, one reed basket at a time, and spread it among the neat rows, stepping between spiny stalks and over stone barriers that the blowing sand had worn smooth and featureless. While I labored, Fenin and her companions rested in the shady infirmary, drinking clean water and eating a thin gruel. Years of starvation had loosened their teeth and shrunk their stomachs, but after the first day, Fenin's eyes brightened, and she stood at the infirmary door as three of the priestesses put on their traveling coats and dust masks and filled water skins for their journey to Svilsara.

"Why can't I go with them?" Fenin asked. "I was chosen to lead Svilsara and keep our covenant with the serpent. I need to go back."

"You're too weak, still," I told her.

She scowled, brushing sparse strands of hair from her brow. "I was strong enough to make it here."

"We didn't have a choice then," I said. "Now you're safe. You must rest, and heal, and let these women help your countrymen."

She turned her sharp, dark eyes to me, her face twisted in anger. What little strength she had gained had all turned to rage against the one who had brought her here. "Without me, the serpent will devour them on the road," she said. "They'll never make it to Svilsara."

I bent over a patch of shriveled beans, gathering them into a large basket. "The same serpent who was going to devour you?"

"I was chosen from birth," she argued. "Untouched and unsullied—the purest of sacrifices. I should be the one to bring back his favor. Not an outlander."

"Don't insult your benefactors," I said, picking up the basket. "These women have saved your lives, and they'll save your people. Let them work."

She crossed her skeletal arms over her chest. The priestesses had given her a green tunic, and it hung from her shoulders like a tent. "How dare you speak to me, unbeliever?" she snarled. "You should have been eaten."

I let the basket drop to the dusty stone path. The wind caught a few hulls and took them away across the garden. "Your serpent is dead," I said before I could still my tongue. "I slew him upon the sacrificial stone. He will never devour anyone, willing or not, again."

Fenin's split lips parted, and then pressed into a thin line. "You lie."

I should have held my tongue, but the dam had been breached, and the truth poured forth whether I willed it or not. "Why else would everything in your city change all at once?" I asked. "At the moment of his death, his magic unraveled, and his illusions fell from your eyes. You were never beautiful, Fenin. You never ate a full meal, or bathed in clean water, or sheltered from the sun in a lush, green garden, not until now."

"You *lie*," she said again, this time a faint whisper lost to the blowing dust.

"Believe me or not," I replied. "It makes no difference."

She slammed the door, and she did not speak to me again for the remainder of my brief stay. She must have warned her companions away, as well, for they kept to the infirmary and avoided me on the rare occasions they stepped outside. Her authority as priestess persisted much longer than the illusions of her god.

These new, green-clad priestesses had little reason to converse with me, either, so I labored in silence, drawing water and gathering the harvest. My only companion was Bran, who followed behind me to eat the weeds I pulled from between the garden rows.

In the evening, while Fenin and the others ate the last of their four small meals of the day, I entered the temple to refill the water stores and sweep the steps. The goddess gazed upon me with an expression of indistinct patience.

She was the goddess of rain and of green, growing things; of mothers and children; of healers and charity. Her figure in white stone possessed only hollows for eyes and the vague suggestion of a beatific smile under the smooth, shallow ridge of her nose. Khalim might have liked her for her resemblance to the god who presided over the rice fields, but to me, she bore too much of a resemblance to the empress of Phyreios, Shanzia of the shining face and emerald eyes, who could bewitch with a look. Shanzia, too, had been queen and mother and bestower of plentiful harvests. She had perished under the rubble along with her divine kin, but this face in the desert temple, bright as a full moon, could have been hers. Shanzia's stone counterpart, standing beside her carved throne in Phyreios, bore a similar smile.

What a cruel irony it would have been if I had taken Fenin and her companions from the clutches of one hungry god just to leave her in the hands of another. Would Isra demand the blood of travelers, like the Ascended did?

After sunset, when the priestesses had finished their prayers and the lights in the infirmary had gone out, I rose from my bed and went to search the temple. I placed my hands against the walls and felt for hidden latches, I looked under every bench and table for a drain to carry blood away to some hidden chamber, and I lifted the cloth from the altar, finding only smooth stone.

I lit a torch and wandered the grounds, searching beside the well and behind the infirmary. One by one, I opened the doors to the outbuildings, and found only the three survivors from Svilsara asleep, the priestesses bunked in orderly rows under a faint cloud of incense, and a sleek, gray cat hunting mice in the grain store.

At last, in a squat, cubic structure behind the priestesses' quarters, I found something unexpected: a library, lined in shelves that reached from floor to ceiling. Bound books covered two walls, their leather spines inscribed in gold and silver, while scrolls lay in piles on the third. I could read their titles no better than I could the text inscribed in the book I carried with me.

The priestesses, however, could read them. Why else would they have kept such a trove?

The next morning, I took the book from my pack and brought it to the temple. Lady Nasrin, the only priestess who had deigned to give me her name along with my tasks for the day, knelt before the altar, with an offering of wildflowers and sweet grasses spread out before her.

She finished her prayer and stood, surprise crossing her sun-browned face. "Good morning, Eske," she said. "I trust all is well?"

I bowed. "All is well," I said, and it was mostly true. Fenin had seen me from the infirmary window and drawn the curtains closed, but Bran and I had enough to eat, and the well continued to produce water, hour after hour and day after day. "I was hoping to ask your assistance."

"Of course," she said.

I handed her the book. "I have traveled west to find the place where this volume was written," I explained. "I cannot read it, but I saw your library. You know your letters. Can you tell me where I need to go."

Lady Nasrin turned the pages with gentle hands. Images leapt out in the morning light: the stag with its crown of branches, the flayed man, the gate of bone, a spiraling labyrinth of fading red ink.

"Where did you get this?" she asked.

"On an island far from here," I said. "A wicked sorcerer had it in his possession, and I took it from him. I seek the gate you see in its pages, and I have dreamed of the stag in the forest. Can you tell me what these images mean?"

She frowned, and she closed the book with a snap that echoed under the temple's peaked ceiling. "You knew this man did not have good intent, and yet you kept his book. Why?"

"I have communed with gods and men and great beasts," I said, "and I have found little to help me on my quest. I know one book cannot contain all the answers I seek, but if you can tell me anything about the people who inscribed it—"

She held up a hand to silence me. "This is an evil book, Eske of the North. It was written in the necropolis of Ksadaja, and even the tomb-keepers there would regard it as a work of heresy. You are fortunate to be unlettered, because no good will come of reading it. It would be best for it to be cast into the fire, to free us all from its presence."

I seized the book from her before she could do so. Her eyes went wide in surprise, and I bowed, apologetic. In my hands, the black leather binding was as warm as living flesh. "I'm sorry," I said. "There may come a day when I burn this book myself, but for now, I must pursue my course. I have spent so long wandering without answers."

"Then you must leave this place," Lady Nasrin said. "We will give you supplies for the road, but you cannot linger here with that book in your possession."

Before the sun had set upon Isra's well a third time, Bran and I walked west once more, our backs laden with water and our tracks vanishing into the sand as soon as we made them.

I would find the origin of this terrible book, I swore, even if I were to burn its pages only a moment later. I had to know what the wizards of the West knew. Once I did, I would keep my own council, and make my own judgment.

I would not see Fenin or the people of Svilsara again.

~ XXI ~

THE CITY OF THE DEAD

I left the tiny commune around Isra's well, and I left the serene face of the goddess, and for another season I wandered across the desert to the lands of the West. My thoughts wandered beyond the northern horizon, where the lands of my people lay, where our gods walked the plains of endless ice, and my dragon-headed ship lay beneath water cold and dark as death. My journey would not lead me back there. I had to press forward.

I would see Isra again in a sand-etched ruin several days from the coast. She stood beside her consort, in a line of seven statues scarred by a century of wind. Like hers, the others' faces had been smoothed away, and they held the faded implements of their stations in their stone hands: a shepherd's crook, a set of balancing scales, a smith's hammer. They towered over the dunes, their eyes long since etched to nothing, the hands who had carved their figures long buried beneath the sand. At their feet, the remains of their temple crumbled to dust.

Once, Aysulu had told me of the gods of the West. There were seven of them, she had said, like the seven Ascended of Phyreios, though they moved between legend and metaphor and not in the streets of their cities. The sight of them filled me with the same dread the Ascended had, but their presence signaled that I neared the long-sought coast.

Bran and I walked under the endless blue sky, while the wind howled over the ruins and dust spiraled in towering vortices. My eyes ached and my legs trembled as loose sand grasped at my feet. We walked in the early morning, as the sun climbed behind us and turned the world to fire, and in the evening, as it stained the sky blood-red and cast illusions of pooled water before us.

At last, a shimmering band of water remained even as the sun lowered itself behind it, and it appeared again in the morning, widening as we crossed the last stretch of sand. I had come once again to the sea.

Distant white sails crept like low clouds against the horizon. They would not come to this remote stretch of beach; they drifted south, to a port that lay beyond my sight.

Bran and I followed them. The sand gave way to a rocky shore and clusters of tall, sharp-edged grass. I cast a net in the surf for fish, and found a freshwater spring emerging from the scrub. With our stores replenished, we continued on. I walked at the edge of the water, letting it wash over my feet, and it was something like coming home.

We came upon the port five days later. A city of silver spires and stone columns the color of old parchment emerged from the remains of the desert haze, and the sound of its harbor met my ears: a murmur of countless voices and creaking timbers, of clanging bells and crashing waves. Months had passed since I had last spoken to anyone but Bran. My throat tightened at the thought of conversing with so many people after so long in silence.

I made camp outside the city, as the last light of the sun pooled like burning oil upon the sea. For the first time since leaving the last waystation, I took the book from my pack. It fell open to a second flayed man, his breath moving in inked whorls through his chest, his eyes lidless and staring. Inscrutable characters danced in the space beside him. If I could interpret them, I would have no need to seek out the place called Ksadaja, a name that Lady Nasrin had uttered like a curse.

I stared at the page until my fire turned to dull embers, but still the writing remained a mystery. I dreamed of the undead that night, of the king under Kannaoka, his clouded eyes gleaming. Blood pooled at his feet, and he raised his skeletal arms in a triumphal pose, declaring with a voice like a death rattle that he would live forever.

I woke, trembling with a nameless fear, to find the book open to the same page beside my bedroll.

I snapped it shut with one hand and buried it at the bottom of my pack, underneath parcels of dried fish and my spare set of clothing, and vowed not to remove it until I had found someone who could read it and was willing to do so.

I did not wish to live forever, I told the last fleeting memories of my dream, and neither did I wish it for Khalim. I wanted one lifetime for him, one spent at my side. I had no plans to endure the ages of the world from an underground tomb, a lightless place that surely Khalim would not bear.

I was nothing like the ruined king of Kannaoka.

With my camp packed and Bran's saddlebags returned to their places on his back, we walked the last miles to the city gates. The spires shone bright as tiny suns in the morning light, piercing my eyes whenever I lifted them from our narrow, rocky trail. We passed a pair of small goats, chewing the spiny grasses, and then their minder, a boy of no more than ten, asleep beneath a prickly shrub with his dark hair tangled in its branches. Vast, tilled fields stretched out all around the city walls, turning the seaside hills into a familiar quilt of gold and green. I had seen a pattern like it hanging on the loom of Khalim's mother, in the now-distant village of Nagara.

The wall around the city was yellow stone, worn smooth by the wind and encrusted in a faint layer of salt. Two heavy wooden doors, painted a soft sky-blue, formed its gate. Two men dressed in turbans wound around their pointed helmets examined my bags and my weapons.

"What's this?" the first man asked, gesturing to the dragon-tooth head of my spear. Though his accent was strange, I recognized the words from many a tale the crew of the *Lady of Osona* had told to me. If I lingered long enough here, I thought I might see that fair ship again.

"A fishing spear," I told the watchman. It was not quite a lie. Attempting to fish with the lightning weapon might cause more trouble than it was worth, but it was the same size and shape as its mundane kin.

He hefted the spear and, finding nothing amiss, handed it back to me. His companion opened my pack, removing some rations and my desert cloak before returning them to their places. If he saw the book, he noticed nothing unusual about it. I was permitted to enter the city.

I did not find the *Lady of Osona* in its harbor. What I found instead was the *Sun's Flame*, a sleek, shallow vessel underneath one brilliant yellow sail. Her captain was a tall, broad-shouldered man with his hair in countless tiny braids that glinted with golden ornaments. He read some question on my face and asked if I needed a ship.

"I am going to a place called Ksadaja," I said, forming the foreign syllables carefully. "Have you heard of it?"

I waited for this man to deny that he had ever heard tell of such a place, or to curse me for my evil intent in seeking it out, but he only smiled. "Of course," he said. "I was born there, in the city among the tombs, in the shadow of the great trees. Are you a pilgrim?"

"I suppose I am a pilgrim, of sorts," I replied.

He smiled a knowing smile. "I am Ramla, son of Tau. The sea called me away from Ksadaja many years ago, but I have returned from time to time. For the right price, I could be persuaded to make another journey there."

He did not inquire as to the nature of my pilgrimage, and in turn I would not ask what had called him to a life of sailing. The call of the sea is a terrible, wonderful thing. It had summoned me in my youth, and as much renown and adventure as it had given me, it had taken much more in payment. I would not demand that Ramla give me an accounting of all that he had gained and lost.

I gave him the last of my coins, and a portion of the dried fish I still carried, and persuaded Bran to climb the plank to the deck. After so long on the shifting sands, he had felt solid ground beneath his hooves and eaten fresh greenery for only a short time. I promised him that we would return to a green land again.

My road turned south, then, across the summer sea—no mountains of ice floated among these sapphire waves. I might have called them gentle, in comparison to the sea in the north, but I knew better than to trust their appearance. On the first evening, a bank of low, violet clouds foretold of a storm coming to disturb the water.

But Ramla steered us ahead of it, and by the time it reached us, it had diminished to only a little rain on the deck and enough wind to fill the golden sail. We crossed the last miles with the gods' own swiftness, and soon a green-black mass arose in the south, cut through with the pale shapes of towering obelisks. Here was the great forest, emerging from the waves. Before it lay the city of tombs.

These stepped pyramids of red stone, huge and ponderous, encircled the harbor. In their high halls and in the labyrinth of tunnels underneath them, the bodies of the esteemed dead awaited the call of their gods, who at the end of an age of calamity would bring them once again to life and place them as rulers over the transformed world. The obelisks, carved with prayers to the same gods, stood like sentries between the temples, greeting us as Ramla's ship made its way into the harbor.

In the shadows of the tombs, the people of Ksadaja went about the business of the living, smiling and laughing as though death did not haunt their every footstep. They dressed vibrant colors and intricate patterns, the fabric wound around their tall, lithe forms and draped over one arm to stir in the breeze from the ocean. One woman carried a basket atop her head, her back as straight as the shaft of a spear, and her small child clung to her garment, watching me disembark with huge, dark eyes until his mother pulled him away toward the market.

I led Bran down from the ship and onto the dock. His hooves struck the salt-stained boards, and he took off ahead of me at a trot. I ran to catch up, worried he'd startle the folk in the market and draw more eyes to me than I wanted.

The presence of a steppe horse, however, lifted only a few eyes from the market stalls. Two more horses walked into view, pulling a heavy cart on four wooden wheels. These were great beasts, their shoulders as high as my head, their coats mottled in the colors of sand and clay. Bran's only notable feature was his diminutive size.

I bade farewell to Ramla, and thanked him for the journey and all that he had told me of his home.

A flock of gulls darted screaming overhead, announcing the arrival of a well-laden fishing boat. Stands selling food and trinkets from beneath colorful awnings lined the docks, with merchants adding their own cries to the cacophony.

"Spices from the southern isles!" proclaimed one. "Silks from the East!" declared another.

The silks and a fine collection of golden jewelry shimmered in the sun. The heavy smell of mingled spices hung in the air like a fog, spreading out from the harbor and well into the city. The temples and the trees beyond, each as high as the Iron Mountain itself, cast a twilight shadow onto the farthest shops even at midday. Not in the jungles of the South nor the mountains of the North had I ever seen a forest so magnificent. Its canopy was like the roof of the world, its boughs so thick and so tightly woven together that sunlight did not reach the forest floor.

"Buy a charm, my lord," the high voice of a young merchant said, piercing through the din of the harbor. "For yourself, and for your lady. You'll never grow ill or feel the bite of a weapon."

Even here, where death was so close at hand, it was something to be feared and avoided. I turned. A young girl, tall and thin as a reed, held out a clever device of knotted silver wire hanging on a fine chain. It caught the sunlight, and a dazzling pattern of reflected light fell across Bran's black flank.

"It's a pretty thing, but I have no lady," I told her, "and nothing can make a man live forever."

She smiled, showing a gap between her front teeth. Her black hair was gathered in two braids that fell to her waist, and she wore a plain dress of a dull, dark green hue, at odds with the colorful array of the others in the marketplace. From her bare arms and her slender neck hung an array of silver bands and dangling chains. "By the grace of the tomb-gods, death comes for all of us," she said. "But one can delay it, even for many years, by the wisdom of my master. All of these charms are made by his own hand. This one will protect you from storms at sea, and this one will hide you from the eyes of your enemies." She held up two more silver baubles.

"Who is your master?" I asked.

A jangle of metal sounded as she folded her arms over her chest. "You must be newly arrived to Ksadaja," she said. "My master is Deinaros the All-Knowing, of the upper city. He can cure any illness and see into the future, and the specter of death is his intimate friend. Ask anyone, and they will tell you."

I doubted most of these claims, but here was a self-professed prophet who claimed knowledge of death and who sent a child out to exchange promises for coin. Surely he lacked the scruples of the priestesses of Isra's Well. "Does this Deinaros know how to read?" I asked.

The girl's face turned to disdain. "Of course he does. He's all-knowing."

"My apologies," I said. "I would like to meet your master. Where does he live?"

"I'm not supposed to tell just anyone that," she said.

"But I am a champion of the great tournament of Phyreios, and I have traveled a great long way to meet a sage such as this one. I'm sure he'd allow an exception."

She considered this, sharp dark eyes examining me in a way that was too like the appraising gaze of the priestess Fenin. I feared the next words out of her mouth would be to condemn me to die in the desert.

"We shall see," she said. "Follow me, then, great champion. If you can keep up, maybe my master will agree to see you."

The girl led me through the market, her trinkets ringing like tiny bells and catching the afternoon sunlight, glittering from shoulder to wrist. I guessed her to be about twelve years of age. She wore straw sandals with fraying edges, and her steps on the stone pavement whispered like wind through a stand of reeds, disappearing under the din of the market and the roar of the surf receding behind us. The streets sloped upward toward the tombs, but my guide's steps neither slowed nor faltered as she climbed. She glanced over her shoulder once, to see if I still followed, her face indifferent.

At the edge of the square, a grain merchant stepped out from behind her stall and into my path. She held up a hand to stop me, and Bran and I came to a halt. The girl continued on, passing underneath the obelisks.

"Why are you following that girl?" the merchant asked. She was tall and stately, with her hair covered in a silk wrap the color of the sea.

I bowed, watching over the woman's shoulder to find where the girl had gone. She would not come back for me if I fell behind. "I wish to speak to her master," I said. "I mean her no harm."

I must have appeared sincere, because the merchant lowered her hand. "Her teacher is a heretic."

"It makes little difference to me what gods he worships," I said. "I have questions that perhaps a heretic can answer. The consequences will be mine to bear."

"Be careful, then." She retreated to her stall and busied her hands with sweeping chaff from her table. "He is a treacherous man. The will of the gods of the tombs means nothing to him, and thus he has instructed the girl. If you are slain on the forest floor, and your body is consumed by the fungus, never to rise again, you cannot claim you weren't warned."

"I thank you for the warning." I could subdue a young girl, if the need arose, and I did not imagine this Deinaros would pose more of a threat than the priests who had held the book I now carried. As for the rest, I would rather have been returned to the sea after death, but a quiet rest on the forest floor sounded much more appealing than resurrection.

The road from the market square to the forest was a wide, paved thoroughfare scattered with dust and fallen leaves. It passed between two of the grandest tombs: towering stone edifices covered from the ground to their peaks in carved characters, filled in with paint in deep black and brilliant blue. The colors shone in the sun as though they were freshly painted, shimmering like gemstones or the surface of the sea.

The girl crouched at the corner of the left-hand pyramid, leaning against the corner. "I thought you'd gotten lost already," she declared.

"Not yet." With a nod to the painted words behind her, I added, "What do the carvings say?"

She stood, glancing at the stone face of the tomb. "Prayers, protective spells, words of scripture," she said. "They were carved centuries ago, and the priests maintain them. Very few can read the text now, and fewer still can write it."

"Can you read it?" I asked.

She shook her head. "My master can, though. He says the gods who gave us the script abandoned us long ago, and they deserve to be forgotten, so he hasn't taught it to me."

I pulled Bran closer. The shadow of the forest fell at my feet, and the wind coming from the darkness blew cold and smelled of wet earth.

"Come along, champion," the girl said. "Don't touch the mushrooms. They are better used for holy days."

Above, the trees closed in, and the sky disappeared behind their woven branches. They formed an arch higher than even the tallest of the sepulchers. As my eyes adjusted to the sudden darkness, the lights of the upper city appeared, flickering and golden in the distance. The city behind us, under the clear sky, grew darker. Even the temples receded into shadow.

The trees were so large that I could have believed we walked between walls of mountain stone. Each trunk filled the span of my vision, rising ever upward into the black clouds of the canopy. Fifty men with their arms outstretched could not encircle a single tree.

Dead leaves, damp and sticky, covered the pavement in vast drifts. Some time ago, laborers had cleared the road with shovels, but more had fallen since. Each leaf was nearly as long from tip to stem as I was tall. Bran's hooves left crescent marks in the veined surfaces, which bled green under our feet. The lights in the trees grew stronger, but they hovered in the air hundreds of feet above our heads.

The girl strayed off the path to a hollow between the rises of two great roots and pulled out a cloak and an oil-soaked torch. She rummaged in her pockets for a flint and steel and sent a shower of sparks falling to the rotting vegetation at her feet, where they sputtered and died. A pool of orange light chased away the nearest shadows. Thus we made our way through the uncanny, premature night.

"How much farther?" I asked.

"Not far," was the answer.

From the gloom appeared the fungus. Low hills, colored a shadowy purple and ridged with a pale, sickly white, rose from the forest floor. Beyond them, the mushroom stalks rose, blooming into discs that stretched across the road. If I let my eyes linger upon them, they appeared to expand and contract with slow, steady breaths. More fungus climbed the trunks of the trees, jutting out like stairs, brilliant orange and pale yellow.

Bran exhaled against my shoulder. I touched his nose with one hand, reassuring him. The sunlit city stood at my back. If I had to flee, I could find it again.

More lights emerged, this time at eye level. As I followed the girl, they resolved into lanterns encased in glass, flanking a magnificent staircase that spiraled around one vast trunk. It rose into the canopy until the broad branches and fluttering leaves hid it from view.

Another staircase appeared, and then another, one as broad as the steps climbing the pyramids and the other as narrow as the steps that led from the deck to the belly of a ship. Above, the lights of the upper city were as a tapestry of golden stars.

The girl darted between two trees and climbed a path hidden under low branches. I tethered Bran to the carved railing, leaving him with a portion of dried grasses and hardy grains. He snorted and tossed his head.

"It will be all right," I said. "Wait here for me."

I followed the girl. I tired before she did, ascending the spiral stair, the heavy air weighing down on my chest and slowing my steps. From the boughs emerged the upper city, the trees ringed in platforms of lacquered wood, with elegant carvings around doorways that led into the bodies of the trees and bridges spanning the air between them. Patrols of guards paced the walkways, dressed in golden armor. They wore tall boots with hard soles and carried spears balanced for throwing in their hands. Short, curved blades hung at their hips. They spoke to one another in a language I did not know, though I recognized a few words—*evening* and *tomorrow*, *mother* and *friend*. Moss and climbing vines hung from each platform and the underside of each bridge.

The girl reached a high platform and set off across a narrow bridge. It swung under my weight, pitching like a ship at sea. I clung to the moss-laden ropes that served as a handrail and pulled myself across. My eyes strayed to the edge of the bridge and the black abyss beneath, crossed with more bridges, and my stomach turned.

We arrived at another platform below the crown of one tree, overgrown with vegetation and scattered with bits of dead leaves. A high doorway had been carved into the trunk and fitted with a heavy wooden door, its brass fittings shining under a layer of oil to protect them from the damp. The girl pulled a leather cord from the collar of her dress, untangling it from the mass of silver chains.

"You're here," she said.

"It was not so difficult to follow you," I replied.

She put the key in the door and turned it with both hands, her trinkets jangling. "It's easy to find my master, but he only helps the worthy."

"And how does he decide who is worthy?"

The door opened. The girl's torch illuminated a cavernous space and the shape of a spiraling staircase in the center. Around it, an austere entry hall took form, with carved stone seats against walls covered in woven tapestries, but the darkness was too thick to discern what images they showed, even in the presence of the light. A strange smell lingered about the place, like copper and burning herbs, overcoming the scent of wet leaves.

She affixed the torch to the wall beside the door and shed her sandals before crossing the room to mount the steps. "Why do you want to see my master?"

I entered the room, and the door shut behind me, shaking the structure. "I've brought him a book from the southern isles," I said. "I was told that it was first written here, in the necropolis of Ksadaja. I've come to find someone who can interpret it."

The girl smiled, a cold, mirthless grin that did not match her young features. "You are wise. Many can read a book, but few can interpret it."

I could do neither, but I would not tell her so. "When can I see the all-knowing one? Is he above?" The stairs descended into the depths of the tree, as well as ascending. I frowned and studied her small, brown face again. The grain merchant had mentioned her teacher, but had not said anything about having ever seen him. "Or are you the all-knowing one, and this is but a test I must pass?"

She laughed, the cold smile falling away to reveal childish delight. "No, he is at the top of the tree, observing the movement of the sun. He will come down soon. You may ascend one floor and wait for him."

With that, she climbed the stairs, disappearing into the deeper darkness above. I went after her, ancient wooden steps creaking under my weight.

I arrived at the next floor, a mirror to the first, though this one possessed slitted windows at regular intervals around its circumference. The dim lights of the upper city provided little illumination, but a pair of oil lamps burned from a set of shelves against one wall. Bundles of dried herbs, the husks of insects the size of my hand, and crooked, shriveled things that might have been roots and might have been severed fingers lay scattered in the wavering pools of light. Small, fanged skulls gleamed white between them.

"What is this place?" I wondered aloud.

The girl, already a floor above me, ignored my question. "Wait here," she said, and climbed away out of sight.

I walked around the circular tower, examining the tapestry and the herbs and avoiding the unidentified objects. From the bottom of the ascending stairs, my guide had hung several more bunches of herbs wrapped in twine, as well as a second dress in a faded blue, still damp from washing.

What little sunlight made its way through the canopy disappeared from the windows, and the city lights went out, one by one. Night was falling, and I was trapped here, in a room of strange trophies that was also the dwelling place of one small girl, with my horse on the forest floor far below. I tugged at the strap of my spear. This space was too cramped to throw it, if the need arose. The weight of my pack made my shoulders ache, but I refused to remove it—I would keep the book on my person.

The girl appeared again, bare feet first. "Ascend," she said. "Deinaros will see you now."

~ XXII ~

THE SORCERER'S TOWER

I climbed the stairs. The walls of the hollow tree, etched with the marks of a hundred or more chisels, constricted around me. Even within them, the forest's damp air, tinged with growth and rot in equal measures, clung to my skin and filled my nostrils.

On the third floor from the arched entrance, a diminutive man in a long garment sat in a high-backed chair, facing the staircase. A pair of tapestries flanked him, each tattered on the bottom edge, the stark white figures of dancing skeletons picked out in thread against a soft, dark background of swirling blue currents. The girl stood to one side, half-hidden in shadow, her hands tucked into hidden pockets in her skirt. She had shed her many baubles.

"Welcome, outlander," the man said. His voice was a low, rasping murmur, too easily lost in the sound of the wind through the branches outside.

I bowed, and I dropped my pack from my shoulder at last. "I have come here to seek your help in the matter of a certain book," I said. "I have heard that you are called the All-Knowing. I hope you can aid me."

"Let me see the book." He reached out a hand.

He was younger than I had expected, his hair deep black, falling around his shoulders in a cascade of braids, and his eyes sharp. A long, thin hand emerged from his voluminous sleeve, the dark skin smooth and unlined. On one finger sat a silver ring, set with a deep blue jewel.

I produced the volume from my pack and held it out, hesitating. As much as I detested it, I had carried it for so long that giving it away was like parting from an old friend. In the damp, the leather cover stuck to my fingers, warm as living flesh.

I placed it in Deinaros' hand.

Deinaros took the book and opened it, laying it flat across his outstretched palms. Another drawing of a man's carcass, hollow but for the swirling currents in his chest, stared out from the page with blackened eyes.

"How did this book come to be in your possession?" Deinaros asked.

"I took it from a king who wished to live forever, and the priest who performed the necessary rituals, on an island far from here," I said.

He turned the page, revealing the gate of bone, rendered in exquisite detail. "You will tell me of your journey," he said. "But for now, I ask you this: is it your wish to evade the clutches of death? You are a young man, yet, but I see the scars of battle upon you. You would not be the first to come to me with such a request, but no others have brought me such a treasure."

"I will die when fate decrees it," I said. "I wish only to travel beyond death for a short time—as long as it takes to retrieve one who did not die, but was unjustly stolen from life."

Deinaros' smile was kindly, though his eyes remained flint-hard. "I have entertained many a pilgrim in these long years. Some come to me like you did, from lands beyond the sea. Others fall out of favor in the upper city or the lower, fail to pay their tithes, and turn to me in their hour of need."

"And what do you provide for them?"

He closed the book, holding it with loving care between his elegant hands. "Shelter, of course, and protection from the golden-armored guards. My home has many rooms. Mostly, though, I offer hope that the world will be different, when the gods return, than what has been promised."

"In the marketplace, they call you a heretic," I said.

"They always have, and they will for a great while longer." He raised a hand, and the girl curtsied and moved around the room, lighting lamps that smelled of rancid oil. In the wavering light, the embroidered skeletons on the walls danced.

"The priests of the lower city tell of the return of the gods," Deinaros continued, "when the world will be remade, and those who rest in the great tombs will rule at the right hand of the divine, while those buried in common graves will serve at their pleasure. The priests of the upper city tell a similar story, though their tombs are high among the trees, cradled in living wood. When the gods come, the honored dead will rule as they did in life, and those whose hands and backs built both kingdoms will labor as they always have."

"It's an old story," I said. "I have heard its like before." In my homeland, we told tales of hunting great beasts alongside our gods in the world beyond. Only the strong would be given such an honor. Those who could not hunt and fight in life were destined for the fields of ice, a cold, blank stretch of land where they would wander forever.

Only now did I understand that this fate might be unjust. Most of the companions I had met and loved since then had been warriors, yes, but not all of them. I would not condemn Khalim to an eternity of wandering because he took up his charge as a healer, nor Garvesh for pursuing a life as a scholar and orator. Even this Deinaros, I thought, heretic though he might be, deserved a better afterlife than that.

"An old story, yes," he said. "But it isn't the only one we can tell. There are other gods here, in this holiest of lands. There are also other means by which a mortal man can claim power—even the power over death. This book contains a certain ritual that I have long sought but could not find. It will require much of you, outlander, and more of me."

"My name is Eske," I said.

He rose, his robes flowing around him like spilled water. He was taller than I had assumed; nearly as tall as I. "Well done, Eske," he said, holding the book aloft. "This copy is nearly complete. The lengthy musings of my former master are the only things missing. Everything useful is here."

"Your master wrote it?" I asked. "He must have traveled as far as I have."

He folded his arms into his sleeves, and the book vanished in folds of cloth. "He penned the original, centuries ago. He never left the city of his birth. His followers, myself among them, made copies, and those who found those copies made more still."

My heart sank. With so many of these books loose in the world, how many ambitious rulers became like the king of Kannaoka, their souls clinging to their bodies even as their flesh rotted and fell away from their bones? A second, selfish question followed the first: how many ill-starred lovers, grieving parents, and lonely widows had found the book and attempted the same task I had undertaken? Had the gods already taken up arms against a sea of sorrowful humanity, building their defenses in preparation against one such as I?

"Very few now remain," Deinaros said. "It was purged from the kingdoms of the West. So many were burned that the pyres reached the heavens. I have not seen a word or line from this book in many years."

That was a small relief. "I do not wish to defy death," I said. "Nor do I wish to bind a soul to my will, draping it in an object, or to sacrifice the blood of innocents to extend a life. I want nothing but what the gods grant to each of us."

"And what might that be, outlander?" asked Deinaros. His garment shimmered in shades of blue and violet. All-knowing or not, he was a wealthy man.

"One life, returned to him from whom it was stolen, and with which to do as he chooses," I said.

A thin smile split Deinaros' face. "That sounds rather like defying death, but I am not here to sit in judgment against you."

"Judge if you wish, as long as you'll help me," I said. "Khalim did not die. A god took his body and sent his soul to the place beyond death. It is this god whom I wish to defy, and bring Khalim back to the world—no more and no less."

Deinaros brushed past me, making his way toward the stairs. His footsteps were quiet on soft-soled shoes, and the lamps wavered as he passed. "We will have plenty of time to argue the specifics," he said. "For now, I will study the book and regain the memories I have lost in the long years since last I laid eyes on it. You may rest here. The girl will see to your needs."

He ascended the stairs in a sweep of rich fabric. A door opened on oiled hinges and closed again.

The girl waited for me, shifting her weight between her feet. Her eyes lingered on the floor, and her small mouth twisted into a scowl. "Come with me, I suppose," she said with a sigh.

"Your hospitality is appreciated," I said, offering her a smile. "What's your name, little one?"

"Cricket," she answered.

My grasp of the language must have failed me. "Cricket?" I repeated.

She nodded. "The guest rooms are on the floor below the entrance. You're not permitted to descend any lower without an invitation from Deinaros. If you try, I can't help you."

"Does your master keep a great beast chained on the lower floors?" I asked with a grin. "Or has he woven magics that will sap my strength and steal my blood for his rituals?"

Her answer was a look of utter disdain. "Find out for yourself, if you're so curious."

"I can do as I'm told," I said, and bowed.

She took a lamp from the wall and led me into the bowels of the tree, past the receiving room with its grotesque collections and the great door that led to the city suspended in the air. The guest quarters were eight arched doorways, each carved into living wood and set with a heavy door. By some logic unknown to me, Cricket chose one on the right and opened it. A narrow bed draped in a woven blanket and a thick, gray fur sat beneath a darkened window. Another fur lay on the ground, halfway under the bed frame. Wax from an old candle pooled on the windowsill and dripped down the wall.

It was better than my tent. I had so rarely slept in my own room, enclosed in four walls; I had spent my youth sleeping six to a room, side by side in another lord's hall, or pressed in between rowing benches on a longship. This small room was as luxurious as it was lonely.

"I should see to my horse," I said.

With unexpected enthusiasm, Cricket bounded toward the stairs. "I'll do it."

"There's no need," I said. "Surely you have more pressing matters to attend to."

She stopped, turning on her heel. "Master Deinaros wants me to dust the library again, as soon as I've seen to you," she said. "And I hate dusting the library. The books are so old, and the spines are weak, and things try to escape." She held out one arm, turning it to show a long, thin scar reaching from her wrist halfway to her elbow.

"I see." The book I had carried, ominous though it was, had never attacked me in the night. I thought she might be testing my credulousness, and the scar was nothing but the relic of an encounter with an ornery cat or a tumble from the lower branches of the trees.

"My master collects books," Cricket continued. "I'm not permitted to read them. I can, though, and write, too."

I entered the small room, placing my pack on the bed and taking the spear from my back. "You're quite accomplished for your age," I said. "But you're young to have taken on such an apprenticeship. Deinaros demands much of you."

She spread her arms in a languid shrug. "He bought me from the flesh-market in Nyssodes. It's a lot of work, but I'm learning magic. Someday I'll have a tree of my own."

"And your own collection of forbidden books, I suppose," I said.

Cricket nodded. "But not the ones that bite."

She assured me that she had handled a horse before, and I was not the first pilgrim to have brought one to the foot of the upper city, and bounded up the stairs again.

I thought to ask her, when next she appeared, what else this tower might be hiding, or what sort of books unleashed creatures upon their caretakers, or what lay below the room where I was to sleep, but I decided against it. I had only to wait, and to care for Bran, and to complete whatever tasks Deinaros had for me. He was no High Priest Ucasta, sacrificing young girls to maintain a life long expired; though she was a little overworked, given the size of the hollow tree she had to maintain, Cricket was hale and well. Surely this place was an improvement over the flesh-market, a term that conjured images of the bodies of humans and animals strung from butcher's hooks to bleed dry.

I had crossed half the world, I reassured myself as I went to sleep. All that was left was to wait.

~ XXIII ~

INTERLUDE THREE: THE BROKEN ROAD

Khalim took a breath. Cold spread from the inside of his chest, where his heart only shivered instead of beating, down to his feet and the tips of his fingers.

The beast rose out of the underbrush, its forelimbs as thick as tree trunks. Under its weight, the earth groaned, the only sound in the rain-scented darkness. Thick, black hair covered each arm and the shadowed body, wet and shiny in the scarlet glow of its eyes. Below its white mask, two rows of sharp teeth stretched out in a sinister smile—the smile of a man, Khalim thought, not of a wolf baring its teeth. A bright, sinister intelligence stared out from behind the mask of bone, and it fixed its gaze on Khalim.

"Is this your mother?" he whispered to the child still clinging to his back.

In response, the boy released his grasp from Khalim's shoulders and slid to the ground, where he crouched beside the ridge of a buried flagstone and hummed a low, flat note.

Here, in the heavy quiet over the ruins of an afterlife long forgotten, the gray shades of the other dead had all disappeared, their ghostly cries of despair and confusion fallen silent. Even the wind was still. The shapes of trees, black in the glow from the creature's eyes, closed in around Khalim, and the cold was like a weight bearing down on him. Fragments of pale stone erupted from the earth, grasped in dark roots. He had believed himself alone among the other shades as they had followed their wandering paths unseeing and unhearing. Now he was truly without help.

"I mean you no harm," he said.

The beast only grinned, lowering its enormous head. The child left Khalim's side, striding on all fours like a monkey, and climbed up the pillar of the creature's forelimb. Other shapes, black on black, moved in the beast's thick coat, the edges of their masks catching slivers of red light.

As the great creature bent down, sniffing the air with nostrils obscured behind its mask, its eyes glowed brighter, setting its body, the trees, and Khalim ablaze in cold light. The mask was as wide as the reach of Khalim's arms, its polished surface pitted and scarred. He backed away from the spearhead teeth, his feet finding the ridges of the buried highway.

The forest canopy lowered behind the creature's head. No, that wasn't right—the beast wore a mantle of crooked branches, a grove of twisted trees growing from its shoulders, fur tangling among the roots like grass. The blaze from its eyes cast eerie shadows on deep knots and rough, ridged bark. The knots made faces in the trees, open mouths and hollow eyes limned in red, frozen into expressions of horror.

The creature's breath stirred Khalim's hair. He held up his hands. "I—I brought the little one back," he said, useless as it was. The little one had led him here. He stood now in the jaws of a trap, just as the child had.

A face in the tree just above the beast's left eye stretched its mouth into a huge, dark hollow and screamed.

Khalim ducked under the vast bone mask and ran between the creature's towering limbs. The light vanished, and his feet slipped on roots slick with recent rain, his hands striking smooth bark and damp earth. The beast turned, slow and inexorable as time, shaking the earth with every step.

He stumbled over the crests of rubble, and thorny vines caught at his hair and his ragged clothing. His chest ached with cold and the habitual, futile attempt to breathe. No matter how much of the mist passed through his body, he took slow, clumsy steps, his feet mired in wintry chill.

The creature pursued. On its back, the faces of the trees moaned and cried, a chorus of pain and suffering that drowned out even the crash of its footsteps. Their faces were too like a human being's, their voices too much like children in pain. Here, then, were the missing spirits, rooted in place instead of wandering, the twisted branches of their limbs stiff and immobile and their faces masks of terror, able to do nothing but scream.

In the citadel, Khalim had turned to stone. Here he would turn to wood, or else he would be eaten, torn apart between the beast's bladed teeth.

His hands found the wet bark of a giant tree. He followed the curve of its trunk, groping his way over the ridges of its roots. The bark compressed beneath the heel of his palm, releasing the sickly smell of rot. Its branches shuddered as the earth shook.

He placed the tree between himself and the advancing beast. A jagged black tear, devoid of even the reflected light of the creature's eyes, opened into a hollow space in the trunk—a lightless, airless chamber that stank of decay and a long-forgotten fire.

Khalim had no hope of outrunning the beast. He slipped between the edges of splintery bark and fell into the tree.

His back met soft, wet wood, rotted into an earthy mass that cushioned his fall and grasped at his hands. Something with many tiny, prickling legs crawled over his arms, chittering in agitation.

I'm sorry, he thought, not daring to speak. *Please, please be quiet.*

The opening in the tree lay above his head, a gash of dark gray against the blackness of the hollow space. He drew his knees to his chest, dragging himself away from the stretch of obscured sky until a wall of wood met his back. The tree shook with the approach of the beast, raining splinters onto his head, and the wind sang with the keening cries of the cursed grove upon its back. Unseen insects moved around his ears, fleeing into their tiny burrows and hidden nests.

Khalim closed his eyes and clenched his fists, reminding himself not to breathe. Wet splinters bent between his fingers. If the power of the white city could turn him to stone, and whatever eldritch power this masked behemoth possessed could turn a shade into a twisted tree, then perhaps he could turn to rotting wood for a short while and avoid the attention of this glowing-eyed monstrosity and its young. Loud, snuffling breaths whistled past the creature's bone mask as it approached.

He wanted to pray, but there was no one to listen. Once, he had carried a god with him, and though he did not ask for much, whatever he had sought had been granted: safety, reassurance, the power to heal—and, only once, the power to kill. With these gifts, he'd had nothing to fear. Nothing could harm him in any way that mattered.

He should never have left the citadel.

This was no punishment. He had no pretensions of the continued attention of the god he had abandoned. No, he had met the predictable consequences of wandering with no guide, no plan, and no protection. The moon-faced owl had warned him.

Huge, dark claws scratched at the bark of his hiding place.

If Khalim had possessed a spear, or even a sharpened stick, he might have wedged it through the gap in the bark and injured the creature. But Khalim had never had a spear. He'd never held a weapon. There had never been any war to be waged in Nagara, over its few miles of rice fields and muddy embankment deep in the woods. Besides, he had been a healer, trained as well as divinely blessed. Even if broken flesh hadn't called out to him to be made whole in a voice that could not be ignored, as it had when the god had been with him, he would have been far more useful away from the fighting.

And what was he now? Another lost soul in the spirit wilds, about to be consumed and then forgotten, his name lost and his face worn by a god upon the earth. No one, living or dead, would remember that Khalim had ever been.

Red light flickered at the edge of the hollow like tongues of flame.

He put his arms over his head—the insects had long since hidden themselves away, and no more pinprick legs troubled his skin—and prayed to no one that what came next wouldn't hurt.

The beast paused, its earth-shaking footsteps stilling. The chorus of fear and pain that followed it quieted to a murmur. Its claws tapped together with a series of metallic clicks as it rummaged through the underbrush.

I'm just a ghost, Khalim said silently. *You can't see me. I'm a ghost, and you're a lot of ghosts, and none of this is real.*

If he had stayed in the white city, he would have been safe now. He'd have turned to stone, a silent watchman over an empty square, years passing like minutes as the sun stood still above the pale horizon, but he'd be safe.

But he had left, and here he was. He had his name, at least.

I'm not here, he pleaded with the creature. *I've gone away, I'm somewhere else where you can't find me, and you can go back to your home.*

A single red eye blazed in the gap in the bark. The tree cracked under the weight of a massive paw.

I'm not here.

Light—bright, yellow sunlight, something Khalim could only just remember ever witnessing—flooded the tree. The rotten trunk gave way beneath him, and he fell, slipping between gnarled roots and softened splinters. He covered his eyes against the blaze. The night had endured for so long, and before that he had seen only endless twilight. The wind tore at his clothing as he plummeted through empty air, squirming insects and bits of wood falling around him.

He should have been afraid, but there was no time. He landed hard on solid ground, dry grass crunching under his back. He opened his eyes to a vast stretch of blue sky, shimmering like water.

Where am I?

He got to his feet, blinking in the searing daylight. An undulating sea of grass, all the color of gold, surrounded him on all sides. It was beautiful, and it went on forever.

Khalim was lost again.

He turned in a slow circle, marking each identical horizon. The forest was gone, so far away that it didn't even make a dark spot in the distant sky. No smiling, sharp-toothed monster emerged from the grass. Instead, a wandering shade far in the distant cast a faint shadow, and another picked its way through, sending ripples across the field.

"Did I do this?" he said aloud. His voice was lost in the wind sweeping over the plain.

He reached out and broke a stalk of grass between his fingers. The edges of the blade scratched at his skin, and it smelled of heat and dust.

Khalim walked in the land of the dead—the land of gods where faith and will held sway, and distance was a matter of thought. He could go anywhere he wanted; anywhere he could possibly imagine.

The grass shifted around him, and the wind sang a song of long roads. Khalim's heart, or the memory of it, shivered. Cold fear settled into his belly.

He could go anywhere he wanted. Not once in his life, not until he had left the white city, had he ever chosen where to walk. His god had directed him, and so had others—Reva, who wanted to keep him hidden from the Ascended, and Eske, who would have done anything to save him. Despite all their efforts, here he was.

Khalim walked, alone, through the field of ghosts.

~ XXIV ~

AMONG THE HERETICS

For nearly three years I would dwell in the tower of Deinaros the All-Knowing, at once a guest, a servant, and a student, much like the girl Cricket. Had I known at the start of my period of servitude that I would remain in Ksadaja so long, I might have left, abandoning the book and its interpreter alike, and continued my journey alone. As it was, I remained, the promise of the ritual tethering me to this place day after sunless day.

Each morning, I left the tree by way of the hanging bridges and the long, spiraling staircase to tend to Bran and accompany Cricket to the market in the lower city. Cricket had placed my horse among the towering steeds of the city watch and the broad draft-horses that carried goods between the harbor and the forest. In heavy carts, they pulled bolts of silk in a spectrum of colors, fish, and grain to the upper city's waiting attendants, and left the next day laden with dried fungus that granted prophetic dreams when consumed with wine and carefully selected timbers from the great trees.

With his even temperament, Bran had no quarrel with his larger neighbors. He was, by my reckoning, about nine years of age when we arrived in Ksadaja. He would serve valiantly for a number of years hence, but if my journey were to continue further, I would one day have to bid him farewell or risk his safety.

Surely, I thought, it would not come to that. I had delivered the book and its terrible images to one who could read it; a follower, no less, of the man who had first set feathered pen to vellum page and inscribed its secrets. He would summon me to his study on the upper floor at any moment, and I would cross through the gate of bone to find Khalim at last.

But days passed, and weeks, and I saw Deinaros but rarely. He kept strange hours, his footsteps moving above my tiny room, tracing recursive, circular paths at all hours of the day and night. If he ever slept, it was in short bursts at odd times.

Other pilgrims came to his door: furtive folk from the lower city, hoods and scarves obscuring their faces; travelers from across the sea with pale eyes and paler skin, seeking more powerful charms than the ones Cricket sold in the marketplace; noblemen from elsewhere in the trees, each accompanied only by a single bodyguard with an impassive face, sworn to secrecy on pain of death. One evening, as I returned from my daily wanderings, I witnessed Cricket opening the door for a man with the face of a lion, wreathed in golden fur. She showed neither surprise nor wonder at his appearance. I, too, had once seen such a man—in the Cerean Tournament, so long ago.

Cricket left the tower each morning to sell her trinkets at the harbor. Most days, I accompanied her, if only to spend some time in the sun and give Bran some needed exercise. I feared the girl might be robbed, at best, weighed down as she was by such a quantity of silver. At worst, I had only just learned of the flesh-markets of Nyssodes. A clever kidnapper needed only to coincide with a waiting ship, and Cricket would never have returned to the tower.

She bade me keep my distance, though, when we reached the docks. She had charms to sell, and my looming presence frightened away her customers. I asked if she were afraid, and if she had the means to defend herself if need be.

In answer, she showed me two objects on her person: a sharp knife hidden in a skirt pocket, the length of a finger and curved like a claw, and a thin golden chain around her neck, hidden under the abundance of silver. Each link was no bigger than a grain of sand and no thicker than a spider's web, and it had no clasp and could not be removed except by severing it.

"There's magic in it," she explained. "Deinaros can find me if he ever loses me."

I did not ask what sort of magic this might be, and neither did I inquire what would happen if Cricket were to be killed before Deinaros could locate her. Deinaros had the book now, and with it he might bind Cricket's soul to her flesh, like the high priest had done for King Sondassan, ensuring that his apprentice could return to the market the next day with only a grayish cast to her face to suggest that she was only pretending at life. For that transgression against the ways of the gods, I would bear the blame, as I had given this strange man the artifact that others had encouraged me to burn.

I silenced these doubting thoughts, insisting to no one that I'd had no other choice. I had communed with gods and crossed the southern sea, walked the breadth of the desert and broken bread with the people of Nagara. I had spoken with the dragon at the top of the eastern mountain, and I had witnessed Khalim departing from the white city where he was once confined. None of these things had brought me any closer to his side.

If the gods could not help me, then I would turn to the heretic. I believed I had nothing to fear from him. He was only a man, not a god or a demon of the wastes. Whatever power he might have possessed, it would collapse with the death of his mortal body, and I had a weapon that was more than equal to the task. I kept my spear close at hand, even at night. I was prepared to use it at the first sign of a threat to myself, Cricket, or the pilgrims that begged Deinaros for aid.

But weeks passed, and I saw little of Deinaros, and everyone who entered the upper floors of the hollow tree emerged again unscathed. I spent my time wandering the harbor, keeping a distant watch over Cricket, and waiting. The seasons passed strangely under the forest canopy, out of the sun, and the sea breeze chased away both the heat of high summer and the chill of deep winter. It was as though the city of the dead were sealed away like one of its tombs, and time and weather could not touch it.

I woke early one morning, some months after my arrival, to the creaking of timbers and the sound of a child's scream, muffled behind layers of damp wood. I leapt to my feet, gathering my tunic and my spear from underneath my bed, and thus half-dressed dashed down the spiraling staircase. Cricket cried out a second time, and I followed the sound to a closed door two stories below my borrowed quarters. Its lintels shook with heavy footsteps.

"Cricket?" I called out.

Her answer came as a terrified sob. "In here!"

The door was locked. With a searing curse in my native tongue, I braced myself against the stairs and kicked the door below its latch. It groaned, its planks bending.

Another kick, and the door sprang free, the iron fastenings tearing from their housing. Within, the wavering yellow light of a hanging lantern spilled over a vast library. Books, both bound and in scrolls, lay in piles like drifts of snow and lined shelves that stretched from the wooden floor to the high ceiling. The room receded into darkness, far wider than the hollow tree that contained it. A cool, dry wind whistled through the shattered door, sending a sudden chill across my skin.

Cricket stood a short distance away, her bare feet planted between fallen books, a broom in her hands like a weapon. Her hair had sprung free from its braids and floated around her head, and dust streaked her plain dress.

I ran to her. "What happened?" I asked. "What's wrong?"

She only shook her head, lifting the head of her broom to indicate a shadowed place between the library shelves. Beneath the towering rows of books and scrolls moved a hulking shadow, four-legged and hunched, its eyes gleaming in the lamplight.

It was a bear of the North, great and shaggy, its claws like daggers. I had met such a bear before, during my solitary exile in the North. Then, I'd had only a branch and a sharpened bit of flint with which to defend myself. It was a monster, whispered of in songs and sagas, never mentioned by name for fear of summoning it, and then foolishly described in parchment and papyrus and sealed between the walls of this uncanny room. Here before me stood the evidence of Cricket's fantastic stories of creatures escaping from the crumbling spines of Deinaros' older volumes.

I grasped the girl by her shoulder and pulled her behind me, bringing my spear forward. The bear shook its heavy head and advanced, sending tremors through the floorboards. On its shadowy fur, the mottled brown of decaying wood and paper, a spiraling pattern was etched in gray, shifting over its powerful muscles in a way not unlike the movement of my own tattoos as I gripped the weapon. I had seen this bear painted on shields and banners and inked into the skin of my brethren. What foolish scribe had brought it here to this forbidden library?

It raised a paw and swiped at me with the sound of wind rustling through the pages of a book. I stepped back, pushing Cricket toward the door. Tongues of lighting crackled over my fingers.

With my spear in both hands, I widened my stance and braced for the bear's charge. It opened its black hole of a mouth, showing paper-white fangs, but no sound emerged. It lowered its head and barreled down the aisle between the shelves.

A crack of thunder filled the room. The hanging light flickered as it swung madly from its chain.

The bear had not struck me. It had vanished like a dream, leaving only a wisp of smoke that smelled of burnt paper. Faint scorch marks marred the edges of the books around me.

I lowered the spear. "There's nothing to fear," I said to Cricket. "It's only a memory, trapped in paper."

She came up behind me, her small brown face contorted in a frown, and swiped her broom through the air where the bear had stood. The smoke swirled and dissipated.

I slung the spear over my shoulder and finished tying my tunic. Even if the bear had not been a threat to me or the girl, I wanted to leave this place. "It's early," I said to Cricket. "You should be in bed."

"Master Deinaros wanted me to find a book for him," she said. She peered around the adjacent shelf, brandishing the broom. "Is it really gone?"

"It's gone." I beckoned to her and picked my way toward the door. "Did you find the book?"

Her face fell. "It's not here."

"Are you certain?" If I could have interpreted the titles etched on the spines of these volumes, or the text within them, I would have spent several days searching the library and not seen half of it. I had the advantage of longer arms and a greater stature, besides, to reach the higher shelves.

"I've been looking all night," said Cricket. With her head low, she followed me to the door.

Anger, bright and hot, flared in my chest. I pushed it aside. The girl had no need for the scolding of a second stern man at this hour. "Go to bed, child," I said. "I will deal with Deinaros."

"He doesn't like to be disturbed," she argued.

"Let me worry about that."

I shut the library door behind us, wedging a large fragment of wood underneath to hold it in place on its broken hinges. Cricket ascended the steps, and I went after, climbing past the guest quarters and the entry hall to the receiving room above. Early morning light, turned green and gold as it filtered through the forest, streamed through the windows.

Cricket's bed lay unrolled under the stairs another floor up, surrounded by more hanging herbs and her collection of silver baubles. With her safely ensconced between her blankets, I climbed yet another floor, and I struck my fist against the closed door.

It opened before my second knock, and my hand fell through empty air. The sorcerer's study lay within, its walls hung with tapestries embroidered in arcane symbols I had no hope of interpreting, silver thread on ancient, faded black. On a table against one wall lay the book I had carried here—in my mind, I called it *my* book, a thought that turned my anger at Deinaros for his treatment of his apprentice to ice. Enough time had passed that I had forgotten what it had been to carry it. The memory of its weight on my back, of the sickening heat that came from its binding whenever I chanced to touch it, returned to me in a wave of revulsion.

And yet some part of me wanted to touch it again, to prove to myself that I had not imagined the images within, and that I had not wasted years of my life in bringing it across the world.

From the shadows, Deinaros emerged, his voluminous garments blending into the darkness. He regarded me with surprise, looking me up and down, one dark brow raised in surprise. "Ah, Eske. What are you doing here?"

"I'm here on behalf of your apprentice," I said. "You've had her searching the library all night."

He sat behind the desk and lit a candle with a shadowed gesture. His other hand covered the book, hiding it from my sight. I tore my gaze away. Had my face betrayed some desire for this accursed tome that I could not read?

"Yes, I remember," said Deinaros. "The volume I seek isn't there. It was taken from my library some years ago."

"And you didn't think to tell Cricket?" I demanded.

He waved a dismissive hand. "She would have come to me when she didn't find it."

I crossed my arms. My spear shifted on my shoulder. "What now, then? What is this book that you seek, that is so important as to keep a young girl awake all night in a library full of apparitions, but can wait for her to abandon the task?"

A flicker of annoyance flashed in Deinaros' sharp, black eyes, as though I was supposed to disappear with his previous gesture and had failed to do so. "If you must know, it's a record of the rituals of my master, Maponos the Ever-Living. It was taken from my collection by a student of mine, who has since gone into hiding." He folded both hands over the book, and the sleeves of his garment flowed over the edge of the desk to pool on the floor. "But while you're here, pilgrim, tell me this: have you lain eyes on the bone gate in your travels?"

"I witnessed it in the ritual of the Dreaming Eye, on the isle of Hanowa," I said.

"Tell me of this ritual."

I hesitated, recalling Hamilcar's promise that he would never ask me of it, and his admonition that I never do the same. "The priestesses used a particular herb to induce a trance, and I communed with their goddess in the deep," I said. "Is that sufficient?"

Deinaros made a sound deep in his throat. "A hallucination. Nothing more. Anyone could do the same with the mushrooms that grow under the trees."

"As you say," I replied. Arguing with a sorcerer could never end well.

"You've never seen the gate in the waking world?" Deinaros asked. "At sea, during the long night?"

His meaning eluded me. I frowned, shaking my head. "Only in the abyss," I said.

"Then we shall simply have to bring it here," he said with a broad smile, and I found myself swayed by his confidence, forgetting all the doubts I had carried into this room. If Deinaros were careless with his underlings, what did it matter? Most great men were, and I could protect Cricket from any creature the library might disgorge.

The smile vanished. Deinaros waved his hand again. "Now, begone. I must scry for my erstwhile student. I will send the girl to fetch you when you are needed."

***

I waited for many weeks, until I had all but forgotten about the bear among the books, and my doubts as to Deinaros' commitment to helping me had grown wild again. He might have had none of the power he pretended to, the strangeness of his surroundings was his only claim at sorcery. I paced the market, Bran at my heels, until I could navigate it by the count of my steps. Cricket returned to her daily tasks, and nothing else emerged from the library to threaten her. A long, sweltering summer had passed over the forest, and already yellow leaves fell again from the branches surrounding the hollow tower.

On one warm day, when fog covered the forest floor, Deinaros summoned me again to his study. The man who had taken the book from him, he said, had been imprisoned for the same heresy Deinaros practiced openly. He languished beneath one of the tombs, where the honored dead might visit him in the dark and admonish him for his sins. He had yet to recant.

Thus I found myself descending the grand staircase to the forest floor and traveling on foot to the sunlit lower city in search of the heretic known as Kural, son of Irreni. For thirty years, Deinaros said, Kural had been a student of his, living in the tower as I did and studying the great library. His tenure had not coincided with Cricket's service, and she had no memory of this man's face, only that he had visited once on a dark winter's night, when a storm shook the trees, and conferred with his former teacher until dawn. I could only guess that he had taken the missing book with him when he had left.

The wind stirred the sea that morning, and waves lapped against the docks and the bellies of ships anchored there. How sweet was the song of the ocean, and how much more appealing was the thought of boarding one of those ships and leaving this cursed shore, rather than remaining to entangle myself in the affairs of sorcerers and priests.

I had come too far to abandon my quest now. I bent my head against the wind and turned toward the palatial tombs.

Deinaros had been content to let me find my own way to the dungeon where Kural languished, but Cricket had drawn me a rudimentary map. It showed the step pyramid of Alaba, king of Ksadaja when it had been nothing more than a port at the edge of the forest, and the passage behind his grand sarcophagus that would take me underground.

She had darkened the hollows of my eyes with earth, giving me the desperate, mad look of the most unfortunate pilgrims—the ones most likely to wander from the priests, chasing new revelations known only to them. I could not hide my height or the breadth of my shoulders, but with the ragged garment that had protected me in the desert wrapped around me, I made a passable imitation of the sort of person Cricket had in mind.

I climbed the stairs to the temple's grand entrance at the back of a line of supplicants, each carrying offerings of flowers and incense. The heady scent of their gifts mingled with the smell of the sea and the dank, still air of the tomb. At the head of our column walked a priest robed in white, his shaved head gleaming in the sun and his neck weighed down by a heavy key on a silver chain. He had no use of it, for the towering wooden doors shuddered open at his gesture, and allowed the procession to enter Alaba's tomb. I pulled my hood over my eyes, hiding my face.

The narrow corridor opened into a wide, rectangular chamber. Its walls were a tome unto themselves, covered from floor to ceiling with the same arcane characters that decorated the tomb's exterior, all plated in gleaming gold. Coals burned in golden bowls suspended from the ceiling. A golden statue of the dead king stood with his arms outstretched at the far end of the room, welcoming the pilgrims, and a pair of emeralds glittered darkly in his eyes. More gems, red and blue, formed his magnificent collar and hung from his carved ears. A murmur of awe went up from the otherwise silent procession.

"I hope I will serve King Alaba, when the day comes," the pilgrim beside me, a pale young man with furtive eyes, whispered.

I bowed my head and pretended I did not hear him.

We knelt before the image of the long-buried king, and stood at the direction of the priest. The procession formed a line again to leave their offerings at the foot of the statue. With my hands pressed together as if in prayer, I followed.

A second carved image of the king adorned his sarcophagus, lying supine with its jeweled eyes open and its hands crossed over its chest. Its bare feet shone with the polish of hundreds of hands paying their respects, year after year, wearing the details smooth. If both carvings were accurate, he had stood head and shoulders taller than any of the supplicants here. Even so, five men of his size could fit inside the tomb with room to spare.

More coffins stood against the walls—smaller ones, adorned with images of vague, faceless figures, carved of black stone with veins of white. These, the priest intoned, were the king's honor guard, buried with their weapons and the hounds they trained to fight alongside them.

This room was darker than the previous one, with only a single brazier to light it. I found it easy enough to fall behind the crowd at Alaba's feet and disappear into the shadows. True to Cricket's map, a door opened between two of the entombed honor guard, and I slipped through and closed it behind me.

I descended a winding stair into the bowels of the tomb. The sounds of chisels on stone rang through the corridor in higher tones than the picks and shovels had rung against the bedrock of Kannaoka. Still, I quickened my pace, fearing that a quake would bring the temple down on top of me. The mountain of manufactured stone remained still but for the constant industry of death: the carving of sarcophagi, the hollowing of tombs, and the manufacturing of jeweled images.

The first door I passed led to a workshop, where guards in hammered breastplates kept watch over an army of artisans and an array of colorful gems. I pressed myself against the corridor wall, keeping to the shadows, and darted past the doorway.

I was well underground, now, below the water and the city streets alike. Only a small part of the pyramid stood in the open air. The rest was hidden below, and the machinations of the city of the dead proceeded day after day out of sight. I lost count of hours; it had been early morning when I had joined the pilgrims, but this was something like the land of the dead, where neither time nor weather could touch the souls that dwelled here.

The prison lay still lower, at the end of a smoky hall that must have cut underneath the marketplace. The rooms above had been pristine, swept each day by attendants, but here the dust gathered. And here in the ruin and rust of forgotten time, Kural the heretic lingered, in a cell behind an iron grate.

"You've gone the wrong way, pilgrim," he said in a voice raspy from disuse. "You'll find no enlightenment here."

His skin was cracked, his hair a mass of knots, but his dark eyes were bright and sharp. I could only guess at his age, but he appeared thirty years older than his former teacher, and like he might have languished here for that long.

I pulled the hood from my head. "I'm not looking for enlightenment," I said. "I'm looking for a book."

He rose from the shadows, placing empty palms against the bars. "One such as I would not be permitted any books, stranger. Return to the other pilgrims, and perhaps the priests will give you a scroll of blessings."

"I've come here from the house of Deinaros the All-Knowing," I said, approaching his cell and lowering my voice. But for the soft, tuneless singing of another prisoner, the corridor was quiet. "You took a volume from his library some years ago, and he wants it returned."

Kural's eyes narrowed, deepening the creases around them. "And he has you performing his errands, now? What happened to the little girl?"

"She's none of your concern."

He left the bars and returned to his cot, a dry laugh rattling his chest. "I was like you, once, you know," he said. "Doing as I was bid, crossing the upper city and the lower in search of relics. I even sailed across the Summer Sea, once, to find the works of the man he called teacher, but I was a hundred years too late. What do you think he'll give you if you perform every task he asks of you?"

I had succeeded where this man had failed—I had brought the work of Deinaros' teacher back to him. Any pride the deed might have given me died as I beheld the lightless prison in which his last student was confined. "In exchange for my labors," I began, "he will perform a certain ritual. I am neither his student nor his servant. Now, will you tell me what became of the book you stole from his library?"

Kural sat straight-backed, as if he were holding court in a palace. "I took many a volume from his hoard over the years. You'll have to refresh my memory."

"It's a book of rituals," I said. "The rituals of Maponos the Ever-Living."

"Ah, yes. Maponos, master of us all, even long after his passage from this world." Another mirthless laugh scratched against the stone walls about us. "It is the pale reflection of the rituals practiced in this very tomb. Where the priests of this house of death wish to quiet the dead, Deinaros wishes to rouse them. Where the priests wish to honor the gods, Deinaros wishes to defy them. He, as Maponos did before him, twists the words of the ritual and believes he has invented something new."

I dismissed his words with a shake of my head. "Tell me where to find it, and I'll leave you be," I said. "I have no concern for its contents or the efficacy of its spells."

Kural placed his elbows on his knees, leaning forward and resting his head atop his hands. His face, already drawn from his years in the dungeon, turned even more grim. "Your ignorance will not spare you, in the end."

"I do not fear Deinaros," I said, "and I don't fear you."

"Let it be on your head, then," said Kural.

"That is how I prefer it."

He laughed. "Very well, errand-boy of Deinaros, but I'm afraid you've come here for naught. The book was destroyed, along with all my possessions, when the guards came for me that night so long ago. The smoke from that fire reached the very highest places in the upper city, though I do not wonder that Deinaros did not notice. He has not set so much as a foot out of his tower in three score years."

Deinaros had not seen sixty winters, and neither had this man, aged as he was by his time in the dungeon. "How do I know you tell me the truth?"

Kural spread his arms wide. His ragged fingernails scraped against opposite walls of his cramped cell. "What have I to gain by lying? I will die here, and my bones will be burned just as my books were, so that I may not pollute the risen kingdom with heresy. This will come to pass whether you believe me or not." His hands dropped to his sides, and his last airs of mystery and dignity fled. He stood with his shoulders hunched and his head hanging to his chest. "If only the knowledge I gained could have been burned, as well. I cannot now pretend at believing that the coming world will be just, and thus gain my freedom. I pray you do not meet the same fate."

I began to speak, but found I had words neither to defy or comfort him. Footsteps approached from the opposite end of the corridor, and the light of a torch grew near.

"Begone," Kural said. "If I see you here again, I will call for the guards. You're no pilgrim—you'll find yourself in one of these cells."

I left him, then, empty-handed, and I made my way back through the temple in time to join the pilgrims after their devotions. If my absence had been noted, I was only another worshiper on the brink of madness, harmless as long as he was found in time.

***

Evening had fallen by the time I reached the foot of the upper city and began my climb of the narrow, aging staircase that led to the tower. Autumn rains had made yellow fungus grow from the edges of the steps, and the feet of travelers had battered and bruised their flesh, leaving dark stains on the moss beneath.

Deinaros had not taken to his bed, despite the lateness of the hour when I arrived at his study. A hundred candles, pale as bone, turned the room brighter than any day under the forest canopy, and the light fell on his shimmering robe in a way that made my eyes ache to look at it.

"The book?" he said as soon as I crossed the threshold.

I showed him my empty hands. "My apologies," I said. "I spoke to Kural. Everything he possessed was burned the night of his arrest. The book you seek no longer exists."

Deinaros' upper lip pulled back from his teeth in a snarl. "How like Kural, to steal my property and then lose it. He was always an ungrateful student."

I could only shrug. "What now?"

He rose from the desk. His shadow towered above him, bending in half at the join between wall and ceiling, looming over me as I stood in the center of the room. "Away with you. I must think."

"How will you conduct the ritual?" I asked. "I have waited so long already. If you cannot help me, I should be on my way."

Pale light flashed in Deinaros' eyes. The candles shivered. "Do not presume to tell me what I can and cannot do, Eske. Leave if you must. I have no need of you."

I thought to do so—with or without the book I had brought him. I was about to turn and storm from the study to fetch my spear and be on my way, heedless of the late hour, when the terrible shadow faded. Deinaros returned to his desk.

"But if you wish to pass through the gate of bone," he said, "I am your best and, indeed, only means to do it. I must consult my books. Surely you can wait a while longer."

As much as I detested him at that moment, I had to admit that I could. He would give me another promise, and I would wait, and so it would go until the end of the world. I went to my bed, feeling much like a child, and listened to Deinaros pace the floors above. He spoke, but to whom I was not certain, and I could not understand his words through layers of hollow space and swollen wood. Sleep overtook me, and I dreamed of the path through the gray forest, and the great stag just out of sight. If I could only catch up to him, I thought I might be granted passage through the world of dreams, and thus find Khalim without Deinaros' help or his artifacts. He ever eluded me.

I spent those next days keeping watch over Cricket in the marketplace, or climbing to Deinaros' door only to find it locked and barred, and I spent the nights retracing the same path through the woods, pursuing the stag. Days turned to weeks, and weeks to months. The trickle of pilgrims to the tower slowed, and when Deinaros would not open his door even to them, they stopped. We three—Deinaros, Cricket, and I—lived each alone in the house together, rarely speaking and never occupying the same room at the same time.

Under the eyes of two indifferent men, Cricket was growing into womanhood. I noticed one morning that she had reached the height of my shoulder, and her plain dresses barely came to her knees. Deinaros had given her no money for a new garment, and when the dry season came, she traded three of her charms for a gown of the sort the women in the market wore. If he noticed either the clothing or the missing trinkets, Deinaros said nothing. He remained in his study, speaking to Cricket only to order her to bring him more books from the library, and to me not at all. With the pilgrims gone, he conversed only with whatever spirits he conjured, alone in the upper reaches of his tower.

What little education Cricket had been receiving in the ways of the arcane came to an end. She grew bored, neglecting her chores and leaving the marketplace to wander the lower city. I was neither her father nor her teacher, and so I only waited for her to return before making my way back to the tower. Deinaros had a way to scry for her location if she became lost, but I doubted that he would think to use it, consumed as he was with his work. I admit that I was not entirely unselfish, keeping my distant watch over her. Should some ill fortune have befallen Cricket, I did not want to be the one Deinaros summoned to search for his next book.

So it was that the time passed, and one bright summer morning, I was summoned at last to Deinaros' study—not with a barked order or even a polite word, but with a crash. I leapt from my cot and took up my spear, fearing that Cricket had again run afoul of something in the library, but the sound came from above.

I found a book on the stairs, its spine cracked down its length and its pages torn and crumpled. The text within provided me with no indication of its subject matter. I set it aside.

The door to the study was open, and within was a second library, smaller than the first but equally crowded with stacks of books and drifts of scrolls, burying the table and obscuring the tapestries on the walls. The candles had all gone out.

Cricket crouched in the doorway, a stack of books balanced on one knee. She gathered more fallen volumes from the floor, her head bowed. Deinaros was a towering shadow behind her, his arms spread and his voluminous sleeves like black wings.

"You've been skulking about the library," he said in a hoarse voice. "I am called all-knowing for a reason."

"I haven't," Cricket protested. "I hate the library. I'm only fetching the books you ask for."

I slung my spear over my shoulder and bent to take the books from Cricket. Placing them beside the door, I helped her to her feet. "Let me deal with him," I said into her ear.

She scurried away, clumsy on limbs so recently grown long. I entered the study, taking cautious steps over more discarded volumes. Some were only the size of an outstretched palm, their pages fluttering like the wings of fallen moths. One that lay before the desk was as wide as my chest and almost as deep; I could not imagine Cricket hauling it from the library alone.

Without a word from me, Deinaros sank back into his chair. "It is inevitable that the student turns on the master," he muttered.

"That may be so," I said, "but it has not yet occurred. Besides, you and I have an arrangement. I'll ask your apprentice not to slay you before it is fulfilled."

He gave me a contemptuous snort. "It took me a hundred years, one hundred long years, but I killed my master. I smote him down on the cliffs beside the northern sea."

A hundred years. Deinaros did not appear a day over forty. He was mad, surely—the state of the room indicated that well enough. I took a cautious step toward the door.

"In the end, he thwarted me after all," Deinaros continued, placing his head in his hands. "He remains there on that rocky coast, and even with all my arts, I cannot find him. There he will remain, and the knowledge he kept from me—the knowledge I seek—will remain there with him."

"I thought that he wrote all of his wisdom in that book I brought you," I said.

Deinaros lowered his hands, fixing me with a withering look. "It would be the height of folly to give all one's secrets to one's students, Eske of the North, but I do not expect you to understand. What is closer to your grasp is this: Maponos kept from all others the means of summoning the bone gate. Without that knowledge, you and I will never find it."

"Then what do you need?" I had languished so long in this place, waiting for the opportunity to act. "His remains? His ghost? A map of his own devising, written in a clever cipher and buried along with him? I'll travel to the North myself and bring it back."

"His skull," said Deinaros. "He kept his most precious knowledge as the unlettered do, in memory. But he will not keep it from me any longer."

"Tell me where I can find it," I said, "and I'll go."

Deinaros' eyes drifted to something in the center of the room. I looked, but nothing was there.

"My master was a great sorcerer," he said, "try as I might to bury his memory. The tribesmen feared him. His bones will rest in a place of honor, even now, though his name might be forgotten."

~ XXV ~

THE TEMPLE IN THE WEST

I found Cricket in the tower's small kitchen, down a long staircase that descended into the roots of the tree. It was no larger than a ship's galley, dark and cavernous, with only a clay chimney pipe to relieve the smoke. Why it was thus hidden, Cricket did not say, but it was certainly her domain. A selection of copper pots and iron pans hung well within her reach, and I had to duck to avoid another rack of herbs hanging from the ceiling.

"The sorcerer's foul mood has quieted, for now," I told her. "I'm to travel north and investigate the place where his master died."

She stood from the place where she had hidden herself, beside the unlit hearth, tugging at her new clothing. "The place where he killed his master, you mean."

"The same."

Cricket frowned. Her small, brown face showed a pair of pockmarks I hadn't noticed before. "He thinks I will do the same to him."

"Will you be careful while I'm gone?" I asked.

She crossed her arms over her chest and shivered, though the room was warm. "I have places to hide. And I can go to the market. Deinaros won't leave the tower."

"Good." She would be safe, even in my absence. It might have been better for me to stay, to protect her from what was to come, but I was still young despite the years that had passed here. I saw nothing but an end to my long endeavors. If I returned from the

North with Maponos' skull, I believed I would cross over to the realm of the gods within a moon's turn.

Cricket busied herself about the galley, wrapping a selection of dried fish in a thin cloth and handing it to me. "I've never been farther north than Nyssodes," she said. "If you return, you can tell me of it."

"If I return?" I echoed. "You think I won't?"

She shrugged, and the trinkets hanging from her neck clattered softly. "We'll see."

The day's events hadn't dampened her spirit. I accepted the fish, and after it a small sack of bright yellow fruit, dried into brittle rounds. The smell of them reminded me of the isle of the priestesses, and of the food I had received in return for my labors there, and I missed the island so terribly that my chest ached. I wished that I could have had the grandmothers' guidance and not this strange sorcerer's. I wished they could have shown me the way to the world beyond the world, and that I'd had no need to leave them. I would never have found the book, nor spent long weeks crossing the river country or the vast sea of dust.

I was angry with them, and with their great goddess who swam alone in the abyss. The power to cross through the gate of bone must have been there, within my grasp, but for reasons beyond my understanding it had been kept from me. Unknowing, I had carried that anger from the island's shore to this benighted forest half a world away, and now that I realized it, I could not set it aside. I could not return to Hanowa. My anger would have to drive me north.

"I was hoping to ask you how long my journey might take," I said to Cricket. "Deinaros was less than forthcoming."

She handed me another wrapped bundle. This one smelled of spice. "How should I know?"

"You're his apprentice. I'm just a traveler. I was hoping he'd shared more of his mysteries with you."

Cricket wrinkled her nose. "He always said he will, someday, when I'm older."

She was older. The forlorn look that crossed her face told me that she understood, too, that Deinaros never intended to teach her anything.

"I'm his only student," she said, barely above a whisper. "None of the others have lasted as long as I have."

"You can read, can't you?" I asked. "He keeps many books in his sanctum, but there are still more in the library."

She turned to the hanging herbs, selecting several bundles and cutting the twine that held them to the ceiling. "This one is for fever," she said, handing me several strips of bark, "and this is for wounds. This one will slow a poison, if you take it quickly enough."

I studied each one before tucking it away among my other provisions. "Did Deinaros teach you that?"

"I learned it from the women in the market," said Cricket.

I smiled, and I told myself that I had nothing to fear in leaving the girl alone in this tower with the sorcerer, who spoke only to invisible presences and sunk deeper and deeper into madness with each passing day. "You're a clever girl," I said. "And one day you'll make a fine magic-worker, with or without Deinaros."

I should have told her to flee.

***

When I returned to my quarters to add Cricket's food and medicine to my pack, I found a crude, hand-drawn map on my bed, along with a pouch containing ten silver coins stamped with the image of the largest ziggurat of the lower city. I would have no further communication from the sorcerer.

I retrieved Bran from the shelter at the foot of the trees where he spent his nights and rode him down to the harbor. Daily exercise in the sea air had been good for him, and he remained strong and hearty, though it was with great reluctance that he boarded the ship that would take us across the Summer Sea.

"Soon, we'll be in the wilds again," I promised him.

Only spring rains troubled our voyage, and we arrived at the northern port after seven days. A crescent of white walls topped with marble columns rose from the waves. Sea-birds circled around the pair of lighthouses guarding the narrow entrance to the harbor, and a garish statue of a man dressed in blue robes and carrying a set of balancing scales gazed down upon the water. He stood with his weight on one leg, his shoulders relaxed, but his painted eyes were wide in a semblance of rage or fear. Passing under his gaze, I could not tell if the contradictory effect was one of age and weather or of the artist's choice.

Other gods greeted me as I disembarked into a noisy marketplace. A woman in a smith's apron, a hammer in her hands, presided over a forge. I had the smith change two of Bran's shoes in exchange for one of my coins. He turned it over, brow furrowed as he examined the image of the pyramid and the face of some long-dead king, as a living king would not be so honored in Ksadaja. Silver was silver, however, and he recognized it as such.

Under the raucous chorus of gulls, I crossed the city, leading Bran over paved streets strewn with the remnants of the birds' most recent meals. The delicate bones of fish crumbled under my feet. A woman in a grass-green habit swept the stones, the veil over her hair stirring in the wind. Ten soldiers, their breastplates gleaming bronze and their helmets crested in feathers, marched past in perfect rhythm. Voices carried on the sea breeze from the market, and a half-dozen children ran by, chasing a stitched leather ball. The costumes were different, the images of the watching gods in a square-faced style with spirals of curling hair, and the smell of the sea and the detritus from it ever-present, but I could imagine myself in Phyreios before the start of the tournament.

Driven by memory and some nameless compulsion, I climbed the main thoroughfare up the hill to the grand temple. In the sun, its columns gleamed, painted red and green and a bright, golden yellow. The steps were colorless stone, all swept clean.

I left Bran at the bottom of the stairs, beside another horse, dappled white and gray, and I ascended the steps to the great open doors. Midday sunlight cast a bright path across the vast dome, and my shadow upon it stretched tall and thin to fall at the feet of the gods within.

An elderly priest, bent under the weight of his years and a heavy, crimson garment, acknowledged me with a nod. "Welcome to Elisia, traveler," he said.

Opposite the door, the statue of a man gazed down upon the handful of petitioners milling about at his feet. He carried a scepter in the crook of one arm, and stretched the other out across the dome, his fingers spread. The woman to his right carried a sheaf of grain, and I recognized her from the waystation in the desert: Isra, with a face rendered in exquisite detail, as though she was only a moment from smiling upon her worshipers. Another statue held aloft a sword. I could count the eyelashes on the smith-god's face and see the marks of use upon her marble hammer.

I approached the statues, my footsteps loud under the dome of the ceiling. My neck ached with the effort of looking up to take in the great height of these figures, some five or six times greater than my own.

I stood in the distorted mirror of the temple of the Ascended. The marble faces of the gods were sharp and angular, unlike the smooth oval masks of the gods of Phyreios, but here they were, resplendent in the seat of their power: king and queen, smith and warrior, scholar and dancer and keeper of the dead. Which had come first? Had the Ascended taken up these guises when they began their thousand-year reign, after they had devoured two of their companions and reduced their number to only seven? Or had word of their vast empire and their holy city reached even here, the other end of the world, and this temple constructed in imitation of their glory?

I had stood at the feet of the Ascended one morning, before the tournament games had begun for the day, Khalim at my side. Now, only empty air stood beside me. The other petitioners stopped at the base of each statue, bowing their heads and pressing their hands together in prayer, moving around me without even a greeting.

"Magnificent, isn't it?"

The voice came from behind me, and it had a familiar cadence. It was a voice I would have expected to hear in that other temple, the one that had fallen under the weight of the great worm along with the rest of Phyreios. I turned, my mind racing to match the voice to the speaker.

He was dressed in a simple robe of undyed linen that fell to his knees. His boots had been restitched a number of times, and the dust of the road still clung to them. A curved sword hung from his belt, its leather scabbard embroidered in golden thread. His hair was long and glossy black, tied back at the nape of his neck, and his face was all fine angles etched in a rich, flawless red-brown.

This face I knew. This was Ashoka, champion of the Ascended and favored son of Phyreios. As his gods turned against their people, he had left their service at last, leading refugees away from the city. He had cast his weapons at Khalim's feet, there at the gate, and I had not seen him once in the years since. Those years had made him no less handsome and no less haughty, humbled as he might have been then.

"Eske," he said. "I'm surprised to see you here."

"Not as surprised as I am to see you." I had not spared him a thought since the fall of Phyreios. He might have died in the conflagration, or perished when the worm emerged from the mountain, and I would have been none the wiser.

"Why are you not in Phyreios?" Ashoka asked, turning his head to regard the kingly statue. "I have heard tell that your companion reigns as a king there. I thought you'd be enjoying the spoils of your victory."

I lowered my eyes to the polished floor. "There was no victory in Phyreios. You should understand that better than anyone." I took a breath, and a sharp pain without origin shot through my chest. "The man on the throne is not Khalim."

"Then I was mistaken." he said.

Outside of the depths of his despair, betrayed even by the gods he had worshiped all his life, this was the closest he might have ever come to an apology. I had not known him well, but I knew of his pride.

"What are you doing here?" I asked.

The ghost of a smile flickered across his face. "I might ask you the same."

If it was to be a duel of questions, then so be it. I had nothing to hide from this man. "I have traveled the length and breadth of the world to find someone who can help me bring Khalim back. I finally found one who has the knowledge I seek, and I am on an errand in his service."

"Bring him back?" Ashoka echoed. "Back from where?"

"The land of the dead, the realm of the gods," I said. "He did not die, but he was taken from me. That is why a man with his face sits on the throne of Phyreios."

Ashoka considered this, a frown troubling his perfect features. "Whatever it is you're doing, it's a fool's errand. No living being can enter the land of the dead." He waved a hand. "Still, it's no concern of mine how you spend the hours and years of your life."

"Neither is it any of mine what you do with yours," I said, "but I hope you'll indulge me, nonetheless. Why are you here?"

He regarded the towering statue of the marble king once more. "I'm searching for a god," he said. "Time will tell whether I have found one here."

I fell out of his awareness, disappearing along with the city and its people and its summer sunlight as he gazed up at the images of the gods. In Phyreios, he and I had barely spoken—until the very end, he'd believed in the might and benevolence of the Ascended, so we'd had little to talk about. He had called Khalim a charlatan and a sorcerer, and me a barbarian. I'd had no kinder terms with which to address him, had I found the occasion to do so. But here stood a man with a familiar face, who had seen the triumphs and the horrors that I had seen. Here stood a man whose gods had betrayed him. Though the animosity between us remained, filling the temple's air with a tension like a taut bowstring, I could not yet bring myself to turn from him.

"You haven't found a god here?" I said in an attempt at wit. "I count seven."

His aquiline nose wrinkled. "Seven gods, just like the Ascended." He shook his head. "I have visited this temple every day for a year. The priests here tell me of their miracles, of the kindnesses they grant to the faithful. They promise me that I need not fear these gods, only the treacherous men who might turn their righteousness to tyranny. But I spoke to the gods of Phyreios. I heard their decrees and stood in their presence on many an occasion. If I could not trust living gods, how can I submit to these lifeless images?"

"It's better this way," I said. "Let the gods stay in the world beyond the world. We have enough troubles here without their meddling."

Ashoka tore his eyes from the statues and favored me with a raised brow. "Meddling? And this from a man who wishes to enter their realm and steal a soul from them?"

I scowled. "I think of it as undoing their meddling."

"Call it what you like," Ashoka said. "The gods give and the gods take away. That is as much true here as it was in Phyreios, and all the places in between. I would have thought that someone so well-traveled would have learned that by now."

I took a step closer to him, petty pride flaring in my chest as he shrank away, one hand falling to his side where his sword hung ready. I had beaten him in duel once, though only barely, and he hadn't forgotten. "And I thought you had learned the circumstances in which they must be overthrown," I said.

He fixed me with a steely glare and said nothing.

I was treating him unfairly. He was no longer a servant of the Ascended. He had rejected them, once he could no longer reject the sights before his eyes, and he had taken his people to safety. Many in Phyreios could not say the same. Even at the end, there had been men in the same armor that he had worn standing guard outside the colosseum, turning aside anyone who would put a stop to the slaughter within. Ashoka did not deserve my disdain.

"I wish you luck in your search," I said. "I hope you find a god worthy of you, son of Phyreios, in this world or the next."

I turned to go.

"Eske," he said. "Wait."

I stopped. The old priest shuffled between the statues, lighting candles at their feet. When the wind stirred the flames, the carved faces appeared to move.

"You're a fool, Eske of the North," Ashoka said.

Perhaps I had been too generous with him. "There are worse things," I said.

"Let me finish." He glanced at the priest. The old man kept to his task, making no sign that he could hear us. Ashoka turned to me, his dark eyes cold and grim.

"You're a fool, Eske of the North," he said, "but you were once an honest man, and I can only assume you've remained so, as you're unafraid to speak ill of the gods in their own house."

"That's not much of a compliment," I said.

Ashoka shook his head. "It wasn't one. Do you believe that you can cross over into the realm of the gods? That you can retrieve the soul of your companion and return to this world?"

That drew the attention of the priest. He raised his head, holding the long match up like a weapon, mouth open in an unspoken reprimand. I nodded toward the door, and Ashoka followed me out.

Bran raised his head as we approached, his ears flicking back and forth. He scuffed the pavement with one hoof.

"I'd thank you not to tell anyone else," I told Ashoka, "but yes, I do believe it. I must believe it, or all the work I have done these past years has been in vain, and there's nothing left for me to do but wait for my eventual death. Beyond that, I believe it because this world is filled with wandering gods, and magic-workers who study all things permitted and forbidden, the bravery of heroes, and the faithfulness of lovers. How could I not believe that such a thing is possible?"

Ashoka's stony face, as sharp as if he had been chiseled like the statues in the temple, softened only slightly. "What are you willing to give, to do this thing?"

"Anything," I said, and then: "I can only swear to you that I will spend no one's blood but my own. I am not the Ascended."

His hand rested atop his sword. "I will hold you to that promise," he said. "If I find that you have broken it, I will have to kill you myself, or die in the attempt."

I held his gaze and nodded, accepting his oath as he had accepted mine. "I would expect no less."

***

I slept that night in an inn beside the water, and I dreamed that I stood upon the gray strip of beach underneath the strange green sky. The stag stood beside me, its hooves light upon the sand and the moss hanging from its branching antlers brushing its powerful shoulders. Far in the distance, past where I had seen my longship in another, more distant dream, a storm gathered dark and furious on the horizon.

"It will be here soon," the stag said, regarding me with one human eye.

"A couple of hours," I agreed. "We should seek shelter inland."

The stag lowered its great head, pawing at the sand in the same way that Bran would. "It will follow."

The wind came from across the sea, carrying with it the bite of winter. White froth appeared atop the waves. "It will," I said, "but a storm does not last forever."

"It is a storm of your own making," the stag told me. "It will seek you out wherever you might go."

I woke in the early hours of the morning, in gray predawn light, under a clear sky.

~ XXVI ~

THE RING-FORT

I left Elisia and its shining gods behind, and the city receded until it was only a bright spot against a hazy horizon. Then it and the sea beyond vanished, and everything became green, from the canopy overhead to the moss under Bran's hooves. Only the sky remained a stubborn gray. Rain fell in brief fits from an impenetrable layer of cloud, and the wind blew cold. Autumn was coming to the North, and it would reach me before long.

For now, though, birds sang summer songs among the branches. After the first day out of the city, the stream of travelers to and from its gates slowed to a trickle. By the time a week had passed, I saw another traveler only once every few days. I sang, too, as I rode, a rowing song of the frost-cold sea, to warn anyone else on the road of my presence and reassure them that I was not a bandit lying in wait.

I had grown more comfortable riding Bran in these longs months and years. Still, I walked most of the time, giving him an easier journey. He carried most of our provisions, and much of that was food for me, so I would not have to hunt and gather on the road. Here, far from the eastern steppe and at the close of summer, grass grew in abundance, and the streams ran clear. Bran needed nothing else. A steppe horse was a magnificent beast.

My reckoning had become confused after so long on the road, but I guessed Bran had passed eleven years of age, and I nearly twenty-seven. Seven years I had spent in his company. If I ever saw

Aysulu again, I had no hope of repaying her for the gift she had given me.

I had left Phyrieos so long ago. Had I not met Ashoka again, I might have thought that my journey had taken me into another world, one in which Phyreios had never been. This far from the Iron Mountain, no one had heard of the grand Cerean Tournament, nor of the fate of the city. No one had seen the Ascended in their power nor witnessed them brought low. No one remembered my role in what had come to pass except for me.

Meeting Ashoka had been like gazing into a mirror—though I would never call myself as divinely blessed with good looks as the erstwhile champion of the Ascended. All my failings and all my doubts reflected back at me from his eyes. Like him, I had been faithless, searching for someone I could trust in the wide world. Instead of a god, I had found a sorcerer. Ashoka still searched. I did not expect I would see him again.

But the rain was light, and my load not too much to bear. Bran was happy to feel the wet earth beneath his feet and leave the harbor behind. I apologized, yet again, for forcing him to travel by boat. I do not think he understood. I forgot the image that had gazed at me from Ashoka's eyes, and the worries I'd had when I left Cricket alone in the tower. By Deinaros' hand-drawn map, we crossed the miles with blessed swiftness.

The forest thinned and gave way to rolling hills, gentle as the waves on a calm sea. Here also was evidence of the workings of human hands: fields in tilled rows, wooden roofs and stone walls, and, far in the distance, a tower that stood like a lone sentry atop the highest hill. At night, light burned in its upper windows. The shapes of men crossing the fields cast long shadows in the evening and early morning.

A mark on the map, a pair of concentric circles labeled with a curving line of script that the all-knowing one had forgotten I could not read, turned out to be the sort of ring-fort that in my youth I had associated with the lands of the South. I did not know, at the time, that a whole world lay even farther south than this. Bran and I crossed a vast field of golden stalks, approaching the high wall of stone in the center. Laborers sprouted from between the rows, looking up as we approached, silent and wary. They watched us with iron-hard eyes, their hands on their scythes.

I approached the fort anyway. Deinaros' map was sparse in detail, and ended with only the vague suggestion of a coastline some distance from here. I needed further direction.

Around the stone walls, the land was built up in circular plateaus, carved into tiers like a staircase fit for giants. A smooth path led from the road to the small gate, barely the height of a man, set into the wall. Above it, a man stood with a spear in one hand and a tall, narrow shield in the other. I could not see his face, but the dull, metallic dome of his helmet turned to me as I came near.

I called out to him in my mother tongue. "I've come here from Elisia, the city by the sea," I said, "and I've traveled for many weeks through the forest. May I speak with the master of this fort?"

"What business do you have here?" the watchman shouted back in the same language, or one close enough to make little difference, with an accent I could not place.

"I'm here to retrieve something for my employer. I mean you no harm, and I come alone." I held up my hands. "The rest should be discussed in private. May I come in?"

The door was wood and fitted with iron. Rust stained the ground beneath it. Footsteps struck the ground on the other side, and the creaking hinges shuddered to life.

The man on the other side was older than I, and not quite as tall; his hair was the color of the dry fields, and he wore a cloak over one shoulder the hue of old blood, clasped with an iron ring. A metal breastplate, polished to a high shine and shaped to suggest a muscular torso, covered his chest. His hand rested on a short sword hanging at his side, and his square-jawed face imitated the carvings of the gods in the city.

I knew this face, as surely as I had known Ashoka's. The temple in Elisia had been enough like Phyreios that Ashoka had not appeared out of place, but here, with the forest pressing in and the wind blowing cold from the northern sea, I could only stare.

"Gaius of the Golden Road," I said at last, naming both the man and the company with which he had competed in the Cerean Tournament.

"Eske of the Iron Mountain," he answered in kind.

I'd last laid eyes on this man after the chariot race that concluded the tournament. He'd been badly hurt trying to run Aysulu and me off the track at the behest of some agent or another of the Ascended. I had followed at Khalim's heels as he went to lay his healing hands on the bone protruding from Gaius's leg, and he had warned us not to offer such aid to the charioteers from the Tribe of the Lion and Wolf. I had left the city soon after, and Gaius had as well, returning home empty-handed. I would never have guessed that his home was here, at the very edge of civilization.

Gaius collected himself, his face resembling stone more and more with each passing breath. "This fortress and its lands belong to my father, who holds them in the name of King Renatus. What business do you have here?"

I bowed, though I risked only a slight incline of my head. The guards remained above, and the sound of their bows creaking did not escape my hearing. "I'm on an errand. A sage in the city of Ksadaja, beyond the Summer Sea, seeks the remains of his teacher, now long dead. I'd be happy to tell you more, if you would let me in out of the weather."

He had already drawn himself up to his full height, and his eyes darted from my face to my feet, as if comparing the two of us. The easy confidence he had shown at the start of the tournament had not been recovered even after all these years. Another three men, similarly dressed, came up behind him, their hands on their swords.

Gaius held up a hand, and the others stilled. The bowstrings above my head slackened, and arrows returned to their quivers. "Of course," he said. "We remember the rules of hospitality here, even if others have forgotten it. It is good to see you well, Eske."

"And you," I said.

He turned, pulling his cloak around him. The others followed. A muddy path led from where I stood to a central structure dug into the earth, with a thatched roof that hung down to the ground. Stone steps descended from the path to its door, and smoke curled from its chimney.

"Come, then," Gaius said. "Your horse will be cared for, and you will be treated as a guest, but you must leave your weapons at the door. My house is still strong, though its strength has been tested at every turn in recent years."

It was a strange thing to say on this particular occasion—what does a solitary traveler in need of hospitality care for the strength of his host's house? I would have rather heard of the warmth of its fire and the abundance of its cooking pots, or of the quality of its roof in the rain.

I trod in the mud behind the men in their red-brown cloaks. Inside the wall, a tiny village sat out of sight of the outside world, with the dugout longhouse at its center. Chickens milled around an elevated coop, pecking at the earth, and a pair of dark-eyed cows watched me from behind a leaning wooden fence. Two women stood beside a well, each carrying a bucket, their heads covered with thick woolen shawls. One was sallow, her dark hair escaping in curls, and the other's face was the soft brown of good clay. One of the men approached the well and waved the women away with an angry gesture from his short spear. They gathered their buckets and disappeared behind the sagging door of a barn.

More armed men took up places beside the path. They did not meet my eyes, but their gazes burned on the back of my neck.

Bran snorted, tossing his head. Another man came to take his lead, and he shied away, pressing his side against mine. I put a hand on his nose to reassure him.

"I'll come to fetch you soon," I promised. It was not my intent to stay overlong in this place. The midday sun was a pale, distant light shrouded in clouds, and I wanted to be out of the distrusting view of Gaius's cohort and well on my way by nightfall. I handed my spear to the guard at the longhouse door, and my belly clenched and my neck stiffened.

This tension softened as I stepped over the threshold. The central fire chased away the damp, and the smell of woodsmoke and roasting meat flooded my senses. If I closed my eyes, I could find myself once again in the hall of my father, where I had not set foot in many years. Many miles lay between me and my homeland, and indeed one could not even see the shadow of the northern mountains from here, when the clouds hung so low, but perhaps the distance was not so great, in the end.

Long tables stood on either side of the fire. I sat where I was directed, on the worn surface of a split log, and Gaius took the place beside me.

"I told you, Gaius," a wavering voice cut through the smoke. "I will see no more of the barbarians' delegates."

As my eyes adjusted to the dark, the shape of two carved chairs emerged from the gloom, their backs against the earthen wall of the longhouse. One was empty, and the other held a man of perhaps sixty years, a circlet of gold around his head and a red-brown cloak clasped at his shoulder. A soot-stained banner hung from the wall above him.

This must have been Gaius's father, the master of this fort. They had the same strong features and hair that thinned at the temples.

"Take this man outside and cut off his head," he said. "You can hang it from the wall as an example to the others."

I got to my feet. I could summon my spear, and hope the man who had taken it from me possessed the good sense to keep his face clear of its sharp edges, but I had been looking forward to a meal hot from the fire.

Gaius reached out a hand and gripped my elbow. "This man has come from the south," he said. "He is on an errand to recover the bones of a sage."

He mentioned nothing of Phyreios or the Cerean Tournament. "I mean you no harm," I added, and let Gaius pull me back into my seat.

The old man peered at me through the smoke that filled the room, his eyes pale blue and rimmed in red. Those eyes were sharp despite his age, made all the more so by the mistrust I had sparked in them.

"You're painted like one of them," he muttered.

Tattooing had long been a common practice among both my mother's and father's peoples, and I doubted that the ink on my skin was identical to that of this man's enemies, but I held my tongue. "I apologize for any threat you might have perceived," I said instead. "I've come here from far to the south, by way of the city of Elisia beside the sea. I've been a month or more on the road, and I do not know your enemies. Yours is the first settlement I've encountered in many days."

The old man's scowl, already etched into his face as if with a chisel, deepened. "Then you've walked the same road as my father's father's father, through the wilderness once tamed. Did you enjoy the sight, barbarian? Elisia's aqueducts once reached from the mountains to the seas. Its roads cut through these blasted forests. Now there are only cow-paths and wells dug into the mud. I'm sure you feel quite welcome in these lands."

I was feeling less welcome by the minute. I placed my hands on the rough surface of the table. "I will not burden your hospitality for long. My employer has sent me here to recover the remains of his teacher, many years dead. Have you heard of a man called the Ever-Living, by the name of Maponos? I am told he was a magic-worker of no small renown."

A low, crackling sound filled the room. The old man's mouth split into a humorless smile of yellowed teeth and black spaces between them. He was laughing.

But it was not at my expense. "Immortal sages and magic-workers?" he asked. "You should ask my son. He has traveled the world, all the way to the city of Phyreios on the steppe, and returned with his hands as empty as a dry well. But he claims he even met the gods of that city!"

Gaius made a sound deep in his throat. His hands clenched into fists beneath the table.

My heart raced unbidden. I drew in a slow breath, willing my face not to show the anger—helpless, impotent rage, and fear as well, a fear that I had not felt in many years—that washed over me like a tide. This place had more in common with my father's hall than its sights and smells.

I could not listen to this man describe his son in the same tone of barely-concealed anger that my father once used to speak of me. Too often had I sat in his presence, my fists clenched like Gaius's, pretending I did not hear. By the time I was a man grown, I had taken up the habit of leaving whenever my father began to speak, staying away for days or even weeks at a time. Gaius, however, remained here, as surely as if he were tied to his place at the table.

"I've never heard the name Maponos," the old man said. "But if you're looking for the ancient dead, you'd best find the barbarians' burial grounds in the forest. The tombs of my ancestors crumbled into dust long ago."

I made to rise from the table. "I'll do that, then."

The old man stopped me with a gesture. "Stay, traveler. Stay and tell us a story of the southlands. Enjoy the generosity that still remains in my hall. On the morrow, Gaius will accompany you into the woods. Perhaps with your help, he will prove more useful than he did in Phyreios."

An itch started between my shoulder blades and spread across my skin. I loathed the idea of being held up as a more favored warrior, an example to which Gaius would be compared every time we so much as occupied the same room. A number of young men of my acquaintance had played that role in my own home. I assumed that, like me, Gaius had no brothers, or his father wouldn't have needed me to shame him.

But I couldn't very well flee the fort now, and I had no idea where to begin looking in the vastness of the forest. I would have to stay.

More men filed into the hall, taking their places at the two long tables. The murmur of their voices filled the room. Their eyes caught the light of the fire with a small, sharp gleam, and they watched me with their teeth half-bared like wary wolves. Like Gaius, they were fair-haired and sharp-featured, and their faces and hands bore hundreds of scars among them.

A woman in a gray dress, her sleeves turned up to her elbows, handed out cups and poured the ale. Her eyes were shadowed, and she did not raise them from the floor. Another distributed trenchers of bread, and several more took great helpings of a thick stew from the iron pot on the central fire and distributed them to the hungry guardsmen, Gaius, and me.

I wouldn't refuse food when it was offered. I ate, and studied the men watching me, and observed that the carved seat beside the old man remained empty.

He stood with some difficulty and indicated me with a broad sweep of one arm. "We have a guest," he announced. "Tell us your name, stranger, and tell us of your travels. Be welcome in my hall."

Quiet fell around me, heavy and soft, and fifty pale faces turned back to me. With their bellies full, the soldiers no longer resembled hungry beasts. They were only men, and their lord was only a man and—as I reminded myself—so had my father always been. I had not had cause to think of him for some time, and his long absence from my thoughts had made him loom all the larger when this place had brought him back.

I banished him again. I had wandered the world, and I had stories to tell and an audience to receive them, a more immediate concern than the travails of my childhood. Besides, this was a test: I would tell a tale, and if my audience approved, I would receive one in return, and learn the location of Deinaros' dead master and be on my way.

"I am Eske of the Clan of the Bear," I began. "I was born far beyond the northern mountains, where the sun never sets in the summer, and where great mountains of ice float atop the storm-battered sea. I've traveled the endless steppe and climbed the peaks of the East, where the great dragon watches over her faithful students. I've sailed emerald waters and walked among trees so tall that no sunlight has ever reached the forest floor. I've met gods who walked as men do, and men who aspired to become gods. Listen, and I'll tell you of the king of Kannaoka, kept alive by dark magic as his body decayed. I'll tell you how the island shook beneath my feet, and the very walls of my prison threatened to fall upon me. I'll tell you of the brave sailors who came to my rescue, and the warriors who defended their home even against their own corrupted king."

And so I told the tale of King Sondassan, from my arrival on his island to the crowning of the twin princesses. I left out the evil book, and the ambitious priest from whom I had taken it. It made for a better ending.

When I had finished, the feast was eaten and all the ale drunk, and the distant sun hung low above the wall of the ring-fort. Darkness would soon follow. The men returned to their posts, their feet slower than when they had left them, and their eyes a little less suspicious. My tale and I had been judged, and my listeners had found me adequate.

It was a good story. I had expected a more lively response. Now, as the hall emptied, there was only the old man, clapping his hands together in a slow, steady rhythm. Gaius sat beside me, his face unreadable and the muscles at the sides of his jaw working silently.

"You are welcome in my hall, Eske of the Bear Clan," the old man said. "The hall of House Legatus, all but fallen into disgrace. I am Lord Oeneus. You've already met my son, Gaius. If you are as brave as you were in your tale, you will serve me well against the barbarians."

I had begun to detest the word *barbarian*, all the more so because for once in all my travels, it was no longer being applied to me. "It would be an honor, my lord, to serve you, but I'm afraid I cannot linger here. I must find what I seek and return to my employer with all haste."

Oeneus dismissed me with another wave of his hand. "Show him to his quarters, Gaius, and ensure that he stays there for the night. We will discuss this in the morning."

I stood, and let Gaius lead me out of the hall. Three of his red-cloaked men fell in behind me. One of them had my spear over his shoulder.

"May I have that back?" I asked.

The man answered me only with a grim look.

I was to be a prisoner, then. All of Oeneus' talk of the hospitality of his hall had been nothing more than empty boasts. I understood, now, the lackluster response to my tale. The men were only humoring me until I was to be confined.

"Gaius," I said. "In Phyreios, we were enemies, but only for a short while. Khalim healed your wounds."

He did not turn to look at me. "I remember."

"It is for Khalim that I do this. Let me go, and I'll not trouble you again."

The wind had turned cold, and a freezing rain descended upon the ring-fort. The torches on the walls spat and hissed, and the men carrying them grumbled. I bent my head, shielding my eyes with one hand.

"Go where?" Gaius asked. "You're alone. The barbarians will find you before you ever find their burial ground. Even if by some sorcery you could see in the dark, this rain will have washed away the tracks they left when they took the bodies from the walls a fortnight ago."

I drew my cloak around my arms. Corpses hung from the walls did not bode well for my long-term future. "Say I wait until morning," I offered. "What happens to me then?"

"Whatever my father decides," Gaius replied. "I'm sorry."

~ XXVII ~

THE STANDING STONES

Gaius and his companions took me to a house close to the stable. The fire in its hearth had all but burned down, and the air within was only a little warmer than the wind without. Making a show of obedience, I shed my cloak and sat down on the bed.

In the doorway, his elbow raised to rest against the lintel, Gaius glowered. "You are, perhaps, the last person I would have expected to meet here, Eske. I am glad the years since the tournament have treated you well. But we are not friends, you and I—we weren't in Phyreios, and we aren't now."

He was nearly ten years my senior, his golden hair flecked with gray, though he stood as tall and broad as he had when we first met. And still he was under the thumb of his father, the decrepit old man who saw nothing but ancient glory turned to ruin but was too stubborn to abandon the fort and return to the shining capital. Elisia, too, might have faded in the generations since this family had left it, the truth of the city paling in comparison to the dream, and Oeneus might not have been happy there, either.

Gaius would follow him into misery, wherever he might go.

"I understand," I said. Oeneus had ordered me confined, and Gaius obeyed. I would find no help here.

He gave a sharp nod. "Good. Rest well, then." Turning, he shut the door behind him. I counted two sets of footsteps following him. He'd left a guard behind to keep me in place.

What awaited me in the morning? Execution? More demands that I prove my intentions, or a demand that I hunt barbarians for Lord Oeneus? Of the options, I might have preferred a swift death.

Night, black as the center of the earth, overtook the fort. I let the fire die, so that the small house in turn was covered in darkness, and I put on my cloak.

The guard yawned, shuffling his feet. I opened the door by inches, just enough to reach an arm through and grasp him by the collar of his red-brown cloak. Dragging him into reach, I clapped my other hand over his mouth before he could cry out. I pulled him inside and delivered one sharp blow to the back of his unprotected head. He fell into my arms, and I laid him gently beside the remains of the fire.

I waited, listening. Soft rain fell on thatched roofs and stone walls. I drew my hood over my head and slipped outside.

Bran stood, half-asleep, in the first stall, and my saddle lay over the gate. He woke, snorting, as I tightened the girth under his belly.

"Hush, now," I whispered.

Together, two dark shapes in the gloomy night, we made our way to the gate. The mud muffled our footsteps. Patches of wavering light clung to the walls and the steps down to the longhouse, but shadow cloaked the rain-soaked paths.

I put my hand to the swollen wood of the fortress door. Moss slicked the beam across it. Above my head, the light shifted and the platform creaked under the weight of the watchman staring out into the dark.

"Ready?" I breathed, more to myself than to Bran. Sensing my worry, he nosed at the wet cloth on my shoulder.

I lifted the bar with both hands and lowered it into the mud. The soft squelch of its weight was as loud as thunder to my ears, but the guards above remained in their places. Louder still was the screech of the rusty hinges as I flung the doors open.

A cry of alarm went up around me. Booted feet moved across wet platforms and soft earth. I leapt into the saddle and kicked Bran forward, harder than I had intended. He let out a whinny of protest as we crossed the threshold and galloped into the storm.

I reached out my hand and felt the tremor in the air that was the song of my spear. Another cry cut through the darkness, and the weapon came to me, its strap snapped neatly in its center.

The first arrow struck the ground behind Bran less than a heart's beat later. A volley of them followed, whistling through the wet air and thudding into the grass. Someone in the ring-fort struck an iron bell, again and again, shattering what stillness remained. Thunder rolled over the hills.

I turned Bran north, cutting through the yellow field turned deep gray under the coming storm. Dry stalks scratched at my legs. Another arrow struck the ground an arm's reach away.

A horse was as valuable as the warrior he carried; more so, if horses were in short supply, and I had not seen many in recent days. The archers might have tried to spare Bran. I was less certain about myself. I risked a glance over my shoulder, and the lights that poured from the fort's open gate burned spots into my eyes.

The fields whispered in the night wind, and we tore through them, heading toward the black shapes of the trees. The forest welcomed us with a shadowy embrace, obscuring our pursuers and their torches, hiding us from their eyes. I looked, again, and the lights receded and fell away.

It was then that Bran stumbled and threw me, headfirst, from the saddle.

With the gods' own luck, I covered my face with my arms and landed in the mud. My elbows struck the ground first, sending a shock of pain to my fingertips and my shoulders. My feet tumbled over my head, and I lay flat on my back, gasping for breath.

The lights from the fort had driven away what little sight I'd had in the darkness. I saw only vague shapes, the colorful remnants of each pursuing torch, and then utter, impenetrable black.

"Bran!" I called, but he was gone, darting off into the woods. Thunder covered the beat of his hooves.

I dragged myself to my feet. Mud soaked through my cloak and into my clothing, and I shivered in the sudden cold. I reached out, and my hands met a tree, slick with rainwater, and I stumbled over its roots to put it between myself and the fort. The wind whistled through the forest, hiding the sounds of any arrows that might have pursued me.

I pressed on, moving from tree to tree—even my own grasping hands were lost in the darkness. One by one, my pursuers slowed and fell back, their lights receding. The forest closed around me, and all the signs of habitation—the smell of smoke, the burning lights, the rows of crops, and the sounds of conversation and industry—all disappeared. I had crossed into the wilds.

An owl cried in the distance. With no other heading, and boundless night on all sides, I followed it. I tapped my spear against each passing tree trunk, as much to direct my footsteps as to make sound to discourage the pursuit of beasts, and sang my rowing song in a low voice. I'd walk for a while, I thought, and put some distance between myself and the fort. I'd find some sort of shelter and wait until morning, and then search for Bran.

The owl called a second time, so close that it might have perched beside my ear. It was an illusion, surely, brought about by my lack of sight. Wherever it might be, I had nothing to fear from an owl.

An answering call came from somewhere behind me. This one was wrong, somehow—a little too low in pitch and resonance. Before I could question whether it was indeed an owl or a man imitating one, two pairs of hands grasped me by the arms. A foot kicked my knees in from behind.

A single flash of firelight seared my eyes. As I turned away, a blindfold fell across my face, and rough hands tied it tightly at the back of my head.

"Who are you?" I asked. "I mean you no harm."

Muffled words were exchanged over my head, and my weapon was pried from my fingers. The language was familiar, though it possessed an odd cadence: a dialect of the deep forest. Its only contact with the tongues of the outside world was what might be shouted across a battlefield.

"I'm here on an errand," I said. "To recover the bones of one long dead. I have nothing to gain from attacking you."

"Did the lord of the fort send you out here in the dark?" a man's voice asked. "Your loyalty is poorly repaid."

I shook my head, and the blindfold's knot shifted against the back of my skull. "I came here from the south. Lord Oeneus wanted to keep me prisoner in the fort, and I've escaped. Are you the forest folk of whom he speaks? Let me go, and I'll fetch my horse and gather what I came for and trouble your lands no longer."

"What are you after, then?" the same voice asked. "Some dusty bones?"

"I'm told I will find them in the burial ground," I said. "That's all, I swear it."

Their single lit torch shone bright against the blindfold. The shadow of a man moved between it and me, wavering like the apparition of a spirit.

"If that's what he wants, then we may as well show it to him. Saves us the trouble of bringing him there later," another voice said. To me, he added, "On your feet, then. This will be easier for you if you cooperate."

Hands gripped my arms again. The rough fibers of a rope scraped at my wrists. By instinct, I pulled away.

"Or we can cut your throat here and leave you for the wolves," said the first man. "It's your choice."

I fell still and let them tie my hands and lift me to my feet. With one of these strange men on either side, I was marched deeper into the forest. With every turn, I tried to keep the fort in my mind, and remember in which direction it lay, but I lost it before long. If I survived the night—the offer to take me to the burial ground was no better than a threat—I'd have to find my way out of the woods by the position of the sun.

My feet caught on roots and undergrowth, but my captors kept me upright, bearing my weight between them. They were shorter than I, and not as tall as the folk of the ring-fort, but their arms were strong and their shoulders sturdy. By their footsteps, I counted six or seven of them. Not one spared me a word as we walked.

I lost all sense of time. I hoped in vain that morning would come and save me from the black abyss in which I traveled, interrupted only by the obstacles underfoot and the men holding me captive. Whoever bore the torch had either put it out or moved far enough behind me that its light was gone. Darkness persisted, and the night went on, and on we marched, until at last my feet found the edge of a clearing.

The men at my sides dropped me to my knees. A thin carpet of moss kept me from gaining any new bruises. Someone lit more torches, and the world around me went from black to a dim orange. Unclear shapes cast looming shadows through the light.

Someone else tore the blindfold from my face. I closed my eyes and turned my head away.

"Well," said another of the men, a different voice than those I had heard. "Here we are."

I blinked the ache from my eyes and looked up. I knelt at the edge of a circle of standing stones, each twice as tall as a man and as wide as the span of my arms. Others, just as large, lay atop the pillars, forming a ring of towering arches. On each, a fine chisel had carved a map of spiraling currents, green with moss against the dull gray stone.

I knew these spirals. Similar ones had been inked down my arms and on the shaved sides of my head when I had come of age.

Cairns were piled between the standing stones, crumbling under the weight of undergrowth and rainwater. Then there were the bones, protruding from the earth and piled in a decaying mockery of the gate that I had so long sought. Deinaros' vague description had given me little idea of how long ago Maponos the Ever-Living had finally given up his title, but it mattered not. Time was lost in this place.

"Welcome," a familiar voice said. The first man who had spoken to me in the forest sauntered into view. He wore a cloak of hide, as did his companions, but on his head of black curls balanced a headdress made from the skull of a deer, its antlers polished and shining. Vibrant blue paint covered his face in more interlocking spirals.

He spread his arms to indicate the circle of stones. "I suppose this is what you were looking for?"

I sat back on my heels. I had only one chance to talk these strange folk out of killing me, or hope that I could retrieve my spear fast enough to cut my bonds and escape. "I'm not sure," I said. "I'm a stranger to these lands. My employer bade me recover the skull of his master, a man long dead by the name of Maponos."

The man grinned, baring his teeth, and his eyes gleamed in the firelight. "That's quite the story."

"I have better tales, if it's a tale you want," I said.

"Later, maybe, if I decide to let you live that long," he replied. "So, you've traveled across the world and run from the legendary hospitality of Lord Oeneus to scratch in the earth for some bones. Unfortunately, I can't let you anger the gods of this grove by disturbing the rest of our brothers and sisters, so soon laid here after hanging from the walls of the fort."

I tried to draw my feet underneath me and stand, but the toes of my boots slipped against wet moss and fallen leaves. "I'm afraid I must insist," I said.

Two of the others moved in the darkness, and I heard the unmistakable sound of spears crossing at my back. I stopped, willing my shoulders to relax and my arms to stop straining against my bonds. In my wet clothes, I shivered, my breath coming in ragged pants and steaming in the air before my face.

The first man dropped his own spear, and it clattered to the wet earth. A knife appeared in his hand, its blade sharpened to a wicked point. Quicker than my eyes could follow, he dropped to his knees, bringing the knife up under my chin and tilting my face to his.

This close, his skin shone pale where the paint had cracked around his mouth and between his brows. The pigment did not hide a scar through the corner of his lip. He grinned, again, though by now I understood it was more of a snarl. "Then I'm afraid I have no choice but to kill you," he said.

My neck strained to keep the soft flesh under my skull away from the knife. I twisted my hands, but the knots held. "I'm not your enemy," I said through my teeth.

"No?" He tilted his head to one side, studying my face. "You come here from the hall of a man who has slain our siblings, burned our lands, and stolen our children, and the first words out of your mouth are that you intend to desecrate the last of our sacred grounds. If you're not our enemy, then you're no better than a rat in our grain stores."

With his face inches from mine, I could see him clearly: he was no older than I, under the paint, with delicate features and liquid dark eyes. Even as he stared me down, his knife to my throat, doubt made him hesitate. He didn't want to spill my blood—not here in this sacred place, while I was at his mercy. The others looked to him for leadership, and he took up its mantle only reluctantly. He might have hidden from them the way his eyes darted about for some sign to tell him how to proceed, but he could not hide it from me.

"I can help you," I said. "I have no love for the men in the ringfort. I am a warrior like you. I hunted the lind-worm in the far northern sea, and crossed the mountains alone. I competed in the tournament of Phyreios and emerged a champion. I have faced gods and monsters and the wicked ambitions of men, and still I lived to tell the tale. I'm worth more to you alive."

The knife lowered. A single trickle of blood, hot against my frigid skin, ran down my neck.

"Let's say I leave you alive, then," the man said. "Will you come back here with a shovel at the first opportunity?"

I hoped it would not come to that. "I'll go only where I'm told," I promised. "But in the meantime, I hope you and the gods of this place will give me the chance to prove that my cause is just."

His only answer was a smirk. He got to his feet, retrieving the spear and sheathing the knife. "Cut his bonds. He's coming with us. If he tries to run, kill him."

***

A thin cast of predawn light fell over the forest as we approached my captors' hidden stronghold. The rain came to an end, but the clouds remained, shrouding the sky in gray. Here, the trees had been cleared in a wide circle, leaving no place to hide as one approached. At the center, a high palisade wall stood in a ring. Smoke rose from several fires within.

All at once, I returned to the fortress upon the Iron Mountain, where I spent my days digging holes for a similar palisade and my nights with Khalim. That peace, I believed then, could have lasted forever, but it had been little more than a space between breaths, a quiet moment just before the arrival of a storm. I had seen that storm approaching even as I denied it, as Khalim dreamed each night of the terrible things to come.

The gate cracked and then shuddered open, the sound shaking me from my reverie. I filed in with my captors, my head down in what I hoped was a posture of contrition.

Inside the wall, the village woke with the morning sun. An oilcloth hung over the door of a makeshift longhouse, leaning against the opposite wall of the palisade, and a fire glowed from within. Two dozen short-legged sheep ran from the gate as we came in, and a small boy with a staff chased them. The sound of the forge reached me before I saw it, its bellows panting and the smith's tools clanging as she set them out.

I was taken to the longhouse, where my host, still clad in his deer-skull headdress and peeling facepaint, spoke with a dark-haired woman. She wore a plain dress and a woolen shawl about her shoulders, and carried a child of no more than two on her back. Even with the differences in their costumes, the man and woman were nearly identical—siblings, I guessed.

After a hushed discussion, the woman left the longhouse, pausing only to favor me with a measuring look. The child slept with his head on her shoulder, heedless of the world.

The man pulled a blanket from somewhere in the shadows and tossed it across the room to me. "You can sleep here for a while. When you wake, I'll decide what to do with you."

Exhaustion weighed down my shoulders, and my eyes ached. I nodded.

A frown crossed his face, further cracking the paint. "What's your name, stranger?"

"Eske of the Clan of the Bear," I said. "World-treader, erstwhile champion, and your grateful guest."

That drew out the flash of a genuine smile. "If I only had the time to listen to your tales," he said. "I am Cullen, son of Bearach, now first of the warband."

The title fell from his lips with bitterness. He'd not been long in his position, and he resented it. Had his predecessor been hung from Oeneus' wall and then buried among the standing stones?

I bade him good morning, and found a quiet corner beside the fire to rest. I slept without dreaming. When I woke, a small gathering of men ate a cold meal of bread and dried meat by the fire. They regarded me without surprise, and without speaking, invited me to partake.

I left the longhouse, walking out into another soft, steady rain. Thunder complained in the distance. Somewhere in the gray forest beyond, Bran was alone. I had to find him, and find some way to recover Maponos' skull for Deinaros, for whatever wisdom he meant to extract from it. I was no closer to that aim than I had been in Oeneus' fort, but I was alive.

Cullen found me standing in the rain like a fool. He'd washed off the paint and removed the antlered headdress, wearing instead a hooded cloak of the same gray-green as the rainy woods. He was no longer the apparition in the forest, bedecked in bones and skins. By the look of him, he was rather ordinary: short and almost slight, but with a strength in his arms that suggested long years of fighting and labor upon the palisade walls. His great dark eyes gave him the brief impression of innocence, but there was a hungry look to his face. He didn't trust me, not yet. I could not say that he should have.

"The rain will pass soon," he said. "You should come hunting with us." He took from his back my dragon-tooth spear. Thick, clumsy stitches repaired the place where the strap had broken.

He was giving me the opportunity to betray him, to lose myself in the woods and find my way back to their sacred grove or out to the fields surrounding the ring-fort. I was no fool—he and his men would hunt me down, surely. Their knowledge of these lands was far superior to mine.

But this was more like freedom than what I'd had in Oeneus' custody. "I would be honored to accompany you on a hunt," I said. "Thank you, truly."

I could keep Cullen's company until I found Bran. Everything else would have to wait.

~ XXVIII ~

INTERLUDE FOUR: A PLACE BETWEEN

"You've been busy," the moon-faced owl said. It hovered on silent wings above Khalim's head, just outside the reach of his arm, the same wind that stirred the golden grass to either side keeping it aloft. Its shadow fell onto the winding path.

"Not really," said Khalim. "I was in a forest for a long time. Some kind of great beast tried to eat me. Then I was here."

The owl shook out its black wings. It might have been laughing at him, low and rasping. "That's all?"

"That's all." Khalim lifted his head, squinting against the low, golden sun that hung at the edge of his vision no matter which way he turned his head. The hollows around the owl's eyes were like the shadowed places on the moon—or the faint image of the moon in Khalim's memory. He'd not seen it since before the white city. "It's like a dream. I used to dream that I flew over great distances, and saw the path from my home to the Iron Mountain. Now, I choose where to fly."

"It's not easy for everyone," said the owl.

"It's easy enough for you," Khalim said. "Or did you flap your wings all the way here?"

Huge, glassy eyes regarded him, showing no human expression. "What do you think I am, child?"

"Not an owl. Just like I'm not a child."

Dust, fine and pale as ash, rose in thin clouds around his feet. The grass rippled like water. He reached out a hand to touch it and sent another ripple flowing across the vast plain, breaking into the waves stirred by the moaning wind. The air smelled of smoke, but the sky was a flat, flawless blue.

He had been walking for what had felt like days, following the winding trail half-hidden in the grass. The forest and its ghostly inhabitants were a lifetime away, and the citadel still farther. He had walked, he understood now, looking for the end to this path, trusting that the terrain of this dream-world would make the decision of where to go for him.

This isn't Torr's city, he reminded himself, not for the first time and not for the last. *I could go anywhere.*

He was free. No one could command him, and nothing could hold him in place—and there was no one to protect him, should he run afoul of another beast that consumed wandering spirits for its sustenance.

He had never been more afraid.

Fear kept him to this path. It had boundaries and limits, a way forward and a way backward; it kept him confined just as it provided the illusion of safety from whatever else rippled the grass in the distance. He walked, and when courage bolstered his resolve, he reached out and ran a hand through the golden seed-heads to see what they were made of and what might be hiding beneath them. When courage faltered, he kept his eyes to the ground and his hands at his sides.

I can't do this forever.

Without thinking, he pressed his hand to his chest. The god that used to dwell inside him was gone, taking with him everything Khalim had held dear and everything he'd ever taken for granted. In exchange, for all the years of Khalim's service and any he might have had left, for the breath of life and the sensation in his hands and the faces of all those he'd loved, that god had taken Khalim to the citadel and left him there alone.

He clenched his fist and returned it, stiffly, to his side.

"This is as fine a place as any to spend eternity," the owl mused, flapping its wings once to stay above Khalim's head. "A place between places, where only the lost and forgotten dwell. Not a place I'd have chosen, but to each his own."

"Why are you here?" Khalim asked. The words came out with more vitriol than he had intended. A shadow fell across the field, as though a cloud had passed over the sun, but the sky remained clear.

The owl hovered nearer, turning one great, black eye to Khalim. "Careful, now," it said. "You're not among the living anymore."

Khalim did not need the reminder. He closed his eyes, and felt neither heartbeat nor breath within his chest. When he looked once more, the sky had regained its unchanging color. "I'm sorry. Are you following me? I could have used your help in the forest."

"I was passing through and happened to see a familiar face," said the owl. "You seem to have done just fine on your own."

That was true enough. The sharp-toothed beast hadn't devoured him, and he had found his way here. He could travel again, he was certain, but where would he go?

In the distance, the grass shimmered like heat in the desert, but Khalim shivered.

"Where are you going?" he asked the owl. "Since you're not going to stay here with the forgotten, I suppose."

"I don't stay anywhere long." It lifted its wings, pushing itself into the air, and turned a slow circle through the sky. It spiraled lower, its wings dipping into the grass, sending more ripples across the winding path and toward the far horizon.

Khalim could imagine worse things than wandering. This place had its dangers, yes, but there were also wonders. The dark forest, its trees taller than the mountains, had stood under a sky of wheeling stars. Here, jeweled insects hummed in the grass. With all the time death had granted him, Khalim could see it all. He could traverse the realms of the gods and map the vast reaches of the wilds.

But I don't want to do that. In his own mind, his voice was that of a child. *I want to go home.*

"Do you remember how you died, little one?" the owl said, startling him.

"Not really," Khalim said. "It was dark. I was underground, and I spoke, but my words weren't mine. The place smelled of blood. There was a flash of light, and a terrible sound, like the earth cried out in pain."

He remembered, also, strong arms around him as the underground chamber had collapsed. Eske had tried to save him, even at the cost of his own life. Under the rubble, in the crushing dark, Khalim's ear had been pressed against Eske's chest, and the last thing he had heard in the living world had been the beat of Eske's heart—and the cracking of bone as the stone had fallen inevitably downward.

Then he had found himself standing before the blinding, radiant figure of his god, and then there had been nothing—nothing, until the citadel.

Time folded in on itself. Khalim could have been under Phyreios yesterday or a thousand years ago. Eske might have been dead by now, his body long since turned to dust.

Then he'd be here, wouldn't he? Somewhere in this strange, vast world, I'd be able to find him.

Eske hadn't perished in the collapse. No one had but the Ascended and Khalim—in the brief vision that Torr had granted him, Khalim had seen that much. Eske would have gone on to live a full life, then, and wherever he was, he might have forgotten Khalim entirely.

Someone remembers you, the owl had said, back there among the sterile columns of pale marble. If anyone remembered Khalim—as himself, and not as a vessel for the god he carried—it must have been Eske.

The god had said that there could be no other way. Khalim had failed to prevent the cataclysm, so he had to go, and the god would take his place and correct all that had gone wrong and rebuild all that had been destroyed. He was meant to carry Torr to Phyreios, and no more. His dreams of the future had only served to remove him from his home and send him across the desert. The gift of healing, which he had believed would save everyone doomed to die if only he could reach them fast enough, had been nothing but a divine afterthought. Torr would use it as he led Phyreios. It mattered not that Khalim had possessed it as well.

And now he had none of it. He could not heal, and he neither slept nor dreamed. He only walked.

A dark, violet-gray cast spread over the sky. Icy rain fell, bursting when it struck the waving stalks and the dusty path beneath with a shimmering, discordant sound.

"If you're going to keep doing that," the owl said, "I'm leaving."

Khalim put a hand over his eyes. The rain was like tiny needles against his skin. "I'm not doing anything."

The owl flapped its wings again, a look of avian disdain on its moon face. "I suppose I should be off, anyway. I will see you, or whatever eats you and steals your face, elsewhere."

Khalim looked at the ground. A peal of thunder split the sky. "Farewell, then," he said.

With a rush of feathers, the owl was gone, and Khalim was alone once more.

He took a breath, or an imitation of one, forcing the sudden burst of anguish in his chest to dissipate. The rain slowed, and the sky lightened, and the endless field returned to what it had always been: bright and gentle, with only a late summer wind to trouble it. Khalim was only a ghost in world of ghosts, haunting this place like a spirit from a story meant to frighten children.

"What am I to do now?" he asked aloud.

There was no answer. He hadn't expected one.

What good does it do me to travel through the world of the dead? I want to go home. I want another chance to help people. I want to see Eske again.

I want the god who betrayed me to look me in the eye.

Anger was still foreign to him, though it had come to him before in this strange place. It burned in his belly and turned his hands to ice. With deliberate effort, he quelled the fire and returned warmth to his fingers. The sky trembled with distant thunder.

All Khalim had to do was imagine the citadel, and his next step brought him to its gates. Wind howled across the empty plain, scratching against the towering marble walls. A red sun cast bloody light on the pale stone.

This place belonged to Torr. It was part of him. If Khalim was to find him, it would be here.

The doors were shut. They had closed behind Khalim when he had left, and he had not intended to return.

He raised one fist and knocked.

~ XXIX ~

FRONTIER OF THE FALLEN EMPIRE

The sun burned away the mist as we departed the palisade gate, the warband and I, and we entered a forest as gold as the treasure-hoard of any of the pirates of the southern seas. Early autumn turned the trees' crowns yellow as sunlight, and bright patches marked the path beneath our feet. The air was heavy with the scent of the recent rain.

Inside the palisade, the village was small, and the population of fighters smaller still. Cullen led twelve capable warriors, and three accompanied us on the hunt: Diarmuid, tall and scarred; Lugaid, fair-haired and broad-shouldered; and Ailbhe, her hair cut as short as a man's and arms thick and ropy from drawing a bow. I believed, as we ventured out, that they regarded me with suspicion, but it was not my presence that stilled their tongues.

"There were thirty of us, not two months ago," Cullen said. "A year before, our village numbered five hundred. Some ran for the coast and joined with the other clans. Others were not so fortunate."

Grief, then, hung over the heads of every soul in the forest. "Why did the rest of you stay?" I asked.

"It's our home, isn't it?" said Cullen. "It was our home when we herded cattle over the grasslands and through the forests, in our great-great-grandfathers' time, and it's our home now."

"As long as we can keep it," added Diarmuid.

The cattle were gone—so long gone that not even the invaders had managed to keep hold of them. I imagined the battles of that age long ago, when the bronze-clad armies that Lord Oeneus dreamed of went to war against a forest full of archers and spearmen, paint on their faces and armor of bone and hide on their breasts. Both forces had dwindled to thin shadows, but the fighting continued. After Oeneus met his death, Gaius would reign over an empty country, its fields lying fallow and the forest overtaking the ring-fort just as it had covered the places where the cattle had roamed.

"There," Cullen said, interrupting my melancholy reverie. He pointed to a patch of earth some distance away, in the shadow of a towering tree. "A horse's hooves. Could be yours, Eske."

I climbed over a fallen trunk and examined the patch. Two crescents marred the soft soil. "You have a sharp eye," I said.

"If only he used it to spot a boar for our dinner, rather than a runaway horse," Ailbhe mused, slapping Cullen on the shoulder like an elder sibling might. He shrugged her off, but he smiled nonetheless. It was a glimpse into an earlier time, before Cullen had been named their leader. Then both recalled who and where they were, and their smiles faded, and Cullen turned away.

Bran's footprints turned south, toward the edge of the forest. I offered to follow them alone, and let the others continue on their hunt, but they refused. I was to be watched.

I considered myself a fair tracker, in my time, though I'd not had opportunity to practice for many years. I'd spent too long on city streets and the decks of ships. The hunters with me followed the hoofprints at a swift pace until we emerged, blinking in the bright sunlight, upon the fields surrounding the ring-fort.

I made to leave the cover of the trees, but Cullen's hand on my arm held me back. "Wait. Their aim isn't as true as mine, but they'll see you well enough."

"What's become of my horse?" I asked, unable to keep the fear from my voice. I could not lose my only friend, not when I had so many miles more to travel. Deinaros' tower was half a world away.

"Inside the fort, no doubt," said Lugaid. "The invaders wouldn't waste a horse."

Bran was safe, then, and had not fallen lame in the tumble we had taken. I hated the idea of one such as Gaius—or, worse, Lord Oeneus himself—imposing upon Bran, but he was not to be treated ill. He could wait until I had earned the trust of the forest folk enough to venture out to recover him.

I left the forest's edge with reluctance, and vowed to return before long.

We found no boars for the village in the trees, but we did slay a speckled deer, and Diarmuid found a patch of berries that might have, long ago, grown under the watchful eyes of his nomadic ancestors.

That night, my belly full and my heart lifted a little, I took watch upon the palisade with Cullen. I'd do whatever he asked, and whatever the rest of the warband required of me as well, I decided, until I had enough of their trust to mount an expedition to recover Bran and make an argument for the exhumation of the skull of Maponos.

A circular gap in the trees overhead showed a tapestry of brilliant stars. How strange it was to watch constellations that I knew from my youth rise above these boughs. The lind-worm twined its way across the sky, its stars as blue-white as sea ice, and a cold wind came in from the north. I gathered my cloak about me and turned my eyes to the ground outside the wall.

"I think your people and mine were kin, long ago," I said.

He placed his hands around the sharpened points of the palisade and gazed into the darkness. "Could be," he said. "You don't look like my kin, though."

I shrugged. "An age or more has passed since then. My people decided to set off across the mountains. We are nothing if not stubborn." If I stared into the trees, I thought I could see the lights of the fort flickering in the distance. "Not that you aren't. Stubborn, I mean."

"You sound like my sister."

I turned away from the imagined lights. All around us, the village closed its doors and put out its fires, and the song of insects replaced the sounds of human life. I longed for my tent on the Iron Mountain more than I had desired anything in all my years on the earth. I still had it, rolled more tightly than a sacred scroll in the bottom of my pack, but I never dared to take it out and see what time and weather had done to the charcoal drawings on the canvas.

I returned to this camp in the forest with some effort. "Is that a good or a bad thing, to sound like your sister?" I asked Cullen.

"Oh, very bad indeed. It suits you poorly," he said with a wry smile. He bowed his head and ran a hand through his hair. "No, that was unfair of me. Ciannait is all I have left."

"I'm sorry," was all I could say.

"Don't be. It has nothing to do with you." He looked up, and in the darkness his black eyes reflected the sky like still pools of water. "Her little boy, Faelan. He'll be king one day, when he's old enough. King of a patch of earth and a few dozen hungry people. I don't envy him."

I had seen this melancholy before, this exhaustion in the face of hopelessness. Khalim had possessed it at the end, when the city had been all aflame and every second thing he had spoken was in the voice of the god and not his own. Cullen had endured it longer; the demise of his people was a slow one. He had seen many a conflagration, and would see many more.

The impulse to wrap my arm around his shoulders and hold him to my chest, as I had done with Khalim, overwhelmed me. I tucked my hands into my cloak instead.

"What do you call that one, where you come from?" Cullen asked, interrupting my thoughts.

He extended a hand above his head, pointing to the serpentine line of blue stars, tracing it with a finger.

"The lind-worm," I said. "It hunts whales and unsuspecting sailors among the floating mountains of ice in the northern sea. I saw it once, in the flesh, and it cost me everything I had."

Cullen nodded, as though my brief recounting had answered all the questions he might have had. "We call it Gilla, the ridge-backed eel," he said. "In the old days, it circled the holy isle, and emerged every third year wreathed in a mighty storm to demand a sacrifice."

"And it does no more?" I asked.

"It's quite the story, if you'd like to hear it. It was my favorite when I was a boy."

I told him that I would, and thus we passed the watch.

Here is the tale, as best as I can recall it. In the days of gods and great beasts, when the North Sea was covered in an unbroken plain of ice even through the summer, there lived a maiden on the holy isle. Her name was Sorcha, and when she was a girl, and her three small siblings were but infants, their parents were both lost at sea in a terrible storm. From this storm came Gilla, whose back was like the ridge of the mountains that hid my people from the lands of the south. As the constellation that I called the lind-worm rose above the horizon, so too did Gilla emerge from the depths to approach the island, demanding the blood and flesh of its people.

The next stars to emerge from the trees formed the suggestion of a human figure, arms spread wide. This was Sorcha, chained to a stone a short distance from the shore of her island. She had grown to womanhood caring for her siblings, while others fed the slow but inexorable appetite of the eel, but this time she was not so fortunate. At sunset, her fellow islanders secured her to the sacrificial stone, and there she would wait. Gilla would arrive at midnight and devour her whole, leaving only her hands and feet in the iron shackles—and, more importantly, leaving the waters surrounding the island safe for fishermen for another three years.

Here, I rubbed at my wrists, recalling the bite of the rope that bound me to a similar stone upon a sea of dust.

Sorcha waited, and she called out to the gods of the island and the sea, and she feared what would become of her young siblings with no one to care for them. The eel's fin, blacker than night, emerged from the sea and circled the rock, spiraling ever nearer. Just as she thought the gods had not heard her, a ship appeared on the far horizon. Its sails were red, and its figurehead was a winged dragon, and at its prow stood the hero, Herela. As the hour passed, the red star of his ship came into view. Upon its emergence above the horizon, Cullen said, it could be used to find true east—the direction in which the holy isle had once lain.

Herela's ship came near on swift oars, and his enchanted harpoon leapt from his hand and slew the great eel. The sea carried its body to the shore of Sorcha's island. With his sword of black iron, a gift from the gods, he cut the chains from Sorcha's wrists and ankles and brought her safely onto his ship. When morning came, he stood atop the corpse of Gilla, and announced that he would be taking Sorcha away to the west to become his bride.

But Sorcha refused. Though he had saved her from certain death and slain the beast that had enslaved the island for many years, she did not know this man, and when she asked if the young children under her care could travel with them, he forbade it. For Herela lived under a prophecy, and it said that his heirs would one day murder each other for his throne, plunging his kingdom into a thousand years of war. He would marry the fairest maiden on land and sea, he declared, and pass his crown to his firstborn son, and he would permit no others to make a claim by right of birth or bond. Sorcha's three siblings would have to remain on the island, among those who had sent their sister, and many others, to a terrible death upon the waves.

Herela offered her all the riches of his kingdom, but she refused again. He threatened to sack her village and carry her off in chains, but she refused him a third time. Herela returned to his ship, promising that he would come for her at sunrise, and she would be his bride whether she wished it or not.

And so Sorcha prayed again, this time to the goddess of the deep, whose name must never be uttered aloud and thus has been forgotten. She prayed for a place where she would be free of the stranger Herela, and where her family could remain together.

I did not offer to Cullen the name Nashurru, though it rose in my mind like the goddess herself from the depths.

When night fell, a silver boat washed up beside the body of the eel. Sorcha placed her three siblings inside and climbed in herself, and she pushed off from the beach. That boat took her over the horizon and beyond the last island, to the sea of eternal night, where the sun never rose. As our watch concluded, a bright silver star shone above our heads—Sorcha's boat, still sailing in eternal night, tracing a path through the southern sky. She found a harbor there in the darkness, Cullen said, but when she left it, she and the children never were seen again.

If only I had a boat, I thought, and I could set sail into the eternal night. Surely then I might find the gate of bone at the end of Sorcha's journey, and I would have no need of Deinaros nor the skull of his master.

Our watch ended, and I slept beside the fire in the longhouse again, along with others of the warband. And so the next weeks passed, hunting and keeping watch in something resembling peace. If I had come here at the end of my long winter in the mountains, rather than setting off across the sea to the steppe, I might have stayed here until the day I died.

It was not long, however, until Oeneus' men brought their torches to the forest and shattered the illusion of safety.

***

They came before dawn, the men from the ring-fort. Their lights hovered like fireflies in the distance, darting and bobbing, appearing as harmless as insects. From my place upon the palisade that fateful morning, I watched the lights come closer, wondering if I had drifted off to sleep, or if the warband had neglected to inform me of any wandering spirits in the mist. Fog lay on the ground in a heavy blanket, turning the trees into soft shadows and hiding the undergrowth.

I cried out an alarm when the first spear point reflected its bearer's torch. These were neither spirits nor dreams emerging from the forest, but men, armed and armored for battle.

Gaius led them from the back of a black horse—Bran, wearing a saddle I did not recognize and flicking his ears in agitation, coming out of the trees like a specter of death. The rest of the men marched on foot. Their crested helmets showed ages of tarnish, and their red-brown cloaks were threadbare and patched, but they formed straight lines and even blocks, their shields raised and their spears ready. The predawn light deepened the scowls on their faces, turning their eyes to dark hollows.

My hand tightened around my spear. Gaius was riding my horse. How dare this obsequious coward, plaything of whatever tyrant plied him with promises, presume to ride *my* horse? He had only seen the steppe from the walls of Phyreios. He had never fought alongside the daughter of the stargazer to earn her respect, nor had he walked with Bran over the endless miles that had led us here.

In truth, I could only blame myself. I'd not yet mounted my planned expedition to recover Bran from the ring-fort, distracted as I was by the endless tasks that kept the village alive. He had been chosen for me for his even temperament and willingness to follow instruction, even if his rider had never sat on a horse before. He'd listen to Gaius as well as he might listen to me.

If Gaius wanted to bring Bran directly back to me, then, I could only thank him.

Cullen was upon the battlements beside me, bow in hand, almost as soon as I had shouted. This had been a watch we had not shared, but he did not sleep well. No matter when I took my shift upon the wall, I would see him wandering the encampment at least once.

"Archers!" he called. With one foot still on the spindly ladder, leaning out into empty air, he bent his bow and strung it.

"Be careful," I warned him. "That's my horse he's riding."

His first arrow struck the man beside Gaius as he emerged from the trees, clashing against his mail hauberk. The force of it knocked the man to the ground. The fog swallowed him, and more soldiers came forth to take his place.

Gaius raised one gauntleted arm. "The forces of King Renatus have been mustered against you, barbarians," he declared, and the crest on his helmet fluttered like the wings of a ragged, red bird. "We have your fort surrounded. Surrender, and your homes will not be burned."

Cullen's face contorted into a snarl as he nocked another arrow. "He lies. Shoot them down before they come any closer."

"My horse," I protested.

The arrow flew. It struck Gaius on his mailed shoulder, at the battered edge of his sculpted cuirass. Three rings burst and fell, glittering, onto the mist-covered ground. Gaius reeled back, and Bran staggered beneath him.

"I never miss," Cullen said.

Gaius clutched the arrow's shaft with his other hand. Beneath the long nose-guard descending from the iron cap of his helmet, his face was a mask of rage and pain. He steered Bran around with his knees, disappearing behind the treeline.

The warband assembled upon the narrow battlements, and their arrows fell like rain upon the advancing line of Gaius's men, tearing through mail and flesh alike. The soldiers marched onward, the gaps between their shields tightening. Like a single beast, they advanced, a hundred legs under a shielded shell.

I brought my spear to my shoulder and threw it over the sharpened tips of the palisade. With a flash of violet lightning and a crack of thunder, it lanced through the fog and struck one of the forward shields. It tore through the hide covering, leaving a ragged gash. The shaft tangled in torn leather before the head could meet flesh. I recalled it to my hand.

The men beside me spared half a second to stare, wide-eyed, as I caught the weapon in midair. It was the first time I had done so since leaving the ring-fort.

The smell of smoke and burning oil took our attention back to the ground beneath the battlements. The shield formation had reached our gate, and from underneath their shell, they set about lighting the palisade.

Days of rain and endless damp quelled the fire, but with enough oil, anything could burn. I slung my spear onto my back and climbed down the ladder, leaping to the earth from halfway down its rungs. Smoke replaced the morning fog, darkening the sky even as the sun crept above the trees. My boots carved furrows in the mud as I ran across the village, toward the swollen wood of the gate, just beginning to smolder.

A terrible crash shook the entire encampment. The gate bowed inward, the bar across it straining. Gaius's men had brought a ram, a felled tree, and they slammed it against our door even as arrows rained down on them from above.

Far more men than had occupied the ring-fort stood outside the palisade. Lord Oeneus had called in others, collecting the far-flung fragments of the empire he loved so well into an army that far outnumbered those within our walls. They had their own line of archers, now, and one of the warband fell from the battlements, landing in the mud beside me with an arrow in his brow.

If the gate came down, this settlement would die. I slung my spear onto my back and ran.

I put my hands to the bar across the gate, and it pricked my palms with splinters. The ram struck again, and the whole wall heaved into my body, pushing me backward. Three more of the warband, Ailbhe among them, came down to join me, pressing themselves against the buckling wood, but it was no use. The gate cracked.

I grabbed the shoulders of the two nearest me and pulled them away. "Get back!" I shouted.

The bar split in two, its halves clattering to the soft ground, and the door swung freely open. Smoke poured from the open passage. I readied my spear, covering my face with my free hand, but my eyes ran with tears as burning ash descended upon me.

I blinked them away. The silhouettes of men carrying spears and shields emerged from the smoke. In the gloom, a ceramic jar shattered, and the odor of burning oil grew stronger.

The first man to reach me swung with his shield, trying to knock my weapon away. I stepped back, striking forward, and caught the wooden rim of his shield with one dragon-claw barb. I tore the shield from his hands and struck him across the chest. He crumpled, gasping for air.

Out of the haze came the sound of hooves against the muddy ground and the shape of Gaius, the arrow still protruding from his shoulder, atop my horse. He kicked at Bran's sides, but Bran shied away. Even such a well-tempered beast as he was feared the fire.

The man at my feet groaned in pain and crawled at the earth, but he remained where he was. I ignored him. "Gaius!" I called out. "Give me back my horse!"

He slid from the saddle, a renewed burst of pain crossing his face. Blood stained his mail and trickled across his cuirass, and he tucked his left arm against his side, stiff and useless. He drew his sword with his right hand, leveling it at me, and placed himself in front of Bran.

I struck first, my spear darting toward his unshielded left side. He twisted away, the wide blade of his sword seeking my eyes, slicing a gash through the smoke in the air.

I slipped in the mud as I backed away and ducked my head under the arc of his slash. More of his men formed up behind him, blocking Bran from view, and others marched past me through the open gate. The battle-song grew loud in my ears, and I could see no one but Gaius, briefly a friend and much longer a foe.

I knocked his next blow away and swung the dragon's tooth toward his throat. I missed his flesh, but I caught the arrow stuck in his shoulder. More blood welled up from the wound. He cried out in pain and staggered backward, his knees buckling.

With my spear raised to deflect his blade, I charged at him, my shoulder meeting his abdomen and folding him in half. The wind fled from his lungs with a grunt. He dropped to the mud.

I drove the wicked head of my spear into the space at the top of his cuirass, breaking mail rings and biting into the flesh of his throat. Gaius gasped once, his lungs filling with blood, and then was still.

His men closed in around me, their shields raised.

I lifted the spear. I wished for a shield of my own, but not one lay within reach. In my fugue, I had left the palisade wall, venturing out into the clearing that lay between it and the forest.

Under their helmets, the shield line's eyes shone white in surprise. A terrible crash shook the forest from behind me. The fort itself had finally caught, and it crumbled, a chorus of panicked shouts and the crackling of the fire growing louder as the wooden supports failed at last.

Another detachment of soldiers placed themselves between me and the falling palisade. I could not reach the warband. I ran, slipping in the mud and breathing in smoke, reaching the end of their line.

I spotted Bran at the edge of the trees. He shied away from me as I came near, turning his head to examine me with one eye. Only then did he let me take his reins in hand and climb, clumsy as ever, into the saddle.

More shadowy figures poured form the gaps in the palisade wall, bent under the burdens of their children and belongings. They fled into the forest.

"Men of Lord Oeneus!" I shouted, my voice hoarse from the harsh air. "I've slain your captain. Come, avenge him!"

With the army at our heels, I steered Bran again into the forest. We darted between hazy beams of sunlight and the blackened trunks of trees, evading their spears. I pulled Bran to a slower pace when I had put distance between us and them, encouraging their pursuit and drawing their attention away from the fleeing folk of the village.

It was all I could think to do.

~ XXX ~

THE BURNING PLAIN

I had made a terrible mistake, and the knowledge of it came to me by degrees as I steered Bran through the forest. Instead of remaining with the warband to defend the gate, or even to put out the fire, I had left the palisade to pursue Gaius with a focus born of battle-rage. If I had stayed, I might have had a hand in preventing the loss of the fort. I cursed my foolishness, my words for myself no less harsh than the shouts that followed me into the trees.

Gaius's men, and the men he had rallied from other isolated fortresses along the crumbling border of what was once a mighty empire, pursued me on foot. One by one, they fell behind and out of sight in the shade of the trees. Clouds overtook the sun, bringing another bout of autumn rain, and even the glint of their mail and the heads of their spears vanished. So too had the forest folk, fleeing the burning palisade.

I dismounted, the ache in my legs making itself known. I had spent too long out of the saddle. Bran shook his head, rattling his harness, and bent to chew at the underbrush.

"It's good to see you, my friend," I said.

Gaius had fed him, and some stablehand had kept his coat glossy, but the marks of misused spurs—crescents of raw flesh—showed half-healed on his flanks. My anger flared, but exhaustion smothered it. I had not slept since early evening the day before. My rage was spent.

I checked his shoes and loosened the girth of the saddle, and we wandered together into the evening. The hidden paths through the forest were known to me now, after many days spent hunting with the warband, and I placed the faint halo of the setting sun on my left and headed north.

Bran's steps slowed, and so did mine. We were both of us much older than when we had begun this journey.

I found the camp of the forest folk at nightfall. They lit no fires, but enough daylight remained that I could make out the shapes of temporary shelters, little more than blankets thrown over frames of branches. The stones of the burial-ground stood a short distance away, like giants hunched and brooding in the darkness.

Many had escaped. Many others had not. Night fell, and I could not count those who remained.

I removed Bran's saddle and left him at the edge of the encampment, and alone I entered the great ring of stones. It was there I found Cullen, standing before the piled bones. Dried blood clung to his face and hands, and a deep violet bruise crept up his neck from the collar of his leather jerkin.

"Give me something," he begged the god of the grove. "Anything. Do you want to see your people suffer and die? There are so few of us left."

No answer came. He bowed his head, covering his face with his hands.

I had no words of comfort for him, nor any verse to describe the ache in my heart that bloomed like a terrible flower at the sight of him in pain. He looked up at my approach, and he allowed me to place a hand on his shoulder.

We stood like that for a long while, silent. The god was more so.

"If you were hoping for another chance at your old bones, my friend," Cullen said at last, "I'm afraid your luck has run out. There's no power here. There hasn't been for a long time."

He turned, his shoulder twisting away from my hand, and busied himself with striking a flint. Sparks bloomed from his fingers to die upon the mossy ground. His torch, an oily rag wrapped around a splintery fragment of wood that might have come from the palisade, flared to life and bathed the standing stones in firelight.

My arm dropped to my side, my hand suddenly cold. I lowered my head. "That's not why I'm here."

He raised the torch, and I could feel his gaze on my face. "No?"

"I was looking for you," I said. It was true, though now that I was here, perhaps I had followed a similar impulse to what had led him to the standing stones. I'd wanted absolution for my errors, or reassurance that all was not lost, despite the loss of the village. Even after so long, some part of me wanted to reach out to the gods.

The torch crackled and spat. "I'm sorry," Cullen said. "You fought well. You don't deserve mistrust after you risked your life for us. I should thank you."

I shook my head. "I've done nothing worth your gratitude. The village was my home, if only for a short time. I should have better defended it."

"You defended it no worse than I did." He moved to stand beside me once more, the light falling on the mounds of rock, the hollow eyes of old skulls, and the spirals etched into the standing stones. "My brother led the warband before me. Lord Oeneus' fair-haired son killed him, the last time he and his men came this way with their torches and spears. They put his head on a pike and strung his body from their wall—him, and my sister's husband, and our father, the old king. The women they buried in a shallow pit at the edge of the forest."

I bit back my empty words of sympathy. He had no need of them. What he needed was my silence as he told his tale.

"I brought them here. My father, my sister's husband, my brother, and three more of my friends. I cut them down myself.

I smelled of rot and old blood for days. The others I didn't find, not before the wolves and the crows got to them. My cousins, my friends, my former lover. The ravens ate her eyes."

In the camp, someone had lit a small fire. The trees danced in low, red light. Someone else was weeping.

"They took Ciannait and Faelan this time," Cullen said. "And half a dozen others. I have to get them back."

"Do you think they still live?" I asked.

He turned, as if he had just recalled I was there. "I don't know. It doesn't matter. They need to come home." Half a mirthless smile flashed across his face. "Or to what's left of it, anyway."

All thoughts of Deinaros and the task I had been sent here to complete fled my mind—though I still thought of my quest, and of Khalim, and the hollow cavern where once my heart had been. It was especially empty now. Cullen was a warrior born and bred, just as I was, and so unlike the man I had loved. Only in the most superficial sense did they resemble each other, but I could not help but find a similarity in the set of Cullen's jaw and the grim acceptance of the impossible task before him.

"I'm yours to command," I said. "I will help in any way I can."

Hadn't I said something like this to Khalim, so long ago? I could not remember. With a pang of guilt, I found that I could only just conjure the image of his face.

***

That night and the next day were spent in rest, and in searching for what supplies could be found in the fire-scarred underbrush and among the trees, standing there in their apathetic vigilance. The hollow that was once the last refuge of the forest folk stood black and empty. Gaius still lay in the mud, his face bloodless and streaked with ash, and there I left him. My anger toward him was a small, petulant thing, and he did not deserve it, as much as he might have deserved his ignoble end.

For my efforts, I recovered a few arrows and a handful of iron spearheads from the cinders, and a hunting knife I was permitted to keep with me. Of the fort's supply of food and clean water, however, I found nothing.

As the sun went down again, I set out with Bran through the trees, a bright torch in my hand and my spear on my back. The forest loomed over me, black against the black sky, and the lights of the ring-fort beckoned me onward. I took a winding path through the woods, leading my horse over fallen branches and in wide loops, so that the trail I laid behind me could not lead the men of Lord Oeneus back to the burial ground and the people sheltering there.

I had slain the son of the fort's master and taken back my horse. With my light the brightest flame other than the setting sun, the eyes of the invaders would all turn to me as soon as I emerged onto the plain. I was ready, as was the war-band following in the shadows behind me.

The western sky glowed red, and the yellow grasses undulating in the evening were like a field of fire. Shrouded in shadow, the ring-fort hunched upon the hill, the domes of the watchers' helmets pacing back and forth behind the edge of the wall. I slowed Bran's pace as we came nearer. The first man spotted me with a shout.

More helmets gathered on the ramparts, their dull crests quivering. I lifted my spear to my shoulder and threw.

It sliced through the heavy, damp air, whistling as it went, and landed at the base of the wall with a thunderous crash. The men above ducked, disappearing behind the ramparts.

They need not have worried. The lightning weapon left only a black scar upon the stone before it returned to my hand. I urged Bran onward toward the gate.

"Lord Oeneus!" I called out. "Your son is dead by my hand. I had no choice but to slay him. Release the people you took, and I'll see that his body is returned to you."

Oeneus was not upon the wall. He remained in his longhouse, ranting to the fire about a past age he had never seen, cursing the name of the son that he blamed for its loss. He could not hear me.

His men, however, took heed. The first arrows came down from the indigo sky, swift and deadly as a tempest wind. I dropped my torch, and it rolled across the wet ground and went out. Bran took off at a gallop, leaving me clinging to the saddle, his hooves tearing at the mud. Bits of earth stung my face and splattered on the ground behind us.

I steered him around, both hands on the reins and my thighs straining. A second volley of arrows fell to the ground. There lay the extent of the archers' range, marked by trembling feathers in the grass. Against his whinnying protests, I urged Bran onward, back toward the killing field and the gate. If no one sallied out to meet me, our scouts could not enter the fort and rescue those inside.

Yes, I did think of them as *our* scouts. How quickly I had come to count myself as one of the forest folk.

Arrows and wheat stalks snapped under Bran's hooves. We galloped in a wide circle, arrows pursuing us through the darkness. A red stain on the horizon was all that remained of the day. I threw my spear again, and blinding violet light tore through the sky, striking the fortress wall and leaving a searing streak through my vision. Screams followed the thundercrack.

"Lord Oeneus!" I shouted again. "I'll bring this wall down on your head!"

I did not believe even my weapon was capable of striking the foundations of the ring-fort, but the men inside did not know that. My hand curled around the shaft, and I let it fly once more.

After the lightning flash, the gate creaked and shuddered. Two men on horses emerged, shadows in front of the wavering lights of the fort, carrying shields and spears. A dozen men on foot came after.

More swift shadows emerged from the trees, under the cloak of night. The warband had arrived. I would keep that gate open if it meant my death.

The riders chased me across the field, closing the distance between us. One turned toward the forest to head me off as I circled around. Like a hedge of deadly branches, the other soldiers made a line of spears in front of the fort, bracing to skewer Bran as the riders drove us toward the wall.

More arrows darted out of the night, this time from the ground. The spear line collapsed, ducking behind their shields, and the warband fell upon them. Iron blades glinted in the fort's lamplight.

I pulled hard on Bran's reins. We slipped away from the spears and flew down the hill, and Oeneus' riders came after us.

The base of the fort was a field of broken arrows, casting long, interwoven shadows. Mud and splinters flew up as we went, stinging my face and the backs of my hands. I reached for my battle-rage to keep the pain and exhaustion at bay, but it would not come to me. My legs ached and my eyes strained against the arrival of night, and worse still was the growing dread like ice in my belly as I turned Bran back toward the gate. In the confusion, the doors remained open, but I could not tell whether the men still standing there were ours or the ring-fort's.

A torrent of arrows greeted me as I came near. One glanced across my cheek, leaving a streak of pain like fire in its wake. More littered the ground before me.

One found its home in Bran's flank, sinking into his unprotected flesh. He screamed, kicking his back legs, and I tumbled from the saddle a second time to land in the mud. The broken shafts of arrows cut into my palms and the meat of my arms. With a deafening noise, the pursuing rider from the fort thundered by, close enough for me to touch. I covered my head with my arms.

I pushed myself to my feet, my bleeding hands slipping against the churned earth of the field. Each step sent more pain through my legs and into the bruises forming on my back. Where was the fury that would propel me to victory? All I could summon was a mundane, helpless anger that my companion was injured and had disappeared from my sight, and my allies fought at the gate, so far from me now that I was on foot. The fort burned with light, its doors hanging open and smoke rising to the cloudless sky.

In the light of the rising moon, Bran's shadow limped toward the edge of the forest. I meant to call out to him, but the shout died on my tongue. I could not draw the riders back to me. Clenching my teeth to keep from complaining, I stumbled after Bran.

He shied away when I caught up to him, his eyes shining white. Blood ran around the shaft of the arrow and down his leg, fever-hot in the evening chill. I reached for his bridle, but he turned his head away, his nostrils flaring. His hooves tore at the ground.

"It's all right, my friend," I said.

At the sound of my voice, his frantic movement slowed, and he sniffed at my offered hand. If he had run, then, I might have deserved it. I had only just recovered him from his captivity in the fort, and already he had been wounded.

Working by touch, I grasped the shaft of the arrow where it entered Bran's flesh. I took my knife and made two tiny cuts there at the base. Bran stamped his feet and snorted in displeasure. With the barbs free, I drew the arrow out and cast it aside.

Blood welled from the wound, shining bright and wet under the moonlight. I tore a strip from the bottom of my cloak and pressed it against Bran's flank. "It wasn't deep," I said, reassuring myself more than him. "You'll run again before long."

One of his dark eyes turned to me with something like doubt. He would need proper care if he were to heal fully, care I could not give him on the field of battle. "Stay here," I told him. "I'll come back for you."

I left him there, in the trees out of sight of the ring-fort, and ran toward the pillar of smoke rising above the hill and spreading into the black sky. It burned my eyes and throat with every step I took. My body was as heavy as if it were carved of stone. Cursing my foul luck, the rage that would not appear to bolster me, and the memory of Gaius, I climbed through mud and broken arrows. The recent rain kept the fire low, and the dead grasses smoldered with tiny tongues of fire. My boots put them out, and more smoke curled around my feet.

At a wordless shout from the gate, I raised my head. A man in filthy chainmail, soot and mud and drying blood streaked across his face, drew his short, wide sword and charged at me.

I willed my exhausted legs to move. His wild swing cut through the air, singing as it went, and I backed away and took my spear in hand. A second blow missed my face by a hair.

"Die, barbarian!" the man cried. His voice broke on the last syllable, his teeth shining white in his dirty face. Madness had taken him. Even if he survived the night, it might never have let him go.

His next strike came directly toward my abdomen. I grasped his mail sleeve in my free hand and drew him in, letting the sword pass harmlessly under my arm. He stumbled. I let him go and grasped the crest of his helmet. Scarlet hair came free in my hand as the helmet lifted from his head. Underneath, his own hair was dark, cut short and sticking up at odd angles. He looked suddenly very young.

With the shaft of my spear, I delivered a single sharp blow to the back of his head. He fell to the ground.

He might have died there. He might have woken some time later, free from madness and the commands of his lord, and lived a long life. I would never know.

Leaving him where he lay, I staggered into the fort. The smoke thickened, trapped as it was inside the circular wall. The longhouse was a hunched shadow within, its roof burning slowly with the hiss of steam. Other shadows, the shapes of the barn and the house in which I had been confined for a short time, emerged as I made my way inside, spear at the ready. The thatch covering the house was all alight, pouring great clouds into the air, through which a handful of indistinct figures moved.

The roof sagged, sending out a shower of sparks to die in the mud. A scream cut through the night, high and frantic—the voice of a child.

I ran for the house. A man in a hide cloak, his face too obscured by ash and dirt for me to recognize, reached into the front window, shouting in a hoarse voice for anyone to answer him. More smoke wreathed his arms.

The door had been barred and the house set afire. The split log lying across it glowed hot at its edges, and the steam coming from it made my shirt cling to my chest.

At last, my fury came to me, and I took the searing bar in both hands and felt nothing. I threw it toward the stable and planted one foot against the edge of the door. Rotting wood came apart in a cascade of splinters.

A thick, black cloud poured from the open doorway and washed over me, robbing me of light and breath. Sparks burned cloth and flesh alike, but the pain remained at a distance. There was only the open door and the people beyond it. I wrapped my arm in my cloak and brought it over my face, and blindly I stepped over the threshold.

I lowered my arm, squinting into the stinging fog. Black sky showed through the burning roof. Beside the open window, with the silhouette of a desperate man reaching, sightless, into the smoke, the bed linens had gone up in flames. The structure of the building, permeated as it was with rain, only hissed and sputtered. Six shadowed figures huddled against the opposite wall. They coughed, thin and weak, as they unfurled themselves.

"Keep your heads down," I said, but my words died in the smoke and steam.

A familiar face—Cullen's, but softer and streaked with soot—came out of the darkness. Here was Ciannait and her young son, left to burn alive. "Where's my brother?" she asked.

I took her hand and led her out of the smoldering house. The man at the window—Diarmuid, now that I stood with the light of the fire at my back—came to bring the others out into the cold night. Ciannait stopped on the path with a fit of coughing, pulling at my hand.

"Come on," I encouraged her.

She shook her head. "My brother," she said again, her voice a rasping whisper that I had only heard before from the dead.

"I'll find him," I promised.

I placed her and the boy Faelan into Diarmuid's custody, and I turned back to the burning village encircled in stone.

A handful of soldiers, their crested helmets streaked with ash and their eyes reddened from the smoke, stood before the door of the longhouse. The same madness that had plagued their companion outside the gate stared at me from behind their dented nose-guards, a bestial rage that, in a stroke of irony, saw the forest folk as inhuman and themselves as the only men worthy of life and succor. I understood, then, the purpose of Oeneus' rambling speeches, and it was not only to shame his son. It was to make these men dream of the empire long fallen, to love it more than life, to be willing to die in fire and blood for it and for him. That after nearly forty years of this, Gaius had been capable of holding a conversation with one such as I was a credit to him.

I placed myself between the soldiers and the fleeing captives, my spear planted in the earth. Let them defend their lord, I thought. As long as the forest folk escaped alive, these men could do as they wished.

Harsh, yellow light flared above the roof. A sharp whistle cut through the sounds of crackling flame and groaning timber. A figure stood atop the spine of the longhouse, holding aloft a torch that burned bright with lamp oil.

The soldiers turned. Cullen drew back the hood of his cloak, showing a wolfish grin, and dropped the torch at his feet.

The damp thatch went up in a blinding flash and the smell of burning oil. Cullen's shadow reeled backward and dropped from the roof, the flames at his heels. I picked up my spear and threw it at the soldiers' feet. The light of its thunderous strike was brighter even than the fire consuming the longhouse.

It returned to my hand as the first of three soldiers reached me. I braced for the oncoming sword-cut, catching it upon the shaft of my spear and turning it aside. The second man drove his own spear under my right arm. I twisted away, and it sliced through my clothing, leaving a bloody gash against my ribs. For now, I felt no pain. I drove the dragon's tooth into his belly with both hands, bursting mail rings and plunging into flesh.

The third man raised a sword dented and pitted with abuse. With my spear embedded in his fellow, I had no means by which to defend myself. I raised an arm and took a step backward.

He fell to his knees, the leather-wrapped handle of a dagger protruding from the base of his neck where the mail failed to reach. Cullen emerged from the cloud of smoke, a second dagger in his hand, his leather bracers and the hem of his sleeve scorched black.

I had no time to thank him, nor even to take a breath of the foul air in order to do so, before the first soldier took two strides across the rutted ground and slashed his blade in a swift arc across

Cullen's belly. The thick leather of Cullen's jerkin prevented his innards from spilling to the mud, but he bled freely, his face going pale.

I wrenched my spear from the dead man's belly with a sickening squelch. Broken mail rings flew into the air. I swung, and my spearhead rang off the side of the soldier's helmet like a discordant bell. He stumbled to one side, his hands raised in a feeble, confused defense.

I did not wait for him to regain his senses. I grasped Cullen by the arm and lifted him over my shoulder, ignoring his weak protest, and I ran from the fort.

The world had turned dark. Clouds covered the moon, and a soft rain began to fall, on the trees and the town and on the soldiers and the forest folk alike.

***

Morning came, the sun rising pale gray behind the growing storm clouds. Blood and water soaked my skin as I trudged through the woods, from Cullen's wound in his belly and my own, less dire; from the wound in Bran's flank, reopened as I encouraged him to keep pace. My battle-rage was spent, and it left me more bereft than I had expected. My steps slowed, and Cullen grew heavier with each passing minute. I stopped to tie another strip of my cloak around him and stanch Bran's wound, but still Cullen's face paled, and still blood ran down Bran's black flank. I could not dismiss the growing sense of dread warning me that I had made another terrible mistake.

I had a sailor's sense of direction, even after my years away from the sea, and the way to the encampment was not so long. I had wandered halfway there alone, in the dark, when I had first left the ring-fort. In daylight, it was no more welcoming than it had been at night, with its fire cold and the tents running with rainwater. Ciannait took Cullen from me, and I tended to my wound and Bran's under a canvas stretched between two branches.

The rain chased away the last of the smoke. The forest would stand for another season, as would the ring-fort, though I could not say what would become of the people living in either.

As the day went on, I made my way to the burial ground, and I stood there among the stones and listened to the rain and the silence of the gods. The skulls at my feet outnumbered the living people in the encampment. Still more had been buried, in mounds or in graves, layers upon layers of earth and death—a grim record of all who had lost their lives in this land.

I would never find the skull of Maponos, no longer ever-living. I had no skill in magecraft; no talent as a shaman. If indeed his mortal remains rested here, I could not tell them from the hundreds and thousands of others. Deinaros must have known that I would not succeed when he sent me here.

Had he intended for me to die, and thus rid himself of an unwanted houseguest and a and my demands for a task that even he, all-knowing as he claimed to be, could not complete?

I raised my hand to the stone before me, and I watched rainwater run through the spirals carved into it and over the same spiral, tattooed on my arm. Then I left the grove, this place at once familiar and strange, and returned to the encampment.

Ciannait waited for me beside the remains of the fire. Her son lay at her feet, wrapped in an oilcloth and fast asleep. One day, he would learn what was expected of him, but today he could rest easy.

"Your name is Eske, isn't it?" Ciannait asked, keeping her head lowered. She brushed a lock of black hair from Faelan's brow. Her hands were clean of mud and ash, but she had torn her nails during her captivity, and the ends of her fingers were bloody.

I crouched a short distance away, extending my hands to the fire. Winter had arrived without my noticing it, with its absence of snow, but the air held a sharp, bright chill. "It is," I said. She'd had little reason to use my name. We had barely spoken during my time here.

"Thank you, Eske," she said. "My brother may be a fool, but he's all I have."

A knot in my chest loosened. "He'll live?"

"He'll not bend a bow for at least a season, but yes, he'll live. He wanted to see you."

I thanked her, and I stood and bowed to her. I had never seen her lift a weapon—though most of the forest folk had learned to fight out of necessity—and yet she was as brave as any warrior who had ever walked this war-torn land.

"Make sure he doesn't try to move about," she added as I ducked into the tent.

Cullen's face had turned moon-white from the loss of blood. Under two thick blankets, his chest rose and fell with shallow breaths. His eyes cracked open and found me in the fading light. "I've made a mess of things, haven't I?" he said.

"I'm not the one to ask," I told him. I had done worse in my time. "What happens now?"

With some effort, he brought one arm out from the bedclothes to draw a hand across his brow. "Diarmuid will lead the warband. My brother should have chosen him to begin with. We'll stay here a while, until we're all back on our feet, and then—" He struggled through another breath, staring hard at the seam of the tent. "North, I suppose, to find what's left of our kin."

"You dealt Lord Oeneus and his king a blow," I said, "though I can't say I'd agree with your tactics."

He laughed, a short, painful snort through his nose. "Lord Oeneus died in his hall. I'm sure of it."

"They'll want vengeance." I had seen it in the mad eyes of Oeneus' soldiers. "Whether they will have the capability of taking it remains to be seen."

Cullen's grim face told me that I did not need to remind him of this. He knew his enemies better than I ever could. "What are you going to do now?" he asked.

"I'm going to look after you for the evening," I said. "If you tear out your stitches, Ciannait will have my hide."

He laughed, again, and groaned, dropping his hand to his side. Outside the tent, the day was dying, and his face fell into darkness except for a thin, illuminated profile, like a sliver moon. He turned to me, and the light fell on the scar on his mouth. "And after that?"

I had no answer.

His hand, warm and rough, crossed the worn blanket and wrapped around mine. "You could stay," he said. "The gods know we could use your help. And I, well, I quite like your company. It's a hard life, here, but there's a life here for you, if you want it."

I saw that life spool out before me. The days would be long, but the years would be short. I'd have a home again, and a family, and though I'd have to fight for each meal and each roof under which I lay my head, I would no longer walk the world alone.

But could I fight for another ten years, twenty, or as long as I should live? As a young man, I had not expected to see thirty, but now I believed I might die old, should fortune favor me. I felt again the hollow where my rage should have been. Instead there was only exhaustion, enveloping me like a cocoon.

I would raise my spear again, if fate forced my hand, but I could not choose to fight. And as much as I had come to care for Cullen, I could not forget Khalim. I could not allow my tale to end without fulfilling my promises.

So I would return to Deinaros, without the skull, and I would continue on until I found the gate of bone or died in the attempt.

I let Cullen's hand go. "In another lifetime," I said, "I would stay with you. In this one, I still have a long way to travel. I'm sorry."

~ XXXI ~

THE EMPTY TOWER

I stayed until the turn of the moon, to help the forest folk prepare for their journey. After the fall of their village, they had very little to pack, but they welcomed a strong pair of arms. In truth, I was delaying my last farewells: to Cullen, to Ciannait, to this beautiful, terrible place, and to Bran.

Bran, my faithful companion, the bravest of horses and the last gift that I still possessed from Phyreios, had endured enough in my company. He deserved solid ground beneath his hooves, green growing things to eat, and the open sky over his head. After his ordeals here, how could I force him to endure another weeks-long trek over land, burdened by my weight and the weight of my pack, or another sea voyage confined belowdecks? And after I had returned to Ksadaja, how much more would I have to ask of him? Let him carry the children of the forest folk north. Let him hunt with them, and teach them to ride, and flee with them to safety. Let him spend the rest of his years in one place, in what little peace he might find.

So I left him behind, and with him remained a piece of my battered heart. I thought it a fitting tribute.

On the day the migration of the forest folk was to begin, I too departed, setting off on foot for the old imperial highway that would take me south. I would return to Deinaros, and report to him that the power of his slain teacher was no more—and that I had survived whatever he might have intended when he sent me to the grove.

Without a horse, my road stretched on for the better part of a year, through a late, mild winter and a stormy spring into a cloudless summer. Days passed where I did not see another soul; weeks went by between the occasions when I had reason to speak. Even the traders accepted my offers of coin or furs without needing to make conversation. I became, once again, a strange, quiet thing, my stories and boasts dying unspoken on a clumsy, inelegant tongue.

I arrived in Elisia on midsummer's eve, haggard and filthy from my travels and wanting nothing more than a bath and a meal I did not have to forage for myself. Ashoka had long since left, his unending pilgrimage carrying him out of the city and out of my story. In his absence, the temple of the seven strangers sat hollow and still upon its marble stairs, without a word of doubt to disturb its serene austerity. I found, standing beneath those carved images with their faces untouched by the travails of the world, that I missed him. I'd harbored some small hope that I would find him again. Who else might offer a listening ear to the tale of the silent gods of the forest folk and the people they had abandoned?

It was a foolish thought. Our shared time in Phyreios and a moment in this temple had not made a friendship between us. He had gone his way, and I would go mine, taking a ship out of Elisia and across the Summer Sea. I paid for my passage with the very last of the treasure I had acquired in Kannaoka.

I arrived in Ksadaja at the close of summer, and the city of tombs welcomed me with its usual antipathy. In my absence, the market's borders had expanded to the docks and into the deeper shadows of the larger tombs, the brilliant scarlet and azure stripes of their tents turned dull and gray in the darkness. The heavy scent of the forest, dank and earthy, filled the bustling streets.

I wandered for an hour or two, acclimating myself to the press of humanity and the cacophony of their voices. Even the ship's berth had not been so crowded. I was searching for Cricket, as well, in the hope that I would find her before my long walk to Deinaros' tower. I would have asked her of her teacher's moods, of the location of the book I had brought him, and of her own well-being. As clever as she was, I had left her in a measure of danger.

But I could not find her. Her characteristic jangling of silver trinkets was nowhere to be heard. Disheartened, I headed into the forest.

Three times I had seen the seasons change in this eldritch place, and yet to me it appeared eternal. Leaves fell and collected in great hills between roots rising from the earth like the serpentine back of the lind-worm. Sunlight shone gold and green far above, and there it remained, leaving the forest floor and the road that cut through it in darkness.

I climbed the stairs to Deinaros' door and found it locked. I raised a fist and struck it above the rusted iron handle, shaking it in its frame. From the way it shuddered, it had been barred as well, a measure Deinaros had not taken in all the days I had sheltered here.

No matter, I thought. The sorcerer was absorbed in his books, or pacing the floor in his study, or whatever he did to pass the time. Cricket would have to leave for the market soon, or attend to another of her long list of duties, and she would find me on the doorstep and grant me entry. I took a piece of dry bread from my pack and sat on the platform to eat it, my back against the door. Cricket would provide me with better rations, at least.

I felt, rather than heard, the door unlock and the bar slip from its brackets and fall to the floor. With a great creaking of hinges, the door opened, spilling me into the entry hall. The spiral staircase ascended above me, diminishing as it climbed into the tower's height.

I got to my feet, rolling to my knees and stowing the last of my bread. The odor of old rot hung in the air, mixed with the smell of dusty parchment and drying herbs. The herbs themselves were absent. Bits of knotted string dangled from underneath the stairs.

Thin, watery lamplight from a higher platform fell in a pool before the doorway. Something that might have been soot blackened the windows. I took a cold torch from the wall and lit it with my flint, and it illuminated an eyeless, grinning skull lying on its side at the foot of the steps.

"That wasn't here last time," I said aloud. The oppressive silence was a physical weight on my skin and pressure in my ears. I raised the torch, and it revealed a rib cage, turned ocher brown from decay and age and caved in on itself. On the other side of the room, a broken pelvis stood upright on the tiled stone like a dropped ceramic vessel. More bones, thin and brittle, lay scattered across the floor, crumbling to dust as I failed to avoid them, picking my way over to the skull.

Cricket would be furious, I thought, when she returned from her errands to see that someone had made a mess of the place. She would not enjoy having to sweep up these bones and scrub the dark stains they left on the floorboards.

"Deinaros!" I called out. "I've returned from the lands to the north, and I would speak with you."

The tower answered only with more silence.

My torch raised, I climbed the stairs, leaving footprints of bone dust as I went. Light streamed through the windows of the second floor, and here the room was strewn not with bones but with books—unfurled scrolls, heavy tomes spilling crumbling pages from broken spines, and thin volumes in leaning stacks. The contents of Deinaros' storied library had been torn from their shelves and thrown here, with no regard for sorting or the monsters that dwelled between their covers. Intricate geometric diagrams and illustrations of cadavers stared up at me from between my boots.

Cricket had been neglecting her duties. My heart fell like a stone.

"Deinaros!" I called again. "Cricket? Is anyone there?"

I climbed another flight of stairs, and another, reaching the sanctum of the sorcerer. For the first time, its door was open, and my access to his secrets unimpeded. I stepped into the room.

Instead of the sorcerer, however, I found Cricket, wrapped in a robe of midnight blue and seated atop a tall stool, its four spindly legs draped in the fabric and bending slightly as she shifted her weight. In her lap sat an open book—the book I had carried here from the southern seas, with the illustration of the flayed man gazing out from its pages.

"Eske," she said. "I thought you'd died out on the road."

She had grown older, in the time I had been absent—and in the years I had spent in this tower with her, though I had not noticed it. Her face was a woman's face, long and elegant. She was as tall as the women in the marketplace, her feet almost reaching the floor and the stack of books there. And yet, to me, she was still the bright-eyed girl she had been when first we met. Had I grown so old in my absence, that a young woman of sixteen or seventeen was only a child? I had set out from my homeland at only two years her senior.

"I'm not dead yet," I said.

She closed the book and set it on the shelf beside her. The stool rocked, two of its legs lifting off the floor and coming back down with a loud crack.

"What happened here, Cricket?" I asked. "Where is Deinaros?"

"Deinaros is dead," she answered, her face downturned. She brushed a dark curl out of her face. In the place of the trinkets that had dangled from her neck and wrists, only fading, paler rings on her dark skin remained. "You'd have seen him on the first floor."

I remembered the decaying skeleton lying in pieces at the bottom of the stairs, and I shivered despite the close heat of the room.

"What happened to him?" I asked. I set the torch in a bracket on the wall and approached her as I might an animal in a trap, my hands open. "Are you hurt?"

"I'm fine," Cricket said. "Deinaros was weak, and he had lived too long. I was stronger."

My breath stirred the dust in the air. "I don't understand. Did you kill Deinaros?"

"I did." A grim smile flickered across her face.

A series of visions flashed through my mind—an explosion of magic, like the incantation that had summoned the worm under Phyreios, confined to this small space; Deinaros' ageless, spidery hands raised against Cricket in fear and wrath; the tomes she had removed from the library, with or without her master's permission.

"I've been busy since you've been gone," Cricket said, dispelling my thoughts. "I am the sorcerer of the tower, now. Deinaros thought he could keep all his knowledge from me forever. I cast him down."

This was no boast. "I...I understand," I said, taking another step away from the stairs. I had no desire to follow Deinaros' likely descent down several floors. "I had no love for the sorcerer. I only worked for him because he promised to help me."

"I know," she said.

A small measure of relief eased the tension in my shoulders. I lowered my hands.

Her eyes darted toward the book lying flat upon the shelf. "He was lying to you, you know. Or he wasn't telling you everything. Once you had brought back the skull of Maponos, he would open the way to the other world, and send you to slay the gods of the tombs with your lightning weapon before you ever chased down the soul you lost. You'd have died, there, and stayed beyond the gate forever."

"But he promised—" I began, but I could not continue. My journey to the North and back had consumed so much time, and I had lingered here even longer, and how long had I spent crossing the world with the book in my pack, unable to read it but feeling its evil fester with each passing day?

Cricket stood, and the cloak spilled around her like a waterfall. "He kept the truth from you, just as he lied to me about making me his apprentice. He was never going to teach me."

"Is that why you killed him?" I asked.

"No." For the first time, a shadow of sorrow fell across her face. Despite her trappings, she was still a child, not the robed sorcerer in the tower. Had I been so young at her age? "I didn't mean to harm him. He tried to wrench a book from my hands, and lightning flashed in his fingers. I thought he was going to kill me."

The rest I could imagine. She had turned Deinaros' magic against him, a lesson he had failed to teach her but that she had taken on herself, and he had fallen through his tower until the long years he had spent cheating death had caught up to him at last, and his body had decayed to rotted bones and dust. It mattered not whether Cricket had intended for this to happen, nor if Deinaros had deserved death. He was gone, and Cricket was master of the tower, and I was no closer to finding Khalim than I had been when I left the isle of the priestesses.

"Even if he did tell the truth," I said, "I could not find the skull of Maponos. I'll have to find another way."

Cricket gestured to the room and its books. "You want to go to the land of the dead. I can help you."

"You've been reading?" I asked lightly, trying to hide the despair weighing down on me.

She regarded me with a familiar look of utter disdain. The child Cricket still lived under the troubled face of the young woman. "Of course I've been reading. First, I read the safe books, and I learned to bind the monsters between the pages."

As if in response, the shelf at her side shuddered, its heavy tomes shifting in place. I backed away toward the stairs.

"*Then* I read the others," she continued. "I didn't sleep for four days. I know all of Deinaros' secrets, and some he didn't know."

He wasn't all-knowing, after all. I could not be surprised, after my quest to find the remains of one called ever-living.

Shadows encircled Cricket's eyes. From within, they glowed with an eerie half-light, a pale moon that hung in her pupils and nowhere else. The fading sunlight filtered through the narrow window, placing a mantle of green atop her deep blue robe. She gathered the voluminous sleeves about her, turning the garment into a cocoon. It made her appear very small.

"Have you slept since then?" I asked.

She blinked. "I think so."

I approached her, my hand outstretched. The books shifted again, as though something living hid in the shelf behind them, pushing its way to freedom. I did not look at them. "You should rest," I said. "The books will still be here afterward."

Cricket rubbed at her eyes with the heels of both palms. "There are so many. I don't know which of them will help you."

"I know. But you're young, and you might live as long as Deinaros did. You have time."

"Three hundred years," she said. "He lived three hundred years. Maybe a few more. He was going to take my blood to live even longer."

And I had brought him the book of the undead king, and of the priest who kept his decaying corpse walking. "I'm so sorry, Cricket," I said. I should never have come here. Failing that, I should never have left.

I placed a hand on her shoulder and guided her, step by step, down the stairs to the guest quarters. She hid her face behind one sleeve as we crossed the landing where Deinaros' remains lay. One floor below, I placed her in the first room across from the stairs.

Without the books nearby to whisper to her, she fell asleep in moments.

A search of the tower, avoiding the stacks of books, turned up a few silver coins, and I took these to the market to purchase what I thought she might need—blankets, a few staple foods, lamp oil, and on an impulse, a cloth doll with hair of plaited string and a plain linen dress of the sort Cricket once wore. She was much too old for such a thing, but other than her clothing and the sorcerer's books, she owned nothing.

I returned to the tower and left these objects in a careful stack outside her room, and I went to sweep up the remains of Deinaros the All-Knowing.

***

I lived in the tower for another turn of the autumn moon, and Cricket pored over tome after tome, searching for answers. I reminded her to eat two or three times a day, and took her lamp soon after sunset, to encourage her to sleep. She kept the doll and placed it in the windowsill above her bed, a post from which I never saw it removed. I slept under the stairs, close to the entry, listening for intruders within and without.

The only beast that emerged from the open books strewn about the tower was a scaled, six-legged thing only an arm's length from nose to tail. In the early morning, while Cricket still slept, it scurried from the pages of one book to another and disappeared into its spine. Only a series of tiny scratches in the vellum proved that it had ever been there at all.

That night, in my bedroll upon the floor that still smelled faintly of bone dust, I dreamed of the gray beach one last time. I followed the oaken-antlered stag through the dead forest and came to the banks of a river, so deep its waters were black under the green cast of the sky. The stag crossed, walking upon the water, footsteps lighter than a fallen feather, but I plunged into the frigid depths like a stone and swam against an impossible current. The water became a mass of fish, dark and slippery, lifting me upon their backs and carrying me downstream, their tails beating against my skin. The stag watched me with its soft human eyes from the opposite bank, growing distant as I struggled.

With one mighty surge, the fish ejected me from their school and deposited me on the sand. I lay face down, my arms aching and the earth heaving beneath me. Fearing the stag would depart without me, and I would never find it again, I drew my exhausted limbs up and got to my feet, swaying with the memory of the current.

Before me lay a sea of grass, golden and undulating, underneath a sky the deep blue of the Summer Sea. Insects sang in an aimless, meandering trill, and the wind carried the faint scent of woodsmoke.

On the far horizon, shining like a beacon, stood a high city wall of pristine white marble.

"You have traveled far, Eske son of Ivor," the stag said. Three scarlet beetles alighted on its crown of branches, their shielded wings humming.

"Have I?" I crossed my arms over my bare chest, and the armored pauldron on my left shoulder bumped against the side of my jaw. I was dressed as I had been in the tournament, so long ago, and the air carried a chill here that it had not even on the Iron Mountain. "This is a dream. I'm no closer to Khalim's prison than I ever have been, and he's no longer there, besides."

"You know the way," said the stag. "Will you choose to take it?"

The city shone so bright under the hollow sky that my eyes ached to behold it. "Of course I will," I said.

"Then on you will be the consequences," was the last thing I heard before I woke.

I left my bed and climbed to the study that had belonged to Deinaros, and I retrieved Ucasta's tome from the shelf where Cricket had left it, stepping with care around the books on the floor. The pages fell open between my hands to the image of the stag, and I gazed at it as if its lifeless form in ink would tell me more than the living image in my dream had.

It said nothing. I could interpret neither the drawing nor the text around it.

"Eske," Cricket's voice came from behind another stack of books, thin and dry from the dust.

I returned the book to its place. "Do you need something?" I asked. I was no good to her in matters of letters, but I could always walk to the market again.

"I found something," she said.

I ducked under the stairs and around a stack of moldering volumes that came up to my waist. Cricket sat curled in Deinaros' chair, the blue robe wrapped around her, her hair tied in a faded scarf that might have once been one of her plain gowns. A slim, leather-bound book lay open in her hands, its binding crudely stitched in black thread. More characters I could not read marched in columns across its pages. Blots of faded ink bled in the spaces between them.

"Deinaros wrote this," Cricket explained. "It's a record of the pilgrims who came to his door."

I leaned one elbow on another stack of books, but I straightened and left them alone at Cricket's sharp glance. "He hadn't seen any pilgrims in months, last I saw him," I said.

"This was years and years ago." Her finger traced the column of figures, dry skin rasping against the page. "The man came to Ksadaja on a ship, and he was ill from the long voyage. Deinaros promised to heal him for less coin than the doctor in the lower city."

It was fortunate that I had not fallen sick before I had arrived here the first time. "Did he?"

"It doesn't say." Cricket turned the page. "The man said he was returning from a pilgrimage far to the south, to a harbor at the edge of the world where the night lasted for three weeks."

My pulse quickened. "A day without a sun," I said, recalling Khalim's words to me, so many years ago, and Deinaros' passing mention of a long night. "We have such days in the North, as well, at the other edge of the world. But we do not have such a harbor."

I'd heard of this harbor before, I remembered now: in the tale of the maiden Sorcha, who put her young siblings in a silver boat and sailed first to a harbor in that eternal night, and then into legend. I had not returned quite empty-handed from the forest. I offered Cullen a silent thanks that he would never receive.

"The man wouldn't tell him any more," Cricket said, "only that his fellow pilgrims would come to his rescue. Deinaros tormented him with illusions of fire and darkness, but he would only say that he had seen death already, and he feared it not. Eventually, Deinaros turned the man away, and he left Ksadaja and did not return."

"Then it seems I, too, must leave Ksadaja," I told her, "and seek the harbor at the end of the world."

"He thought he knew where he might be, but he wanted to get there by magic, instead. I can help you." Sorrow darkened her eyes, but her face was resolute. She was master of this tower, now, for all the good and ill that meant. "You could come visit again, someday," she said.

I could not promise her that I would, only that I would try. I could not say if I would ever return from this last journey.

I gathered my few belongings, and Cricket gave me books of maps to aid me on my way, though I could interpret a scant few of them, their inked coastlines unknown to me despite the extent of my travels. After all this time, I had yet to see so much of the world. Standing at the tower's threshold, I longed for the days when all that existed lay between the mountains of ice in the sea and the mountains of stone on the land. In the summer, in the days without night, I could have crossed from one to the other in a matter of weeks.

The thought departed as soon as it arose. It was not by choice that I had left the lands of my birth, but I had chosen not to return, even now, when I turned instead to the other side of the world.

***

I needed a ship, and so I departed from the tower and from the city of the dead, chasing a rumor of the *Lady of Osona*, the ship that had carried me across the southern seas, and of her intrepid captain. I followed the coast to another city, as rich and vast as Ksadaja—Marenni, the jewel of the Sultan of Beddal, whose sword had slain a demon of the desert for each of his seven daughters, the cursed flesh offered as dowries on their wedding days. His palace, overlooking the sea, was home to his great-great-grandson, a man so afflicted by illness that he wore a porcelain mask and never left the palace walls. The image of his mask, bone-white and painted with sapphire to give it the appearance of one eternally weeping, adorned the walls at regular intervals. Despite the mournful appearance of these frescoes, the people in the market were cheerful, and gold and silver, silk and spice, steel and lacquered wood exchanged hands with barely a glance of acknowledgment toward the sad, painted faces.

Hamilcar was there, along with his crew. He recognized me before I did him, and called out to me across the busy square.

"I was wondering if I'd ever see you again, my friend," he said, grasping my arm in a warrior's handshake.

I, too, had worried that my path would never again cross his. "I must ask you again for your help," I said. "I must cross the southern seas and find the harbor at the end of the world."

His eyes widened and his mouth opened, but no words came forth. Then he laughed, throwing his head back in delight. "I would expect no less from you, my friend. Come, let us talk. The crew will want to hear your stories."

~ XXXII ~

THE LAST, LONELY HARBOR

If I had gained nothing else from my term in the service of Deinaros the All-Knowing, I had obtained several volumes of esoteric maps and the goodwill of the new master of the sorcerer's tower, a boon far more valuable than that of her predecessor. These I gave to Hamilcar, in exchange for his aid on this most perilous of journeys.

We would sail west first, out of the Summer Sea and into the vast, unforgiving ocean. We would then turn south and sail as long as the *Lady of Osona* could withstand the wind and the waves. She was a sturdy vessel, reinforced with the best shipbuilding techniques known to all the peoples of the trade routes, but Hamilcar warned me that even she would not hold together in the waters at the end of the world. Already he planned to sail farther than he had ever dared before now, the siren call of adventure louder in his ears than the voice of caution. I would have to traverse the last miles over land, alone.

For twenty-seven days, we outran the coming winter. Its winds carried us past Ksadaja and Elisia alike, while dolphins danced alongside the ship's hull, hunting shining silver fish just out of reach of the oars. Seabirds circled overhead, hoping for a share of the catch, their wings gleaming white in the slanting sunlight.

As the weeks stretched on, the sun would grow scarce. When we reached the narrow strait that served as a gateway between one ocean and the next, a gray ceiling of sky stretched out between the cliffs that rose up on either side. The water rose around us, and the current drove us toward the spearing rocks. Hamilcar stood at the rudder, his hands white-knuckled. With salt spray in my eyes and lashing against my skin, I brought down the last sail. It fought and kicked against the wind like a living creature.

Water surged beneath the ship, lifting her toward the sky. The cries of the crew, half triumph and half fear, crescendoed and fell abruptly quiet as we fell into the trough of another wave, wind screaming in our ears and tearing at the moorings. Clinging to the mast, I shielded my face from the driving wind. Walls of stone pressed in on either side.

We passed through the strait, our passage like being spat out from the mouth of a great serpent. Quiet, or something like it, covered the soaked deck. Waves broke upon the hull, no higher than the rail, and the wind's roar dropped to a lonely keening. Rain, soft and heavy, fell from the gray dome of the sky.

We did not escape that rain on our way south, not for many weeks. I shivered in my hammock and through my meager rations as I broke my fast each morning, and I shivered until my work at the oars warmed my blood at last. My clothes grew damp and did not dry. For days, the air smelled of wet wood, and then I ceased to notice it.

This last foolhardy quest notwithstanding, the *Lady* was still a trading vessel, and we stopped at a port on the western coast of a vast, mist-shrouded continent. We exchanged chests full of lengths of silk, sealed carefully against the damp, for grains and dried fruit. Some of this bounty we would consume ourselves on the long journey, while the rest we would trade in the farthest southern reaches, where the rocky earth brought forth neither crops nor trees.

"You've been this way before?" I asked Hamilcar.

He shook his head, adjusting the jaunty tilt of his feathered hat. "Never. Your books told me of where this coast will lead. We may have to part ways sooner than I anticipated."

I would disembark at the last safe port, wherever that might lie. This was a great boon that he and his crew had granted me, and one that I might never repay. The odds that I would ever see them again dwindled as the days grew shorter and the storms battered our sails. I might not ever return from the other world; Sorcha and her siblings had not. It was a sort of death I was undertaking, and early crossing over to the realm of spirits. That I intended to bring along my living body meant little. I could easily lose it, as Deinaros had expected I might, and spend the rest of eternity as a wandering spirit, or dwell among the stars for all eternity as Sorcha had. I could only hope that once I reached those shadowed borderlands I had seen only in dreams, I would find Khalim before any ill befell me.

As I prepared for this almost-death, I still intended to bring him back, to give him the life that the god of Phyreios had taken from him. But the sky darkened, and the winds howled, and the work of rowing chased away all thoughts beyond the next stroke. The image of that life, one Khalim might spend with me, faded to a shadow.

We descended the coast, and the shining cities and bustling ports dwindled to seaside hamlets and then to empty, rock-strewn beaches. The other broad-sailed ships that had accompanied us south caught the trade winds and turned back north, and even the tiny fishing boats of the coastal villages disappeared. The sea lay slate-gray and wind-battered under the grim sky, without another soul or work of human hands as far as even the watcher in the crow's nest could see.

It was then that the whales appeared.

I could not hear them singing, but I felt their terrible, beautiful song when I put my hand to the inside of the hull. It seized hold of my body, shaking my very bones, and I feared the timbers would come apart under its magnificent force. I escaped it only when I returned to my hammock in the middle of the night, and it returned to seize me by both legs as soon as my feet touched the beams the next morning. My oar shook in my hands.

I welcomed them. Even here, so close to the end of the world, the whales had made a well-traveled road. Their broad backs rose like islands from the waves, and fountains sprayed from the breaths of their vast lungs. We kept well away from their enormous flukes, and before long, they took their world-shaking chorus away into deeper water.

Another month passed before we saw another living thing. Even the birds did not venture far from the distant coast, and any fish that dwelled in these waters lay far beneath our keel, where our nets could not reach them. Hamilcar weighed and measured our supply of food at the end of each day, to ensure enough would remain for the voyage to friendlier seas. My time here was coming to an end.

One last ship emerged on the horizon before the day came that I was to depart. It was a squat, ugly thing, little more than a wide raft with a shelter erected at the center. Several hunched figures walked in procession around it, their steps steady despite the tossing of the sea. They sang a high, piercing chant that carried upon the wind.

"What are they doing?" I asked.

Hamilcar spread his arms in a shrug. "Your books made mention of floating monasteries—ascetic communes that drift upon the waves until they're either wrecked or wash up on one shore or another."

The storms came in twos and threes now, one after another. This flat vessel with neither oars nor sails would not last much longer. "Whom do you think they pray to, all the way out here?" I wondered.

"The books did not say," Hamilcar replied.

Winter came in a gust of wind from the south. Snow fell upon the deck and collected in the open sails. As in the North, a pale mountain of floating ice drifted across the horizon. It was time.

Hamilcar guided his ship clear of the icebergs and into a shallow bay surrounded with spires of pale stone. Like a hedge of briars, they grew too closely to allow the *Lady*'s entry. I bade him farewell, and wished the crew a safe journey home, and I swam the rest of the way to shore with a pack balanced on my shoulder. It was a familiar cold that pierced my body. I might have swum in the frigid waters of the North.

Once ashore, I built a fire of driftwood and dry grass and waited for my clothes to dry. The scarlet sails of the *Lady of Osona* receded to a tiny jewel on the horizon and vanished into the oncoming night.

The days had already grown short, and they shortened further as I walked south, navigating by the distant, pale light of the veiled sun. Low, twisted scrub grew in fissures in the striated rock, grasping at my feet. Frost covered the ground, and soon it clung to my hair and clothing, turning me as white as the landscape. I expected to make this last part of my journey alone, as I had once climbed the mountains and walked the tundra, starving and mad. After a handful of brief days, however, I came across a procession of robed pilgrims tracing a narrow path through the scrub with bells upon their walking staves. I followed them deeper into this strange, bare continent.

They communicated with each other and me by signs and gestures, having traveled here from the world over. They were going to the far southern coast, they said, where soon the sun would hide, and a passage would open upon the sea. They had come only to glimpse it, and thus complete their pilgrimage and return, after many months of walking, to the lands from whence they came.

The unfortunate prisoner of Deinaros' record had been one of them. I was to be another, though my return was less certain.

I reached that final shore at last, where the wind-sharpened rocks allowed no trees to grow. Still, there was wood to be found: shattered, salt-stained timbers, some bearing the fragmented images of their figureheads or scraps of rotted rope. It would be enough.

In the cold and dwindling sunlight, in the company of these strange people, I set about crafting a sturdy canoe from the wreckage of a hundred or more ships. I cut apart the robe that had kept the sun at bay in the desert to stitch into a sail; an oar I found in the hollow of a cracked hull in a frozen tide pool. Water and weather had split its shaft almost in two, but I lashed it together with rope and sinews, and it held well enough.

Each morning, the sun rose lower, and at the end of each brief day, it set more swiftly. I worked by firelight. The pilgrims maintained a bonfire of driftwood and animal dung, carried with them from the southernmost herding villages. We ate from our shared stores and from what little we could gather in the tide pools: tiny shrimp and spiny urchins, as well as kelp and seaweed, green-black and tasting of salt. I speared a seal soon after my arrival, and that fed us well for many days and earned me a place among the pilgrims.

How they stared at me, day and night, watching me work. They were a strange, pale lot, with sunken eyes and bent backs from carrying heavy packs and eating little for months at a time. They had walked, they said, for the better part of a year. When the bitter winter ended, they would make their return journey, carrying with them all that they would need.

They whispered about the coming long night, and the vision that it promised them, but they said nothing of which gods spurred them to take the long road here. Still, when a great squid washed up on the shore, its dead flesh shining like still water and reeking of the deep, they left it alone. One must not eat the flesh of a god, they said.

I disagreed, but I left the squid alone, out of respect for my hosts.

As I sorted through the wreckage for a suitable mast for my boat, one of the pilgrims approached me. His cloak wrapped twice around his shoulders and covered his head, and he carried a staff of gnarled wood, its surface worn smooth from his hands. No trees grew in this desolate place, nor anything taller than a hand's breadth, so he must have carried it for some time. The scar of an old burn, red and shining in the firelight, crossed his face. His shadow lay long and thin upon the frozen ground.

"You're not a pilgrim," he said.

I raised a broken spar to my eyes to check its straightness and set it down a short distance from the waterline. I turned to him. He stood almost as tall as I, his back straight, and his hands were sun-darkened where they gripped his staff. "Neither are you," I said.

"I'm a sailor." He gathered his cloak around his legs and sat cross-legged on the sand, his back to the bonfire a short distance away. Shadows pooled at his feet. "Or I was. I have not set foot on a ship in many years, and likely will not for many years more. But I know these waters, and I know this land well enough, and the pilgrims keep me fed and warm in exchange for my guidance."

I flexed my frozen fingers. Even at midday, the air was icy, and the fire only did so much to chase the cold away. "They're a generous people, though they have so little," I said.

"It is so in much of the world," said the sailor. "You're building a boat."

On the other side of the bonfire, the frame of my canoe lay like the ribs of a beached whale. "I am."

"Why?" The scar rendered his face expressionless, but he tilted his head to one side rather like a bird.

I tucked my hands under my arms. I'd made a coat of sealskin and wrapped my fingers in the remains of my robe, but the winter ever proved stronger. "I'm going through the gate of bone," I said. "That's what your charges are here to see, isn't it? It will appear with the final departure of the sun."

"They walk all this way to see it, to catch a glimpse of death," said the sailor. "Some gain more than a glimpse, on the way here or the way back. I will do all I can to keep them safe, but they claim such is the will of the gods."

"The gods ask much of them," I said. I chose another timber from the wreck of what might have once been a merchant vessel, weighing it in my hands.

He pushed his hood back and looked out over the water. A distant, red sun shone on his face. "They do not ask the same of you," he said. "You're not one of these pilgrims. You've neither learned their scriptures nor sung them yourself. By all accounts, you should not even know that this place exists. Why have you come here?"

"To breach the gate of bone on a day without a sun," I recited. Ten years had passed, and I still remembered them. They were clearer to me than Khalim's face.

"Surely you don't intend to take to the sea in *that*," he said, gesturing toward the unfinished skeleton.

Once finished, it would hold together on open water. I could not say if it would weather a storm. "It will take me out," I said. "I will concern myself with the return journey if and when I reach it."

"You still haven't answered my question," he said. "Why are you doing this?"

I leaned against the broken hull beside me. "Do you have time for a tale?"

"Tell me. It will pass the evening, and on another long evening I will tell it again to the pilgrims. They've heard all my tales by now."

"Then listen," I said. "Let me tell you a story."

And so, I told him why I had come here, and why I spent all the hours of the day and night building a craft out of refuse, and why I was so willing to undertake this voyage from which I might not return. I told him of my ill-fated hunt of the lind-worm and of Fearghus, of my year spent alone in the mountains; of my chance encounter with Aysulu of the Tribe of Hyrkan Khan and our trek overland to Phyreios; of the Cerean Tournament, the Ascended, and Khalim.

He listened, his head resting on one weathered hand, and the sun sank below the horizon, bringing on another long, dark night.

Over the next brief days, I finished the building of my boat, installed a suitable mast, and raised my sail, so that when the sun set after a day that lasted only a few minutes, I was ready.

As that last sunset faded into darkness, the pilgrims began to sing.

The keel of my little boat scraped against the rocky beach. The water took hold of it with grasping hands, shoving it back against me and then drawing it out into the black water, fighting against my grasp. Without a sun, the sea was cold as winter ice—cold as death. My feet ached, the cold slicing through the leather of my boots.

I gave my boat one more push and leapt over the rail. The sail unfurled, and the timbers creaked, but I trusted my boat. It would carry me to the gate of bone.

Whether it would carry me back remained to be seen.

The winter wind filled my sail, driving the boat into the roaring dark. It howled in my ears, and the crashing waves sprayed me with ice, and the pilgrims' bonfire receded into a tiny, burning point. Their song followed me for another verse before it, too, disappeared.

I hung a lantern from the prow, and it cast a tiny halo of gold as the sea tossed it from side to side. All else was black. The absent sun had taken the moon and stars alike with it when it had vanished, and the sky became a cloak of impenetrable darkness drawn over the world. Below me lay the abyss.

"Nashurru, goddess of the deep," I shouted over the clamor of the sea. "Forgive my trespass against you. I will pass through the gate of bone, with or without your permission."

The great fluked goddess gave me no answer, nor did she rise from the fathoms below to cast me down with an enormous hand. Even here, in the place between the living world and the realm of the gods, I was alone, without either guidance or condemnation.

I crouched beside the mast, one hand on the rope to guide the sail and the other on my oar, placed in the stern as a rudder. I had no means by which to navigate. An hour passed, and another, my hands growing numb and my legs trembling. The featureless horizon encircled me like a waiting snare.

"Am I lost?" I asked the tumbling waves. The boat surged and bucked underneath me, the creaking of the hull taking up a steady rhythm. "Is it my fate to die out here, after all?"

Once, I had boarded a similar boat, crafted by my own hands, and set out to sea, fearing that I would drift on even after my death. Then, I had arrived half-starved on a strange shore.

Now, the gate of bone rose at last from the waters before me.

I had seen it before, in the vision of the goddess of the deep, but it was far grander and more terrible here. Two columns of sun-bleached white death stood upright in the roiling water. An arch of ribs stretched between them, shrouded in black cloud. An alien moon, dim and blue, lit it from within, illuminating the domes of skulls and the ridges of spines. Interlaced bones spanned the space between the columns, barring any entrance.

Here was the gate of bone, on a day without a sun. I had only to breach it.

I braced one foot against the mast and raised my spear.

The waves drew me closer and closer, relentless as a river rushing downhill. Strange moonlight assaulted my eyes, and I released the sail and covered my face with my arm.

The point of the dragon's tooth met rigid bone. A horrible, awesome sound, of the earth rending in two and the sea pouring into the fissure, of the sky shattering and the stars falling, of a heart breaking, flooded all my senses. I screamed, my throat burning. The world turned blank and blue-white.

All fell still. The rocking of the boat calmed, and a gentle breeze, cool like the beginning of spring, stirred my hair and tugged at my rough coat.

I uncovered my eyes. A sunless sky, now an eerie green, stretched out overhead. A gray beach lay before me, and beyond it a shadowed forest. My keel scraped against dark gravel as my boat came to a stop.

I knew this place. It felt like a dream.

Someone stood on the beach—tall, copper-haired, and wearing a fur-lined cloak clasped at the shoulder. He was too far for me to see the design of the circular clasp, but I knew what it was: two hounds, facing each other with their teeth bared, the symbol of Fearghus's clan.

Fearghus was here. I had crossed over to the realm of spirits.

I climbed out of the boat and dragged it onto the beach. It moved with reluctance, and my limbs were heavy. I fought to breathe against the weight of my body.

"Eske," Fearghus said. "It's good to see you."

He was exactly as I remembered him. I had grown older, in the time since his death, but he remained the same. He was barely twenty winters old, freckled and bright-eyed.

"But you're not here for me, are you?" he asked.

He had been my first love, my companion in the stormy, early days of manhood, when I had struggled against the burden of my father's expectations. Fearghus had accompanied me on the hunt for the lind-worm, letting me persuade him to do so. He had always said I was the braver of us, and he had been wrong. I had been running from my father when I boarded the longship that fateful summer day.

He had deserved a better life—and a better end to it—than I had given him. He also deserved someone who would have passed through the gate for him alone, and not for another.

Guilt and sorrow stilled my tongue. I could not answer him.

~ XXXIII ~

INTERLUDE FIVE: THE WHITE CITY

Khalim's fist struck the vast wooden door and made no sound. The wall of the white city loomed above him, high as the red twilit sky, its perfect, flat surface marred only with faint, gray veins. The seam between the doors let none of the perpetual low sunlight escape. The city was as Khalim had left it—flawless, impenetrable, and silent.

He did not belong here. His hand was dark, held out against the marble flagstones, the tattered threads of his clothing brighter than even the sky. He had left the forest and the grasslands behind, but dust still clung to him, leaving a crescent mark on the polished iron fittings of the door.

He knocked again, scraping his knuckles against the metal. It only appeared smooth.

"I know you're there," Khalim said to the door. "I spent fifteen years in your presence. I could find you again even now, even in this place."

With a low rumble like distant thunder, the door shuddered open. On either side, the statues that had once been Jahan and Ihsad stood watch, each regal profile framed in scarlet light.

At the threshold, Khalim hesitated. He had left the citadel once, at the risk of angering its god. If these doors shut behind him, he might not receive another chance at freedom.

I came here with nothing more than a thought. I can go wherever I want. Not even these walls can stop me.

But he could not go to the land of the living. That barrier remained in place.

The city's central thoroughfare stretched out before him until it reached the sealed temple, where the sun bathed the columns in red. How long had he spent under those silent arches, waiting for the night that never came and the morning that never followed? That thought, that an age had passed before he had left this place, and everyone that he had ever known and loved was long dead, frightened him more than the wilds, more than the walls towering over him.

Khalim stepped over the threshold.

He stopped, but his feet retained the appearance of flesh and his hands moved at his command, uncurling from the anxious fists he had been holding. Jahan and Ihsad stared down at him, unblinking. They almost seemed to breathe, each hair on their heads and fold in their clothing so exquisitely carved that they might have stepped down from their pedestals and walked, but there they remained.

"Hello, Khalim."

He recognized the voice, but it came from neither of the vigilant statues. With a start, Khalim lowered his eyes, and he found himself looking at his own face.

He'd seen his own reflection before—in the rice fields, when they flooded, and in the polished armor of the soldiers of the Ascended. He had some idea of his own appearance. This was something quite different, without distortion of form or color, alive and moving.

This man's eyes, however, were the bright gold of a new coin.

"Welcome home, child," he said in Khalim's voice. "You've been wandering a long time."

The owl had said Khalim might have his face stolen. Had it known that he had already met that fate before it had ever flown over the citadel walls, or even before Khalim had first found himself here?

He remembered the sensation of his own mouth forming another's words, and all the anger he had gathered in his wanderings fell away. Only sorrow remained. "You," was all he could say.

The god smiled with Khalim's face. "You are always welcome here," he said. "I'm sorry you felt the need to venture outside my walls. I'm glad nothing befell you out there."

"This is a prison," Khalim whispered. "You thought I would stay?"

The reflection of his face adopted a look of concern and pity. "The others don't think so. This is a place of protection, a reflection of the kingdom that Phyreios once was, and will be again."

"But it's empty," said Khalim. "Your kingdom has no people in it. Only statues."

Another smile, beatific and patronizing. "I had hoped you would be the first."

A shiver traveled down Khalim's spine and shook his shoulders. He welcomed it; it meant he had not yet turned to stone a second time. "Who are you, really?"

The man—the god—who looked like Khalim shimmered, becoming as transparent as a trick of the light. He turned into a shadow, half again as tall, and solidified into a figure dressed in armor that glittered red in the low sunlight. His shoulders were broad, his face sharply angled. He looked like the Ascended, as beautiful as they were terrifying— or like the Ascended once had appeared, Khalim thought, before centuries of consuming blood and faith had made them something even less human. This god's skin was still soft and brown, his hair shining with perfumed oil rather than metal filament.

"I had a name, once," he said, "but it has long been forgotten. I am called Torr now, the First Hero and the King of Phyreios."

For the first time, Khalim looked upon the face of his god. In all the years they had spent together, he had not imagined the presence he carried to have a face. That presence had always been a sensation, a reassurance, a promise that Khalim would be granted whatever he needed to move forward. It had been the soft sunlight glow of his magic as it knit together torn flesh and broken bone. It had been the terrible visions that he dreamed each night as the downfall of Phyreios grew closer.

It had been the scent of scorched flesh as fire had fallen from the heavens to strike the assassin where he had stood.

"Torr," Khalim repeated, holding the name in his mouth and feeling its weight and its contours. Names in his mother tongue had soft edges and syllables that flowed into one another like music. Here was another division between the god and him, another sign that Torr was no longer a part of him, and never had been, really. "I know," he said. "Jahan told me."

The god had a name now, and a face not so unlike a man's face. He was more than human, nine feet tall with eyes that shone like the sun, but not so much more. He was no worm from under the mountain, or titan with skin of bronze and a hunger for blood. But he had the look of a hero, far more than Khalim ever had. He was the image of the champions of old, made greater with each retelling of their tales.

How Khalim hated him.

"I don't understand," Khalim said. "You could have slain the worm yourself. You could have cast the Ascended down. You didn't need me at all."

The magnificent face softened around the eyes. "I could not. I had been away from the world for so long that I could not act upon it alone. I needed a vessel to take me to Phyreios."

"That's all I was, then," Khalim spat. "A vessel. An empty basket. You needed someone to carry you across the desert, and you cast me aside when you were done with me."

Torr reached out a strong, long-fingered hand to caress Khalim's face. Khalim pulled away.

"Is that what you think?" Torr asked. "That you were chosen at random, that you were interchangeable? That anyone could have done what you did? That I abandoned you?"

Khalim spread out his arms to indicate the stone visages of Ihsad and Jahan. "If you wanted to save Phyreios, if you wanted someone who could have ruled there and restored your kingdom for you, you would have chosen someone better."

"No," said Torr. "You were always my chosen. That's why I brought you here."

"You brought me here when you were done with me," Khalim shouted. It stirred no birds from the stunted trees, and the stone men by the gate did not complain. "Everything—the magic, the dreams, the horrible dreams, it was all to make me take you to Phyreios so you could rule. I thought I was supposed to save the city, but so many died anyway, even before the ritual. I couldn't stop the Ascended. I didn't make a difference. Why couldn't you have just left me alone, and found someone else to bear you to your throne?"

Torr's face, beautiful and alien, looked upon him with pity. "Oh, my child. I understand that you're angry. Most mortals are, especially when they meet an untimely end."

Khalim bit his tongue. The taste of blood was only a memory.

"I did not intend to return to Phyreios to rule. I had hoped to leave it in the hands of its people, to a mortal king and his council, but the Ascended had become so much worse than I'd anticipated. So much damage had been done. I had to help them rebuild. When it is done, I will place the city into mortal hands again." Torr sighed, an almost human sound. "You're angry because you could not live longer. Even those who live to an old age possess the same rage. It will fade with time."

"I'm angry because you took me away," Khalim argued. "I didn't die. I was still breathing when—when you—"

His words failed him, and then his memory, leaving only the image of the crushing dark and the shaking of the earth. It seemed to him that the sky darkened and the marble columns trembled.

"You were moments from death," Torr said, placating. "The city had fallen upon you. It would not have been an easy passage."

"I don't care. You should have let me die a mortal's death. How could I be mourned when you walk the city streets wearing my face? How could I find peace, trapped here and turning to stone away from all my ancestors? Away from everyone who ever loved me?"

Torr's answer was flat, his face stern. "You would not say these things if you had perished under the rubble."

"You could be right," Khalim said. "But it doesn't matter, does it? You lifted my body out of the pit. I could have lived. You didn't have to send me away."

"Enough." Torr drew himself up, shedding the pretension of humanity. His voice shook the towering walls of his city. "I chose you, but you are still a mortal soul. You cannot see what I see. In another thousand years, you might begin to understand. I offer that to you now—time and understanding. Will you cease your foolishness and stay in the place I offer you? Or are you going to wander the wilds again, with no one to protect you?"

The gates remained open. Beyond them lay all the realms that mortal minds had ever dreamed of, and still others besides, with all their wonders and dangers alike. Khalim had only to walk over the threshold, and Torr would let him go.

"I don't need anyone to protect me," Khalim said.

Torr nodded. His golden eyes held an ancient sorrow, more vast than Khalim ever could comprehend. "So be it," he said.

He turned, and the city rippled like a still lake disturbed by a stone. Khalim stumbled toward the gate, wheeling his arms for balance, his hand striking the pedestal on which Jahan stood. With a quickening of his remembered pulse, he looked to the god's retreating back.

But it was not Torr's wrath that troubled these marble streets. He turned, eyeing Khalim with an ungodlike confusion. "Something has happened," he said, not quite accusing. "Someone has breached the boundaries of this world."

The city remained the same: here stood the gate, and Jahan and Ihsad watching over it; there lay the temple with its impenetrable doors, all carved of pristine marble. But something had changed. The air sang with a subtle vibration, and deep below Khalim's feet, far beneath the paving stones, the earth shifted. A new fear grasped at his shivering heart. What could have happened to trouble even the manifestation of a god in his own realm?

The answer came not from the city around him but from his own troubled memory.

"Eske," he said, and laughed in breathless disbelief. "Eske is here."

~ XXXIV ~

THE LONG WALK

Fearghus waited for my reply, ginger brows raised in an unspoken question. He'd always called me impatient, and said that his fiery hair belied which of us was the more hotheaded. I had missed him so—even in the long years when I had thought of nothing and no one but Khalim, I had carried Fearghus with me. I dared not reach out to touch him for fear that he would vanish into the thin, shimmering air.

"What are you doing here?" I said, finding my voice at last. "You should be upon the summer plains, hunting with the gods of our people. Please, tell me you haven't been banished to this desolate place."

The gray sea broke against the shore in a whisper, lifting my boat and pushing it against the rocks. My hand lay heavy on the prow. I could not tear my eyes from Fearghus's face.

He smiled in the way that he always did, as if the two of us were sharing a secret. "I came here to meet you. I always thought I would, when one day you crossed over from the land of the living, but I never thought you would come here still alive." He studied me, brows furrowing, his head tilted to one side. "And you are alive, aren't you? I didn't believe it at first."

"I sailed here from the end of the world," I told him.

"What could have driven you to do such a thing?" Fearghus asked.

The answer would not come to me. I could not bear to look into his eyes and confess that I had crossed the world and back and sailed alone into the winter darkness, all for the love of another. I deserved Fearghus's anger, not his welcome. I had caused his death, all those years ago, and through some accident of fate escaped it myself. And what of the others, the brave men who had sailed out with us in pursuit of the lind-worm? I could no longer recall their names or their faces. Wasn't my responsibility to them and to Fearghus no less than mine to Khalim? And what of the lives I had trampled through on my way here—Fenin and the people of Svilsara, Kannaoka without its king, Cricket alone in her tower, Cullen and his people fleeing north through the forest?

Despair fell on my shoulders, and my feet sunk into the sand, my body heavy as a stone. I struggled to breathe. All that I touched turned to ash, and everyone I had loved had met with a terrible fate.

But I had arrived here on this strange shore. I had breached the gate of bone on a day without a sun. I had a task to complete, even if I deserved nothing more than to remain here among the dead while Khalim returned to the world I had just left. I was unworthy of the summer plains, but I was accustomed to wandering. I could become a pilgrim in the land of spirits.

"There's someone I have to find," I confessed to Fearghus.

"I might have guessed," he said. "You've changed, Eske. You're no longer seeking glory for its own sake, or to spite your father. I can see it even in your eyes."

This was no empty praise. Fearghus had no use for such things. He had not changed in more than ten years. I, on the other hand, was not yet an old man, but no longer a young one, and the years weighed on me. "I suppose you're right," I said. "Glory has been far from my mind for some time."

"Well, you'll have it anyway, if you manage to return." Fearghus looked at my boat, and I was pleased to see him smile, impressed. He lifted a hand to touch it, but drew back.

With some effort, I could move again. I grasped the boat and pulled it out of the reach of the surf. "After the lind-worm wrecked our ship, I washed up on a distant shore," I began. "I crossed the mountains and the tundra to a different sea, and from there I landed upon the vast eastern steppe. I traveled then to the city called Phyreios, and engaged in a contest against the champions of that city's tyrant gods. I met a healer there, a prophet of another god, long forgotten. He was meant to save the city. His god took him away, sending his spirit here and keeping his body with which to rule the city in the wake of its destruction."

"And you loved him, this prophet?" Fearghus asked.

I had hoped to avoid speaking that particular truth aloud. Fearghus had always known me the best of any. "Yes," I said, and then: "I'm sorry."

Fearghus's face softened. He gave me a sad smile. "I'm not an angry ghost to be placated, Eske. I wanted you to survive. Even as seawater filled my lungs and the world turned dark, I hoped that you would go on to live a full, long life—and I kept that hope when I did not find you upon the summer plains." He sighed, and his eyes fell again on my boat. "This is not what I would have wished for you. You're alive, Eske. You should be among the living."

"I hope to return," I said. I might not have merited such a fate, but I desired it, nonetheless. "I have to find Khalim first. He, too, should be in the living world. Once I've corrected this injustice, I'll return to where I belong, wherever that might be."

"You will do as you've always done, with or without my counsel," Fearghus said. "I wish I could join you for one last expedition." He rested his hand on the driftwood prow, and his skin shimmered like the illusion of water in the desert. His fingers curled, passing through the solid wood.

He could not come with me, and I could not stay here. The sand shifted under my feet, pliable as new clay, and water flowed around my ankles. My boat listed starboard toward the surf.

"Will I see you again?" I asked.

Under the deep green sky, Fearghus was so vivid that my eyes ached to look at him. His hair was too red, his cloak too blue, the silver clasp bright as the sun. "You might," he said, "at the end of your life, some time from now, I hope. Seek me out."

"I will," I promised.

He reached for me, his hand lingering in the air. "Be cautious. Do not trust a stranger, even if he wears a familiar face. The wilds are full of strange creatures, and of ghosts less welcoming than I. Find your healer and go back to the living."

"I will be swift and careful," I said. "I swear it."

Fearghus pulled back before he touched me, sorrow in his eyes. He held out his arm to the bare gray forest, and a path that opened between two gnarled trees. It wound between twisted branches and over buckling roots and disappeared into the gloom.

I knew this road, and I knew what waited for me in the shadow of the trees.

"Thank you, Fearghus," I said, but he was already gone, vanished into sea spray and wind, returning to the summer plain where he would hunt in the company of the gods of the North until the end of time.

With my spear on my shoulder and my boat stowed upon the rocks, I walked into the forest.

***

My feet fell heavy upon the path, and the earth answered each step with an echoing tremor. A salt-scented wind rustled the dry branches, a whispering sound that might have been words, too soft and distant to understand. A storm tinged the sky in violet shadow, but it remained at a distance, and the sun hung suspended over the water, never moving from its place. Though I followed a narrow, winding way among the trees, when I looked over my shoulder, the path behind me was straight as an arrow. It led all the way back to the shore.

Each tree possessed a face, a detail I did not recall from my dreams. Knots in the rough bark formed pairs of eyes, lidless and sightless, while the scars left by a woodsman's axe gave them mouths open in despair. Joining them in their silent moaning were the ghosts, pale and hollow, standing still as the trees.

"Who are you?" I called out. "Do you know the way to the citadel?"

Even the effort of speaking shortened my breath and drained my strength. The thin, rarefied air provided no relief. I put my spear to the ground and leaned on it like an old man, gasping and coughing. The shades regarded me with wide-eyed fear, saying nothing. They backed away, cloaking themselves in darkness, their shimmering forms fading to wisps of fog and vanishing.

They might have been illusions—tricks of the strange light, meant to lead me away from my path. Fearghus had warned me not to trust a stranger. Despite his warnings against those who might appear familiar, I trusted him. I had known him since we were both children, long before we had ever become lovers; so long ago that I could not recall when and how we had met. I trusted I would be able to spot an impostor.

The passage of years had not made me any wiser than I had been at twenty.

I steadied myself with another labored breath and picked up my leaden feet. In my dreams, I had crossed the forest in a matter of hours. Now, it seemed to me that I had walked for days, weeks, or years, that I had dreamed my passage through the gate of bone and the life that had preceded it.

Even time had been lost to me. I had only the path ahead.

I heard the stag before it appeared, its footfalls light and swift as it moved unseen through the trees. It kept pace with me, a shadow among shadows, and the pale shades parted to allow it to pass.

"I thought I might see you, sooner or later," I said.

It turned, human eyes gazing at me from either side of its long face. A shake of its head dislodged dry leaves and bits of moss from its crown of oaken antlers.

"Nothing to say?" I gasped, my voice strained as I dragged my body through step after endless step. I envied the stag and the hovering ghosts, who moved about without the weight of this strange world upon them. "I recall you had much to tell me when last we met."

Those eyes blinked once, slowly, and the stag quickened its pace, leaving rings of light where its hooves touched the wrinkled earth. With both hands on my spear, I dragged myself after it, and in my wake the path turned straight and broad—a scar carved into the world.

It led me to the edge of the forest. The gloom fell away, and the sun, now rising from the plain ahead, burned golden in a white sky. As in my half-remembered dream, the roar of the river assailed my ears, its black depths capped with white and singing of all the souls it had drowned.

"The river of memory, deep as the sea," I recited.

The stag held my gaze. Above the trees, the storm gathered in a great, twisting spiral, and the path I'd carved through the forest turned dark as night. Even without speaking, my sometimes guide's meaning was clear enough: I had made my choice. What had been done could not be undone.

I took another breath and bowed to the stag. Some strength had returned to my limbs, or I was becoming accustomed at last to this place after so long walking. "Will I see you on the other side?"

It only bent its head, returning my bow. I put my spear on my back and waded into the river.

Another step, and the bank fell away, plunging me into the water. I had anticipated cold, but it was warm as flesh, wrapping around me like an embrace and pulling me under the surface. My arms strained against the pull of the current. Absent were the masses of fish from my dream; I might have sworn that hands grasped at my ankles and arms wrapped around my neck. I opened my eyes, but all around me was black.

I had not come this far only to drown in memory. I mustered my failing strength, reaching for the sky that had vanished above my head, and kicked against the river's ensnaring grasp. The river's roar was quiet here, reduced to a bare whisper. It bore no words, but it promised rest in the smothering dark.

My face broke the surface. I drew in a gulp of air, and it tasted of smoke. Water, warm and cloying, ran from my hair and down my cheeks like a flood of tears. Sunlight seared my eyes.

I would not leave my body behind and find Fearghus on the summer plain only to report that I had failed in my task. I would not die after completing only one of the challenges Khalim had lain before me on that last night outside of ruined Phyreios. I swam, and the river pulled at my clothing and wrapped me in its warm embrace, and the water washed over my head and filled my nose and mouth. Memory, as the sages say, was both bitter and sweet.

My hands met dry earth, and it crumbled between my fingers. I clawed great furrows into the riverbank, scattering sand and dry grass on the surface of the water, where it sparkled like snow and vanished into the current. Pain shot through my right knee as I crawled free of the river, and blood soaked through my sailor's trousers and stained the ground. I'd cut myself on a buried rock.

I got to my feet. Before me lay a field of golden grass, rippling like a sea, dotted with tiny white flowers and humming with the sound of thousands upon thousands of insects. They hovered in the dusty air, shining like jewels, their ruby wings stretched open. I looked over the river's roar and beheld the stag as it bowed its antlered head once more, turned, and darted into the forest, light as an autumn leaf on the wind.

I, in contrast, had grown only heavier without the water to buoy me. I dared not lie down to rest. Though I could not say how much time had passed, I had walked long enough that I should have felt hunger and thirst. Instead, there was only the weight, and a throbbing pain where my knee still bled.

I tore a strip from the bottom of my tunic and tied it around the wound, and I set off into the grass. As long as this reprieve from my body's mortal weaknesses lasted, I would press forward. The insects gathered around me, their song buzzing in my ears and across my skin, and the vegetation parted to show bare, black earth as I walked. If my dreams had shown me right, I wasn't far from the citadel, but I had never fully trusted my dreams.

In the distance, a tendril of smoke broke the flat monotony of the sky. I followed it until it grew into a column, rising from a fire of timber and bones piled as high as I was tall. Around it, a dozen hunched figures gathered in a small clearing, feeding more bones and the husks of giant insects, larger than two hands, to the flames.

"I mean you no harm," I called out, raising my hands to show that they were empty. "I'm looking for the citadel of the god Torr. Can you help me?"

The figure nearest to me lifted his head. His face was that of a deer, long and narrow, with velvet ears that twitched as I came closer. He stared at me, his eyes wide and fearful.

To his left, another figure rose. He wore a black robe that covered him from his neck to the ground, stretched over the huge, rounded shape of his back. His eyes were small and black, and his teeth needle-sharp. A pale, gray hand emerged from the robe, pointing a bony finger at the bandage on my leg. "Flesh," he said, the syllable hissing through the points of his teeth.

"Behave yourself, Kelast," the deer-headed one murmured.

A third figure, this one a woman with a narrow, human face and white hair that reached her knees, waved both of them away. They shuffled around the fire, still watching me.

"Come," the woman said. "Eat with us. The bread will ease your pain."

I bowed. "Your hospitality is generous, but I cannot stay," I said. "I need to find the citadel. Do you know how I may travel there?"

The sky had turned dark, the sun hiding behind a bank of cloud. The dark spiral of the storm loomed overhead, its wet wind stirring the fire. Burning bones hissed and popped. Where I had walked through the field, the grass curled and blackened, leaving a wide path.

"There's no citadel here," the sharp-toothed one, Kelast, hissed.

"We are a long way from the realm of any god," the woman said. Her eyes, the color of sea ice, filled with sorrow, but her words were cold. I heard them as a threat: no god would come to my rescue if these people decided to throw me onto their bonfire. My trek here, with the storm at my back, had made me fearful.

I had long since abandoned the hope of any god granting me divine help. I had come here, after all, against the wishes of even those who might have looked upon me with sympathy. I bowed a second time, smiling in a way I hoped was placating. "Then I must take my leave," I said.

What might occur if I lingered here, scarring the landscape and bringing on the storm, I could not say, and I did not wish to find out, for my sake and the sake of these strangers. Even if the bones charring upon the fire had not come from unsuspecting passersby, I would not stay.

A fourth figure stood up from the fire, and this one looked like Khalim.

"Flesh," the sharp-toothed one repeated, a keening whine that made the fine hairs on the back of my neck stand on end.

"Hush, Kelast," the man said in Khalim's voice, soft and gentle.

He was dressed in roughspun brown: a tunic that reached to his knees and a cloak with a fraying hem. I searched his face, looking for some flaw that might give away a shapeshifter, or a detail that would prove that my eyes did not deceive me. There were his dark eyes, untainted by the deceiver's gold. There was his smile, warm and guileless.

Khalim had left the citadel where the god Torr had confined him—that I knew. I knew also that he would seek out the lost and wounded, and how else could one describe these people gathered around the fire? They showed no injuries on the hands and faces that emerged from their loose clothing, but their eyes—the eyes of deer and frogs as well as of men—were hollow and hungry.

"Come," he said. "Sit. Rest a while."

Thunder cracked the sky.

"There's no time," I said. "Come with me, Khalim."

In those warm eyes, no flicker of recognition stirred. He knew neither my face nor the name I had called him. I reached out, and the image of Khalim did the same, but my hand passed through his. I drew it back, startled.

"You really are made of flesh," he said, awe and wonder on his face.

Kelast made a sound halfway between a laugh and a sob.

A knife appeared in the hand that wasn't Khalim's. Its blade curved to a point like the talon of a great hunting bird. If I'd had any doubts, this would have dispelled them. Khalim had never held a weapon.

The assumed face fell away. Behind it was a flat, lacquered mask, split across the bottom in the semblance of a mouth. Two blank, white eyes stared out from deep, chisel-scarred holes above its empty grin.

In a new voice, dry and brittle, it said, "Give it to me."

The deer-headed man rose to stand at my left, wringing long hands as his eyes rolled from side to side. Kelast approached me from the right, his teeth chattering. From the obscuring light of the bonfire emerged more figures: one with the sunken eyes of a desiccated corpse, whose arms reached almost to the ground; another with the teeth of a great cat but the mouth of a woman; yet another that buzzed with the sound of a swarm of flies, whose face was a shifting mosaic of wings. The others were only shadows, lurking in the smoke.

I reached for my spear. Lightning crackled over my hand as I took it from my back. "Let me pass," I said, "or by the dragon who created this weapon and the dragon who keeps the warriors' temple, I will kill you where you stand."

"You can't kill us, living man," the pale-eyed woman said. "But we can kill you."

The masked figure reached for me. I took the spear in both hands, and lightning caressed my fingers, sharp as a knife and gentle as a kiss. It darted out ahead of the dragon's tooth and spread across the figure's dark clothing, lighting up the deep hollows of his eyes.

He staggered backward toward the fire. I struck at Kelast, aiming the spear below his rows of needle teeth. The point met flesh, or something like it, and the man-creature keened and fell to his knees. Black blood poured from a wound beneath his chin, open like a second mouth.

The deer-headed man, his eyes darting from one horizon to another, crept closer and seized me by the left arm, wrapping both hands around my elbow. I pulled against his intangible grasp, but his touch against my skin was as painful as bare ice, and he took hold of me again as soon as I slipped free.

"You smell of life," he whispered in my ear.

I took the spear in my right hand and swung it in a descending arc. It sang through the air, white light trailing behind it, and struck the deer-headed man across the forehead. Thunder cracked. An answering peal of thunder resounded in the sky. The fire flickered and dimmed.

The man released my arm, covering his face with both hands. In his place, the masked figure advanced once more, his curved knife gleaming.

I ran, pushing past the masked figure and the insect-faced man and wading into the tall grass. It bit at my legs with tiny, invisible teeth, dragging at my clothing and cutting narrow welts into my skin. Kelast shrieked and giggled, chasing me down the scar I carved through the field, uninhibited by the wound in his throat. A single exclamation of "Flesh!" followed me across the plain.

The citadel, the citadel—my solitary goal ran through my thoughts like a drumbeat, urging me forward. The earth gave a hollow sound with each of my heavy footsteps. An unnatural night fell around me as the storm covered the sky, swirling black and purple as a bruise. Its thunder shook the world.

My pursuers fell behind, disappearing into the gathering dark. If it was my fate to become a wandering spirit, I would not meet it now, not at their hands.

I walked, and the storm gathered, and the ground beneath my feet and the air I breathed turned cold and brittle. Pain bloomed from my injured knee and in my chest as I labored to breathe. *The citadel, the citadel,* I repeated, a voiceless chant that drowned out all other thoughts, and I walked. The storm followed. The grass withered in my wake.

And when I lifted my head, a wall of stone white as floating ice rose from the great grass sea. I had carved a path across the world to find it, and here it was, stark and painfully bright. I had to turn my eyes away.

My head lowered, contrite as a penitent, I put the spear over my shoulder and kept walking.

The gates stood open as I arrived, framing a livid sky, red sunlight slanting through black clouds. The heavy doors were carved of polished wood, seamless and flat. Wind rushed down streets of the same white marble as the walls, screaming as it passed shuttered buildings and the smooth, unadorned pillars of the empty central square. On either side of the gate, a colossal statue of a man in armor stood watch. I knew their faces.

There in the doorway stood a human figure, dressed in fraying clothes, tiny beneath the towering statues. He looked out through the gate, over the endless plain, hands in the pockets of his thin, woven coat.

Khalim wasn't here, I thought. He had left to wander the wilds years ago. But I knew his relaxed posture, his quiet patience—the things neither the creature by the fire of bones nor the serpent in the desert had managed to imitate. Those who had known him as a child had said he had always been listening. Now, he was listening for me, and watching me as I crossed from grass to bare earth to marble flagstones, hard and cold beneath my feet.

"Eske," he said, and all my doubts fled from me. He smiled. "You're here."

How much I had forgotten in the intervening years between this city gate and the gates of Phyreios. He was as tall as I, though I had remembered him as shorter. He was slight, but when he reached out to take one of my hands in both of his, his grip was as strong as a warrior's.

His hands were cold, and like water, as though my fingers would pass through them if I held him too tightly.

Ten years of exhaustion caught up with me at once. I fell to my knees. It hurt when my bones struck marble, but the pain receded in favor of the wave of relief and sadness that enveloped me—the grief I had kept locked away and hidden for all this time, buried beneath bravado and a dogged determination to see this task through. Now that my labors were done, I had barely the strength to stand.

"Come with me," I said. How many details of his face had I forgotten? He was as young as I had been when the god Torr had taken him away, but faint lines showed around his mouth and at the corners of his eyes, evidence of his easy smile. Stubble shaded his jaw. His dark eyes caught the last light of the bloody sun and turned it into the comfort of a hearth.

"Eske," he said again. I'd forgotten the sound of his voice. "You're not supposed to be here."

My heart sank. "But I came all this way to find you."

He smiled again, but his eyes were sad. "I know. I'll thank you for it later. For now, you're bending the world around you, and the longer you stay, the worse it will get. The god of this place—Torr—he wants to send you away."

"Let him." I staggered to my feet. "I'm not leaving without you."

His smile faltered, and my heart dropped to the flagstones. "Unless," I said, "you don't want to come with me."

He opened his mouth to speak, but before he could utter a word, the gates of the citadel slammed shut. The impact shook the world, scattering dust and setting the grass to trembling. Lightning flashed across the roiling sky. I closed my eyes, covering my face with my free arm. With the other, I held tight to Khalim.

A sudden chill crawled across my skin. I opened my eyes, and the citadel was gone, as was the vast plain. Khalim and I stood in a dark forest, the trees pressing in around us, shadowed and damp. Something vast and four-legged shuffled by in the distance, and specks of violet light hovered in the air. Lightning flashed across the sky.

Khalim frowned, and he set his jaw in the stubborn way that I had both adored and dreaded in our short time together. He took my hand and stepped forward. I had no choice but to follow.

I fell, wind roaring in my ears and my stomach turning over, and half a heartbeat later I found myself standing on the marble road again, this time inside the great doors, where the statues looked down upon me from their lofty pedestals. My head spun and my vision blurred.

Khalim's hands were almost solid on my arm, keeping me on my feet. "You can't keep me out," he called to the city and the god that made it.

In response, the world inverted. My heart flew into my throat. Now we stood upon the shore of a vast, black ocean, under a sky of unfamiliar stars. White-crested waves curled around our feet.

"Are you all right, Eske?" Khalim asked.

I could only nod.

"Stay with me," he said. "I'm going to send us both home."

We traveled again, quick as a thought, and when we arrived in the citadel Torr was there to meet us.

I had never seen this form before, only the face he had stolen from Khalim, but I could not mistake him for anyone else. In beauty and might, he was the equal of the Ascended, tall as a legend, but his skin was soft and brown and his eyes, gold as they were, lacked the haughty distance and inhuman sheen of his erstwhile successors. Even in the darkness, his bronze armor gleamed.

All around him, the pillars trembled and leaned. Cracks showed on the perfect marble.

"Cease this foolishness," he commanded. "You know not what you do."

"I know exactly what I'm doing," Khalim said.

Torr's imperious face cracked, revealing the barest hint of something that might have been anger, disbelief, or even a grudging respect. "This is a realm of spirits," he said. "The passage of this living man will destroy everything. Release him, and you'll be welcome back here, since that appears to be what you wish."

"You'll release us both," Khalim said, "and give back what you have taken from me. Let the people of Phyreios govern themselves, and let me live a mortal life."

"You ask for too much," Torr intoned. His hand went to the curved sword at his hip, but it rested there, waiting. "What if I refuse?"

Khalim looked him in the eye, his gaze unflinching. "Then I'll take Eske to and from your city as many times as it takes to watch the world crumble."

If ever I had loved him before, it had been nothing compared to how much I loved him in this moment, as he stared down the god. Here was the courage I had so admired, and the watchful patience, and the *anger*—he had possessed it in Phyreios, helpless as he had been then, and I had forgotten it.

I caught my breath and found my voice at last. "I go," I began, swallowed, and tried again. "I go with him willingly. Let this be another city that falls around you, Torr. I am only thankful that this one, it seems, is empty."

"You know nothing of what you speak," Torr said. He reached out, an offer of peace or a command to stand down, I could not tell which.

Khalim's hand on mine was still cold and insubstantial, but it was more solid than the stone around us. "Maybe not," he said. "I'm only a man, and you are a god. But I can bring your city down. What say you, then? Will you let us go, and return what I've lost?"

Thunder tore across the sky. Under my feet, the stone cracked and shifted.

"Very well," Torr said. "You will have your wish. Let what is to come be on your head."

"I take it willingly," said Khalim.

He turned to me and took my face in both his hands. "Find me in Phyreios," he said, and everything went black.

~ XXXV ~

THE NEW PHYREIOS

The sound of water lapping against the hull of a boat stirred me from a slumber that might have lasted an age. I woke with reluctance, longing for the warm embrace of sleep—the air bit at my face, piercing a haze of frigid numbness. I knew this lethargy well, and it was a false comfort. I was freezing to death.

An indigo sky greeted me as I opened my eyes, and innumerable stars danced in it. I stretched out my arms. Even with the cold stiffening my joints, the leaden weight I had felt as I crossed the other world was gone. I pushed myself up. I lay in the hull of my boat, in a layer of water a hand's breadth deep. The sea around me was black, stirred by the whistling wind that lifted my tiny craft and pushed it toward some unknown destination. With no landmass to obscure them, the stars stretched down to the horizon in all directions. I was lost.

Had I dreamed all of it? My landing on the gray beach, my conversation with Fearghus, my trek across the plain, my long-awaited and ever so brief meeting with Khalim?

The gate of bone had vanished. Either it had disappeared just as it had come, or I had drifted far away.

I moved to the stern and took up my oar, gathering my sealskin coat around me. In a small measure of good fortune, the fur remained mostly dry, and feeling began to return to my hands and feet. I found my flint, but my lantern was empty of oil. I would have to find my way in the dark.

My sail hung in tatters. I used scraps of it to plug up the gaps that cold water had forced between the timbers of my boat. Time had passed, but I could not tell how much. In a night that lasted the full turn of the moon, time was an ephemral thing.

In the persistent cold, my thoughts moved slowly—too slowly to be afraid. I had also, burning in my chest, the hope that all I had seen had not been a dream, and Khalim had told me to meet him in Phyreios.

So, to Phyreios I would go.

I knew these stars. I had spent long evenings underneath them, constructing my boat. Over the horizon behind me, a constellation the pilgrims had called the wineskin of the gods hung in the sky. It would lead their way home after the day without a sun, they had said, and they would make the months-long journey on foot back to wherever they had come from.

The wineskin would not lead me home, but it would show me the way back to shore. I plunged my oar into the icy water and turned my battered craft around. Its driftwood sides creaked, and water stirred around my feet, but it held together. I rowed toward the unassuming oval of stars in the distance, the muscles in my arms protesting against the cold.

It had not been a dream. I had walked the forests and plains of the world of the dead, my mortal body bending the earth around me, as wandering spirits pursued me for a pound of my flesh. I had met Khalim at the gate, and stood before the god Torr, and now I was on my way to Phyreios once again.

I had returned to the world of the living, as strange as this landscape may have appeared. Splinters dug into my palms as my oar pulled my boat along. Hunger churned in my belly. As I crept forward, the sea lay unchanged behind me, as though I had never passed this way at all.

As the gods' wineskin dipped below the horizon, my boat met the rocky shore. A sharp, black spire pierced my hull, and water rushed in. I gathered my spear and leapt onto the land.

The pilgrims had gone. The remains of their fire lay cold and dark in a ring of stones. Above the eastern horizon, the first rays of an unexpected morning crept into view, pale and faint against the depths of the sea. I was alone.

They had left me a small bundle, tied in a scrap of cloth. In it was a small portion of grain from their stores and the last of the seal meat. It wasn't much, but it would get me on my way.

I ate my fill and wrapped myself in my coat for a few hours' rest. Dark had returned when I woke again. With my spear as a staff, I set out over the rocks, stumbling through the long winter night. The wineskin of the gods hung low in the sky, taunting me from just out of reach.

I walked, and the days grew longer, and the constellation I followed climbed up from the horizon. The land flattened and grew green with moss, and soon I passed among low, twisted trees, as bent as I was in the howling wind.

My meager stores lasted me only a fortnight. I hunted what I could catch and dug tubers from the ground. I was hungry, but I had been hungry before. I'd made a similar journey once, on the opposite side of the world, wandering because death was the only alternative. Now, I had a destination.

I came to a port—a tiny, windswept village with a battered pier, but it had fishing boats sturdy enough to venture farther up the coast. I bartered with the fishermen until one agreed to let me row for him in exchange for passage.

"Are you strong enough to row?" he asked me, looking me up and down, his eyes two bright sparks in the weathered bark of his face.

"To row, to fish, to fend off pirates," I answered. "Yes, I'm strong enough."

He lay down his nets and crossed his arms over his narrow chest. These were a wiry, strong people, aged before their time by sun and wind. "You look like you've been to the deepest hells and crawled your way back," he said with a shrug.

"You're more correct than you could possibly know," I said.

He asked me no more questions as we pushed off from the pier and into the winter sea. The fisherman had a family to return to once he had filled his nets, but I found another village, another port, and another boat after his, and then another. I rowed and cast nets and dined well on fish, regaining the strength I'd lost in my winter wanderings.

And with each passing day, I came closer to Phyreios.

The waters turned from gray to blue, and I arrived upon the Summer Sea as the winds grew warm and the towering forest that held the upper city of Ksadaja in its branches turned green. I hoped to meet Hamilcar again in the harbor of the lower city, but he had gone elsewhere, pursuing his own ends. Perhaps our paths would cross again one day.

Across the Summer Sea I went, then, in a ship with tall, white sails; its swift rowers and clever pilot brought me to a new port, a city built of pale yellow stone with domed roofs painted blue as the sea. People in colorful dress crowded the streets, calling to one another in more languages than I could count. It reminded me of Svilsara—the illusion of Svilsara. Its serpent god must have gleaned his inspiration from a place like this.

Four weeks later, in the company of a caravan of traders, I came across the real Svilsara. Sand had swept over it, smoothing over the ruins of its buildings until the city was all but invisible. No footsteps sounded on its buried streets; no one sang hymns in the shadow of the temple's remains.

Svilsara had emptied at last. After dark, as the caravan went to sleep, I ventured to the edge of the ruined wall and bowed to the absent folk, asking for their forgiveness. I hoped they had found true safety at last.

I might have begged forgiveness from so many others. I'd left Cricket alone in her tower, and Cullen and his people to flee the invaders' swords at their backs. I had brought grief to Taherah's door in Nagara, and left it there upon my departure. I had trespassed against Nashurru and her priestesses, and against the dragon of the mountain.

One day, perhaps, I would see them again, and keep the promises I had made. For now, I could think of nothing but Phyreios.

With the caravan, I crossed a river valley well in bloom, where insects sang in a raucous chorus and birds hunted fish among the reeds. We turned north to where the green country turned once more to desert, rust-red with iron. I left these brave merchants and joined another caravan, this one of horse traders, who brought the fabled beasts of the steppe to the lords of the river valleys, and returned north with silk and spice. They told stories of a tribe led by a woman, who broke the chains of the enslaved and brought them into her warband. She had amassed a herd of ten thousand horses, and the dust kicked up by their hooves, the merchants said, could be seen for miles.

It was everything Aysulu would have wanted.

"And what of Phyreios?" I asked. "Do you have news of the city?"

"Some time ago," the caravan leader said, "the king left his throne, and his council rules in his stead."

His brother nodded, staring into the campfire. "It wasn't so long ago that the earthquake claimed the lives of their last rulers. The place is cursed. Soon, no one will rule it."

"The city was rebuilt," the ladder argued. "I think he decided his work was done, and he'd rather spend his days doing whatever kings do when they pass on their crowns. Maybe he has a garden, or he writes poetry."

A smile crossed my face. Khalim might have liked a garden.

The Iron Mountain rose in the distance, half the height it had reached when I had first laid eyes on it so long ago. As the days passed and we came nearer, the spires of the new temple complex rose white and shining before it. A layer of gray-green scrub covered the sides of the hills, unmarred by footpaths, and the black maw of the mine remained closed, perhaps never to be opened again. The towering forge had not yet been restored, and the place where it had once loomed over the industrial quarter was only empty sky.

In my memory, the city was a ruin, its pale stone scarred by fire and cast down to lie in broken piles. I had not seen it in more than ten years. How strange it was to behold the walls rebuilt, the great gate remade and standing open, a procession of travelers and merchants passing to and fro. The streets lay smooth and even, cleared of debris. Guards in white tabards stood smiling in the sun, greeting each passer-by with a nod. Overhead, a new aqueduct came down from the mountain, its water sparkling like silver and babbling like the laughter of children. There were children, too, clean and well-fed, running through the market square, asking the shopkeepers not for money but for sweets. The dark, reeking slums outside the walls were gone. In its stead, colorful tents spread out like the wings of brooding birds, and fresh water flowed from a pump beside the wall, where the women of the caravans gathered with their baskets and jugs. It was as if the passage of the great worm was the dream of a dream, forgotten upon waking.

This was an illusion. I passed through the gate, and the stones that made up the arch above my head bore the marks of the fire. The columns holding the aqueduct aloft were rough with chips and scratches. As I wandered away from the market, the city fell quiet, and empty houses with dark windows sat in silence on either side of a spotless thoroughfare. Even now, with travelers coming and going each day, the city was too large for the few people who remained. It remembered as well as I did what had transpired here ten years ago.

I followed the aqueduct toward the remains of the mountain. More channels reached out across the city, unfinished for want of laborers, but the work continued, the sound of hammers ringing out across the streets. I turned a corner as I approached the new temple, a rectangular structure with columns not unlike those I had seen in Torr's pristine, sterile city in the world beyond the world, and piles of cracked stone greeted me like old friends.

Here was the Phyreios I remembered. I walked on, and my feet carried me to what was once the industrial quarter and the footprint of the great forge. I retraced a path I had walked so many times during the Cerean Tournament, from the colosseum to the rented house where my companions and I had slept. The arena was gone, as was the house. A few small dwellings had sprung up around the low ring of weathered stone, the only evidence that the forge had ever stood.

On the first door, the emblem of an open hand had been painted in a vibrant blue.

I pushed it open, finding it unlocked.

Dim embers smoldered in a hearth of red bricks. The single room smelled of smoke and herbs, and so many plants of every hue and shape hung from the rafters that I thought I might have walked into a forest. A plain wooden table, rough with splinters, stood by the door, scattered with rolls of linen bandages. The only sounds were a quiet whisper of a pestle grinding herbs and the wind from the door stirring the hanging plants. I pushed the nearest ones aside.

"Watch your head, there," a soft voice said. "What can I do for you?"

Khalim sat beside the hearth, his hands stained green. His dark eyes went wide as he lifted his head to look at me, and he stood, crossing the small room in two strides.

I could not speak. I held out my hands, and he took them in his, and he was warm and solid and alive, at last. I ran my thumbs over the calluses on his fingers, and the green spread from his flesh to mine.

My knees buckled, but he pulled me into his arms and held me there, my face against his neck and his hand in my hair. His chest rose and fell with each breath, and his blood pulsed against his skin. He was alive. I had found him.

"Eske," he said. "I've been waiting for you."

I stepped back and took his face in my hands. He was still so young, but time had touched him at last. His hair had grown long enough to tie back at the base of his neck. A recent nick from a razor shone red on his cheek, and the sun had turned his brow and his hands a darker shade of brown.

"I had to cross the whole world again," I said. "I thought you might not have waited."

He smiled. "I knew you were on your way."

I could have stood there for an age. If I turned my eyes away, if I removed my hands from his face, I feared he would vanish into the air.

"Have you eaten?" he asked, releasing me from my stupor.

I could not recall. I shook my head. He took my hands and led me to a wobbly chair, and left me there to busy himself with stoking the fire.

I watched him move, slow and careful, just as he had been in the house that had once stood here. We had cooked meals together, along with Aysulu and Garvesh the scholar, in the days of tournament. Tears ran hot down my face, and I wiped them away.

"You're working as a healer?" I asked, my voice thick.

"I have no magic anymore," he said, "but I learned some things over the years, and a few more in the months since I came back. They tried to keep me in the temple, Roshani and Reva and the others, to see if Torr would return. When he didn't, they let me go. I think he's gone for good."

"Even the Ascended couldn't keep him away," I said. "Not forever."

Khalim sat back on his heels, watching the fire. "I don't dream anymore."

He stood and moved around the room, adding water to a copper pot and placing it in the hearth. I should have offered to help, but I could only watch him and listen to his feet on the crude wooden floor and his breath stirring the hanging herbs.

"The city is in good hands," he said. "He planned to leave them, eventually, like he had the Ascended. It might have been a hundred years from now, but he didn't mean to stay forever."

"I spent so long trying to find you, but you didn't need me, in the end," I said. "You freed yourself."

Another smile. I would never tire of them. "You helped me," said Khalim. "If you hadn't crossed over, if the world of the spirits hadn't rejected you, I wouldn't have convinced Torr to let me go. Not for another hundred years."

With his arms laden with rice from the south and spices from the east, he returned to the hearth. The small house filled with a familiar, warm scent. How long had it been since I had felt at home? Was it in the house beside the forge, or the tent on the mountainside, before Phyreios had fallen and stood again?

"The world of the dead will be forever changed because of what we did," Khalim said to the fire. "I suppose one day, we'll have to face that. But not yet."

Not yet. Even after all my labors, there was a lifetime still to live. "Ten years I searched for a way to reach you," I said. "Compared to that, our time together was so short. I never got the chance to know you, not really."

He looked up. "I suppose I don't know everything about you, either—only that you are the bravest of men, and the most faithful. And I don't know who I am, now, without the god." He held out a hand. "I'd like to find out. With you, if you'll have me."

I took the offered hand between both of mine. "Neither death nor disaster, nor the vast distances of the world, could keep me from your side."

"I'd like to see it," he said. "The world is so wide, and I've only seen a fragment of it."

I could have told him so many tales, but there would be time for that later. "It's cruel and rough, most of the time. But there's beauty there, if you look."

"I want to see it all. Even the ugly things. I'm free now. I can go wherever I choose." He got to his feet. The wind stirred the hanging herbs, and the fire crackled and spat. "And I choose to go with you. I've been given a life, thanks to you, and I want to spend it knowing you better."

"All the time I have left is yours," I said.

And all around us, the city went on, broken and battered but living still.

An earlier draft of *Journey to the Water* was published serially on my website, spacewhalespress.com, between September 21, 2021 and July 31, 2024.

Madeline Crane studied Medieval literature and English education before becoming a writer and part-time cryptid. She lives in Wisconsin with her husband and two cats. *Journey to the Water* is her third book, following *Beyond the Frost-Cold Sea* and *The Book of the New Moon Door.*

www.ingramcontent.com/pod-product-compliance
Lightning Source LLC
LaVergne TN
LVHW041738060526
838201LV00046B/845